Something in the Water

Something in the Water

A Novel

Catherine Steadman

• • •

Ballantine Books
New York

Published in the United States by Ballantine Books, an imprint of Random House, a division of Penguin Random House LLC, New York.

BALLANTINE and the HOUSE colophon are registered trademarks of Penguin Random House LLC.

Library of Congress Cataloging-in-Publication Data
Names: Steadman, Catherine author.
Title: Something in the water : a novel / Catherine Steadman.
Description: First edition. | New York : Ballantine Books, 2018.
Identifiers: LCCN 2018005086 | ISBN 9781524797188 (hardcover) | ISBN 9781524797195 (ebook)
Subjects: LCSH: Married people—Fiction. | Honeymoons—Fiction. | GSAFD: Suspense fiction | Psychological fiction
Classification: LCC PS3619.T4265 S66 2018 | DDC 813/.6—dc23
LC record available at https://lccn.loc.gov/2018005086

Printed in the United States of America on acid-free paper

randomhousebooks.com

1 2 3 4 5 6 7 8 9

First Edition

Book design by Susan Turner

For Ross

If a victory is told in detail, one can no longer distinguish it from a defeat.

—JEAN-PAUL SARTRE, *Le Diable et le Bon Dieu*

I'm going to smile, and my smile will sink down into your pupils, and heaven knows what it will become.

—SARTRE, *No Exit*

Something in the Water

1

The Grave

Have you ever wondered how long it takes to dig a grave? Wonder no longer. It takes an age. However long you think it takes, double that.

I'm sure you've seen it in movies: the hero, gun to his head perhaps, as he sweats and grunts his way deeper and deeper into the earth until he's standing six feet down in his own grave. Or the two hapless crooks who argue and quip in the hilarious madcap chaos as they shovel frantically, dirt flying skyward with cartoonish ease.

It's not like that. It's hard. Nothing about it is easy. The ground is solid and heavy and slow. It's so damn hard.

And it's boring. And long. And it has to be done.

The stress, the adrenaline, the desperate animal need to *do it,* sustains you for about twenty minutes. Then you crash.

Your muscles yawn against the bones in your arms and legs. Skin to bone, bone to skin. Your heart aches from the aftermath of the adrenal shock, your blood sugar drops, you hit the wall. A full-body hit. But you know, you know with crystal clarity, that high or low, exhausted or not, that hole's getting dug.

Then you kick into another gear. It's that halfway point in a marathon when the novelty has worn off and you've just got to finish the joyless bloody thing. You've invested; you're all in. You've told all your friends you'd do it, you made them pledge donations to some charity or other, one you have only a vague passing connection to. They guiltily promised more money than they really wanted to give, feeling obligated because of some bike ride or other they might have done at university, the details of which they bore you with every time they get drunk. I'm still talking about the marathon, stick with me. And then you went out every evening, on your own, shins throbbing, headphones in, building up miles, for this. So that you can fight yourself, fight with your body, right there, in that moment, in that stark moment, and see who wins. And no one but you is watching. And no one but you really cares. It's just you and yourself trying to survive. That is what digging a grave feels like, like the music has stopped but you can't stop dancing. Because if you stop dancing, you die.

So you keep digging. You do it, because the alternative is far worse than digging a never-ending god-awful hole in the hard compacted soil with a shovel you found in some old man's shed.

As you dig you see colors drift across your eyes: phosphenes caused by metabolic stimulation of neurons in the visual cortex due to low oxygenation and low glucose. Your ears roar with blood: low blood pressure caused by dehydration and overexertion. But your thoughts? Your thoughts skim across the still pool of your consciousness, only occasionally glancing the surface. Gone before you can grasp them. Your mind is completely blank. The central nervous system treats this overexertion as a fight-or-flight situation; exercise-induced neurogenesis, along with that ever-popular sports mag favorite, "exercise-induced endorphin release," acts to both inhibit your brain and protect it from the sustained pain and stress of what you are doing.

Exhaustion is a fantastic emotional leveler. Running or digging.

Around the forty-five-minute mark I decide six feet is an unrealistic depth for this grave. I will not manage to dig down to six feet. I'm five foot six. How would I even climb out? I would literally have dug myself into a hole.

According to a 2014 YouGov survey, five foot six is the ideal height for a British woman. Apparently that is the height that the average British man would prefer his partner to be. So, lucky me. Lucky Mark. God, I wish Mark were here.

So if I'm not digging six feet under, how far under? How deep is deep enough?

Bodies tend to get found because of poor burial. I don't want that to happen. I really don't. That would definitely not be the outcome I'm after. And a poor burial, like a poor anything else really, comes down to three things:

1. Lack of time
2. Lack of initiative
3. Lack of care

In terms of time: I have three to six hours to do this. Three hours is my conservative estimate. Six hours is the daylight I have left. I have time.

I believe I have initiative; two brains are better than one. I hope. I just need to work through this step by step.

And number three: care? God, do I care. I care. More than I have ever cared in my entire life.

| | |

Three feet is the minimum depth recommended by the ICCM (Institute of Cemetery and Crematorium Management). I know this because I Googled it. I Googled it before I started digging. See, initiative. Care. I squatted down next to the body, wet leaves and mud malty underfoot, and I Googled how to bury a body. I Googled this on the body's burner phone. If they do find the body . . . *they won't find the body* . . . and manage to retrieve the data . . . *they won't retrieve the data* . . . then this search history is going to make fantastic reading.

Two full hours in, I stop digging. The hole is just over three feet deep. I don't have a tape measure, but I remember that three feet is around crotch height. The height of the highest jump I managed on the horse-riding vacation I took before I left for university twelve years ago. An eighteenth-birthday present. Weird what sticks in the memory, isn't it? But here I am, waist-deep in a grave, remembering a gymkhana. I got second prize, by the way. I was very happy with it.

Anyway, I've dug approximately three feet deep, two feet wide, six feet long. Yes, that took two hours.

To reiterate: digging a grave is *very* hard.

Just to put this into perspective for you, this hole, my two-hour hole, is: 3 ft x 2 ft x 6 ft, which is 36 cubic feet of soil, which is 1 cubic meter of soil, which is 1.5 tons of soil. And that—that—is the weight of a hatchback car or a fully grown beluga whale or the average hippopotamus. I have moved the equivalent of that up and slightly to the left of where it was before. And this grave is only three feet deep.

I look across the mud at the mound and slowly hoist myself out, forearms trembling under my own weight. The body lies across from me under a torn tarpaulin, its brilliant cobalt a slash of color against the brown forest floor. I'd found it abandoned, hanging like a veil from a branch, back toward the layby, in quiet communion with an abandoned fridge. The fridge's small freezer-box door creaking calmly in the breeze. Dumped.

There's something so sad about abandoned objects, isn't there? Desolate. But kind of beautiful. I suppose, in a sense, I've come to abandon a body.

The fridge has been here a while—I know this because I saw it from the car window as we drove past here three months ago, and nobody has come for it yet. We were on our way back to London from Norfolk, Mark and I, after celebrating our anniversary, and here the fridge still is months later. Odd to think so much has happened—to me, to us—in that time, but nothing has changed here. As if this spot were adrift from time, a holding area. It has that feel. Perhaps no one has been here since the fridge owner was here, and God knows how long ago that might have been. The fridge looks distinctly seventies—you know, in that bricky way. Bricky, Kubricky. A monolith in a damp English wood. Obsolete. Three months it's been here at least and no collection, no men from the dump. No one comes here, that's clear. Except us. No council workers, no disgruntled locals to write letters to the council, no early morning dog walkers to stumble across my quarry. This was the safest place I could think of. So here we are. It will take a while for it all to settle, the soil. But I think the fridge and I have enough time.

I look it over, the crumpled-tarp mound. Underneath lie flesh, skin, bone, teeth. Three and a half hours dead.

I wonder if he's still warm. My husband. Warm to the touch. I Google it. Either way, I don't want the shock.

Okay.

Okay, the arms and legs should be cold to the touch but the main body will still be warm. Okay then.

I take a long, full exhalation.

Okay, here we go. . . .

I stop. Wait.

I don't know why, but I clear his burner phone's search history. It's pointless, I know; the phone's untraceable and after a couple of hours in the damp October ground it won't work anyway. But then, maybe it will. I place the burner back in his coat pocket and slip his personal iPhone out of his chest pocket. It's on airplane mode.

I look through the photo library. Us. Tears well and then streak in two hot dribbles down my face.

I fully remove the tarp, exposing everything it conceals. I wipe the phone for prints, return it to its warm chest pocket, and brace my knees to drag.

I'm not a bad person. Or maybe I am. Maybe you should decide?

But I should definitely explain. And to explain I need to go back. Back to that anniversary morning, three months ago.

● ● ●

2

Friday, July 8

Anniversary Morning

We woke up before sunrise this morning. Mark and I. It's our anniversary morning. The anniversary of the first day we met.

We've been staying in a boutique pub hotel on the Norfolk coast. Mark found it in the *Financial Times*'s "How to Spend It" supplement. He has a subscription but the supplements are the only bits he ever gets time to read. The *FT* was right, though; this is "the cozy-country bolt-hole of your dreams." And I'm glad this is "how we're spending it." Of course, it's not my "it" we're spending, really, but I suppose it will be soon.

The hotel is a perfect country nest of fresh seafood, cold beer, and cashmere throws. Chelsea-on-Sea, the guidebooks call it.

We'd spent the past three days walking until our muscles were loose and heavy, our cheeks flushed from English sun and windburn, hair smelling of forest and salty sea. Walking and then fucking, bathing, and eating. Heaven.

The hotel had originally been built in 1651 as a coaching inn for customs officials making that bumpy trip to London and had since boasted famous Norfolkian and Battle of Trafalgar winner Vice Admiral Horatio Lord Nelson as a regular patron. He stayed in room 5, the one next to ours, and came here to collect his dispatches every Saturday of his five-year unemployment, apparently. Interesting that Lord Nelson had stretches of unemployment. I suppose I always thought if you were in the Navy, then you were just in the Navy. But there you go. It happens to the best of us. Anyway, throughout the years, livestock auctions, assizes, and all the fun of the Jane Austen fair had been hosted here in the hotel.

The coffee-table book in our room had gleefully informed us that the preliminary hearings for the infamous Burnham Murderers trial had been held in what was now the private dining room downstairs. "Infamous" is questionable. I had certainly never heard of them. So I read up.

The story began in 1835 with the wife of a shoemaker violently retching up her stomach at the family dinner table as her husband watched. Mrs. Taylor, the retcher, had been poisoned with arsenic. The flour in the larder had been laced with the stuff, and arsenic traces were later found in her stomach lining at autopsy. An inquest into the poisoning found that Mr. Taylor had been having an affair with their neighbor, a Mrs. Fanny Billing. And Fanny Billing had recently purchased three-pennyworth of arsenic from a local druggist. That arsenic had made its way into the Taylors' flour bag and consequently into the dumplings that ended the life of Mrs. Taylor. I guess Mr. Taylor was abstaining that evening. Perhaps Mr. Taylor was on a no-carbs diet.

Further information supplied by another neighbor at the inquest stated that a Mrs. Catherine Frary had had access to the Taylors' home that day and had been heard telling Fanny before her questioning, "Hold your own and they can't hurt us."

Upon further investigation it was found that Catherine's husband and her child had also both died very suddenly the previous fortnight.

Foul play was suspected. Catherine's husband's and child's stomachs were shipped to Norwich, where analysis confirmed they too contained arsenic. A witness at the Taylor house attested he had seen Catherine attending to the sick Mrs. Taylor, post-retching, and he had seen her add a white powder "on the tip of a knife from a paper packet" into Mrs. Taylor's gruel, poisoning her a second time. This time fatally. The two women had also poisoned Catherine's sister-in-law the week before.

Catherine and Fanny were hung in Norwich for the multiple murders of their husbands, as well as Mrs. Taylor, Catherine's child, and Catherine's sister-in-law. According to the *Niles' Weekly Register* of October 17, 1835: the pair were "launched into eternity amidst an immense concourse of spectators, (20,000 or 30,000), above one-half of whom were women." *Launched into eternity*. Nice shipping reference.

Odd to put "the Burnham Murderers" in the hotel information booklet, especially considering the nature of weekend getaways.

The alarm wakes us at four-thirty in the morning from our warm bundle of goose down and Egyptian cotton. We dress in silence, our clothes laid out the night before: thin cotton T-shirts, walking boots, jeans, and woolen sweaters for before the sun rises. I make us some coffee using the little machine in the room while Mark fixes his hair in the bathroom. Mark's not a vain man by any standard, but like most men in their thirties, his getting ready seems to be mainly hair-based. I like his dithering, though, a little chink in his perfection. I like that I can be ready quicker. We drink our coffee fully clothed on top of the duvet, windows open, his arm around me, silent. We'll have enough time to jump in the car and get to the beach for the break of dawn. Sunrise is listed as 5:05 on the daily information card by the bed.

We drive in relative silence to Holkham Beach, breathing and thinking. We're together, but alone with our thoughts and each other. Trying to hang on to the thick sleepiness that hasn't quite faded away yet. There's an innate sense of ritual to it all. We have that sometimes; things just happened that way for us. A little bit of magic creeps into our lives and we nurture it like a succulent. We've done all this before; it's one of our things. Anniversary morning. As we pull in to park I wonder if we'll still celebrate this day after we're married, two months from now. Or maybe that will be our new day?

We get out to thick quiet at Holkham Hall. Silence pierced intermittently by bursts of rich birdsong. A herd of deer in the adjoining field look up as we slam the car doors, and freeze. We hold their gaze, all momentarily caught in stasis, until their attention drops back down to the grass.

We are one of the first cars of the day in the clay gravel car park; it will get much busier later—it always does—with dogs and families, horseboxes and riders, family clans eking out the last of the good weather. Apparently this heat won't last. But then, they say that every year, don't they?

No one is in sight yet as we make our way along the gravel tracks down to the great desert stretch of Holkham Beach, four miles of golden-white sand skirted by pine forests. The North Sea wind bends patches of wild grasses and whips sand up into the air along the ridgebacks of towering dunes. Miles of freshly blown sand and sea and not a soul in sight. Unearthly in the predawn light. A fresh barren landscape. It always feels like a clean start. Like the New Year.

Mark takes my hand and we walk out toward the shore. At the water's edge we squeeze off our boots and slip into the icy North Sea, jeans pushed up to our knees.

His smile. His eyes. His hot hand tightly gripping mine. The sharp taut feeling of the icy water on my feet, bursting into a fluid white heat up my legs. *Burning* cold. We'd timed it exactly right. The sky starts to lighten. We laugh. Mark counts down to 5:05 on his wristwatch and we look patiently east across the water.

The entire sky lightens to twilight before the sun crests the silver water. Yellow streaks the horizon and ombrés out to peaches and pinks as it hits the lowest clouds, and beyond—the whole sky blazes blue. Azure blue. Ha. It's so beautiful. So beautiful I feel nauseous.

When we can't stand the cold anymore, I wade back to shore, bending to clean the sand off my feet in the shallows before I put my boots back on. My engagement ring catches the full glare of the sun refracting through the crystal water. The early morning mist is gone, the air full of moisture, salty and crisp. So bright. So clear. The sky in high-definition blue. The best day of the year. Always. So much hope, every year.

Mark asked me to marry him last October, after his thirty-fifth birthday. Although we'd been together for years, it had still been a surprise, somehow. I sometimes wonder if things pass me by more than other people. Maybe I don't pay enough attention, or maybe I'm just not that good at picking stuff up. Things often surprise me. I'm always surprised to find out from Mark that so-and-so didn't like so-and-so, or somebody was attracted to me or had some other strong reaction. I never notice. I suppose that's probably for the best. What you don't know can't hurt you.

Mark notices things. He's very good with people. People light up when they see him coming. They love him. People often ask me, on the rare occasions that we do anything separately, "Isn't Mark coming?" with a tone of bemused disappointment. I don't take it personally, because that's how I feel too. Mark makes all situations better. He listens, really listens. He holds eye contact. Not aggressively but in a way that reassures people—his look says: *I'm here, and that's enough for me.* He's interested in people. Mark's look has no angle; he's just there, with you.

| | |

We sit high on a dune, looking out across the wide flat expanse of sky and sea. It's windier up here. The air howls in our ears. I'm glad of the thick sweaters. The coarse Irish wool gives off the scent of animal as it warms. The conversation turns to the future. Our plans. We've always made plans on this day. Like resolutions, I suppose, mid-year resolutions. I've always enjoyed planning ahead, since I was a child. I like to plan. I like to take stock. Mark had never really done resolutions before we met, but he took to it instantly—it suited him, the progressive futurist nature of it.

My mid-year resolutions aren't out of the ordinary. The usual: read more, watch TV less, work smarter, spend more time with loved ones, eat better, drink less, be happy. And then Mark says he wants to focus on work more.

Mark works in banking. I know, yes, boo hiss. But all I can say is: he's not an arsehole. You'll have to trust me on that. He's definitely no Eton, drinking-club, polo-team alumnus. He's a Yorkshire lad made good. Granted, his dad wasn't exactly a coal miner or anything. Mr. Roberts, now retired, had been a pensions adviser for Prudential in East Riding.

Mark moved forward fast in the City, passed his regulation exams, became a trader, specialized in sovereigns, got poached, got promoted, and then it happened. The financial crash.

The bottom fell out of the financial industry. Everyone who understood was terrified from the first day. They could see it all spooling out ahead of them. Technically, Mark was fine. His job was safe—if anything, it was safer than before because he specialized in the exact thing that everyone needed help with after the crash, sovereign debt. But bonuses plummeted for everyone. Which was fine, we weren't exactly on the breadline, but a lot of his friends got laid off, which was terrifying. It scared me at the time, watching grown adults failing; they had kids in schools, and mortgages they couldn't afford anymore. The wives hadn't worked since pregnancy. No one had a backup plan. That year was the year that people came to dinner and cried. They'd leave our house apologizing, smiling bravely, and promising to see us once they'd moved back to their hometowns and got their lives back on track. We never heard from a lot of them again. We'd hear that they'd moved back in with their parents in Berkshire or moved to work in Australia, or divorced.

Mark switched banks; all his colleagues had been let go where he was and he'd been left doing five people's jobs, so he took a chance and went somewhere else.

The new bank, I don't like. It's not quite right. The men there manage to be fat and yet sinewy at the same time. They're out of shape, and they smoke, which I didn't used to mind at all, but now it has that air of nervous desperation. That worries me. It smells of bile and broken dreams. Mark's colleagues sometimes come out with us for drinks and sneer and bitch about their wives and kids, as if I weren't there. As if were it not for those women they'd be on some beach somewhere.

Mark isn't like them; he looks after himself. He runs, he swims, he plays tennis, he keeps himself healthy, and now he sits in a room for eleven hours a day with these men. I know he's strong-minded but I can see it's wearing him down. And now, on this day of all days, on our anniversary, he announces he wants to focus on work more.

Focus means I'll see him less. He already works too hard. He gets up at 6 A.M. every weekday, leaves the house at 6:30, has lunch at his desk and gets home to me totally exhausted at 7:30 at night. We have dinner and talk, maybe watch a film, and he's in bed with the lights out at 10:00 to do it all again.

"That's what I want to change, though," he says. "I've been working there for a year now. When I moved there they promised I'd only be in this position initially, until we restructured the department. But they won't let me do that. They won't let me restructure. So I'm not actually doing what they hired me to do." He sighs. Rubs his hand up and down his face. "Which is fine. But I need to have a proper conversation with Lawrence. We need to talk about my end-of-year bonus, or changing the team, because some of these jokers have no idea what they're doing." He pauses, then looks at me. "I'm serious, Erin. I wasn't going to tell you this, but after that deal went through on Monday, Hector rang me crying."

"Why was he crying?" I ask, surprised. Hector has worked alongside Mark for years now. When Mark left the other bank, when everything was going wrong, Mark promised Hector he'd find him a position if he moved. And he kept his promise. Mark made Hector part of his deal when he moved. They came as a pair or not at all.

"You know we were waiting for the figures the other day to sign off on the deal?" He looks at me searchingly.

"Yeah, you took the call in the car park," I say, nodding him on. He'd slipped out of our pub lunch yesterday and spent an hour pacing the gravel while his food went cold. I'd read my book. I'm self-employed, so I know the "phone wander" well.

"Yeah, he told me he'd got the figures. The guys on the trading desk had been really hard to even get in the office over the holidays and they'd made it pretty difficult for him. They've called a meeting once we're back to discuss overtime hours and fair practice. It's ridiculous. Anyway. Hector spoke to New York, tried to explain that no one was in and why the figures were late and they went fucking mental. Andrew . . . You remember Andrew in New York, right? I told you about the—"

"That guy I heard swearing at you through the phone at Brianny's wedding?" I interrupt.

He snorts and smiles. "Yeah, Andrew. He's . . . highly strung. But anyway. So Andrew screams at Hector on the phone, and Hector freaks out and just prices the deal and hits send. Goes to bed. Wakes up to hundreds of missed calls and emails. Turns out they'd put an extra zero in the figures. Greg and the other guys on the desk put it in to slow down the deal. They thought Hector would look it over before sending and get them to redo it next week once we were all back in the office, but Hector didn't check it. He signed off on it and sent it. And that is a legally binding contract."

"Oh my God, Mark. Can't they just say it was an error?"

"Not really, honey. So Hector rings me and he's trying to explain that he just assumed it would be right and he always, always, usually checks . . . but Andrew said send it and . . . and then he just starts crying. Erin, I just . . . I feel like I'm surrounded by absolute—" Mark stops himself and shakes his head ruefully. "So, I'm going to put feelers out for somewhere else. I'm one hundred percent happy to take a bonus drop, or a salary cut; the market's not going back to the way it was anyway. Who are we kidding? I just don't need this stress anymore. I want my life back. I want you and babies, and our evenings again."

I like the sound of that. Very much. I hug him. Bury my head in his shoulder. "I want that too."

"Good." He kisses my hair lightly.

"I'll find a good place, hand in my notice after this Hector stuff settles, take my garden leave for the wedding and honeymoon stretch, and start back hopefully around November. Just in time for Christmas."

He's done "garden leave" before—everyone who works in the financial sector has to take a mandatory leave between jobs; it's supposed to stop insider trading but it's essentially a two-month paid vacation. This does sound like a pretty good plan. Good for him. But I could definitely take a few weeks away from my work too. We could make a thing of it, get some serious honeymooning done. I'm working on my first feature-length documentary right now but I'll have completed the first stage of filming by the wedding, and then I should have a good three- to four-week gap before I start on the second stage. That three to four weeks could definitely work in our favor.

A warm feeling spreads through my chest. This is good. This will be better for us.

"Where shall we go?" he asks.

"Honeymoon?"

This is the first time we've really talked about it. It's two months away now, the wedding. We've covered all of that but this we've left fresh. Untouched, like an unopened gift. But I guess now is as good a time as any to broach the subject. I'm excited by the possibility of it all. Having him all to myself for weeks.

"Let's go crazy. It might be the last time we have the time or the money." I throw it out there.

"Yes!" he shouts, matching my energy.

"Two weeks—no, three weeks?" I offer. I squint, thinking through the filming schedule and interviews I have to do. I can manage three.

"Now we're talking. Caribbean? Maldives? Bora Bora?" he asks.

"Bora Bora. That sounds perfect. I have no idea where it is but it sounds glorious. Fuck it. First class? Can we do first class?"

He grins at me. "We can do first class. I'll book it."

"Great!" I've never flown first class before.

And then I say something I'll probably live to regret.

"I'm going to scuba dive with you. When we go. I'll try it again. Then we can go down together." I say it because it seems like all I can give Mark to show him how much I love him. Like a cat with a dead mouse in its mouth. Whether he wants it or not, I drop it at his feet.

"Seriously?" He stares at me, concerned, the sunlight creasing his eyes, the breeze ruffling his dark hair. He wasn't expecting that.

Mark's a qualified diver. He's been trying to get me to go with him on every trip we've ever been on together, but I've always chickened out. I had a bad experience once, before we met. I panicked. Nothing serious, but the whole idea really scares the shit out of me. I don't like the idea of feeling trapped. The thought of the pressure and the slow underwater ascents fills me with dread. But I want to do this thing for him. New life together, new challenges.

I grin. "Yes, definitely!" I can do it. How hard can it be? Kids do it. I'll be fine.

He looks at me. "I fucking love you, Erin Locke," he says. Just like that.

"I fucking love you too, Mark Roberts."

He leans in, tilts my head, and kisses me.

"Are you real?" he asks, fixing my gaze.

We've played this game before, except it's not really a game at all. Or is it? A mind game perhaps.

What he's actually asking is, "Is *this* real?" It's so good it must be a trick, a mistake. I must be lying. Am I lying?

I give it a second. I let the muscles of my face fall as he studies me. I let my pupils contract like the universe imploding and calmly reply, "No." No, I'm not real. It's scary. I've only done it a few times. Absented myself from my own face. Made myself disappear. Like a phone reverting to factory settings.

"No, I'm not real," I say simply, my face blank and open.

It has to look like I mean it.

It works best when it looks real.

His eyes flicker and jump across my face, searching for a hook, a crack to hang understanding on. There's nothing there. I've disappeared.

I know he worries. He worries deep down that one day I will actually just vanish. Leave. That this isn't real. That he'll wake up and everything will be the same in the house but I won't be there. I know that fear; I see it fluttering across his face at random moments when we're out with friends or standing on opposite sides of a busy room. I see it, that look, and then I know that *he* is real. I see it on his face now. And that's enough for me.

I let the smile creep out of me and his face bursts with joy. He laughs. Flushing with emotion. I laugh and then he takes my face in his hands again and puts his lips to mine. Like I've won a race. Like I'm back from war. Well done, me. *God, I love you, Mark.* He pulls me into the salt marsh reeds and we fuck, desperately, hands full of woolen sweater and wet skin. As he comes I whisper in his ear, "I'm real."

3

The Phone Call

Last year I finally got co-funding from a prison charity to finance my first solo project. It's now coming together after years of research and planning: my very own feature-length documentary. I've managed to get all the research and preproduction done while taking freelance projects along the way, and I'm due to start filming the face-to-face interviews in nine days. I've put so much of myself into this production and I hope, more than anything, that it all comes together. There's only so far planning can take you, then you just have to wait and see what happens. It's a big year. For me. For us. The film, the wedding—everything seems to be happening all at once. But I honestly think I'm at that magical point in my life where all the plans I set in motion in my twenties are finally coming together, all in unison, as if somehow I'd deliberately orchestrated it that way, though I don't remember consciously doing that. I guess that's the way life works, isn't it—nothing, and then everything at once.

The idea for the film is simple, really; it came to me one evening when I was telling Mark about what it was like at boarding school. At night after lights-out we girls would spend hours in the darkness talking about what we would do when we finally got home. What we would eat when we could choose our own food. We'd fantasize endlessly about those imagined meals. We'd obsess over Yorkshire puddings in gravy or cocktail sausages on sticks. We'd imagine what we would wear when we could choose our own clothes, where we would go, what we would do when we had our freedom. And then Mark said it sounded like prison. That we'd dreamt of home in the same way prisoners dream of home.

So came the idea for the documentary. Its format is simple. It will follow three different prisoners during and after incarceration, through interviews and fly-on-the-wall coverage: two women and one man charting their hopes and dreams about their freedom before and after release. Today I'm doing my last introductory telephone conversation with my final prisoner, then I'll be conducting face-to-face interviews with each of the subjects in prison before their release. So far I've spoken several times to the two female candidates, but it's been much harder to secure access to my male candidate. Today we've finally got our hard-won phone call. Today I am waiting for a phone call from Eddie Bishop. *The* Eddie Bishop, one of the last remaining East End London gangsters. One hundred percent authentic, chop-you-up-with-a-hatchet, nightclub-casino, cockney-rhyming gangster. An original Richardson Gang member and, more recently, the center of the largest criminal gang in London operating south of the river.

I stare down at the house phone. It's not ringing. It's supposed to be ringing. It's 1:12 and I've been waiting for an incoming call from Pentonville Prison for twelve—no, now thirteen—minutes. My other subjects', Alexa's and Holli's, calls came through exactly on time. I wonder what the problem is, and pray that Eddie hasn't pulled out, changed his mind. I pray the prison board hasn't changed theirs.

It was hard to get approval from the prison board on anything, so I'll be conducting the face-to-face interview portions on my own. Just me and a locked-off fixed-position camera. It'll be raw footage at that stage, but then that fits the content, so I'm happy. During the second stage, once my candidates are out of prison, Phil and Duncan are joining me.

Phil is a cameraman I know and trust implicitly—he's got a great eye and we share a very similar aesthetic, which I know sounds a bit pretentious but I promise it's important. And Duncan and I have worked together a couple of times before. He's fun, but more importantly he's much better than I can afford. Duncan and Phil will both be taking a hit on the money front for this; the funding's good but it's not great. Thankfully, they love the concept as much as I do and they've got faith in the project.

I look through the plastic wallets containing my hard-won permissions papers from the Ministry of Justice and Her Majesty's Prison Service. More than anything, I want the documentary to overcome the conventional representation of prisoners by trying to show these three people as individuals separate from their convictions. Both Holli and Eddie have sentences between four and seven years for nonfatal crimes. Alexa has a sentence of "life with parole," so fourteen years. But do those sentences say anything about who they are as people? Does that tell you who is more dangerous? Who is a better person? Who you can trust? We'll see.

I pull the phone, cord and all, over to the sofa and sit down with it in a patch of sunlight under the window. Leafy North London sun instantly warms my shoulders and the back of my neck. Somehow the British summer is lingering. We usually only get a couple of days of proper summer but the sunshine is still going strong. We've had three weeks of it already. They're saying it won't last, but it has so far. Mark's out at work and the house is silent. Only the muffled rumble of lorries and the buzz of scooters reach me from distant Stoke New-

ington High Street. I look out of the Georgian sash windows into our
back garden; a cat wanders along the back wall, black with white paws.

I've had to call in favors from everyone to get this far. Fred Davey,
the film director who gave me my first job, vouched for me in a letter to the Minister for Justice. I'm pretty sure Fred's two BAFTAs
and the Oscar nomination helped my cause a damn sight better than
the synopsis I wrote for the film proposal. ITV has already expressed
an interest in picking up the doc after general release, and Channel 4
vouched for my work in another letter—they've already aired two of
my shorts. My film school backed me, of course. The White Cube
gave me a reference, for what *that's* worth to the Ministry of Justice.
So did all the production companies I've freelanced for and Creative
England, which has helped so much with funding and support
throughout the process so far.

And then of course I have Eddie Bishop. He's the real coup, an
absolute dream for a documentarian. This interview is why I got my
funding. So this phone call is kind of a big deal. Eddie is kind of a
big deal.

You might not know it, but Eddie's story is British crime history.
He joined the Richardson Gang at the age of eighteen when the
gang was at the height of its power, just before its fall in 1966. It was
the year England won the World Cup and the year it all kicked off
with the Krays.

Eddie had an aptitude for crime. He was reliable, he was straightforward, he got things done. Whatever the job was. No muss, no
fuss. He quickly became indispensable to the Richardson brothers,
so much so that when the Richardsons were finally arrested that
summer in 1966, Eddie Bishop was there to keep everything running smoothly while the brothers, and the rest of the gang, were
behind bars.

Eddie allegedly rebuilt the whole syndicate in South London and
ran it for forty-two years, until his arrest for money laundering seven

years ago. Four decades Eddie ran South London, murdered, slashed, and extorted his way across the city, and all they could give him was seven years for money laundering.

Ring, ring.

The phone pierces the silence. Shrill, insistent, and all at once I'm nervous.

Ring, ring. Ring, ring.

I tell myself it's fine. I've done this before with the other subjects. It's fine. I take a shaky breath and lift the receiver to my ear, to my mouth.

"Hello?"

"Hello, is that Erin Locke?" The voice is female, curt, mid-forties. Not what I was expecting. Clearly not Eddie Bishop.

"Yes, this is Erin Locke."

"This is Diane Ford, from Pentonville Prison. I have a call from a Mr. Eddie Bishop for you. Can I connect you, Ms. Locke?" Diane Ford sounds bored. She doesn't care who I am, or who he is. To her, this is just another call.

"Er, yes, thank you, Diane. Thanks." And she's gone. The faint click of a disconnect and a hold tone.

Eddie's never given an interview. He's never said a word to anyone about any of it. Ever. I don't for a second believe I'll be the one to crack the case wide open. And I'm not sure I'd want to. Eddie has been a professional criminal longer than I've been alive. I don't know why on earth he's agreed to be part of my documentary, but here we are. He strikes me as the kind of man who does things for a reason, so I guess I'll figure out what that reason is soon enough.

I take another shaky breath.

Then the line connects.

"This is Eddie." The voice is deep, warm. A rich cockney glottal stop of a voice. Strange to finally hear it.

"Hello, Mr. Bishop. It's nice to finally speak to you. This is Erin Locke. How are you doing today?" A good start. Very professional. I hear him shuffle at the other end of the line, settling in.

"Hello, sweetheart. Nice to hear from you. Locke, is it? Not a Roberts yet then? When's the big day?" He asks it cheerily, off the cuff.

I can hear a smile in his voice. It would be a nice thing to ask someone under any other circumstances and I almost smile back into the phone, but something makes me stop. Because there is no way Eddie could possibly know about my approaching wedding, or name change, or Mark, unless he's been looking into me. And he's in prison, which means he must have *had* me looked into. And looking into me is a more involved process than a quick online search. I'm not on social media. I don't *do* Facebook. All good documentarians know what you can do with a healthy dose of social media information, so we keep off it. So, in one simple sentence, Eddie Bishop has just told me he's been having me professionally looked into. He's had me vetted. He is in charge and he knows all about me. And Mark. And our life.

I take a moment before answering. He's testing me. I don't want to make a misstep so early in the game.

"I gather we've both done our research, Mr. Bishop. Did you find out anything interesting?"

There's nothing too controversial in my past, no dancing skeletons in my closet. I know this, of course, but still I feel exposed, under threat. This is his show of power, a verbal line in the sand. Eddie may have been behind bars for seven years, but he wants me to know he's still got his hands on all the ropes. If he wasn't being so up front about it, right now I'd be terrified.

"Very reassuring, I'd say. Put my mind to rest, sweetheart. You can never be too careful," he says. Eddie's decided I'm safe, but he wants me to know he's watching.

I move on, stand and try to unravel the phone cord, slipping into work spiel. "Thank you for agreeing to take part in this. I really appreciate you agreeing and I want you to know I'm going to handle the interviews in as unbiased and straightforward a way as I can. I'm not in the business of creating straw dogs; I'm just going to tell your story. Or rather, I'm going to let you tell your story. The way you want." I hope he knows that I mean that. I'm sure he's had plenty of people try to sell him snake oil in the past.

"I know, sweetheart. Why do you think I said yes to you? You're a rarity. Just don't let me down, aye?" He lets that sink in for a second before shaking off the intensity, lightening the tone. "Anyway, when's all this kick off then?" His tone is bright, industrious.

"Well, our face-to-face interview is scheduled for September 24, which is about two and a half months away. And then your release is sometime in early December. So we can arrange nearer the time when we'll do your post-release filming. Would you be happy with us shadowing you on release day itself?" I ask. I'm in my element now; this is where all my planning is coming into its own. If we can film Eddie's actual release fly-on-the-wall style, that would really be something.

His voice comes back, warm but clear. "I'll be honest, love, it's not ideal for me. I'll have a bit on that day, if you know what I mean. Maybe give me a day or two, aye? That work for you?" We're negotiating. He wants to give me something—that's definitely a good sign.

"Of course. We'll iron it out as we go along. You have my number, so we'll just keep in touch on those dates. Not a problem." I watch the cat outside creep back along the fence, its back hunched, its head low.

Eddie clears his throat.

"Is there anything else about the interviews or schedule you'd like to ask about at this stage, Mr. Bishop?" I ask.

He laughs. "No, I think we're done for today, sweetheart, apart from you calling me Eddie. Nice to talk to you finally though, Erin, after hearing so much about you."

"You too, Eddie. It's been a pleasure."

"Oh and give my regards to Mark, won't you, darling? Seems like a nice fella." It's a throwaway remark but my breath catches in my chest. He's been looking into Mark too. My Mark. I don't know what to say. The little pause I've left grows into a silence on the line. He fills it.

"So how did you two meet then?" He leaves the question hanging in the air. Shit. This isn't and shouldn't be about me.

"That's none of your business, Eddie, now is it?" I say it with a forced smile in my voice. The words come out smooth and confident and, weirdly, with a hint of sexuality. Entirely inappropriate but somehow perfectly appropriate.

"Ha! No. Quite right, sweetheart. None of my business at all." Eddie roars with laughter. I hear it echo along the prison hallway at the other end of the line. "Very good, love, very good."

And there we go. We're back on track. It seems to be going well. We seem to be getting on. Me and Eddie Bishop.

I smile down the phone, a genuine grin this time. I smile in my empty living room, by myself, bathed in sunlight.

4

How We Met

I met Mark in Annabel's, a private club in Mayfair. Let's be clear: Annabel's is not the sort of place either of us frequents. It was the first and last time I've ever been there. Not for any terrible reason; I'd had fun there—God, I met the love of my life there—but it was just pure chance that either of us was there in the first place. If you've never heard of Annabel's before, it's a strange one. Nestled under a nondescript staircase in Berkeley Square and open for the past five decades, it has seen everyone from Nixon to Lady Gaga tip-tap down its staircase. Opened by Mark Birley at the suggestion of his close friend Lord Aspinall in the 1960s as a casino, more along the lines of a Connery Bond location and less of a one-armed-bandit arrangement. Birley was tied up with royalty, politics, and crime, so, as you can imagine, he pulled in a pretty sexy crowd. He created a quiet little supper club/pickup spot, run by the establishment for the establishment. That night, I wasn't a member, but I was with one.

I met Caro on my first job out of the National Film and Television School. It was a TV documentary on the White Cube galleries. I'd been so excited to get it. My professor had put in a word with the producer and passed along my first short, which she'd loved. I was camera assistant to Fred Davey, one of my absolute heroes. The man who would eventually help me get my first feature documentary into production. Thankfully, we got on well—I tend to be quite good with tricky people. I'd turn up early and set up—bring coffee and smile. Trying to be invisible yet indispensable, walking that tricky line between flirty and reliable.

Caro had done some talking-heads stuff on the documentary. She was the smartest person I'd ever met, or at least the most thoroughly educated person I'd ever met. She'd been the most recent recipient of a starred first in History from Cambridge, following in the footsteps of Simon Schama and Alain de Botton. Not short on job offers after graduation, she'd unexpectedly taken a job running a new gallery bankrolled by her best friend from prep school. Five years later that gallery had reputedly discovered the next generation of great British artists. She'd invited me out for drinks after we'd wrapped on the first day of filming, and we'd been fast friends ever since.

Caro was fun. She had a habit of elliptically referring to her heritage; I'd catch glimpses of blue-stockinged, cigarette-rolling badasses through the folds of her allusions. She was exciting and glamorous, and a couple of weeks after we met she took me to Annabel's.

The first time I saw Mark I was on my way back from the toilets. I'd been hiding there trying to dodge a hedge-fund bore who'd gotten it into his head that my sporadic nodding coupled with determined crowd-searching somehow indicated interest. I'd had it on good information from a Spanish girl that Hedge Fund was still hanging around outside the ladies' room entrance with a fresh drink, waiting for my return. So I took the opportunity to brush up on current affairs via my phone. I gave it ten minutes, then made a break for it. Hedge Fund was gone. Gone a-wooing some other lucky lady, no doubt. I made a beeline back to the bar, spotting the back of Caro's dull golden dress through the crowd. She was speaking animatedly to someone. Then, as she twisted to the right, she revealed her talking partner.

I literally broke step. My body deciding, before my brain, that my presence would not be needed in their interaction. Caro was gorgeous, a tall confident amazon of a woman. The lines of her gold lamé dress skimming every curve of her body. She was clearly not wearing underwear. She looked like a glossy magazine perfume ad and this man was her magazine equal. He was perfect. Tall, substantial, he looked muscular without giving the impression that he worked out. Maybe he was a rower, or it could be tennis. Maybe he chopped trees down. Yes, he'd be very good at chopping trees down. I remember feeling an unnaturally strong desire to watch him do that. Short brown tousled hair. Slept in, but still just about business-appropriate. He smiled broadly at something I couldn't quite hear, and Caro burst into laughter. I don't know why but for some reason I sped up. I like to think my body took over, a cellular need. Anyway, I pulled myself to my full height without a clue what I would say when I got there and entirely not in control of my actions. His eyes caught mine at least ten steps away and took me in, his gaze doing a dance over me that I would come to recognize and yearn for the rest of my life. His gaze searching my face, tripping and darting from my eyes to my mouth, looking for *me*.

I'd had time to change before we left the shoot and had opted for a vintage jumpsuit in dusty pink and rose-gold cage shoes. It was my Faye Dunaway *Network* outfit, for emergency evening situations only. I looked good in it. I know this because men like Hedge Fund don't go for personality.

Caro turns her head toward me, following the brown-haired man's look. "Hey, honey! Where the hell have you been?" She beams at me, obviously happy with the effect we are both having. I feel a blush begin at my neck but I shut it down.

"Mark, this gorgeous creature is my friend Erin. She's an artist. She makes documentaries. She's a genius," she coos, slipping her arm through mine in a surprisingly territorial way. It's nice to be wanted.

"Erin, this is Mark. He works in the City, he enjoys collecting modern art. Although we've ascertained he's not a fan of anything featuring Kalashnikovs or human fingernails. But aside from that, he has an open mind. Right?"

He smiles and extends a hand. "Lovely to meet you, Erin."

Those eyes holding me, taking me in. I take his hand in mine, making sure to match his grip. I feel the whole of his warm hand wrapped around my fingers, which are still cool from the washroom.

I let him have a smile, let it spread across the corners of my lips and up to my eyes. I gave him some of myself.

"And you," I reply.

I needed to know who he belonged to, if I could have him. Could I have him?

"Can I get anyone a drink?" I offer.

"Actually, hon, I'm just going to nip to the loos. Toilet relay. Back in a min," Caro trills, and exits, leaving only a waft of rich perfume behind. She's left him here for me. But then, I guess hot guys are ten a penny to the Caros of this world.

Mark loosens his tie slightly with his forefinger and thumb. Dark navy suit. Fuck.

"Drink, Mark?" I offer.

"Oh, God, no, sorry, let me." Champagne is ordered with a nod and a wave. He gestures over to a nook and we sit down together at a low table. It turns out that he's only just met Caro and he's here alone. Well, he came with a friend named Richard.

"Who is talking to that lovely lady over there." Mark points to a woman who is very clearly an escort. Latex knee-length boots and bored wandering eyes. Richard doesn't seem to be too bothered by the lack of conversational input and appears to have the talking covered for both of them.

"Wow, okay. Interesting." I was not expecting that. Wow.

Mark grins and nods and I completely fail to intercept my full-on *snort* of laughter. He laughs too.

"We're very close, Richard and I," he intones with mock solemnity. "He's over for the day from a Swiss bank. I'm basically his minder. Or carer? Who knows. I just have to take him where he wants to go. Which is apparently . . . there. What sort of documentaries do you make?"

"At the moment, not many. But I've only just started, really. I've done a short on Norwegian fishermen. Like a kind of homage to Melville, it's sort of *Local Hero* meets *The Old Man and the Sea,* you know?" I check to see if I'm boring him. He smiles and nods me on.

We talk for two hours straight, going through two bottles of Krug together, which I assumed he'd be covering, as the bill would be equivalent to a month's rent in my flat. It flowed easily, the conversation and the champagne. In the moments where he smiled, my thigh would tense involuntarily.

Finally the spell breaks when Mark's friend catches his eye from across the room and gestures that he and his lady friend are off. Having come to some kind of hard-fought agreement, one would imagine.

"On that magical note, I'm going to have to call it a night, I'm afraid." Mark gets to his feet reluctantly.

"You have to see him back?" I stall. I don't want to ask for his number; I want him to ask for mine.

"God no, that would be just . . . no, thank God. I'll put them in a cab and my work is done. You?"

"Caro's place is just around the corner. I'll probably crash on her couch tonight." I've done it before and in all honesty her sofa bed is far more comfortable than my bed.

"You're North, though, right? Your place? Usually?" He's stalling now too. Over his shoulder I see Richard, loitering passive-aggressively by the stairs. His date must already be up on street level being bored by passersby.

"Uh, yeah, North, Finsbury Park." I'm not sure where this conversation is going now. We're floundering.

He nods his head decisively. A decision made.

"Great. Um, okay, so long story short. I got this projector for Christmas from my sister and I'm really having a bit of a moment with it. I've got it shining onto this blank wall in my apartment. It's pretty fucking epic. If you fancied it? I've got some documentaries. Long shot but I've been meaning to watch this four-hour doc on Nicolae Ceauşescu?"

I look at him. Is he joking? Ceauşescu? I really can't tell. This might be the most brilliantly odd invitation I've ever received. I realize I haven't answered him. But he continues to talk, not letting the air out of the situation just yet.

"Former dictator of Romania. Sang 'L'Internationale' at his own execution. Too dark? Probably. Fancy it? Pretty sexy stuff, right? He had his own tour bus. Well, Ceauşescu-bus."

He hangs there for a second. He's perfect.

"Amazing. That was amazing. I would actually love that. Sign me up." I pull a freshly minted business card out of my clutch and hand it to him. It's the third time I've done this since I picked them up from the stationers after graduating last month. But it looks well practiced. Fred Davey's got one, Caro's got one, and now Mark Roberts has one.

"I'm free next week. Let's watch the four-hour Ceauşescu."

And with that I disappear back into the heart of Annabel's.

It takes all of my self-control not to look back over my shoulder before I turn the corner.

5

Wednesday, July 20

Interview One

Mark calls me from work at 7:23 A.M. Something's wrong. There's panic in his voice. He's stifling it, but I can hear it.

I sit up in my chair. I've never heard even an inkling of this tone in his voice before. I shudder slightly, even in the warmth of the room.

"Erin, listen, I'm in the loo. They've taken my BlackBerry and I've got to leave the building right now. They've got two security guards outside the bathroom waiting to escort me off the premises." He's breathy but he's holding it together.

"What's happening?" I ask, visions of terror attacks and shaky mobile-phone footage racing through my mind. But it's not that. I know it's not that. I recognize the bones of this story already. I've heard it from enough people by now. It's eerie in its sterility. Mark's been "let go."

"Lawrence called me into his office at seven o'clock. He told me he'd heard through the grapevine that I'm looking elsewhere and he thinks it's better for all concerned if I take leave from today. He's happy to offer references but my desk has been emptied already and I'll have to hand in my work phone before leaving the building." The line goes silent for a second. "He didn't mention who told him."

Silence again.

"But it's fine, Erin. I'm fine. You know they make you go straight into an HR meeting after they let you go. They lead you out of the room and straight into another one with an HR rep in it! They cover their fucking backs, by God. Such a load of bullshit! The rep asks, Was I happy here? And then I have to say, 'Yes, it's been fantastic and it's all worked out for the best in the end. Lawrence has done me a favor. Freed me up for the next challenge, blah blah.'" Mark's ranting. He can sense my worry through the phone.

"It's fine, though, Erin. It's going to be fine. I promise you. Listen, I've got to go with these guys now but I'll be home in an hour or so."

I'm not at home, though.

I'm currently in Holloway Prison, about to do my first face-to-face interview. He can't have forgotten, can he? I'm in a prison holding room. Shit! *Please don't need me there now, Mark. Please be okay.*

But if he needs me, I'll go.

Oh fucking hell. Those two constantly tugging needs: your own life and "being there." Your relationship or your life. No matter how hard you try, you can't have both.

"Should I come home?" I ask.

Silence.

"No, no, it's fine," he says finally. "I need to make a fuckload of calls and sort something out. I need to get in somewhere else before this gets too big. Rafie and Andrew were meant to get back to me yesterday—"

I hear banging on the door on his end.

"Fucking hell. Just a sec, mate! Christ. I'm taking a piss!" he shouts. "I gotta go, honey. Time's up. Call me after the interview. Love you."

"Love you." I make a kiss noise but he's already hung up.

Silence. I'm back in the hushed holding room again. The guard glances over and frowns, his dark eyes kind but firm.

"Didn't want to mention it, but you can't use that in here," the guard mumbles, embarrassed to be playing the role of hall monitor. But it is his job; he's doing his best.

I put the phone on airplane mode and set it on the table in front of me. More silence.

I stare at the empty chair on the other side of the table. The interviewee's chair.

I feel a brief shiver of freedom. I'm not in that washroom with Mark. The whole world is still open and clear for me. It's not my problem.

The guilt follows immediately. What an awful thing to think. Of course it's my problem. It's *our* problem. We're getting married in a couple of months. But I can't make that feeling stick. I don't feel Mark's problems like I feel my own. What does that mean? I don't feel like something devastating has happened. I feel free and light.

He'll be fine, I reassure myself. Maybe that's why I don't feel anything. Because it'll all be fine by tomorrow. I'll get home early tonight. I'll make him dinner. I'll open some wine. Wine and fine.

A sudden buzzer blast from the electric doors snaps me back to the present. It's followed by the low clunk of sliding bolts. I straighten my notepad. Realign my pens. The guard catches my eye.

"Any point you feel uncomfortable, give me the nod and we'll terminate," he says. "I'll be staying in the room, I'm sure they told you."

"Yes. Thank you, Amal." I flash him my most professional smile and press record on the camera, lens trained on the door.

Amal presses the door release. The buzz is deafening. Here we go. Interview one.

The door release thunders again and a short, fair-haired girl comes into view through the wire-meshed window of the door. A pair of eyes land on me, bore through me, before sliding off.

I'm standing before the impulse reaches any decision-making area of my brain. The buzzer blast thunders around the room. Then the clunk of bolts, the magnets releasing.

She steps into the room, interviewee number one, all five feet three inches of her. Holli Byford is twenty-three and painfully thin. Her long hair messily piled high on top of her head, her blue prison tracksuit loose and heavy on her tiny frame. Cheekbones sharp. She looks like a child. They say you know when you're really getting old because everyone around you starts to look impossibly young. I'm only thirty. Holli Byford looks about sixteen to me.

The door buzzes shut behind her. Amal clears his throat. I'm glad Amal's staying. The prison called yesterday; although Holli's progressing they're not entirely happy for her to be unsupervised just yet. Holli continues to stand there, unselfconsciously, halfway into the room. Her eyes play lazily across the furniture, the camera. They skip over me. She hasn't acknowledged me yet. And then her eyes alight on my face. My body tenses. I brace myself. The gaze is hard. It hits me. It's solid. It makes her seem far more substantial than her slight frame.

"You Erin then?" she asks.

I nod. "It's nice to finally meet you in person, Holli," I reply.

Over the past three months our telephone conversations have been brief. Mainly consisting of me talking, explaining the project, and silences occasionally peppered by her distracted "yeah's" and "no's." But now that I can see her, I understand that those silences, which sounded empty over the phone, were actually very full. I just couldn't see before what they were full of.

"Would you like to sit down?" I offer.

"Not really." She holds her ground by the door.

A standoff.

"Sit down please, Holli, or we'll take you back to your cell," Amal fires into the heavy silence.

She drags the chair across from me slowly out from under the table and sits demurely, small hands in her lap. She looks up to the frosted window high on the holding room wall. I flick a look over to Amal. He gives me a reassuring nod. *Go ahead.*

"So, Holli. I'll just dive in with the questions, just like we discussed over the phone. Don't worry about the camera, just talk to me the way you normally would."

She's not looking at me at all, her eyes still lingering on the square of light above. I wonder if she's thinking of the outside. The sky? The wind? I suddenly imagine Mark in a taxi on his way home, a file box of his belongings on his lap, trapped in his own mess. What is he thinking right now as he glides through the City with nowhere to go? Now I look up to the skylight too. Above us two gulls swoop in the open blue. I take a deep breath of bleached prison air and drop my gaze back down to my notes. I need to stay focused. I push Mark to the back of my mind and look up into Holli's sharp face.

"Okay, Holli? Is that clear?"

She lets her eyes flop back down onto me.

"What?" She asks it as if I'd been talking gibberish.

Okay. I need to get this back on track. Plan B. Let's just get this done.

"Holli, can you tell me your name, age, sentence length, and conviction, please." It's an instruction plain and simple. My tone has slipped into that of Amal's. We don't have time for whatever game this is.

She sits up slightly in her chair. For better or worse, this dynamic she understands.

"Holli Byford, twenty-three, five years for arson in the London riots," she answers briskly, by rote.

She was one of the thousands of arrests over the five days of rioting across London in August 2011. The riots began when a peaceful protest at the unlawful shooting of Mark Duggan swiftly escalated into something else entirely. Opportunists, fueled by a sense of self-righteousness, quickly took advantage of the mayhem, and Tottenham descended into chaos. Police were attacked, shops burnt, property destroyed, and shopping malls looted. The chaos spread across London over the next few days and nights. Rioters and looters, realizing they were one step ahead of the police, started to coordinate their attacks via social media platforms. Looters gathered, united, and raided stores, then posted trophy shots of their hauls online. Stores closed, people stayed away, terrified of being attacked or worse.

I remember at the time watching the grainy camera-phone footage of people smashing into JD Sports, desperate for sneakers, desperate for sports socks.

Don't get me wrong; I'm not belittling it. You can only taunt people with the things that they can't have for so long. You can only push people so far. Until, for better or worse, they push back.

London was in free fall during those five days in August 2011.

Of the 4,600 arrests made over those days, a record 2,250 of them went to court. The sentencing was rapid and it was harsh. The authorities feared that if examples weren't made of the young people involved, then troubling precedents would be set. Half of those charged, tried, and sentenced were under twenty-one. One of them was Holli.

She sits across the table from me, her gaze once again on the window above.

"And what did you do in the riots, Holli? Talk us through that night, as you remember it."

She stifles a laugh, her eyes flashing across to Amal, looking for an ally, then slowly traveling over to me, her face hardening again.

"As *I remember it*"—she smirks—"it was the weekend they shot Mark Duggan. I look on Facebook and everyone's doing this crazy stuff—they'd broke into this retail park thing and they've got all this stuff, like clothes and that, and the police don't even care, and they're not even going there to stop anyone." She adjusts her messy bun slightly. Tightening the knot. "My mate's brother said he was going to drive us up there to get some stuff but then he got worried about his license plates coming up, so he didn't." She stops and looks again at Amal. He's looking blankly ahead. She's free to say what she likes.

"Anyway, on Sunday it all kicked off for real everywhere. I got a text from my mate Ash saying they were about to do the Whitgift Centre. It's like the main shopping center in Croydon. Ash says we've gotta wear hoodies, cover our faces, for the CCTV. So we go down there and there's loads of us. There's crumbled glass all over the ground in the street and everyone is just standing around. So Ash starts smashing into the electric doors of Whitgift. The alarm starts going then, so we all join in together 'cos we think there's not gonna be much time till the police come. But no one goes through; we just stand there. Then this guy who's running past just pushes straight through the crowd and he's like, 'What you fucking waiting for, you Muppets,' and he goes straight in. So then we push in too.

"I get some clothes and some nice stuff. Is this what you're after?" She breaks off. Her dead-eyed stare on me, again, hard.

"Yes, Holli, it's exactly what we're after. Keep going, please." I nod her on, trying to stay blank, impassive; I don't want this thrown off track.

She smirks again and shifts in her seat. She continues.

"Then we get hungry and wander back along the main street. People are throwing stuff— those newspaper dispensers, bricks, bottles on fire. Blocking off the road with those big bins. Anyway, Ash joins in and then when we see the police we run for it, Ash and me and his mate, back toward the bus station. It's quiet round there, no police, and there's this bus stopped right in the middle of the road, lights on with some people still on it. We wanna get safe for a bit, so we try and get on the bus too but the driver won't open up the doors. The driver starts having a fucking meltdown, shouting and waving his arms around. Then someone opens up the end door and the people on the bus start pouring out the other end 'cos they're scared we're gonna jump 'em or something. The driver's shitting himself 'cos now the door's open he's not so brave anymore. Then he runs for it too and we've got the bus to ourselves."

She leans back into her chair, satisfied, eyes cast up to the glass again.

"It was nice. We went up top and had a lie-down on the back seats and ate some chicken. Had a drink. That's when they got all our faces." She says it pensively.

"Anyway, I poured some Jack Daniel's on the back seats and lit it up with one of those free papers, as a joke. Ash starts laughing 'cos he didn't think I'd do it, and the whole back bit of the bus goes straight up in flames. So we're all laughing and throwing more papers on it 'cos it's fucking messy up there anyway. And it's burning really hot and stinking, so we go outside to watch. Ash is telling everyone I did it. And now the whole double-decker's on fire. People passing are high-fiving and fist-bumping me 'cos it looks completely mental. We got some insane photos on my phone. Don't look at me like that," she snarls. "I'm not completely retarded. I wasn't posting the pictures up online or anything."

"Holli, how did you get caught?" My tone neutral.

Her eyes slip off me. Challenge dropped.

"Turns out I'd been caught on someone's mobile phone footage, of the bus on fire and us watching it. Ash saying I'd done it. There was a photo on the front page of the local paper the next day. Me watching the bus burn. They used it in court. They got the footage of us on the bus too."

I've watched the burning-bus footage. Holli, her eyes bright like a kid at a fireworks display, joyful, alive. Her friend Ash a menacing wall of muscle and sportswear beside her, her protector. It's unsettling to watch, the laughter, the excitement, the pride. It's chilling, given her demeanor now, to know what it takes to make her smile.

"And are you excited to go home soon, Holli?" I have little expectation of an honest answer here but I have to ask.

She shoots another look across at Amal. A pause.

"Yeah, it'll be good. I miss my crew. I wanna put some normal clothes on." She shrugs her loose sack of a sweater. "Get some proper food in me. They're basically starving me in here it tastes so disgusting."

"Do you think you'd ever do something like that again, once you're out, Holli?" I ask. It's worth a shot.

She smiles, finally. Sits up in her seat.

"Definitely not. I won't be doing anything like that again." She's smirking again now. She's not even trying to lie well. She has every intention of doing something like that again. The conversation is starting to make me feel uncomfortable. For the first time, I wonder if Holli has mental health issues. I want this interview over now.

"And what are your plans for the future?"

Instantly her demeanor changes; her face, her posture, shift. She looks smaller again somehow, vulnerable. Her tone of voice is suddenly normal, a normal twenty-three-year-old woman. Polite, open, friendly. The change is deeply unsettling. I have no doubt that this is the face a parole board will see.

"Well, I spoke to the prison charity about helping to speed up my sentence. I want to give back to the community and prove I can be trusted again. They're going to help me get a job and work with my probation officer to help me get back on the straight and narrow," she says, full of sweetness and light.

I press her.

"But what do *you* want, Holli? For the future? What do you want to do with your life once you get out of here?" I try to keep my tone flat but I can feel the flavor of my own words.

She smiles again, innocently. She's getting a rise out of me and she's enjoying it.

"That would be telling. I just want to get out of here first. Then I don't know. You'll have to wait and see, won't you? But expect . . . great things, Erin. Great things." Her unnerving smirk is back.

I look to Amal. He looks back at me.

This is the utterly terrifying shape of things.

"Thank you, Holli. That's a fantastic start. We'll call it a day there," I say.

I turn off the camera.

6

Giving Me Away

We're having a dinner party. I know it's probably not the best time for it, given everything that's going on right now, but the wedding is fast approaching. Five weeks now, and I still need to ask someone a very important favor.

They'll be here in an hour. I haven't changed or washed yet, let alone started cooking. We're cooking a roast. I don't know why. I suppose it's fast and it's easy and it's something Mark and I can cook together. He's doing the meat, I'm the trimmings. Mark very much enjoyed that as a metaphor for our relationship when I said it earlier. A rare moment of levity. The joke has quickly evaporated, though, and now I'm standing alone in our state-of-the-art kitchen, staring at a cold fleshy chicken and a mound of vegetables.

| | |

Mark's not doing well, hence my lateness today. I've sent him off to get ready. It's been just over a week now since he was fired and he's been pacing back and forth ever since—in the living room, in the bedroom, in the bathroom, barefoot, while shouting into the phone at people in New York, Germany, Copenhagen, China. We need a night off. I need a night off.

I've invited Fred Davey and his wife, Nancy, over for dinner to-night. It's actually been planned for a month now. They're practically family. Fred has always been there with support and advice, ever since I met him on my first job, assisting on his White Cube docu-mentary. I really don't think my doc would be in production if he hadn't brainstormed with me and written so many letters with BAFTA letterheads. And lovely Nancy, one of the warmest, gentlest women I've ever met, never misses a birthday, an opening, or a get-together. My surrogate family, my tiny makeshift support structure.

There's still no sign of Mark in the kitchen, so I make a start on the food myself. He's been on the phone for half an hour already, trying to chase up yet another lead on a new job. It turns out that the feelers he'd mentioned on our anniversary morning have come to nothing, and that his "friend" in New York is the one who landed Mark, and ultimately us, in this mess. By the time I got home the day he lost his job, Mark had figured out that Andrew in New York had been responsible for everything. Andrew had rung Mark's desk and somehow mistaken Greg's voice for Mark's voice—I have no idea how this happened because Greg is Glaswegian. Anyway, Andrew mistook Greg for Mark and told him that someone from the New York office was going to be ringing him later in the day with a po-tential new job offer.

Greg, creep that he is, no doubt glowing with pleasure, then went straight to their boss and dutifully informed him of the phone conversation.

Andrew in New York had apparently not responded well to being implicated in this cock-up and had consequently soured the potential New York job offer. All that maneuvering just to save himself the ignominy of apologizing for the mistake he made in the first place. But then, you see, in the banking world apologizing is a sign of weakness. And weakness doesn't inspire confidence, and, as we all know, the market is built on confidence. Bull you win; Bear you lose. Hence Mark, now unemployed, standing half dressed in our living room shouting at the house phone.

He tells me that all's not lost. He's spoken to Rafie and a couple of other work friends and there are at least three possibilities floating around, if not more. He just needs to hang tight for a few weeks. There's nothing more he can do himself at this stage. Even if he gets an offer, he can't start till after garden leave, which means until mid-September. An enforced vacation. At any other time of my life I would absolutely love that idea, but now that the filming's actually started I'm going to be swamped until the wedding. Bad timing.

As if on cue he appears, washed and changed, in the kitchen. He smiles at me; he looks amazing. White shirted and freshly scented, he takes my hand and twirls me. We go on a brief, silent dance tour of the kitchen before he holds me at arm's length and says, "I'm taking over. Get up those stairs and make yourself more beautiful. I challenge you!" He grabs a tea towel and whips me giggling out of the room.

Some might find this switch unnerving, but I love that about Mark. He can turn on a dime, compartmentalize. He's in control of his emotions. He knows I need him tonight, so he's there.

Upstairs I agonize over what to wear. I want to seem like I've made an effort but effortlessly. It's a tricky balance.

Tonight I'm going to ask Fred to give me away at the wedding. It's delicate because Fred's not a relation. He's just the closest thing I have to a father. I respect him. I care about him and I flatter myself he cares about me too. At least I hope so. Anyway, I hate talking about my family. I feel like people place too much emphasis on where we come from and not enough on where we're going, but anyway . . . I suppose I need to tell you about my family so you understand.

My mother was young and beautiful and clever. She worked hard, she ran a company, and I loved her so much it hurts to think about her. So I don't. She died. Her car went off a road and rolled down onto a railway track one night twenty years ago. My dad rang me at boarding school the day after and told me. He came to collect me that evening. I got a week off school. There was a funeral. After that my dad took a job in Saudi Arabia. I saw him on school holidays when I went out there. At sixteen I stopped going, choosing to spend the holidays at friends' houses instead. He remarried. They have two kids now. Chloe's sixteen and Paul is ten. Dad can't make the wedding. And to be honest, I'm glad. He doesn't make it to much these days. I went over for a visit a couple of years ago. Slept in a bare spare room. I know he sees my mother when he looks at me, because that's all I see when I look at him. Anyway, that's it. That's all I'll say on it.

When I finally make it downstairs, the air is filled with the heady scents of dinner. The table is laid. Best plates, best glasses, champagne, and somehow Mark's fished out some cloth napkins. God. I didn't even know we had napkins. He grins up at me as I enter, his deep brown eyes tracing the contours of my body through the dress. I've gone with a minimalist black velvet dress, my dark hair pulled loosely back to reveal the long gold earrings Mark bought me for my birthday.

"Gorgeous," he says, looking me up and down as he lights the last candle.

I look at him silently. I'm nervous. He stands there, solid chested and handsome. He sees it, my worry. He sets down what he's doing and comes over to me.

"It's going to be fine. It's a lovely thing you're asking. It's going to be fine," he whispers into my ear, holding me close.

"But what if he asks about them?" I look up at him. I can't talk about it all again. I don't want to think of her.

"He knows you. He'll know there are reasons you need to ask him. And if he asks, we'll deal with it together. Okay?" He pulls back and meets my gaze.

I nod reluctantly. "Okay," I whisper.

"Do you trust me?" he asks.

I smile. "Implicitly," I say.

He grins. "Well, okay then! Let's dinner-party the hell out of this."

And with that the doorbell rings.

7

Wedding Dress

At knee level, a friendly Irish woman is hemming the folds at the base of my wedding dress. Her name is Mary. I stand there in the delicate Edwardian crepe de chine, observing the whole scene, detached and unsure of how to feel. Caro is looking on, my wedding attaché. She helped me find the dress. She knows a few costume designers who work in film. Costume designers tend to have a lot of vintage stock; they buy it up at auction, copy it for productions, and then sell it online. All in mint condition. This gown is one of those. It's perfect.

We've come to a tailor's basement in Savile Row for a few tiny alterations. The dress doesn't need much; it fits like a glove.

It's the tailor Caro's father used to use when he was alive. I'm not sure how he died, probably a heart attack, he was old. He'd had Caro late in life; I think she only caught his sixties and seventies. I don't know that much about him really—only tidbits slipped into conversations, never enough to grab hold of. There's a check framed and hanging in her house, in the downstairs loo, for a million pounds, payable to him. The house itself, left solely to her, is five floors in Hampstead with a garden the size of Russell Square out the back. He was a proper millionaire, an old-school millionaire; at least that's what I glean. There's a Warhol in the living room, propped casually against a wall.

So anyway, when Caro gives me advice I tend to take it, if I can afford it. They're doing my alterations for free. I'm not sure why, but free I can afford.

"Right, all done, sweetheart." Mary rubs the lint from her knees as she rises.

Back out on the street Caro turns to me.

"Late lunch?"

I'm starving. I haven't eaten since last night. In an unusually irrational move, I decided to skip breakfast this morning, not wanting to distort the dress-fitting measurements. I know, I know; I'm going to eat on the actual wedding day. In fact, I'm very much looking forward to it—the caterers we've chosen look amazing. Booked, deposit paid. The menu tasting is next week. Amazing. God, I'm starving.

"Lunch would be ideal." I check my watch; it's 3 P.M. Later than I thought, but I really need to talk to her. Mark's barefoot pacing is stuck on repeat in my brain. I need to talk about Mark's job. I don't want to but I have to. I have to talk to someone. Even though it feels like a betrayal talking about our relationship to other people. It's usually the other way around, Mark and I discussing them. We don't talk about each other to outsiders. We're our own unit. Impenetrable.

Secure. There's us and then there's the rest of the world. Until now. Until this.

It's not Mark, though; he's not the problem. I just don't know what to do. How to fix what's happening. Caro must read it on my face.

"Come on. We're going to George," she declares.

Yes, George. George will be quiet at this time of day. It's a gorgeous members-only restaurant with a canopied deck set back from the street in deepest Mayfair. Her gallery gets Caro in everywhere. She takes my arm and guides me further into Mayfair.

"What's up?" she demands once the waiter deposits two dewy glasses of ice water and disappears.

I eye her as I gulp my water down, the lemon tapping insistently against my top lip.

She smirks. "There's no use telling me nothing's up; you're an awful liar, Erin. And you're obviously desperate to tell me. So talk." She lifts her glass to her lips and sips expectantly.

I've run out of water. My ice rattles. "If we have this discussion, you have to forget it afterwards. Promise me." I put the empty glass down gingerly.

"Bloody hell, babes. Yeah, fine, promised." She leans back into her chair, eyebrows raised.

"It's Mark. He's been fired." My voice is slightly quieter than before; I'm aware of the businessmen three tables away. You never know.

"Huh? Laid off?" She leans forward, lowering her tone to match mine. What a pair we are. Bloody hell.

"No, not laid off. They're paying his garden leave but there's no financial package. No lump sum. They made him resign in exchange for references. If he said no, they'd have just fired him anyway, no references. Apparently that's what they wanted to do until his boss talked everyone around to the voluntary resignation."

"What!? What the actual! That's just—that's ridiculous! Bloody hell, is he all right?" Caro's shifted up an octave. A businessman swivels in his chair to look over at us. I hush her.

"It's fine. I mean . . . *he's* not fine, but it is fine. It's tricky because I really want to be there for him but at the same time I don't want to . . . you know, emasculate him by actually helping him, you see? It's delicate. I have to sort of fluff him up without him noticing. And don't get me wrong, it's not because he needs bolstering or anything. It's because I love him, you know, Caro. I want him to be happy. But he won't let me make him happy. It's like he thinks the worrying focuses him or something, like it's going to help fix it all. I've never seen him act like this, you know? He's always got a plan, but this one's falling apart. This whole EU situation, fucking Brexit, the bottom falling out of the pound, sterling at an all-time low, the government, the new prime minister, the new foreign secretary, for God's sake. Donald Trump! Everything is fucked. It's the worst possible timing for this total shitstorm."

"Humph." Caro shakes her head in solidarity.

I charge on. "And I know as well as he does, it's ruining his chances of getting something else. And not only that, but even if someone is looking, it's going to be hard to sell the idea to a future employer that he resigned from his job before getting another position. He says they're going to wonder why on earth he did that. It just looks weird, apparently. Well, that's what he's saying. But I say: Just tell people you didn't like it there. Or say you wanted a break from work before the run-up to the wedding. I mean, it's not a crime to take some time off. But then, I do see what he means. It looks weak. To them, I mean. Like he can't handle the pressure and had to 'take a break.' Like he had some kind of breakdown or something. Argh! God, it's so annoying. Seriously, Caro, it's driving me nuts. I can't fix it. Everything I suggest gets batted down. I don't know what to do. So I just sit there, listening and nodding."

I stop talking. She shifts in her seat. Looks out at the street and nods sagely before answering.

"I don't know what to say, hon. It's fucking frustrating. It'd drive me mad. Mark's a smart guy, though, isn't he? I mean—come on, he could do anything, right? Why doesn't he just get another job? He could work in any industry, really, with his experience. Why doesn't he just look for something else?"

The answer to that is simple. It's the same answer I'd give if Caro asked me to change my career. I don't want to do something else. And Mark doesn't want to do something else either.

"He *could*, definitely. But, you know, hopefully it won't have to come to that. We're still waiting to hear back about a couple of things. It's just that the wedding's coming up and it feels like he's checked out of it a little bit."

"Of what? The wedding planning? Or the actual relationship?"

"The . . . the planning? I don't know. I don't know, Caro. No, not the relationship. No." I feel bad now.

"Is he being an arsehole?" Her tone is now uncharacteristic in its extreme earnestness. I can't help but laugh out loud.

Caro looks instantly concerned; I guess I'm not acting very characteristic myself right now. I must look nuts.

"Sorry! No. No, he's not. He's not being an arsehole." I glance at her worried face, her crinkled forehead.

There's no point in this conversation, I realize suddenly. Caro doesn't know what I should do. She has no idea. She doesn't even know that much about me. Not really. I mean, we're friends but we don't really *know* each other. I'm not going to find any answers here. I need to talk to Mark. I'm just making a mess here, with this conversation. We should be talking about flowers and cake and hen weekends. I snap myself out of it.

"You know what, I think I'm just hungry! No breakfast," I confess. "Nothing's wrong, really, I think I'm just getting jittery about the wedding. And low blood sugar. What I need, what I *really* need, is a Caesar roll and some of those straw chips. And wine."

Caro's smile returns instantly. I'm back. Everything is fine, all stress forgotten. Confession erased. Slate wiped clean. I've turned a corner and she's completely on board. We move on. *Thank you, Caro.* And that, ladies and gentlemen, is why she is my maid of honor.

It's late afternoon when I finally leave Caro, joining the rush-hour commuters, tipsy and slow, as they pour underground.

On the tube home I think about what I'll say to him. We need to talk properly. About everything, actually.

Or maybe we just need to fuck. That always seems to reset us. It's been four days now since we slept together, which for us is long. We're usually a, at least, once-a-day couple. I know, I know. Don't get me wrong; I know that's not a usual amount. I know that after the first year has passed, that is ridiculously sick-making. I know because before I met Mark sex was more of a once-a-month ticketed-event type of thing. Overhyped and ultimately disappointing. Trust me, I've been in my fair share of shitty relationships. But we—Mark and I—have never been like that. I want him. I want him all the time. His smell, his face, the back of his neck, his hands on me. Between my legs.

God, I miss him. I feel my pulse racing. The woman in the seat opposite me looks up from her crossword. She frowns. Perhaps she can hear my thoughts.

Underneath my dress I can feel the soft brush of peach silk on skin. Matching underwear. I always wear matching, since I started dating Mark. He loves silk. I cross my legs slowly, feeling skin against skin.

8

Food Tasting

The first wedding-related thing we did, after getting engaged, was to look at venues. We dived straight in. We went to a lot of places: quirky, austere, opulent, futuristic, earthy. You name it, we've had a walk-around tour of it. But it was clear once we stepped into the bookish wood-paneled reception rooms at the Café Royal that that was what we wanted. Whatever *that* was.

Today they're laying on three options of every course for us to taste privately in the reception rooms, along with wine pairings and champagne choices. We've been looking forward to this for a long time, but now that it's here it seems a tiny bit like a formality. It also seems odd celebrating when Mark is going through all this. But we can't put life on hold.

In the underground on the way there, Mark reads news on his phone. I try to do the same. At Covent Garden he turns to me.

"Erin, listen. I know you're excited about this but can we just decide now that we'll go for the cheapest options on food and drink? Like, sure, we'll try it all and it'll be an amazing day, but moneywise, at the end of it let's just go for the cheapest, okay? I mean, it's a five-star restaurant already, so everything's going to be good, so, yeah? Can we agree on that? Is that all right?"

I see what he's saying. He's right, of course. It's dinner for eighty people, we do need to be sensible about it. And to be honest, their house wine is fucking amazing. We won't need anything more than that.

"Yes, okay. Agreed. Can we do it properly, though? Can we make all the right noises until the end? I want to try it all, all the stuff. I mean, why not, right? We're only going to do it once. We'll just try it and then we'll say at the end. Okay?"

He relaxes. "Okay! Great. Thank you."

I squeeze his hand. He squeezes back. Something shifts almost imperceptibly behind his eyes.

"Erin. Thanks for being, you know . . . I've got a lot on my plate right now and I know maybe I'm not expressing it in the best way." His eyes drift around the nearby passengers. They're all absorbed in phones and paperbacks. He leans in to me, quieter now. "I tend to clam up when I'm stressed. And, you know, I don't usually get stressed, so it's hard finding my way through this. So thanks."

I squeeze his hand harder and let my head fall onto his shoulder.

"I love you. It's okay," I whisper.

He shifts slightly, straightening up in the tube seat. He's not finished. There's more. I lift my head.

"Erin. I did something last week—" He falls silent.

He studies my face. My stomach flips. Sentences like that always chill me to the core. Words of preparation for something. Worse news to come.

"What did you do?" I ask it gently because I don't want to scare him off. I don't want him to shut down.

"Look, I'm sorry I didn't tell you this before. I just, I thought it wasn't the right time and then the right time didn't come and then it became a thing and now here we are." He stops. His eyes remorseful.

"I canceled our honeymoon."

"You what?!"

"Not all of it. I just, I've canceled a week of it. Bora Bora is only two weeks now." He studies my face. He waits to see what will happen next.

He canceled our honeymoon. No, he didn't cancel it; he just rearranged some of it, that's all. But without asking me? Without saying anything? Without checking with his future wife? Secretly? And now, now that I've agreed to pay less for the food today, he's decided that it's okay to tell me. Right. Okay.

My mind races as I try to process it. To find out what this means. But nothing comes. Is it important? Maybe it's not. I can't really make myself care. I can't make myself care about a vacation. It doesn't feel like a thing. Dare I say it: I don't mind. Should I mind? But then maybe the point is, he *lied*. Yes. Or did he? He didn't really lie, did he? He just did something without telling me. And, come on, at least he's telling me now. But then, he had to tell me at some point, right? Didn't he? What was the alternative? Not tell me until we were on the plane? No, of course he would have told me. It's fine. I've just been busy. I've been too busy with work. Besides, two weeks on a tropical island is fine. More than fine, bloody fantastic. That's more than some people get in a lifetime. And I don't need any of it anyway. I just want him. I just want to marry him. Don't I?

We'll work it out later. But right now I won't scare him away. Won't make it worse. He's made a mistake and he's sorry, so that's it.

I raise his hand, still interlaced in mine, and kiss his knuckles.

"It's fine. Don't worry about it. We'll have a chat about money later. Let's just have a lovely day. Okay?"

He smiles, eyes still sad.

"Done. Let's have a lovely day."

And it is a lovely day.

In the twinkly mirror-and-oak-paneled ballroom, we sit at a white-clothed table floating adrift on a sea of buffed parquet flooring. A cheerful waiter brings us intricate plates artfully arranged with seasonal fare. Once all the starter options are placed on the table, the maître d' explains each one and hands us a discreet card listing the dishes and prices. And disappears back through the oak paneling, leaving us to it. We peruse the card.

STARTERS:

Lobster with watercress, apple, crème fraîche vinaigrette,
£32 per person.

———

Rock Oysters with shallot vinegar, lemon, brown bread & butter,
£19 per person.

———

Asparagus with quail egg, beetroot & celeriac rémoulade,
£22.50 per person.

Times that by eighty people. And that's just the starter. I look at Mark; he's gone white. I can't help it. I burst out laughing. He looks at me, relief written all over his face. He smiles and raises his glass to toast. I lift mine.

"To not having starters?"

"To not having starters." I chuckle.

We dig in to the delicious entrées. And they're worth every single penny. I'm just glad we won't be the ones paying for them.

We opt for a main course of: *Café Royal Homemade Chicken Pie with Bacon, quail's egg, fine French beans, mousseline potatoes, £19.50.*

For desserts we go for: *Dark Chocolate & Wild Cherries: Dark chocolate crémeux and wild cherry compote, £13.*

Plus thirty bottles of house red and thirty house white and twenty bottles of sparkling wine.

We think we've done a pretty good job until the maître d', Gerard, sits down for a post-coffee chat. Apparently the minimum spend is six thousand pounds. They must have told us that last year when we booked, but we obviously weren't listening, and even if we were, it wouldn't have seemed important then. Gerard tells us not to worry; we can simply bump up to that price by adding after-dinner coffee and a cheeseboard for eighty people. Adding another thirteen hundred pounds to our total. We agree. Well, what else can we do? The wedding is in three weeks.

Afterwards, stuffed and brimming with buyer's remorse, we descend into Piccadilly Station. Before the turnstiles Mark takes my upper arm and stops me.

"Erin, we can't do this. Seriously, it's ridiculous. It's way too much, right? I mean—come on? We need to cancel it when we get home, lose the deposit, sure, fine, but just cancel it. We'll do the wedding part in All Souls and then go to a local restaurant or something? Or up to my mum and dad's, they could do a village hall thing, right?"

I look down at his hand tight around my arm. This isn't someone I recognize.

"Mark, seriously, you're scaring me a bit now. Actually scaring me. Why are you acting like this? It's our wedding. We've got savings, it's not like we're taking out loans to cover the cost. You only do this day once in your life and I personally want to spend my money on this. On us. I mean, not all of my money obviously, but a bit of it. Otherwise what's it all for?"

He sighs hard through his nose. Frustrated, he abandons the conversation, his hand releases me, and we descend underground.

The rest of our journey is spent in silence. I watch other people on the tube. Wonder about their lives. Sitting next to Mark but not talking with him, I imagine I don't know him. That maybe I'm just a girl on the tube going somewhere on my own. That I don't have to worry about what happens next, or with the rest of my life, for that matter. The thought is calming but ultimately empty. I want Mark. I do. I just wish I could shake him out of this mood. I wish I could fix it.

He turns on me as soon as we're through the front door at home. His voice is no longer the whisper it was in the station.

He tells me I don't understand. I'm not *listening*. I've never seen him like this, as if something inside were bursting to come out.

"I don't think you really appreciate what is going on here, Erin, do you? What's actually happening? I don't have a *job* anymore. There is no *money* for any of this. And I can't get another job, no one is hiring. My world is not like it is in *the arts* or your film school or whatever. I can't just jump ship and do something else for a living! I'm an investment banker. That's what I do. I'm not trained to do anything else. And even if I was, it doesn't matter. I can't just set up my own bank or, I don't know, collaborate on a postmodern banking project or whatever the fuck. I'm not like you. I don't come from the same place you do. I spent my whole life getting to where I am now. *My whole life.* Do you know how hard that was? People who went to my high school work in petrol stations, Erin! Do you understand that? They live in council flats and stack fucking supermarket shelves. I will not go back to that. I will not let that happen. But I don't have a backup. I don't have family friends in publishing or journalism or fucking wine-making. I've got a retired mum and dad in East Riding who are both going to need looking after before too long. I've got a total of eighty grand in savings and the rest tied up in this house. And now we're trying to have a baby. I had a real job. I've lost it, and we are screwed. Because unfortunately we don't all have the luxury of being paid for, like you do!"

I feel the bile rise up inside me. I've had enough. Enough of this for today.

"Fuck you, Mark! You're being a fucking arsehole. When have you ever paid for me? When? What am I, a fucking hooker?"

This was supposed to be a lovely day.

"No, Erin, no, you're not, sadly. Because if you were you'd shut the fuck up about now."

My heart skips a beat in my chest. Fuck. Mark has gone, just like that, and a stranger is standing in my living room. Fucking hell. My breathing becomes shallow—*God. Don't cry. Please don't cry, Erin. Just breathe.* I feel the prickle behind my eyes.

Mark looks at me.

He mutters something inaudible, then turns away and looks out the window.

I sit down in silence.

"I can't believe you just said that, Mark," I whisper.

I know I should let it go but—no, no, I shouldn't let it go. Fuck that! I have to marry this man in three weeks. If this is going to be the rest of my life from now on, I want to bloody know.

"Mark . . ."

"What, Erin! What do you think we're going to do after the wedding? If we do have kids? What do you think is going to happen? My job pays for *everything*. It paid for this house."

"No, Mark. No! We both pay for it! I put all of my savings into that deposit too. Everything I had," I blurt out, my voice rising to meet his.

"Okay, great, that's great, Erin. You put your money in too. But you can't pay all the mortgage on your salary, can you? I mean, we don't live in a one-bed flat in Peckham, do we? There's absolutely no way you can cover the mortgage on your own with what you earn. I don't mean to upset you, Erin, but you're just not listening. We're going to have to sell the house. Obviously!"

Sell it? Oh my God. I must look terrified, because he nods now, satisfied.

"I don't think you've really thought about this at all, have you? Because if you had, then honestly, Erin, you'd be just as worried about it as I am. We are going to go under."

Oh my God. I am silent. I've been an idiot. I see that now. This hurts. None of what he's saying had occurred to me. I hadn't thought about the fact that all our plans might simply fall through. That he just might not get another good job at all.

He's right. No wonder he's so angry. He's been dealing with this alone. And I've been flouncing around acting as if . . . But then I remember. It doesn't have to be like that. Like Caro said, he could just do something else.

"But, Mark, you can get another job! Any job! You've got a great résumé, can't you just—"

"No, Erin," he interrupts, wearily. "It doesn't work like that. What the fuck else am I going to do? All I am qualified to do is price and sell bonds, nothing else. Unless you're suggesting I work in a bar?"

"Mark, please. I'm just trying to help! Okay! I don't know exactly how your industry works, do I? I just want to be in this together, so please stop saying I don't understand and just explain it to me. *Please*." I know I sound like a petulant child but I don't know what else to say.

He sags down on the sofa opposite me, drained. His shoulders hunched. An impasse.

We sit in the silence, the low hum of traffic and wind through the trees in the garden just audible.

I get up and go over to sit next to him. I reach out and touch his back gently with my hand. He doesn't flinch away, so I start to rub it softly with my palm. Soothing him, stroking his warm back through the starched cotton shirt. He lets me.

"Mark?" I say tentatively.

"It's okay if we sell this place," I continue. "It's okay. It'll be sad, because I like it here. But I don't care where we live. I just want you. You anywhere. Under a bridge. In a tent. Just you. And we don't need to have kids straightaway, if it's the wrong time. And listen, I know you'd hate to do a different job, but it wouldn't bother me what you did, as long as you were happy. I mean, I wouldn't think any differently about you. You're just you. I never loved you for money or anything like that. It's nice to have it, sure, but I just want to be with you. We can even live with your mum and dad in East Riding if you want?"

He lifts his eyes to me. Smiles in spite of himself.

"That's great, Erin, because that was another thing I needed to tell you: Mum's already made up the futon in the spare room." He's watching me slyly. A joke. Thank God. We laugh and the tension bursts over us. It's going to be okay.

"I genuinely think that would make your mum's year, you know!" I laugh.

He smiles, sheepish, boyish again. I love him.

"Sorry." His steady look. He is sorry.

"Can you let me join in again?" I ask.

"Yes, I'm sorry. I should have told you how I felt before. But I will from now on, okay?"

"Yes please."

"Okay. But, Erin, I know it's stupid but . . . I can't go back to where I started. I can't do all that again."

"I know, honey. It's okay. You won't have to. We're going to work this out together. Because that's what we do."

He takes my other hand, my ring hand, lifts it to his mouth.

"Mark, should I go back on the pill? Should we wait?"

"You know what they say . . ." He kisses our engagement ring. "There's never a good time." He still wants it. Thank God.

He pulls me close. We swing our legs up onto the couch and fall asleep together, spooning in the afternoon sunlight.

9

Interview Two

I'm back at Holloway to meet Alexa, my second interview subject. The guard, Amal, has gone; instead we have a guard called Nigel. He's much older than Amal, mid-fifties, a career prison guard. I'd say by the look of him the novelty of the job wore off back in his early twenties, yet here he stands. We're in the same room as last time. I think of Holli staring opaquely up at the slice of sky, and her face morphs into Mark's. Holli's release date, and our follow-up interview, is set for five weeks from now, but that won't be till after the wedding and, now, after we're back from our honeymoon.

| | |

It's an odd damp day. I sip the staff room instant coffee that Nigel has made for me as I wait for Alexa to arrive. The coffee is hot and strong and that's all that matters right now. I like my coffee like my men. I am joking, obviously. Wait, am I? I didn't sleep that well last night; it's been two days since our argument. I think we're okay now, though. Mark and I. Over the weekend, we canceled the wedding venue and rejiggered a lot of wedding stuff together. It was actually pretty fun. I've been relieved to discover that I'm not a highly strung bride, not by a long shot. We've cut back in some places in order to splurge in others. We're all set now. And Mark seems much happier. More secure. Back to his old self. I think this whole thing has just shaken his confidence a bit. But he's back formulating a strategy now.

I don't care about the wedding as long as he's happy.

Nigel clears his throat loudly and gives me a nod. I turn on the camera next to me and stand awkwardly, as if I'll be greeting someone I don't know. But the funny thing with Alexa is that, since our telephone chats, I feel like I actually do know her, even though I've never met her.

I see her through the reinforced mesh of the door's window, her eyes: warm, calm, serious. She enters looking at me from under soft blond bangs. Her open face. The pale blue Holloway prison-issue sweatshirt, pants, and slip-ons look like they're from a Scandinavian fashion house on her. Like she's trying something new for London Fashion Week. Very minimalist, very chic. Alexa is forty-two. She looks toward Nigel and waits for him to nod before pulling out the seat opposite me. I extend my hand across the white void of the table. She takes it with a muted smile.

"Alexa Fuller," she says.

"Erin. It's great to finally meet you, Alexa. Thank you so much for coming."

"Yes, great to finally put a face to a voice," she says, her smile widening. We take our seats.

I want to get straight to it but Alexa is staring at Nigel. His presence is going to be an impediment.

"Nigel. I've got the camera on now. It's recording already, so would you mind stepping out of the interview? I'll make the tapes available. Just the other side of the door is fine."

I wouldn't have dreamed of asking Amal to do the same during my interview with Holli, but Alexa is by far the safest of my interviewees. Nigel shrugs. I'm sure he's aware of Alexa's history and her crime. He knows I'll be perfectly safe in here alone with her. I'm not so sure how safe I'd be with Holli and Eddie Bishop, though. I wonder if the authorities would ever even allow those two to be unsupervised.

Eddie has requested another telephone interview. I received an email from Pentonville on Sunday. I'm not sure what exactly he wants to discuss. I hope he isn't getting cold feet about filming next month. I hope it's not more game-playing.

I wait until Nigel leaves and the bolt slides on the door before I speak again.

"Thank you, Alexa. I really appreciate you taking part in this process. I know we've talked it all through over the phone, but just to recap: What I'm going to do is record everything we say here today. If something comes out wrong or you're not happy with how you've expressed something, then just let me know and I'll ask you again or I'll rephrase the question. You don't have to worry about performing for the camera or anything like that. Just ignore it and talk to me. Just like a normal conversation."

She smiles. I've said something funny.

"It's been a while since I've had a 'normal conversation,' Erin. So you'll have to bear with me, I'm afraid. I'll do my best." She chuckles. Her voice is warm and deep. It's funny to hear it now in person after hearing it on the phone for so long. We've had three pretty comprehensive phone conversations since we started the process. I've managed to keep off the central interview topics, as I want her to be able to tell me her story in full for the first time on camera. I want to keep it fresh. It's strange to see her now, here, real, in front of me. Of course, I've seen pictures of her in her file, articles in papers, the story Mark read over my shoulder only a month ago, but this is different. She's so calm, so self-possessed. I've seen her arrest photos from fourteen years ago, when she was twenty-eight. She's more beautiful now somehow; she was attractive then but she has clearly grown into her beauty. Her soft dark blond hair is tied back loosely in a low ponytail at the nape of her neck, her naturally sun-kissed skin has a sprinkling of freckles across her nose and forehead.

She's only half joking about the lack of normal conversation. I can see it in her eyes. I smile. I understand why she might have agreed to this project. Cultural homesickness. I can't imagine there are too many people like Alexa in Holloway. From where she's from. We're not the same generation, she and I, but we're definitely the same tribe.

"Shall we give this a go then? Any questions before we start?" I ask.

"No, I'm happy to jump right in." She straightens her already straight sweatshirt and shakes her bangs from her eyes.

"Great! Just to let you know, I'm going to keep my questions short; they'll be more like prompts for you, really, to focus you on a topic or redirect you. I can edit myself out and we can use voiceover later to overlay. Okay. Let's give it a go. Could you tell me your name, age, and sentence?"

I feel my phone buzz silently through my pocket. Mark. Maybe good news. Maybe a job offer? God, I hope so. That would solve everything in one quick stroke. The buzzing stops abruptly. Either went to voicemail or he's remembered where I am today. What I'm supposed to be doing right now.

I snap back into focus. I watch as Alexa takes a soft breath, I let go of thoughts of Mark, and the prison interview room seems to disappear around her.

"My name is Alexa Fuller. I'm forty-two years old and I've been here, in Holloway, for fourteen years now. I was convicted for assisting in the suicide of my mother, Dawn Fuller. She was terminally ill. Pancreatic cancer. I was sentenced for the maximum sentence allowable." She pauses. "Um . . . the maximum conviction ever given for assisted suicide. There had been a lot of press that year around lenient sentencing, lots in the media about assisted-suicide convictions being thrown out of court. There was an inquest where it was decided that the Crown Prosecution Service should take a harder line in the future. I just happened to be first through the door after the rules changed. They decided cases would be treated similarly to manslaughter, even if they clearly aren't manslaughter."

She stops for a second. Looking past me.

"She'd wanted to go to Dignitas in Switzerland originally, Mum, but we told her it would all be fine, she would beat it. She was only fifty-five and receiving the most intensive chemo program available. They all thought it would knock it on the head finally. But she had a heart attack.

"When they stopped the treatments she was too sick to fly; I wouldn't have wanted to take her to Switzerland anyway. Dad and I visited the place whilst she was still in ICU recovering. It was so cold there. Empty, you know, like one of those hotel rooms you get at motorway service stations." She pulls her sleeves down over her hands before continuing. "I couldn't imagine her there. Dying."

For a fraction of a second, I think of my mother. A flash of Mum in a bed, in a room, somewhere, alone. That night after the crash. After they found her, broken, rain-soaked. I don't know what room it was or where it was, whether she was alone. I hope it wasn't a room like that.

Alexa's eyes flick up to my face. "Neither of us wanted to imagine her there. So we brought her home. And she got worse. And then one day she asked me to leave her the morphine. I knew what that meant. . . ." Her voice wobbles.

"I put it on the nightstand but she couldn't pick up the bottle. She kept dropping it on the bedsheets. I called Dad downstairs and we talked it all through together, the three of us. I went upstairs and got the camcorder, Dad set up the tripod, and Mum told the camera, and later the courtroom, that she was in sound mind and wished to end her life. She showed how she couldn't lift the bottle on her own, let alone inject herself, and then she explained that she was asking me to help her. After the video we had dinner. I set the table in the living room with candles. We had champagne. Then I left her and Dad to talk. He came out into the hall after. He didn't say anything. I remember that. He just walked past me, up to bed. I tucked her up in the duvet on the sofa and we talked for a while but she was tired. She would have talked all night with me but she was too tired."

Alexa's breath catches. She looks away. I wait, silent.

"She was tired. So I did what she asked, and then I kissed her goodnight and she fell asleep. Not long after that, she stopped breathing." She pauses before looking back at me. "We never lied, you know. Not once. We told the truth from the beginning. It was just bad timing. With the crackdown. But that's life, isn't it? Sometimes you're the dog; sometimes you're the lamppost."

She smiles her muted smile.

I smile back at her. I don't know how she's done it, stayed sane after being stuck so long in this place for doing what anyone would have done. For helping someone she loved. Would I do that for Mark? Would he for me? I look at Alexa. Fourteen years is a lot of thinking time.

"What job did you do before prison, Alexa?" I ask. I want to get her back in flow again.

"I was partner at a corporate law firm. I was doing pretty well, all told. Mum and Dad were very proud. *Are* proud. I wouldn't go back to it, though, even if I could, which I definitely can't. But I wouldn't."

"Why not? Why wouldn't you go back?" I prompt her.

"Well, I don't need the money, for starters. I made a lot before. I invested well. We have a house already. Well, my dad does. I'm moving back in with my dad; he owns outright, no mortgage anymore. I could retire on my investments and savings. I won't, but I could."

She smiles and leans forward, resting her elbows and forearms on the table.

"My plan . . . my plan is to try and get pregnant." She says it softly, instantly young again, vulnerable. "I know I'm getting on, obviously, but I've spoken to the prison doctor about it and the IVF available now is just light-years ahead of where it was before I came in here. I'm forty-two and I'm out in a month. I've already contacted a clinic. I've got an appointment set for the day after I get home."

"Donor sperm?" I hazard. She's never mentioned a man in any of our phone calls. There aren't many people who can wait around for fourteen years, I suppose. I'm not sure I could.

A burst of laughter. "Yes, donor sperm. I'm a fast mover but I'm not *that* fast!"

She looks genuinely happy. Joyful. Making a person. Making a new life. I can feel my heart beating faster. The idea of a baby. A baby with Mark. A warm feeling. We bask in it together for a second. Mark and I have talked it through already. We're going to start trying. I came off the pill four weeks ago. We're going to try for a baby, and if it happens on honeymoon so much the better. It's strange that Alexa and I are at the same point in our own, very different, lives.

She leans in. "I'm going to try as soon as possible. The chance of success drops every year, but the limit for IVF is forty-five, so I've got three years. Three years' worth of chances. I'm healthy. It should be fine."

"Why do you want to have a baby?" It sounds stupid even as I say it. But she takes the question as I meant it.

"Why does anyone? I suppose so much of my life recently has been endings—endings and waiting. Even before prison: waiting for holidays, or for a better time, or next year, or whatever. I don't even know what I was waiting for. But now I get a new beginning. I don't have to wait anymore. I've done all my waiting and now I'm going to live."

She sits back in her seat, face glowing, lost in a world of possibilities.

I take the opportunity to glance at my phone. We've run over by ten minutes. My one missed call up on the screen. I can see the edge of Nigel's shoulder through the small window in the door. He's not rushing us but I don't want to push my luck.

"Thank you, Alexa." We're done for the day. I stand and press the door release button on the wall. I sneak another glance at my phone and tap the notification. The call was from Caro, not Mark. My disappointment is so sharp I can taste it. I guess he doesn't have a job yet. I was so sure for a second there. But never mind. Early days. Early days.

The claxon sounds abruptly, bolts slide, and Nigel, slightly startled, trundles in.

I turn off the camera.

10

Honeymoon

Words are said. He slips a thin gold band onto my finger.

His eyes, his face. His hands on mine. The music. The feel of the cold stone beneath my thin shoes. The scent of incense and flowers. Of eighty people's best perfume. Happiness. Pure and clean.

We kiss, familiar voices rising loud behind us. And then the bone-shaking organ thundering out Mendelssohn's titanic "Wedding March."

And petals, petals fall all around us as we step out into the autumn air of London. Husband and wife.

I'm woken by a gentle knocking. Mark hasn't woken up yet; he's still sound asleep, nestled beside me in the vast hotel bed. My husband. My sleeping new husband. The gentle taps continue. I roll out of bed, throw a robe on, and tiptoe into the suite's sitting room.

It's coffee. Two tall silver coffee pots on a white-clothed trolley waiting outside in the hall. The room service waiter whispers a "Good morning" and beams.

"Thank you so much," I whisper back, and wheel the trolley around myself into our thickly carpeted lounge area. I sign and return the bill; there's a bloody big tip on there. Today I'm officially sharing the joy.

It's six o'clock on a Sunday morning. I ordered the coffee last night because I thought it might soften the early start. But to be honest, I'm okay. Already wide-awake and raring to go. I'm so glad I didn't drink too much last night. I didn't really want to. I wanted to stay clearheaded, stay focused. I wanted to remember and treasure every moment.

I push the trolley around our plush hotel furniture and into the bedroom and leave it to stand while I pop into the shower. Hopefully the pungent aroma of coffee will wake him up naturally. I want everything to be perfect for him today. He loves coffee. I hop into the rainforest shower and soap myself, careful not to wet my hair as I wash. We need to be out of the hotel and on our way to the airport in half an hour.

Today is, technically, going to be the longest day of our lives. We'll be traveling backward across eleven time zones and the International Date Line, so that after twenty-one hours of air and boat travel we'll be on the other side of the world and it'll only be ten o'clock. I let the hot soapy water flow over my shoulder muscles, my arms, the new gold band on my finger.

Snapshots of yesterday shutter through my mind: the church, Fred's toast, Mark's toast, Caro talking to Mark's parents, the first dance. The last dance. Last night, finally alone. Desperate for each other.

I hear the light clink of china on china. He's up.

And I'm out of the shower in a second and wet in his arms.

"Too early, Erin. Too early," he protests grouchily as he pours the hot coffee out for us. I cover him in kisses and shower water.

He hands me a cup and I stand there fully nude and soaking wet as I sip it. I'm looking pretty good at the moment, if I do say so my-self; I'm in shape. I sort of made a point of it. It's not every day a girl gets married. He drinks his coffee perched on the end of the bed, his eyes playing lazily across my body as he sips.

"You're beautiful," he says, still half asleep.

"Thank you." I smile.

We're dressed and checked out in no time. A Mercedes glides into the Sunday morning half-light outside the hotel. The driver intro-duces himself as Michael but doesn't say much else during the jour-ney to Heathrow. We sail through the abandoned early morning streets, safely muffled in our leather-scented cocoon; the only people about are the occasional revelers, still stumbling home. Somewhere out there in the half-light, out toward North London, through locked corridors of sleeping bodies, lie Alexa, Eddie, and Holli, in bare, sealed rooms I'll never see, about to live a day I'll never really understand. I feel my freedom with renewed clarity.

At Heathrow, Mark leads me past the already-snaking British Airways queues toward the empty check-in desks at the end of the aisle. First. I've never traveled first-class before. I have that odd mixed feeling of excitement paired with middle-class guilt at the idea of it. I want it, but I know I shouldn't want it. Mark has traveled first with clients—he assures me I'll love it. I shouldn't overthink it.

At the desk a woman with a dazzling smile greets us like long-lost friends returning home. Fiona, our check-in assistant, the only check-in assistant who has ever introduced herself by name to me, is infinitely hospitable and helpful. I could definitely get used to this. I suppose money buys you time and time buys you attention. It feels great. *Don't overanalyze it,* I tell myself. *Just enjoy. You'll be poor again soon.*

We glide through security. The guards seem almost embarrassed to check our bags. Once my shoes are back on, Mark points across the security hall to the far right wall. In the wall is a door. Just an ordinary white door. No sign. It looks just like a staff room door. He smiles.

"That's Millionaire's Door." He grins and raises an eyebrow. "Shall we?" he asks.

All I can do is follow. He strides confidently as he crosses the hall, like he knows exactly where he's going, whereas I feel absolutely certain we'll be stopped at any moment. As we walk toward its un-signposted archway, I half expect, at any second, a hand to grab my arm, to escort us into some tiny interview room for hours of grueling terrorism questioning. But that doesn't happen; we make it across the hall unnoticed, through the strange little doorway, and out of the low-level bustle of the concourse into the cool hushed air of the Concorde Room lounge.

It's a secret shortcut for first-class passengers only. Straight from fast-track security into the private British Airways lounge.

So this is how the other half lives? Well, the other 1 percent, anyway. I had no idea.

British Airways apparently pays one million pounds sterling a year in compensation to Heathrow to make sure their first-class passengers don't have to suffer the indignity of having to walk past all those duty-free shops full of shit they don't need. And today neither do we.

It's heaven inside the lounge. It's nice to be on this side of the door, not that I even knew there was a door up until five minutes ago. That's strange, isn't it? When you think you know what a good thing is and then you suddenly realize that there is a whole other level beyond what you knew even existed? Scary, in a way. How quickly what is good can become not good enough through comparison. Maybe best never to see it. Maybe best not to know that everyone else in the airport is being shepherded through retail units designed to strip them of the very little that they have, while you keep yours safe.

Don't overthink it, Erin, stop it. Just enjoy it. It's okay to enjoy having this good thing.

Everything in here is free. We sink down into the leather restaurant booths and order a light breakfast of freshly baked pain au chocolat and English breakfast tea. I look at Mark. Gorgeous Mark reading the paper. He looks happy. I look around at the other people in the lounge. Somehow first class has imbued them all with a kind of mystery, a mystique that drips from every movement, endowing it with a sort of grace. Or perhaps I've imbued them with that because I feel like I've wandered into a glen of unicorns.

Millionaires don't really look like millionaires, do they? Elon Musk doesn't even look like a millionaire, and he's actually a billionaire.

As I look at them, on their iPhones sipping their espressos, I wonder. I wonder, do they only ever travel first? Do they mix with other people? In their everyday lives? Do they mix with Club Class people? Economy people? I know they employ them, but do they mix with them? And what do they all do for jobs? How do they have so much money? Are they good people? I imagine Alexa flying business for her job before everything happened. I can imagine her here somehow. She'd look the part, even in her powder blue prison uniform. And Eddie. I can easily imagine Eddie here, a ghost lurking in one of the shadowy leather-bound corners, coffee cup in hand, eyes restlessly scanning, missing nothing. I returned his email with a call the day before the wedding. It was an odd call. I felt he wanted to say something but maybe he was being monitored this time. I can definitely imagine him here. But not Holli. I can't imagine Holli here the way I can Eddie or Alexa. I wonder if she's ever even left the country. Has she felt the Mediterranean sun? Let alone the wet heat of the tropics? I doubt it. But maybe I'm stereotyping, maybe Holli used to travel all the time. There's that guilt again. *Don't overthink it, Erin, just enjoy it.*

For the first time in my life I board the flight and turn left; everyone else turns right. And if I'm honest it's hard not to feel special, even though I'm aware I've just paid a lot more money than everyone else, money that we only really have by various quirks of fate and birth. But I do. Feel special.

"It's a Dreamliner," Mark leans in and whispers.

I have no idea what he's talking about.

"The plane," he explains.

"Oh, the plane is a *Dreamliner.*" I give him a teasing look. "I didn't realize you were so into planes." I grin.

Mark's into planes. Weird that I've never noticed. I can see why he might want to keep that hobby under wraps. Not the sexiest interest a man can have. But he has lots of other pretty sexy hobbies, so I'm fairly comfortable letting him off on this one. I make a mental note to get him something plane-related for Christmas. Maybe a coffee table book, a nice one. I'll check out some plane documentaries.

Mark and I have the two front-row center seats and my God it's not like economy seating. First has only eight seats. Only two rows of seating in the whole cabin. And even they aren't full. It's quiet up at this end of the plane. Peaceful.

This is to economy what organic farming is to factory farming. The economy passengers way back there, like industrially farmed chickens cramped in for eleven hours. And us, the corn-fed free-range chickens, happily clucking our way through the tall grass. Maybe that's the wrong metaphor; maybe we're actually the farmers?

I sink down into my seat, buttery leather with that fresh new-car smell. The seat walls reach all around us high enough so that I can't see the other passengers in their seats over it, but low enough that I can see the hostess when she passes. She comes around the five passengers and hands out champagne in tall chilled glasses as people take their seats and stow away hand luggage.

We explore our nests, our homes for the next eleven hours; the electronic wall dividing our seats is lowered and we investigate all our new devices together. A flat-screen TV is mounted on the seat wall in front of me, handy little storage cupboards, noise-canceling headphones. A wash kit squirreled away, embossed with "First," full of miniature products that weirdly remind me of the Fisher-Price kitchen set I had as a child. When I used to play house. I find a generously sized fold-out one-person dining table in the cupboard above the armrest. And, yes, I am excited by that! I'm drinking champagne at nine forty-five in the morning; of course I'm excited by that. I'm excited by everything! I slide my carry-on bag into a cubbyhole. It was a wedding gift from Fred. He was so happy to be a part of our wedding. To walk me down the aisle. To stand there beside me. I know it meant a lot to him to be asked. Lovely Fred. Fred and Nancy. They never had kids themselves. Perhaps they could be godparents? When the time comes maybe? I think I'd like that. I wonder if Mark would like that.

And just like that we're in the air.

My mouth is full of champagne when the stewardess pops her head over the wall and asks what size pajamas I'll need. Caught in the act, I feel my neck warm with embarrassment, breakfast-time lush that I am.

"Small. Thank you very much," I manage after I've swallowed.

She smiles and hands me the small navy pajama set wrapped in white ribbons, a white BA logo emblazoned on the left breast. Soft. Snug.

"Just let me know if you fancy a nap later," she trills, "and I'll make up your bed for you, okay?" And she's gone from view.

I've always had a bit of a problem with free champagne. Lovely, lovely free champagne. I find it very hard to turn down. If the glass gets topped up, it gets drunk. It's the one time that the phrase "You'll regret not finishing that" actually resonates with me. So three glasses in, and one in-flight movie down, the stewardess and I are having a nap-related chat.

My bed is made up by the time I'm back from brushing my teeth in the cavernous washroom, the basin being a good three-stride walk from the toilet. The bed looks pretty inviting: thick duvet, plump pillow, all made up on the flat cabin bed. Mark laughs at me through the partition wall as I clamber in.

"I can't believe you're drunk already. We haven't even been married a full day yet."

"I got excited. Now shush, you, I'm going to sleep it off," I say as the electric divider slowly blocks out his grinning face.

"Night, you old alkie." He laughs again.

I smile to myself. All tucked up cozy in my nook, I close my eyes.

I manage a fairly impressive seven hours' sleep on the first flight. And when we land in LAX I'm feeling relatively well rested and thankfully fully sober. I've never been a big drinker. A few of glasses of anything and I'm knocked out. Mark stayed up the whole flight watching movies and reading.

At LAX we find our way to the first-class lounge of American Airlines. It's not quite as impressive as Heathrow, but we've got only thirty minutes to kill now until our flight to Tahiti boards. This is the tricky part of the trip. The midway point. The eleven-hour flight to LAX done. The eight-hour flight to Tahiti about to start, followed by a forty-five-minute flight to Bora Bora and then a private boat trip around the atoll to the Four Seasons hotel.

We get an email from Mark's parents. Family photos they took at the wedding yesterday. There we all are—at least I think it's us, we're pretty blurry and we all have red eyes, but it's definitely us. I suddenly realize I've never felt happier than I do at this very moment.

Mark manages six hours' sleep on the next flight. This time I stay awake, gazing out of my oval window, transfixed by the pinks and purples of the setting sun reflecting off the vast Pacific Ocean beneath us. The clouds: miles and miles of mountainous white, turning peachy in the fading sunlight. And then just blueness, rich, dark velvet blue. And stars.

A wave of hot, wet tropical air slaps us as we step off the plane in Tahiti. The first hint of our honeymoon. We don't see much of Tahiti itself, just a runway, landing lights, an almost empty airport concourse, another departure gate, and then we're airborne again.

Our flight to Bora Bora is via a small plane with brightly dressed hostesses. Somehow Mark sleeps on the short, bumpy flight. I manage to finish reading the magazine I picked up from the Concorde lounge at Heathrow; it's an extremely niche quarterly dressage publication titled *Piaffe*. I know nothing about dressage—my teenage girl's basic riding knowledge doesn't quite stretch to advanced equine showing—but the magazine looked so far removed from anything I'd ever seen before that I had to pick it up. Turns out that "piaffe" is when the horse stands in the middle of the arena and trots up and down on the spot. So there you go. Bet you're glad we found that out. I do like things like that, though; I've always been into reading whatever is lying about, the less I know about it the better. I remember someone at film school suggesting developing that habit: always read outside your comfort zone. That's where stories come from. That's where ideas come from. Anyway, I can highly recommend *Piaffe*. It lost me slightly in the horse-feed section, but, overall, interesting stuff. If not directly for its content, then definitely to wonder at the lifestyles, and habits, of its average reader.

Bora Bora Airport is tiny. Two beaming women garland us upon arrival. The white flowers hang sweet and musky around our necks as a porter leads us toward a jetty in the water outside the terminal. The airport and its runway take up one entire island of their own on the atoll of Bora Bora. The whole airport island is just a long stretch of tarmac, edged with balding dry grass and a terminal building afloat in the blue of the South Pacific. A real-world visual representation of man's dominance over nature.

A speedboat waits for us, beautiful in understated varnished wood, at the end of the jetty, like a Venetian water taxi. Our water taxi driver takes my hand and helps me down into the deck seating. He offers me a warm blanket for my knees.

"It can get pretty breezy when we get going." He smiles. He's got a kind face, like the women in the airport. I suppose there's not that much to worry about out here, no city life to harden you.

Mark passes our bags down and hops on himself and then we're off. It's dark as we speed around the coves and bays. I wish we'd arranged the flights so we could see this in daylight. I bet it's breathtaking, but right now in the darkness I see only the twinkling lights along the shoreline and the huge moon hanging across the water. The brilliant white moon. I'm certain the moon's not this bright back in England. But it must be. Maybe we just can't see how bright it is through all the light pollution back there.

England seems so far away now. Those hedged lanes, the frosty grass. I feel a brief pang for it, nine thousand miles away, misty and cold. My hair whips around my face in the perfumed breeze. We're slowing down now. Nearly there. I turn back to look at the mainland, the shoreline, and the lights of the Four Seasons. And there it is.

The water all around glows emerald, up-lit through the green lagoon water. Soft candlelight bathes the thatched buildings, the communal areas, restaurants, and bars. Flaming torches flicker along the beachfront. Huts on stilts spill their orange warmth out into the thick darkness of the South Pacific Ocean. And that moon. That moon, shining as bright as a high beam on a country road, shining out from behind the sharp towering silhouette of Mount Otemanu, the extinct volcano at the center of Bora Bora's atoll. We're here.

The water laps placidly around us as we slowly *put-put* in. Candles light up the jetty and a welcome party ties us off and pulls us in. More garlands. Sweetly scented, spicy. Water. Cool towels. A slice of orange. And a golf buggy whisks us along the stilted walkways toward our new home.

We've got a fantastic room, Mark made sure of that. The best they have. An overwater lagoon bungalow at the end of the pier.

Private plunge pool, private lagoon access, glass-floored bathroom. We pull up to the door and there's a welcome talk but we're tired now. I can see through Mark's smiles to his tired eyes, and the hotel staff must see it too. We're exhausted. The intro is blessedly brief.

The buggy buzzes away from us back down the walkway, leaving us alone outside our suite. Mark looks at me as the sound of the buggy recedes. He drops his bags and lunges toward me, grabbing my waist with one arm and my thighs with the other and I'm up in the air, cradled in his arms. I kiss the end of his nose. He grins and fumbles us over the threshold.

11

A Storm Is Coming

Four days of the holiday go by. A dream. A turquoise, warm-sanded dream.

Breakfasts canoed across the rippling green of the lagoon to us. Juicy ripe fruits that I don't even know the names of. Padding bare-foot across cool-tiled floors and hot decking. Slipping into clear pool water. Letting the sun soak deep into my tired English skin right down into my damp British bones.

Mark in the sunlight. Mark's glistening body through the water. My fingers running through his wet hair, across his browning skin. Damp sex tangled up in sheets. The soft hum of air conditioning. I model a flipbook of delicate, beautiful underwear every day. Cobweb-thin black lace with glinting crystals, fuchsia blooms, brassy red, cheap white, rich cream, silk, satin. Long, easy conversations across paddleboards and bars. As we decided, I stopped taking the pill seven weeks ago. We make plans.

A helicopter tour of the surrounding islands. The thick thudding of rotor blades through cushioned headsets. Endless blue in every direction, above and below. Forests seemingly growing clean out of the ocean. A heaven on earth.

The pilot tells us that, out past the reefs, the waves tower so high that seaplanes can't even land on the water. This is the second-most-remote island chain in the world. The waves here are the largest waves on the planet. We see them breaking, rolling, through the Perspex floor of the helicopter, through its windows. We are thousands of miles from mainland, from the nearest continent.

Desert islands crest up out of the ocean. Cartoon drawings made real. The smallest circles of sand to the craggiest peaks, all with at least one palm tree. Why do desert islands always have palm trees? Because coconuts float. They float across the ocean, they float alone for thousands of miles, until they beach and plant themselves in the hot sand. Their roots sink deep, right down into the earth until they hit the rock-filtered fresh water far under the ground. Like swimmers finally making it to shore.

A day spent snorkeling in the soft water of the lagoon. I think of the cold weather back at home as I float quietly, surrounded by great gliding manta rays, like gray ghosts made flesh, rippling muscular through the pristine silence.

Mark books out the scuba-training pool for us, just me and him. A session to ease me back in. The bad experience, the one before I met Mark, shall be forgotten, he promises. I was only twenty-one when it happened, but I remember it with crystal clarity. I panicked at eighteen meters under. I don't know why but I suddenly became certain that I was going to die. I thought of my mum. I thought of the fear she must have felt, trapped in that car. I let my thoughts take over and I panicked. I remember people saying at the time I was lucky it worked out the way it did because it might not have. I could have easily taken a great gasping breath of seawater. But I don't panic these days. I don't let my thoughts take over. At least I haven't since then.

I hardly sleep the night before the pool—it's not fear exactly, just low-level anxiety. But I had promised Mark and, more than that, I had promised myself. Every time my mind drifts to the thought of the oxygen regulator, I feel the tension pinching deep in between my eyebrows. Who am I kidding, I'm fucking terrified.

I'm not scared of drowning or water or anything like that. I'm scared of that blind panic. The blind panic that traps rabbits in snares, pulls the noose tighter, and drowns them in their own blood. Silly things happen in blind panics. Things die.

Look, I'm not crazy. I know it'll be fine. It's bloody scuba diving. It's supposed to be fun! Everyone does it. I know nothing will happen. It will be beautiful. So beautiful. Awe-inspiring out under the South Pacific Ocean. Something to always remember. But my thoughts just keep opening up like trapdoors under me. Panic, disorientation, claustrophobia. An accidental gasp of water and thrashing terror.

But no. I'm a grown woman. I can control my fears. That's why I'm doing this, really, right? That's why we challenge ourselves, isn't it? To silence those fears. To wrangle them back into their box. I think of Alexa in her cell, in her cell for fourteen years. We wrangle our fears, don't we? That's what we do.

When Mark and I get to the pool, we slip into the water and start our pre-dive buddy check. Mark guides me slowly through. I'm glad of the cooling effect of the pool water, as the back of my neck is hot with nerves. *Just breathe,* I have to remind myself. *Just breathe.*

"You're doing great," Mark says reassuringly. "You remember all this bit perfectly, and this is the tricky bit, to be honest. I've got your back, okay? I've got you. But listen—" He stops and looks at me seriously now, his hands on my shoulders. "If you feel panic rising at any point underwater, just continue breathing. If you want to shoot up to the top, just keep breathing. It'll only be your brain trying to protect you from something that isn't really a problem. It's no more dangerous down there than it is up here, I promise you. Do you trust me, honey? It'll be fine." He smiles and pats my shoulders. I nod. I will always trust him.

The thing that keeps swimmers afloat is the oxygen held in the lungs. The lungs when full are like two rugby balls inside our chests making sure we stay up. That's why if you lie on your back in the sea you can relax your whole body and float with just your face out of the water. The trick for the diver is learning to use this buoyancy to regulate depth. That's what the weights are for: to drag us to the bottom.

We descend together suspended in pale blue. Tiny bubbles go up and we lower smoothly as if in an invisible elevator. The silence under the pool's surface is amniotic. I can see why Mark likes diving. I feel calm, all thoughts of panic dissipated. Mark glances back at me, beatific through a foot of dense water. It's like we're separated by thick glass. He smiles. I smile back. We feel closer down here than we ever could up there. We exchange the "OK" dive hand signal. You know it; it's the hand gesture "the Fonz" would give you if you asked how his date was going. Mark and I sit cross-legged opposite each other on the scratchy tile floor of the deep end, passing the oxygen regulator back and forth to each other like a twenty-first-century peace pipe. Still I remain calm. The trapdoor thoughts are gone. They feel inconceivable now as I look into Mark's calm face. We are safe. Just us and silence. It could just be the oxygen relaxing me, of course. It's supposed to have a calming effect, isn't it? I'm sure I've read that somewhere, something about oxygen masks on airplanes. Or maybe it's the color of the pool that's soothing me. Or the thick underwater silence. Or Mark. Right now all I care about is that I'm perfectly at peace. I am fixed. Mark has fixed me. We stay under like this for a long time.

| | |

The dream continues. Warm sand at sunset. Ice clinking on glass. The smell of sunscreen. Fingerprints on my paperback. There's so much to see. So much to do. Until day five.

On day five we hear a storm is coming.

Storms here aren't like storms back home. That much is clear. You don't just move your patio furniture inside and cover the roses. Here, storms are serious business; the nearest hospital is an hour's flight back to Tahiti and no one flies in a storm. Storms can last for days, so they're handled with logistical precision. The beaches are cleared, restaurants battened, guests briefed.

After breakfast a friendly manager knocks on our bungalow door. He tells us that the storm should hit around 4 P.M. and it'll probably last until early tomorrow morning. It's only hours away. He reassures us that it will pass the island by; although we'll feel it, we won't get the full brunt of it, so we don't need to worry about being washed away to sea or anything crazy like that, that never happens here. The manager chuckles. The bungalows are in the lagoon, protected from the waves by the atoll, so I suppose it would take a bloody strong wave to crest the atoll and the string of islands, pick us up and carry us off. The lagoon has been here for thousands of years; it's not going anywhere today.

He tells us that the staff will be on duty all night and, in the unlikely event that the storm should change course, we will be alerted promptly and moved into the main body of the hotel. But that hasn't been necessary in the entire time he has worked on the island, he says, and today's storm, although certainly choppy, doesn't look too troublesome.

After he leaves we go out onto our private deck and look out across the lagoon. The sky is sapphire blue and the sun is shining out across the water. Nothing hints at the storm to come. We look at each other; we're both thinking the same thing, *Where is it?*

"Shall we go check the other beach?" Mark asks, suddenly excited. He's read my mind; maybe we can see it coming from that direction. Perhaps the storm is coming from behind us. We grab our sneakers and set off through the carefully preened jungle of the Four Seasons toward the storm front.

On the other side of the resort, the side that's open to the South Pacific Ocean, there's another longer, straighter beach. It's windy here, too windy for hotel guests. The ocean is rough, the waves noisy and powerful, not like the quiet, still lagoon that our bungalow is perched on. The wild side of the island. I want to see the storm; I want to see it coming. The sun still shines bright and warm but the wind whips through our hair and T-shirts as we paddle into the shallows. And then we see it. On the horizon.

A towering column of cloud, ocean to sky, in the far distance. I've never seen anything like it. A wall of rain and wind. There's no sense of perspective here, looking out at the vastness of the sky, no way to know its size, there's nothing to judge it against, but as we watch, it fills half of the sky. At its edges patches of blue sky appear and vanish. A single thrilling pillar of gray, approaching.

We spend most of the day in the calm waters of the lagoon, paddleboarding, snorkeling. We're advised to stay in our bungalows from three-thirty onward; room service will be available as usual.

We hunker down around three forty-five, with snacks, beers, and a movie marathon. Enforced relaxation.

We're halfway through *Close Encounters of the Third Kind* when the storm kicks up a gear. The sounds of waves beneath the bungalow and rain on the roof force us to turn up the volume on the plasma screen. Mark whips out his phone and starts filming me.

I'm tangled like a beached, snacking whale in the sheets. Burying the pistachios under a pillow, I shift myself into a more attractive position, a more camera-ready position.

"What are you watching, Erin?" he asks from behind the camera.

"Good question, Mark! I am watching a movie about aliens while we wait for the world to end outside," I answer.

The sounds of sirens and muffled shouting from the screen.

"Day five of the honeymoon," Mark intones, "and we're sitting out a full-blown tropical storm. Take a look at this." Mark spins the camera to the rain-soaked glass doors.

Gray outside. A thick opaque mist. The wind is blowing all the visible plant life sideways, the trees arching against it. And the thick rain, in sheets, so much rain. He points the phone at the floor now; rain from the deck is pooling in cold puddles around the doors.

"Ghost ship," Mark calls to me, looking out toward the water.

I jump out of bed and trot over to the windows. And there it is. A ghost ship. A yacht anchored out on the water, its sails safely packed in, mast secured, bobbing half-obscured in the fog.

"Creepy," I whisper.

Mark smiles. "Creepy."

The top of Mount Otemanu is gone, swallowed in the gray, only the tree-covered base still visible. Mark zooms in on the boat. He's wondering if there are still people on it. We both stare at the zoomed image on his phone display.

It's then that his phone pings and a text notification flashes up over the video screen. It's only there for a microsecond but my stomach flips. It's from Rafie. It's important. It's about a potential new job. Rafie's been trying to help him out. Mark's been waiting for this text.

Mark fumbles the phone and strides off toward the suite's lounge area.

"Mark?" I say, following him.

His hand goes up impatiently. *Wait.*

He reads, nods, then puts the phone down carefully on the table, distracted, thinking. He swallows.

"Mark?" I ask again.

The hand goes up again, harder. *Wait!*

He paces, paces. Stops. Goes to the bar and starts to shovel ice into a whiskey glass. Oh fuck. That's not good.

I make my way to the table slowly and bend to pick up the phone. Gingerly, tentatively, just in case it's not okay to read his texts.

But his mind is elsewhere. I punch in his code, his birthday. Tap messages. Tap Rafie.

> Bro, sad news. Just heard they've filled the job internally. Fucking curveball. I thought it was sewn up. I'll let you know if I hear of anything else. R

Oh. God.

I put the phone back down softly on the glass coffee table. Mark is sipping his whiskey on the other side of the room. I flick the remote off. The sirens and commotion cease. The clunk of his ice cubes and the muffled storm raging outside are now the only sounds.

Mark finally looks up at me.

"Shit happens, Erin, what you gonna do?" He raises his glass in salute.

I think suddenly of Alexa. *Sometimes you're the dog; sometimes you're the lamppost.*

But he's smiling. "It's fine," he says. "I'm fine. Seriously." His tone is calm, reassuring. And I believe him this time; he is fine. But . . . this is all wrong. What's happening to him is wrong. It isn't fair.

"I have an idea," I blurt out.

I cross to him, take the whiskey glass from his hand, and set it down. He looks surprised, knocked off-balance by my sudden determination. I take him by the hand.

"Trust me?" I ask, looking up into his eyes.

He grins wide, eyes creasing. He knows I'm up to something.

"Trust you," he answers. He squeezes my hand.

I lead him to the suite's entrance and unlock the door. But he pulls my hand back as I try to push down on the handle.

"Erin?" He stops me. The storm rages on the other side.

"Trust me," I repeat.

He nods.

I pull down the handle and the door flies back into my hand; the wind's more powerful than I thought it would be, much stronger than it looked through the window. We step out onto the walkway and somehow I manage to wrangle the door shut again. Mark stands staring out at the maelstrom, the rain soaking fast through his T-shirt, darkening the fabric as I close the door behind us and take his hand again. We break into a run. I lead him along the stilt walkways, over the jetty bridges, onto the mainland of the resort, and on through the puddle-gathering pathways, all the way out to the roaring Pacific coastline. We stumble on through the sand, the wind buffeting us from all sides now. Our clothes, dark and heavy with rain, cling to us as we scramble out toward the waves. We stop at the edge of the South Pacific Ocean.

"Scream!" I shout.

"What?" He stares at me. He can't hear me over the roar of the wind and sea.

"Scream!!"

This time he hears me. He laughs.

"What?!" he shouts, incredulous.

"Scream, Mark! Fucking *scream!*"

I turn to the ocean, the wind, the pounding abyss beyond, and I scream. I scream with every fiber of my being. I scream for what's happening to Mark right now, for what happened to Alexa, for her dead mother, for mine, for Mark's future, for our future, for myself. I scream until I have no breath left. Mark looks at me silent through the storm. I can't tell what he's thinking. He turns, seems to be about to walk away, but then he circles back and he screams, long and hard into the lashing rain and fog. Every sinew poised, every muscle ready, a battle cry into the unknown. And the wind roars back.

12

Saturday, September 10

Things in the Water

By dawn, the storm has passed.

We wake in our suite to the usual gentle tapping of room service. The only evidence of the storm is the occasional loose palm frond, floating past in the lagoon, and our own hoarse voices.

I haven't slept so well in years. After breakfast Mark goes to have a chat with the hotel dive coordinator. Mark wants us to go diving this afternoon. He's going to see if we can go under our own steam. He and the dive coordinator seemed to hit it off pretty well yesterday, so I leave Mark to it and stay behind.

I promise Mark I won't do any work, but the moment he's out the door I've got my laptop open. There are emails from everyone.

Wedding stuff mostly. But I'm looking for work emails, news about the project. I find one.

Holloway Prison has emailed about Holli.

There are new details about her release date. It's been moved forward. It's now set for September 12. Two days from today. Damn. It wasn't supposed to be until after we were back.

I fire off a couple of emails to Phil, my cameraman, and Duncan, the sound guy; we'll need to go to Holli's house to interview her as soon as I'm back. It's not ideal but we need the footage as fast as we can get it after she's out. I also remind them of our Alexa-release filming dates. She'll be getting out a couple of days after I get back, so there's a little more prep time on that.

Another email catches my eye. It's from Pentonville Prison this time. Eddie's release date is set. My interview with him is penciled in for one week after we return.

And then there is a knock on the door. Odd. Mark has a key, why is he knocking? He's up to something. I smile to myself as I head for the door and pull it open dramatically.

A tiny Polynesian woman stands in the doorway, smiling.

"Special gift. You take!" She beams up at me and proffers a misted ice bucket containing a bottle of very expensive-looking chilled champagne.

"Oh, no, sorry, we didn't order—" I begin, but she shakes her tiny crinkly head slyly.

"No. Special gift. Gift from friend. Marriage gift. Yes!" She grins.

Well, that does make sense, I suppose. A gift from Fred and Nancy? Or Caro, maybe?

She nods at me to take it and for some reason I bow slightly as I take the bucket from her. Some unconscious nod to cultural respect, I suppose. I really shouldn't be allowed out of the house sometimes. She giggles merrily, waves her little hand, and wanders back toward the hotel.

Inside the room, I place the bucket carefully on the glass coffee table. Beads of condensation drip down its sides. There is a note. I open up the thick card and read.

To Mrs. Erin Roberts,

Congratulations on the nuptials, sweetheart. Took the liberty of sending you a little gift. A nice Dom Pérignon 2006. Used to be the wife's favorite. God knows we've had our differences over the years but she's got taste, I'll give her that. After all, she married me.

Anyway, I wish the best for you both now and in the future. Make sure he treats you right. Enjoy yourself, sweetheart.

Oh and apologies for the call the other week, I wasn't able to speak freely at the time. But we'll talk again very soon.

I heard they've sent you my release date. So we're all set. Looking forward to meeting you in two weeks. I won't waste any more of your time now. Get back out in that lovely sunshine.

Best Wishes,
Eddie Bishop

Dom Pérignon 2006. How the hell did he do that? He knows exactly where I am, what island I'm on, what room we're in, everything. But then, I already knew he was keeping tabs on me, didn't I? But this? This is creepy.

If I think it through logically, what does it mean? It means Eddie found out where we were staying and phoned the hotel to order us a bottle. He could have found out anywhere. It wasn't as if I was keeping our honeymoon destination secret. Anyone interested could have figured it out without too much trouble. In a way, it's kind of sweet. Isn't it? Or is it meant to be a threat? Whatever Eddie's intention, benign or malevolent, I decide not to tell Mark. He'd only worry.

I hear footsteps along the walkway outside and pop the card into my pocket. I'll get rid of it later. I grab my laptop off the sofa where I left it just as Mark enters.

I'm caught out. He smiles. "You're working, aren't you?"
I shrug, noncommittal, and slip the laptop into a drawer.
"Nope."

Mark's arranged a boat and diving gear for this afternoon. It'll be ready for us on the dock after lunch. Apparently the storm has made underwater visibility around the island quite bad, so the hotel dive instructor, Mark's new best friend, has given him the GPS coordinates of a great wreck a bit farther away. The visibility should be good out there. It's near an island about an hour out by motorboat. Mark's got a skipper's license from a gap year crewing yachts in the Mediterranean, so it shouldn't be too difficult for him to get us there. The hotel has even suggested we take a picnic and moor around the island after our dive. It's uninhabited, so we won't need to worry about disturbing anyone.

I'm pretty excited. A desert island to ourselves.

The trip out is slightly unnerving in the sense that once Bora Bora disappears from sight there is nothing else. Nothing in any direction but blue. I now understand how sailors used to go mad at sea. It's like snow blindness. If it weren't for the dot on the GPS moving steadily toward the destination pin, I'd swear we were going around endlessly in giant looping circles.

An hour out we see the island we're heading toward breaching the waves on the far horizon ahead. Which means it's about three miles away. The horizon is always approximately three miles away from you when viewed at sea level. Good to know, isn't it?

The wreck we're after today is just northwest of the island. It's at a depth of only twenty meters, which Mark promises I'll be fine with. "Technically, you're not supposed to go below eighteen meters. So we'll be sticking to around twenty meters on this holiday, okay? Trust me, honey, you won't automatically explode if you go two meters over your max today; the limit is only meant to be a guideline really. Twenty meters will be absolutely fine. And I'll be right there with you. Okay?" he reassures me. I know he's certified to go down to twice that depth.

A pink sun-bleached buoy bobbing in the waves marks the wreck site. We drop anchor a safe distance away.

As we're suiting up, Mark glances over at me, a shadow crossing his face.

"Erin, honey? Just to give you a heads-up. There are supposed to be a lot of sharks out here, sweetheart."

I literally stop breathing.

He laughs at my expression.

"It's fine! I'm going to be completely honest, okay? I'm going to tell you exactly what's in there, honey, so you know. All right?"

I nod. I couldn't speak if I wanted to.

He continues. "You know those blacktip sharks they've got in the lagoon, right? The ones we saw the other day?"

I nod.

He goes on, his voice smooth and reassuring. "The blacktip reef sharks, you're fine with them; they're perfectly friendly, aren't they? They don't bite people. And they're not that big, relatively speaking—they're only the same size as a person, so . . . not the biggest shark, but then again they're definitely not fish-sized anymore. They're fine, though. You with me so far, Erin?"

I nod again. When I first saw a blacktip shark in the lagoon on Monday, while we were snorkeling, I almost had an aneurysm. They look absolutely terrifying. But he's right, after the initial shock I was fine with them. They didn't bother us at all.

"Well, there'll be lots of them," he continues.

Great . . .

"And there might be quite a lot of lemon sharks too. Lemon sharks are around three and a half meters long—that's about the length of a hatchback car. They don't tend to hurt people but . . . they are three and a half meters long. Just so you're aware."

Wow. Okay. They're big.

"They're fine, Erin, trust me. But, just to be on the safe side . . . They don't like anything shiny, like watches, jewelry, that kind of thing, so—"

I hastily remove both my rings and thrust them at him.

"What else is in there, Mark?" I brace myself.

He takes the rings. "There's a chance that there might be gray reef sharks . . . two meters."

Fine.

"Whitetip sharks, silvertips . . . three meters."

Fine.

"And . . . stingray? Maybe . . ."

Fine too, they're like the manta rays in the lagoon but smaller.

"And turtles," he continues.

Lovely, love them.

"And, maybe, but probably not—and, you know, even if we do see them then don't worry, they'll keep their distance, it'll be fine— but there might be tiger sharks."

Oh. My. God.

Even I know about these. These are real sharks. Big sharks. Four to five meters long.

I'm really not sure about this dive now. I look at Mark. He looks at me, just the sound of lapping waves against the boat's hull. He laughs.

"Erin? Do you trust me?"

"Yes," I say, reluctantly.

"They might come toward you but they will not hurt you, okay?" He holds my gaze.

"Okay." I nod. *Okay.*

Just breathe. That's all you need to do, I tell myself. *Breathe. It's just like the pool. It'll be just like the pool.*

We finish suiting up and slip into the water. It's nice buddy-checking with Mark again. Safe. Plus he's pretty easy on the eyes. He holds my look. *Are you okay?*

I nod. *I am okay.*

Then we slip beneath the water. We descend slowly. My eyes are glued to Mark; I follow every hand signal, every move. And then he points, and I see it.

I could glimpse the wreck through the water from up in the boat, but now that we're under the waves I can see it crystal clear ahead of us. We descend. As my eyes adjust to the light I start to notice fish, darting about our bubbles as they rise back to the surface. I follow a parting fish with my eyes and see it join a shoal, under the shadow of the speedboat, a column of twisting and turning silver.

I look back to Mark. He's controlling our descent, nice and slow. No sudden moves. He's looking after me, his face angled down at his wrist computer, his expression one of intense concentration. We hit five meters and pause for a check. Mark signals *Okay?*

Okay, I signal. We're doing fine.

He signals to continue the descent. He's doing this so completely by the book that I can't help grinning behind my regulator mouthpiece. I'm in good hands.

I look down and see coral on some rocky outcrops a good five meters below us. I look back up. The surface is nearly ten meters away now, dancing brightly above us.

I look to Mark. Suspended in blue. Outside of time. He looks to me and smiles.

We sink. A movement in my periphery view. Not an object, but a change in color depth just beyond my field of vision.

I turn my head and focus hard into the blurred blue beyond us. Straining my eyes to see through the shaded water. Then I see them. They're all around us. They come into focus one by one. With each, my heart skips a beat. The fizz of adrenaline shoots through my veins. The water is full of them. Arcing in great loops over the wreck, and out around the reef. Their hulking bodies hanging weightlessly in the blue-green air around us. Fins, gills, mouths, teeth. Gliding like ocean liners. Sharks. So many sharks. What type they are doesn't seem relevant to my central nervous system, which has taken over.

I'm not breathing. My muscles are frozen, like that nightmare where you can't scream. I look to Mark. His eyes are flicking over them fast; he's assessing the threat.

I manage to lift my hand, terrified the movement will draw their attention. I signal *Okay?* my forearm trembling beyond my control.

Mark lifts a hand. *Wait.* His eyes scanning the waters around us.

I look up. Fifteen meters up. *Breathe, Erin! Fucking breathe.* I draw in deep. Cool, crisp tank air. Exhale slow and calm. I watch my bubbles escape up to the surface.

Good. Good work, Erin.

Mark turns to me in the water. *Okay.*

It's okay.

He smiles.

My whole body relaxes. They're all fine. We're fine.

I look out to them. It's vaguely reminiscent of wandering into a field full of cattle. The size. The vague worry that they might at any instant turn on you. Come at you.

Then I notice their fins. The fin tips aren't black or silver or anything. They are gray. The perspective is hard to judge; I can't tell how far away they are. But they're big. They're really big. Gray reef sharks.

They know we're here. They can see us. But it'll be okay. They won't come for us. They won't attack. It's okay.

We continue our descent.

We pass a huge school of yellow and silver fish, six feet high and densely packed.

When we reach the bottom, Mark signals to follow him toward the wreck. It's not too far ahead of us now along the ocean floor. It comes out of the haze and into sharper focus as we fin toward it.

I look up at the school of fish and sharks above us. A wall of fish, a cathedral wall of fish, suspended in the clear water above us. Wow.

I look over to Mark. He sees it too. Without a word, he reaches through the water and takes my gloved hand in his.

| | |

After the dive we lunch on the empty island, bringing the boat as close to shore as we can. We peel off our suits and swim naked in the shallows, sunbathe on the empty sand. It's getting late by the time we climb back on the boat and set off toward Bora Bora.

Mark stands over the wheel, gaze focused on the middle distance. It might take us longer than an hour to get back to the hotel at this time of day. The wind whipping my hair over my eyes coupled with my exhausted limbs makes it almost impossible to stay awake as we bump along the waves. The flashing green circle on the GPS creeps toward the red one. My eyelids begin to droop.

I'm not sure if I dozed off, but when I open my eyes the speed-boat motor is changing tone and we're slowing. I look up at Mark. We're not back in Bora Bora yet. There's nothing there, just ocean stretching miles in every direction. And then I see what he sees.

In the water all around us. Paper. Sheets of white paper.

We're approaching their source, a circle of papers about ten me-ters wide: I can't tell what they were, magazines, forms, or docu-ments, because the ink has run across the pages, dark and illegible now. The papers stick to the surface of the waves like a film of skin.

Mark glances at me. *What is this?* We can see to the horizon on all sides. Nothing but blue.

Garbage, maybe? We stop in its center. Our boat is in the eye of a giant circle of floating papers. Mark cuts the engine. In its way, it's beautiful. Like a modern art installation floating in the middle of the South Pacific. I reach over the side of the boat and fish out a wet page from the water. The writing dissolves before my eyes as I lift it toward me, the ink running and swirling across the wet white. Who knows what it said. It can't have been that important, though, to end up here. Can it?

Maybe it was the storm that brought it here? I study the swirls of illegible black running across the white pages. If it was important, it's not now.

Mark and I share a glance, the silence thick around us. It's eerie.

Suddenly I have this crazy idea that we died. Maybe we died and this is purgatory. Or a dream.

The silence is broken by a *thunk* against the side of the boat. And another. *Thunk. Thunk.* The waves are knocking something repeatedly into the side of the hull. We look toward the noise; whatever it is, we can't see it over the rim. *Thunk, thunk.* Mark frowns at me.

I shrug. I don't know. I don't know what it is either.

But there's something in his demeanor, something in the set of his shoulders, that makes my blood freeze. Something bad is happening. Mark thinks something very bad is happening.

Thunk, thunk. Insistent now. *Thunk, thunk.* Mark steps toward the noise. *Thunk thunk.* He braces himself against the boat, arms spread, then he inhales sharply and leans over the side.

He doesn't move now. *Thunk thunk.* He's looking down at whatever it is, frozen. *Thunk thunk.* And then he shifts, and he ever so carefully lowers a hand overboard. It disappears from view. *Thunk thu—*

With a grunt Mark heaves a waterlogged object onto the deck between us. It lands with a wet suck on the floor. A few bits of soggy paper stick to it. We stand and stare at it. It's a black canvas duffel bag just under a meter in length. It's too big for a gym bag but too small for a holiday suitcase.

It's clearly good quality but there don't seem to be any labels, no writing. Mark bends to inspect it. No tag. No handy address label. He looks for the zip, hidden black on black, and finds it. The zip is padlocked to the fastening of the bag by a matte black combination lock. Huh.

Okay. Obviously valuable. It's obviously not garbage, right? Mark glances up at me.

Should he try to open it?

I nod.

He tries to force the zipper, padlock and all. It won't budge. He tries again.

He looks up. I shrug. I want to open it too but . . .

He tries the fabric around the zip. Pulls at it. It doesn't give. He partially lifts the bag as he wrestles with it, the wet fabric smacking against the fiberglass deck as he struggles.

The bag has things in it. I can make out hard, angular shapes moving around inside as Mark tries to force a way in. He stops abruptly.

"Maybe we should wait," Mark says. His voice is taut, concerned. "Whoever owns it definitely doesn't want anyone getting into it. Right?"

I guess not. But the allure of finding out what's inside is pretty fucking strong right now. He's right, though. He's definitely right. It's not ours to open, is it?

"Can I?" I gesture toward it.

I just want to hold it, feel it. Maybe I'll know what's in it by weight, by shape. Like a Christmas present.

"Sure, go ahead." He stands back, giving me room.

"It's heavier than it looks," he adds, just as I lift the handles. And it is. Deceptively heavy. I pick it up slowly and it hangs around my calves. Wet and weighted. It feels like . . . It feels like . . .

I drop it immediately and it hits the fiberglass with a familiar *thunk*. Mark stares at me. Shakes his head.

"It's not." He knows what I'm thinking.

"It's not, Erin. They'd have eaten it. They'd have smelled it and eaten it. Especially the grays. It's not," he insists, but it's the way he says it. I know he was thinking it too.

Of course he's right, if it was a body the sharks would have had it by now. It's not organic; it's just some things in a bag.

Probably just someone's business accounts or something, judging by all the paper around. Maybe some dodgy bookkeeping. Just accounting, at the end of the day. I'm sure it's really not that interesting. Right? Just some stuff in a bag.

In a padlocked bag, Erin. Floating in the middle of the South Pacific. Surrounded by ten meters of illegible papers.

"What should we do?" I ask. "Should we even do anything? Should we put it back in the water and just leave it?"

Mark looks at his watch. It's getting late now; the sun will be setting in the next half hour or so and we've still got a forty-five-minute journey back. I do not want to be out in the middle of nowhere when it gets dark. Mark doesn't either.

"We need to get going. I'll note the coordinates and we'll take the bag back with us. Hand it in or something. Okay, Erin? We let someone know about this mess. Whatever happened here." He finds a pad and pencil in a locker under the seat. Jots down the location on the GPS.

I look out across the water at the papers, searching for some other clue to what this strange situation could be. But there's just that familiar blue, all around. Nothing else bobbing in the water. Nothing drifting on the waves. Just paper and blue. I turn back to Mark.

"Yes, okay. We'll hand it in at the hotel and they can sort it out." I sit back down.

It's none of our business really. Someone probably just dumped it.

Mark turns back to the wheel and we're off again. Speeding back toward the hotel and dinner. I watch the bag slide across the decking and lodge under a seat.

I curl up on the bench cushions behind Mark and put on his sweater, pulling the sleeves down over my cold hands. Hair whipping across my face, I close my eyes.

13

The Day After

We bounce out of bed early this morning. All the exercise and fresh air is knocking us out by ten most nights, and I feel great.

We handed the bag in last night when we docked at the hotel. Mark gave it to a porter and we explained that it had been found in the water. Mark didn't think it was worth telling the guy on the dock about the coordinates, or the papers. Best to have a chat with the dive guy about it today instead—he seems a bit more on it and he might actually look into it.

We breakfast in the main restaurant today; it's the Four Seasons Sunday buffet. It's ridiculously opulent, everything you could ever want to eat: whole lobsters, pancakes with syrup, exotic fruit, full English breakfast, sushi, rainbow cake. Ludicrous. That's another great thing about all this exercise: I can pretty much eat whatever I want right now and it'll make no difference.

We've got exciting plans for today, 4x4 off-roading in the forest on the main island, followed by a hike up Mount Otemanu to the Sacred Cave, then back to the hotel for the Sunday evening torchlit dinner on the beach. The boat will be collecting us right after break-fast from the jetty. There's no sign of the dive guy yet. And I need to nip back to the room to quickly grab my bag and sunscreen, so I leave Mark at the restaurant and run back to our room.

I don't see it at first.

As I come out of our bathroom, toothbrush in my mouth, mid-stroke, there it is. Sitting neatly on the floor at the end of our bed. The bag. Someone put it back in our room. It's dry now. Chalky salt tidemarks crust the black canvas. Padlock still safely fastened. They must have misunderstood what Mark was saying last night. And now it's back.

I think of the *thunk thunk* against the side of the boat. The insistence. I wouldn't have ever thought that a bag could be creepy, but there you go. You live and learn.

I'll have to sort it out later. No time now. I finish brushing my teeth, grab my bag, and dash for the jetty. I'll tell Mark later.

After the quick boat trip across the lagoon, we pile into an off-road vehicle. There are four of us as well as the guide in the 4x4. Us and another young couple. Sally and Daniel. We set off. Snapshots of jungle, the edge of a Jeep wing mirror, blurry smiling faces, hot black leather car seats against thighs, the smell of warm forest in the air, wind along the hairs of my arm, bumping hard over steep rugged hills, cool air and warmth.

And then we hike, the breeze reaching us over the treetops, shift-ing stones and dust underfoot, muffled chatter, sweat running down between my breasts, heavy breathing, Mark's darkening T-shirt ahead of me.

By the end of our hike I'm exhausted but satisfied. My legs heavy and loose.

Mark's cheeks have picked up some sun, making him look irresistibly healthy, outdoorsy. I haven't seen him this happy for a while now. Old Mark. I can't stop touching him. His browning skin. On the boat trip back to the hotel, I rest one warm thigh over his. Territorial.

I told him about the bag; he actually thought it was quite funny when I told him about it. *Fawlty Towers* funny. Hotel mishaps funny. I never really got *Fawlty Towers,* to be honest; they always seemed so angry. Disproportionately angry. Maybe that's what's so funny. I don't know. Python I love, but Cleese needs some tempering. Straight-up Cleese is too rich for my blood.

When we're back we dive straight into bed, make lazy love, and nap until sunset.

Once we're showered and dressed, Mark leads me out onto the decking and pops a bottle of champagne. Eddie's champagne. Or as I told Mark, "Fred's champagne."

He offers me a full glass, the fizz misting off its surface. You can tell a champagne's quality by the size of the bubbles, did you know that? The smaller the bubbles, the more there are available to release the aroma and flavor. The carbon dioxide bubbles pick up and carry the flavor molecules; the more there are, the more refreshing and subtle the flavors will feel to your palate. My glass is alive with long strings of tiny, ascending bubbles. We clink.

"Marrying you was the best decision I've ever made." He smiles. "I just want you to know that I love you, Erin, and I'm going to look after you, and when we get home I'm going to get another job and we're going to make a proper life together. Sound good?"

"Yes, that sounds perfect," I reply.

I take a sip, the bubbles bursting over my lip and nose. It's heaven. I smile. *Thank you, Eddie.*

"What shall we do about . . . ?" I nod my head back toward the suite.

He grins. "I'll take it to the dive center tomorrow and give the dive coordinator the area location. He can deal with it. Or maybe he'll just put it back in our room, of course! Either way." He laughs.

Music starts across the lagoon.

On Sunday nights there's a traditional Polynesian dinner show on the beach. I said to Mark, it does sound a little like eighties dinner theater. But he reminded me this is the Four Seasons, so it's a five-star three-course meal on a torchlit tropical beach followed by traditional Polynesian water-drumming and fire-dancing.

"Right, like dinner theater?" I say. They do that at dinner theater, right?

We're seated at a table right at the water's edge. There are only ten other couples, spaced out across the sand lit by candles and flaming torches all along the water's edge. We give the couple from the hike a wave. Daniel and Sally. They smile and wave back. Everyone loose-limbed and happy. The scent of Tahitian gardenia and fire fills the air.

We sip more champagne and talk about the future. What we'll do once we're home. I tell Mark all about Alexa, her plan to get pregnant, I tell him about Holli, everything. I don't mention too much about Eddie, of course, or Eddie's gift. Mark listens, rapt. I think he forgot somehow that I was still living my life while he was so wrapped up in his, but he's interested now. He asks why they're letting Holli out at all. He asks if I think Alexa regrets what she did. We talk into dessert and through coffee. And then the show begins.

Polynesian dancers, male and female, dressed in traditional costume, flip and somersault across the sand with flaming torches clasped in bronzed hands or between clenched teeth. Leaping into the air, diving into the water. Percussionists stand knee-deep in the waves and beat floating drums and the water with open palms.

The music builds, builds and climaxes with the waves flashing on fire for a moment in front of us, a circle of white-hot flames licking up off the surface of the water. And then darkness, claps, and whoops.

We move to the bar afterwards and on to cocktails. We dance, we talk, we kiss, we canoodle, we drink some more, and not until we're the last ones standing do we call it a night and stumble back along the jetty to our room.

And there it sits, waiting. I get some nail scissors from the bathroom and we open it.

14

Flotsam or Jetsam

I wake up late.

Mark is out cold beside me, the smell of booze thick over us. We forgot to order breakfast or even turn the air-con on before we fell into bed last night.

My head is fuzzy and I'm hungry. It looks like we ordered more room service last night. I roll out of bed carefully and wander over to the abandoned trolley.

Melted ice cream and an upturned champagne bottle in a bucket.

How much did we drink? Jesus. My tongue feels fat and dry in my mouth. And I'm absolutely starving. I make an executive decision and head for the phone.

Halfway across the floor, I feel a sharp pain shoot up through my foot and I lose my balance, crashing down hard onto the stone tiles.

Fucking hell, ow ow ow. Fucking ow.

A bright bulb of blood blossoms on the arch of my foot. Fuck. I see the offending scissors kicked up next to me. The bulb of blood bursts into a dribble and runs down and drips to the floor. My head throbs.

Oh, fuck this. I stand slowly, cautiously, and hobble to the phone. They pick up after two rings.

"Hi there. Can I order some room service please? . . . Yes, that's it. Yes. Can I get two full breakfasts . . . poached, coffee for two, pastry basket. . . . Yes, yes, that one. Orange juice for two. And do you have plasters? . . . No. Plasters—Band-Aids? . . . No. Band—? Like a first-aid kit or . . . Oh, oh yes! Yes, that's great. Yes, great. Thank you." I hang up and collapse back into bed, my foot bleeding into the sheets.

Mark stirs next to me. He grunts.

"Twenty minutes," I mumble, and fall asleep.

I wake as Mark pulls the breakfast trolley through the room and out onto the deck. He's wrapped in a hotel robe, bright white against his tanned skin. I grab the first-aid kit they brought and limp out to join him. Oversized T-shirt covering my underwear, foot crusted over with dried blood.

We eat in silence, staring dazed into the middle distance. I hobble back in to fetch us painkillers. Then after putting a plaster over my injury, I make the short move across to a sunlounger and promptly fall asleep again.

When I wake I see Mark has pulled the sunshade over me. God, I love him. I test my head with a gentle nod, a gentle shake. Yes, better. Much better. Maybe a shower now. I hobble back into the room past Mark watching Attenborough on cable and into the bathroom. He blows me a kiss as I pass by.

I let the cool water run over my face and hair. I rub the shampoo deep into my scalp; the massage feels heavenly. I think about last night. What did we do once we got back? I don't remember having ice cream. I remember the scissors, getting the scissors, for the bag. That's it.

I wrap a fresh towel around myself and wander back in to Mark.

"Did we open it?" I ask. I really hope we didn't. There's no way we can hand it in if we've ruined it.

He grimaces and hauls the bag up onto the bed.

It's very clearly got a hole in it. We really didn't get very far last night. God, drunk people are idiots. I notice Mark's hand has two of the Band-Aids stuck to it. I guess he was in charge of scissors last night. I sit down on the bed and inspect the bag. The hole is useless. I can't get a finger in to stretch it wider and I can't see anything through it. Maximum impact, minimum results.

"Can we still hand it in?" I look up at Mark.

"Yeah, of course. We'll just say we found it that way. It was in the sea, right?" He doesn't seem concerned.

"If this hole is passable, would a slightly bigger hole be passable?" I hold his gaze.

He shrugs and chucks me the scissors from his bedside table.

"Knock yourself out," he says, his attention drifting back to Attenborough.

But I don't. I'm scared. I don't know why. It seems wrong to open the bag.

But why? It's just like finding a wallet, isn't it? It's all right to open the wallet and look at the stuff, find out who it belongs to. It's only not all right if you take the stuff inside it. I don't want to take the stuff inside. I just want to know. And that's absolutely fine. It might help us return it. If we know whose it is.

So I take the scissors to the bag again and start to cut. After a while I wander out to the deck with it. There was a sharp knife out there on the food trolley earlier. I find it and force it into the small opening I've already made and start to saw. Inside I hear Mark turn on the shower.

I keep sawing until I can get one hand into the hole, and then I pull with all my strength, opening the tear in the fabric. The canvas rips apart with a long satisfyingly bass-y tear. I'm in. I turn to shout to Mark but he's in the shower. Should I wait before I look?

No.

I tip the bag out onto the wooden decking and look down at the contents.

I blink. A long time passes.

I think about calling to Mark. But I don't. I just look.

Four objects. The largest by far is the one I reach out for first. It's bulky but much lighter than its size would suggest. This was what was keeping the bag afloat. Paper. Tightly packed paper. More specifically, paper money. A clear plastic vacuum-sealed package of money. American dollars. In bundles, each bundle labeled "$10,000" with a paper currency strap. Real money. Actual real money. Lots of it.

It hits me. Viscerally. My stomach flips and I run toward the bathroom, but, impeded by the sharp stabs in my foot, I find myself vomiting halfway through my dash across the room. I lurch to my knees, bracing against the floor as my stomach muscles heave beyond my control. Bile, thick pungent bile. Fear made visible. I moan as I struggle to catch my breath between retches.

We shouldn't have opened the bag.

I wipe my mouth on the bedsheet and stumble to my feet. I limp back outside and squat down in front of it. I stare at the money; the tight vacuum packing has somehow managed to keep the water out, and although, obviously, that wasn't its original purpose, I doubt if we'd have ever found the duffel bag otherwise.

The next item is a cloudy ziplock bag about the size of an iPad mini. It's full of small pieces of something. Something broken, maybe broken glass. The salt water has gotten into this bag and misted the plastic so I can't quite make out what's inside it. I run back into the room and grab a towel. I squat back down and rub at the plastic but the fogginess is inside as well. I grab the scissors again and snip the corner of the baggie carefully. I tip the contents out onto the towel.

Diamonds tumble out before me. Beautifully cut and sparkling back at me in the sunlight. So many. I can't judge the number. A hundred? Two hundred? They twinkle innocently in the sunlight. Mainly princess and marquise cut by the look of it, but I see some heart and pear cut in there too. I know my cuts, colors, and sizes of diamond. We looked at every possible permutation before Mark and I settled on the one in my ring. I look at my hand, my own ring glittering in the sunlight. They're all about the same size. The same size as my stone. That means they're all about two carats. Oh my God. I look down at the beautiful sparkling pile, my breath catching in my throat. The sun glinting colors off of them. There could be over a million pounds in diamonds here. *Oh wow. Wow wow. Holy crap.*

"Mark!" I call, slightly off key, slightly too loud.

"Mark! Mark, Mark, Mark." My voice sounds weird; I hear it coming from me but don't recognize it. I'm standing now.

He runs out of the bathroom bare-chested. My arm goes up and I point at the pile before me. His eyes follow my finger. But he can't see past the crumpled empty bag on the decking.

"Oh, watch out for the vomit," I shout. He dodges it and stares at me like I've gone insane, finally coming out to me in the sunshine, completely confused.

"What the—" Then he sees it. "Oh Jesus Christ! Bloody hell. Right. Bloody—Okay. Christ."

He stares at me. I can read his face as clear as day.

"Jesus."

He's squatting down in front of it all, turning the packet of money over and over in his arms. He looks up at me.

"It could be a million. They're ten-thousand-dollar packs," he says, his eyes bright. He's really excited.

Because, let's be clear, this is really bloody exciting.

"I know. That's what I thought. What about the other stuff?" I say quickly. I squat down beside him.

He pushes the diamonds around on the towel with his finger. He moistens his lips and squints through the sun at me.

"Two carats, right? That what you're thinking?" he asks.

"Yes. How many stones?"

"Hard to tell without counting. I'm guessing a hundred and fifty to two hundred."

I nod. "That's what I thought. So, maybe a million's worth?"

"Yeah, could be more. But that seems right. Fuck." He rubs the stubble along his jaw.

"What else is there?" he asks.

I don't know; I haven't looked at the rest yet.

He picks up another sealed clear plastic bag; just visible through the salt smears is a USB stick. Sealed tight, somehow still protected from the water. He places it back down carefully next to the stones and the money. He looks at me before picking up the final object.

It is a hard plastic case with a handle. He sets it down in front of us. I know what it is before he flips open the plastic latches.

It sits there, dark dense metal nestled in molded foam padding. A handgun. I don't know what type. I don't know about guns. The sort you'd see in a film, I guess. A modern film. That type. But a real one, on the decking, in front of us. Spare bullets nestled in a fresh cardboard box next to it in the foam. Sealed. There's an iPhone in the box too. The plastic gun case must be airtight, because everything inside it is dry, and, I'd imagine, still in working order.

"Okay." Mark closes the case. "Let's go inside for a bit, shall we?"

He gathers the money, USB, and gun case into the destroyed canvas bag and ushers me inside. I carefully carry in the towel of diamonds.

He slides the glass door shut and sets the bag on the bed.

"Okay, Erin. First things first. We're going to clean up the vomit, right? Clean ourselves, and the room, up. Then we're going to have a chat, okay?" He's watching me encouragingly. He's speaking to me in the same, even, measured tone he had yesterday when he told me about the sharks. He's extremely reassuring when he needs to be. Yes, I'll clean up.

It doesn't take me long. I use some of the disinfectant lotion from the first-aid kit to douse the floor. I wash my face, brush my teeth, and pull myself together. Meanwhile Mark's cleaned the rest of the room. The food cart is gone. The bed is stripped now too, the bag the only thing on it. The diamonds sit in a whiskey tumbler. Mark wanders in from the lounge area holding my laptop.

"First of all, I don't think we should contact the police until we know what the fuck is going on. I don't fancy spending life in a Polynesian prison for diamond smuggling or whatever. I suppose we need to know if anyone is missing this stuff. Right? If anyone might know we have it?" he says.

I take the computer as he holds it out to me.

I see, we're going to do a bit of research. Research I'm good at. He sits down on the bed and I sidle next to him.

"So, what should I check the news for, what do we think? Ship- wreck? Missing persons? Or maybe robbery gone wrong? What are we looking for?" I ask. I'm not sure. My fingers hover over the keys. We need something to go on.

He looks at the bag again.

"Well, we have a phone." He lets it hang there.

Yes. Yes, we do have a phone, which means we have a number, we also probably have an email address and emails, and we probably have an actual name.

"Shall we check the phone? See who they are?" I ask.

"Not yet. Wait. Let's just think logically here, carefully. Are we breaking the law right now? Are we, Erin? Have we done anything? Anything at all wrong so far?"

Like I would know. I suppose my moral compass has always been slightly more true than his, but only slightly.

"No. No, I don't think so," I say. "I ripped the bag. But I ripped it to find out what was inside—to find out who it belonged to. It's the truth; that should stand up."

"Why didn't we give it straight to the police or security?"

"We did. We handed it in to the hotel straightaway but they gave it back to us. And then we got drunk and we thought we'd sort it out ourselves. It's stupid, but it's not illegal." I nod. That sounds all right, I decide.

"But this is wrong now," I add. I say it as I think it. "We should call the police right now and tell them about it. The gun and the money are definitely red flags," I say, nodding again.

I study the frayed bag. I can see the corner of the packet of money through the torn canvas. A million dollars. I look at Mark.

"Just a second," I say. "I remember this. It came up in that Norwegian fishermen film." I tap away at Google.

"Basically, flotsam and jetsam, maritime debris, salvage, whatever you want to call it, basically treasure, is covered by international maritime law. Here . . . look at this." I scroll down and read from the gov.uk website.

"*'Jetsam' is the term used to describe goods jettisoned overboard to lighten a vessel's load in emergencies. 'Flotsam' is the term used to describe goods accidentally lost overboard in emergencies.* Blah, blah, blah. *The salvor must declare salvaged goods by completing a 'report of salvage' form within 28 days of recovery.* Blah, blah, blah. *A salvor acting within the law is likely to be entitled to the salvaged goods should the owner not come forward.* Uh-huh. Oh, wait. Shit! *Under the Merchant Shipping Act of 1995 this law applies to all salvage within UK territorial waters—up to the twelve-nautical-mile limit.*" British law is totally irrelevant here. I'm not sure whether we'll fall under French or U.S. law in Polynesia.

I search again. Tapping. Mark stares at the bag, mute.

"Here we go! U.S. Department of Commerce. *'Flotsam' and 'jetsam' are terms that describe two types of marine debris associated with vessels. 'Flotsam' is defined as debris in the water that was not deliberately thrown overboard, often as a result from a shipwreck or accident. 'Jetsam' describes debris deliberately thrown overboard by a crew of a ship in distress, most often*

to lighten the ship's load. Under maritime law, the distinction is important."
I look up at Mark.

"Flotsam may be claimed by the original owner, whereas jetsam may be claimed as property of whoever discovers it. If the jetsam is valuable, the discoverer may collect proceeds received through the sale of the salvaged objects."
I stop.

Mark looks out of the window across the lagoon, frowning.

When he finally speaks he says, "So, I suppose the question is: is this flotsam or jetsam?"

"Uh-huh." I nod, moistening my lips.

We need to go back there and find out. We need to go back to the paper circle tomorrow and see if there's a wreck. If the owner went down in the storm and lost this bag, then that's one thing. If he threw it overboard and ran away, that's another.

If there's nothing there, under the water, under all those papers, then we are two million richer.

"If there's a wreck there, we'll just put the bag back. Then we'll report it. But if there's nothing there . . . If the bag was abandoned, I think we're all right. I think we'll be all right, Mark." I go to the fridge and grab some ice-cold water. I take a sip and pass it to him.

"Yes?" I ask.

He takes a sip. Runs his hand through his hair.

"Yes," he agrees. "We'll go back tomorrow."

■ ● ●

15

A Dot in the Sea

Mark logs the coordinates into the GPS and we head off. It's another perfect day, deep azure above and below as far as the eye can see.

Last night I Googled news stories about the storm. There's no mention of any missing yachts, or missing people. Nothing but holidaymakers' Instagram photos of storm clouds and wind-battered trees.

As the waves fly by on the way there I think of the ghost ship the night of the storm. It was anchored there the whole time, wasn't it? Could that have been them? Did they leave during the storm? Why would they set sail in the middle of a storm? People don't do things like that. Yachts have names, their movements are logged; I'm sure we'd have heard by now if a ship was missing. Wouldn't we? But there is nothing online. No mention of a missing ship.

Who are we kidding? The bag didn't come off that little holiday yacht. The circle of paper in the water, the diamonds, the vacuum-packed money, the phone, the gun? I'm pretty sure that whoever owns this bag isn't in the habit of logging their movements. Whoever they are, I don't think they'll have left a convenient trail for us to find.

I have the feeling of being too near to something I don't want to be near to. To something dangerous. I can't quite see what it is yet but I feel it; it feels close. I feel the trapdoors in my mind creaking under the strain of what lies underneath. But then, of course, it could just be free money and everyone loves free money. Someone might have made a mistake, and if it doesn't hurt anyone . . . then we could keep it. Free money for us. And it's not like we don't need it.

It only takes us fifty minutes to reach the spot today—something to do with tidal stream and drift, Mark says; I'm not really listening. When we arrive there's nothing left of the paper circle. Nothing to say anything was ever here. Nothing but water for miles. If Mark hadn't written down the coordinates on Saturday, we'd never have found this place again.

Ever since Mark suggested the idea of diving to look for a wreck, I've had a dreadful feeling lurking just below my thoughts. I really don't want to find a boat. I really, really don't. But more than that. The thought that I'm pushing down hardest is that we'll find something else. That it won't be sharks hanging heavy in the water this time, it'll be something different. Something worse.

He can feel my tension. We rig up in silence, Mark throwing me reassuring glances.

He thinks it'll be about forty meters deep here. Contextually speaking, that's two meters higher than the statue of "Christ the Redeemer" in Rio. I can only really go to twenty and he knows it. But the visibility out here is damn near perfect, so we should be able to see right down to the bottom without moving a muscle, or at least without having to go all the way down.

Before we slip into the water, Mark warns me again about the sharks. It doesn't seem that relevant today. I stare off into the cloudless sky, letting his words wash over me. I breathe. Trying to let his voice calm me. We're both nervous. And it's not about sharks.

I notice I'm shaking as we do our buddy check in the water. He grasps my hand and holds it tight against his chest for a second. My heart rate slows. The waves are big and rolling us high today. There's a strong breeze but Mark promises it'll be placid once we're underwater. As we finish up he takes my arm.

"Erin, you don't have to do this, you know. I can go down alone. You can stay on the boat and I'll be back in about fifteen minutes. That's all it'll take, honey." He pushes a wet strand of hair behind my ear.

"No, it's okay. I'm fine." I smile. "I can do this. And if I don't see for myself, I'll be imagining worse anyway," I say, my voice distant, slightly off-key again.

He nods. He knows me too well to disagree. I'm coming.

He slides on his mask, signals *descend,* and slips beneath the surface. I place my mask on slowly, securely, letting it suck hard against my cheeks. I can't afford any mishaps today. I take my last breath of sweet fresh air and follow him under.

It's clearer down here than it was the last time. Crystal-clear blue. High-definition blue. Mark is waiting for me just below the surface, picked out in nature-program resolution, a living thing suspended in an ocean of nothing. He gestures to descend. And we let out our buoyance.

Our descent is steady. I look up at the huge waves crashing above us; it's so eerily still down here. Seen from underneath, the cresting waves appear forged from metal as they glint in the sun. Huge sheets of burnished aluminum.

Everything is fine. Everything is fine up until we hit ten meters.

Mark jerkily stops and signals for me to hold position. I freeze.

Something's wrong.

Blood suddenly bursts through my veins at a rate of knots, pumping faster than ever around my body. Why are we stopping?

Is there something in the water? I'm careful not to move, but my eyes search in every direction for what it could be. I can't see it. Should we get back up to the boat? Or is it fine?

Mark signals *It's okay* back to me.

Okay? Then what? Why hold?

He signals it to me again: *hold*. Then he signals *be calm*. *Be calm* is never a good sign.

Then he signals *look down*.

Oh God.

Oh Goddy, God, God. Why look down? Why? I don't want to look down. I don't want to look down, Mark. I shake my head.

No. No, not doing it.

He reaches out and takes my arm. He signals *It's okay* again.

His eyes. *It's fine, Erin.*

I nod, I'm calm. All right. I can do this. I can do this.

I breathe in deep, a cool crisp chemical breath, and look down.

It's beautiful. Papers caught in a slow-motion dance hang in the water all around us. Half sunk, half floating, beautiful.

Then through the gaps between papers . . . I see it below us.

About thirty meters below us on the seabed. A plane. Not a commercial plane. A small plane. A private jet perhaps. I see it clearly below. One wing disconnected, broken off in the sand beneath. A great gaping breach in its main hull. And darkness within. I breathe out, hanging motionless in the water.

I breathe in slow, calm. I look to the door, the airplane's door. It's sealed. The door is sealed. Oh. Oh shit. I feel the panic rise. I feel it fizz through my muscles, through my arms, through my heart, the clenching, the seizing. Fuck. Oh my fucking God. There are people in there.

The trapdoor in my mind bursts wide open and the panic spills out all over me. Images flash through my mind. I can see rows of silent people safely strapped in, in the dark, deep below us. Their faces. Jaws broken mid-scream. *Stop!* I command myself.

This is not real. Stop.

But it is, though, isn't it? It is real. They'll be in there; I know they will. They can't have got out. They didn't even try. Why didn't they even try?

I realize I've stopped breathing.

I gasp in a breath. The gasps come fast in quick succession, panicked pulls on life. Grasping. *Oh shit oh shit oh shit.* I look up. The sun dancing silver above. Ten meters up. I have to get out of the water. Now.

I flail out of Mark's grasp, kicking as hard as I can, up. Up and away from the plane. From the death.

A hand grabs my ankle and I jolt to a stop as it pulls hard, yanks me down. I can't get away. It's Mark. Mark holding me down in the water. Protecting me from rising too fast, from hurting myself. I know it's for my own good but I don't want it. I need to get out of the fucking water, right now.

The surface is still about eight meters above us. I suck in breaths as I struggle to get free. Free from him. He clambers up me to eye level and seizes me by my shoulders, strong and steady. Trying to muffle the panic. Stanch it. He catches my gaze. *Stop, Erin. Stop,* his eyes say.

Breathe.

He's got me. It's okay. He's got me. I'm okay. I breathe. I relax into his hold. Calm. Calm.

I'm okay.

The panic sucks back into its hole and the trapdoor slams shut behind it.

Stillness. I breathe. I signal *okay*. Mark nods, satisfied. He loosens his grip.

I'm okay. But I'm not going down there. There's no way on earth I'm going down there.

I signal *up*. I'm going up.

He looks at me for a while before he replies. He signals *okay*. Then, *You, up.*

He's still going down. Alone.

I squeeze his arms and he releases me. I watch him descend as I kick up slowly. A controlled ascent, now the panic has dissipated. He disappears into the murky darkness as I rise.

Once I hit the surface I remove my tank immediately in the water and haul it onto the boat. I strip off my suit and leave it like a husked skin on the floor. I slump there shivering and wheezing, struggling to catch my breath, elbows on my knees as the tears start to well in my eyes.

Images flash across the backs of my closed eyelids. Their faces. The passengers'. Distorted, distended. The terror. I slam my fists down hard onto my legs. Pain flashes through my body. Anything to stop the images.

I get up and pace the deck. *Think about something else. What does it mean, Erin? Yes, think about that, concentrate on that. What does it mean?*

It means the bag was on a plane and the plane crashed. A storm in the South Pacific. Something happened and they had nowhere to land. We're about one hour by air to Tahiti. I guess they couldn't make it there. Or maybe they didn't want to land in Tahiti. It's obviously a private plane. A private jet. They had money. Other than the money in the bag, obviously. Perhaps they wanted to stay away from public airports. I think about the diamonds, the money, the gun.

Perhaps they thought they could outrun the storm. But they didn't. I look at my watch. Mark must be in there by now. With them. *Stop it, Erin.*

I turn my mind to the logistics of the flight. Where were they going? I'm going to need to look some stuff up once we're back. I rummage through the boat locker until I find what I'm looking for. A pad and pencil. Right, I know what I need to do, what I need to focus on. Not the plane down there. Mark's got that covered.

I note down: *Flight paths over French Polynesia??* God, I wish I'd noted down a tail number or something from down there. I'm sure Mark will.

I jot down: *Plane type, aircraft tail number, max speed, & distance achievable nonstop??*

Planes can only travel so far without refueling. We can try to work out where they might have been heading. I doubt the flight was logged, but we can search online and see if anyone is missing.

At least now our question has been answered. What we have found is flotsam. Our bag was most certainly not deliberately jettisoned. Somehow that canvas bag made its way, along with those bundles of papers, out of the plane's breached hull and up into the Polynesian sunshine. But—and this is a big one—technically, what we have is neither flotsam nor jetsam. This is not a shipwreck. This is a plane crash. What we have is a big bag of evidence from an underwater aviation incident. I take a shuddery breath of cool tropical air.

Our honeymoon feels a million miles away and yet just within reach, if only we could—

Mark breaks through the waves on my starboard side. He fins toward the boat. His expression blank, controlled. For the first time, I truly appreciate how useful his masked emotions actually are. I think if I ever saw him truly scared, then I'd know for sure that we were done for.

He drags himself up the ladder at the stern of the boat, exhausted.

"Water, please," he says as he jiggles his tank off onto the deck. He peels off his suit, discards it like mine, and drops heavily onto the teak seating. I fetch a water bottle from the cooler box and hand it across to him. His eyes are tight in the sunlight, brow tensed against the glare.

"You all right?" he asks. He's watching me, concerned.

"Yeah, yeah, I'm fine. Sorry. I just . . ." I'm not sure how to finish that sentence, so I stop.

"No, it's fine. God. It's good that you came up." He takes a long pull on the water bottle and looks out over the waves, his wet hair dripping slowly onto his bare shoulders.

"Fucking hell," he says.

I wait but he doesn't continue.

"Are they in there?" I ask. I have to ask. I have to know.

"Yeah," he says.

He takes another long swig of water.

"Two pilots up front, three passengers. That I could see. One of them was a woman, the rest men." He looks out again at the waves, his jaw tight.

"Fucking hell." I realize too late that I've echoed him. I don't know what else to say.

"They weren't good people, Erin," he says, looking at me now.

What the fuck does that mean?

I want to know more, I want to know everything he saw, but it doesn't seem right to ask. He's processing. I wait for him to tell me.

But nothing comes. He drinks more.

His words still hang in the air. I try to catch them before they disappear. "What do you mean, they weren't good people, Mark?"

"The things they had with them. Down there. They weren't good people. Don't feel too sad, is all I mean." With that he stands. Grabs a towel and wipes his face, rubs his hair.

I realize that's probably the most I'll get from him right now, and I don't want to linger too long on the thought of the people down there. I'm trying my hardest to stay focused as it is. I change the subject. Well, sort of.

"It's flotsam, Mark."

He stares at me blankly for a moment. I think he'd forgotten all about the bag until now. I continue.

"Well, sort of flotsam, lost by accident in an emergency—it can be claimed by the owners. But you've just met the owners and I don't think they'll be claiming it anytime soon. Will they?" My stab at dark humor. I'm not sure it sounded quite right.

"No, no, they won't." He says it flatly.

I move on quickly. "Mark, did you get the plane's tail number? Anything we can use to identify them? Who they were? Anything helpful?"

He pulls the dive slate off his tank strap and hands it to me. The plane make, model, and tail number. Of course he got it!

"They're Russian," he says as I jot the slate information down in my notepad and wipe it clean again.

I look up. "How do you know that?"

"There were Russian snack packets."

"Right." I nod slowly.

"Listen, Erin. You said no one will claim the bag. Does that mean you're suggesting we don't report this? We don't report a plane crash?" He's scowling at me.

Shit. Yes. I thought that's what we both were suggesting. Weren't we? To keep the shiny pretty diamonds and the free money. To pay off our mortgage and have a family, right? Or am I crazy? Maybe I am crazy.

My mind flits to the people below us. The dead people, rotting in the water. The bad people. Should we keep the bad people's money?

"Yes. Yes, that is what I'm suggesting," I say to Mark.

He nods slowly, processing what that means.

I continue, carefully. "I am suggesting that we get back to the hotel, find out if they've been reported missing, and if anyone is missing them at all, then we forget it all. Drop it back here. But if not, if they've just evaporated into thin air, then yes, I say we keep the bag. We found it floating in the sea, Mark. We keep it and use it for a better purpose than I'm sure it was meant for."

He looks at me. I can't quite tell through the blaze of sun what his expression means.

"Okay," he says. "Let's find out who they are."

16

Tuesday, September 13

Flight Paths

It turns out there's a live online feed of every registered airborne flight in the world. I'm watching it now as different-sized purple triangles flicker across a lo-fi black and yellow map of the world. A real-life version of the video game Asteroids.

A brief touch of the cursor arrow over each of the larger triangles displays its flight number, its origin, and its destination. The smaller triangles—private planes, jets—simply display their craft type: Gulfstream G550, Falcon 5X, Global 6000.

Our plane was, and still is I suppose, a Gulfstream G650. I look up its specifications online. The G650 can fly eight thousand miles without refueling. That's pretty much the distance from London to

Australia. That's a really long way for a small business jet. Its top speed is Mach 0.925, transonic. That means traveling at nearly the speed of sound. *The speed of sound.* It would have been a short flight if they'd made it, wherever they were going. I guess they thought they could outrun the storm.

I look up the most common causes of small-craft accidents. Wikipedia tells me:

> Severe instability can occur at transonic speeds. Shock waves move through the air at the speed of sound. When an object such as an aircraft also moves near to the speed of sound, these shock waves build up in front of the plane's nose to form a single, very large shock wave. During transonic flight, the plane must pass through this large shock wave, as well as contend with the instability caused by air moving faster than sound over parts of the wing and slower in other parts.

That might have been it. Mightn't it? They just hit the storm and at that speed it knocked them out of the sky. I guess we'll never know.

I need to look up the tail number next. R–RWOA. I'm hoping it's a similar system to the car registration system; hopefully, there's some kind of database online.

After a couple of searches it becomes evident that the "R–R" element of the registration is the country prefix. Registered in Russia. Mark was right. People do get quite nationalistic about their choice of snacks, it's true.

I check the national aviation database for Russia and somehow, somehow it works. It just works. The details come up. There's nothing solid, of course. It was registered in 2015 to a company called Aegys-Mutual Consultants. Possibly the least glamorous company name that I've ever heard. Sounds a bit like a recruitment company in

Basildon. Except small businesses in Basildon can't usually afford $60 million planes. Yeah. Yeah, that's how much that plane was worth. Over $60 million. Our house is the most expensive thing we own and it's only worth $1.5 million. And we haven't even paid off the mortgage yet. I'm starting to wonder if, whoever these people are, they'd even miss the contents of the bag. It's obviously not their main business, if it's even a sideline? But it does make me wonder if they have been missed. There must be someone out there looking. Sixty-million-dollar planes, their crews, and their owners don't just vanish. They leave a hole, don't they?

Aegys-Mutual Consultants is a corporation registered in Luxemburg. Which makes sense, I suppose. I don't know much about Luxemburg, but I do know it's a tax haven. I'm pretty sure Aegys-Mutual is a shell company. Mark explained them to me once; shell companies are ghost companies set up to make transactions, but the companies have no assets or services in and of themselves; they're empty shells.

I reopen the flight path feed and scroll over our airspace, the empty black section of screen over French Polynesia: it's completely blank at the moment, no planes overhead. There won't be scout planes this far from the mainland, and as the helicopter pilot told us, helicopters can only island-hop out this far. Helicopter fuel tanks aren't large enough to fly all the way back to the mainland unless they refuel on a plane ship. If someone is looking for this plane, then somewhere between America and Asia is a pretty big search area to cover. But if we had some idea where they were headed or where they departed from, we might be able to work out who they were.

The triangle nearest our island, on the flight map, is currently hovering equidistant between Hawaii and us. A tap reveals it to be a passenger jet from LAX to Australia. Looking at the live feed, it's clear that planes do fly over the vast expanse of the North and South Pacific Ocean. I always thought airlines tried to avoid it because there's nowhere to land during emergencies—isn't it always better to be over land if something goes wrong? At least then there's the chance of landing—better to fly round the endless water than over it. But it turns out there are still a few transpacific flight paths in the skies above us. People being ferried to and fro, although clearly there's less air traffic here than over the bustling Atlantic, which is alive right now with color, planes like swarming purple ants crawling across the screen. Not much directly over us, though. Over us it's mostly commercial airliners from LAX or San Francisco heading to Sydney, Japan, and New Zealand. Then I catch sight of another triangle, higher up on the map than the others. It looks like it's come across from Russia. I scroll over it. Yes. A Gulfstream G550, private jet. Another one. It's heading the opposite way from most of the flights over the Pacific—it's heading left to right, over to Central or North America, I can't tell which just yet.

It's hard to know where to even start to look for these people. These ghost people. Google offers no information on missing flights over the past few days beyond a story about a missing light aircraft in Wyoming. I think I can safely say this is not our guys. Some weekend hobbyist, I suppose, who got carried away, or a crop farmer who made a fatal mistake. I'm sure that mystery will solve itself. Either way, there's nothing to be found online about our missing plane.

I search for private airports in Russia. There are loads, of course, and I'm guessing if you've got money, air traffic control can probably keep you off the grid there, if need be. Perhaps that's true anywhere.

I'm suddenly reminded of the people we saw in the first-class lounge at Heathrow. The millionaires who didn't look like millionaires. Why weren't they flying in their own planes? Or chartering? A quick search reveals that chartering a private jet from London to LAX costs around four thousand pounds for one person on an empty leg flight and thirty thousand for the whole plane. A standard first-class ticket, without using any points, is about nine thousand pounds round trip. If you're rich enough to fly first-class, why not just hire a jet? Hell, why not buy one?

Maybe they're not savvy enough. Maybe they're not rich enough.

Maybe the people in that lounge weren't even paying for their own tickets.

Either way, it all feels very different now. First class doesn't seem quite so impressive somehow. It all feels a bit . . . well, silly in comparison.

These ghost people live in a world that, up until now, I had no idea existed. A world I wouldn't even begin to know how to access.

I'm not sure we're going to find out anything that these people don't want us to find out. I mean, let's face it, I'm not a spy; I don't have access to databases. Resources . . .

But then . . . that does give me an idea.

Maybe Mark would be able to recognize them. He saw them, after all, he saw their faces. Albeit in pretty unnatural circumstances. I try to imagine what he must have seen, those corpses swaying like reeds, bloated in the water. *Don't go there, Erin.*

"Mark, if I showed you some pictures, would you be able to recognize any of them? The pilots? Those passengers? The two men and the woman?"

He takes a moment. "Why? Did you come up with something?"

"I'm not sure yet. But do you think you could?" I tap away at the keyboard, trying to find what I'm looking for.

"Yeah. Yeah, I do. I'm pretty sure I'll never forget what they looked like." That's the first time he's talked about them that way, as if he too is haunted by them. I sometimes forget he feels things too. Does that sound strange? But by that, I mean I sometimes forget he has fears too, weaknesses. I try so hard to suppress mine I forget he must be doing the same. He sits down next to me on the edge of the bed so he can see the screen. I've pulled up the Interpol website. I click on the Wanted Persons tab top right. There're currently 182 wanted persons listed, 182 photographs for Mark to look through. I think it's fairly obvious what we're dealing with now. I know two million dollars is fuck all to people who can afford a sixty-million-dollar jet, but I have the feeling this bag isn't the sum total of their business.

Mark looks up at me. "Seriously?"

"It can't hurt, can it? Scroll through. Check." I hand him the laptop and leave him to it.

I grab my phone and go out onto the decking. I want him to check the FBI wanted list next and the British National Crime Agency list after. I find them easily with a quick Google search on my phone. Rows of FBI mugshots load up just like the Interpol site.

They're a seedy-looking bunch. But then, to be fair, I suppose you could put a picture of Mark's mother on an FBI watch list and she'd somehow manage to look seedy. I glance back at him through the glass door, his face lit up by the screen's glow. It can't hurt to check, can it? Even if he sees nothing, at least we've tried. And we will find something eventually or he'll have to go back down there. We need to find some clue as to who they are, or we'll just have to go back, leave the money down there, and forget the whole thing.

I suddenly remember the iPhone. It's still in the gun box in the bag, which I've hidden at the top of the wardrobe behind the spare hotel pillows. Right at the back. Mark's already vetoed using it, even turning it *on*. He insists we should chuck it. But it could save us so much time if we just used it. Just once.

The battery's dead. I know this because I've already tried pressing the power button. I tried it while he was in the shower earlier. But no power.

If I could just charge it, then we'd know immediately who they were. We could stop searching.

I look at him again through the glass: his face is concentrated, focused. He's worried about culpability, of course; I know he is. He's thinking ahead, he's thinking practically: if something happens, if we have to go to court. If we turn the iPhone on, it'll be solid evidence that we have the bag. It'll pick up signal and the account will show when and where. Even if we put it all back underwater, in the plane, under the sea. It'll show up on some network server somewhere that it was receiving a signal after the crash. It'll prove someone found the crash, the dead people, all of it, and told no one. Hid the evidence.

But then again it might just all be fine. I might just turn the phone on and find out whose it is and that could be it. I mean, if I make sure it's on airplane mode, it won't pick up a signal at all and that should be fine. No mobile phone record. No evidence. I can definitely do this. I can fix this. I know I can.

I'll charge it tonight.

17

The Phone

Something very, very bad has happened.

Last night Mark went to a private squash lesson over in the hotel complex. He needs the distraction—the stress is getting to him and I suggested it would be a good outlet. Plus he loves squash; it's really sort of sanctioned shouting for men, isn't it?

While he was out I took the opportunity to unplug the trouser press that's hidden inside the closet and plug in the iPhone from the bag using our spare charger. I plugged it in, checked it was on silent, and slid it down the side of the press in case Mark looked in the closet.

I woke up earlier than usual this morning, the anticipation of what I was going to do weighing on my mind. I had to wait until Mark had finished his breakfast and got in the shower to slip back into the closet and unplug it. It hadn't turned on by itself. I wasn't sure if that was something that happened automatically—for all I know, it could be broken. And then where would I be? I pocketed it and replaced the spare charger in our suitcase and replugged the presser.

What I need is some more time by myself, just half an hour or so, to check the phone. But it's hard thinking of excuses to spend time alone on your honeymoon, isn't it? Nothing seems important enough to be a credible distraction. I think of Holli's release two days ago. It makes sense that I'd need to Skype Phil to sort out logistics on filming with her as soon as we're back, now that we've missed her actual release. That definitely seems like a good enough reason to leave the room on my own for a while.

I tell Mark I'm going out to Skype my crew. I tell Mark I'll need an Ethernet connection for the Internet—it'll make the call signal stronger, the picture quality better. And rather conveniently I'll need to go to the hotel's business center for that.

He offers to come too but I say it'll be boring for him, and maybe a bit weird for Phil and Duncan, and I'll be super quick. Back before he knows it, I promise. He seems satisfied. I suggest he look through the Interpol missing-persons section today too. Just in case. You never know. But then, I do know—I know they won't be there. These people won't be reported missing. They just won't.

The business center is a small room with a large cream PC and a boxy printer unit. There's a conference table in the center of it taking up almost all the floor space. I can't imagine the room has ever been used for an actual business meeting. Perhaps they use it for staff meetings.

I give the corners of the room a cursory glance, high up along the coving. No cameras. That's good. What I'm doing is going to look odd and I don't want video evidence of me doing it. You know, just in case, in case it all comes out wrong.

I log on to the computer and pull up the search screen. I'm ready. I've been reading up on what to do all morning.

I pull the iPhone out of my pocket and push the power button. The screen floods with white light followed by the tiny Apple logo. I'm going to have to switch to airplane mode as soon as the locked screen comes up. I wait, holding my breath, while it slowly loads itself. How long has it been turned off? Does it take longer to load the longer it's been off? I wonder. Probably not.

Then the screen flashes up. It's not the locked screen. There's no locked screen. No password. Just apps. Straight to apps. Oh my God! No password? That's ridiculous, who does that in this day and age? I hastily swipe up the quick-access Control Center and tap the little airplane button. Safe.

It would have still been possible to switch to airplane mode from a locked screen, which is exactly what I had expected to be doing. My plan had been to bypass the locked screen. Apparently it's fairly easy to do, according to the Internet. But I don't need to do any of that now. The owner obviously wasn't too worried about people checking his phone. I suppose putting it in a case along with a handgun is probably security enough.

My heart is hammering.

I have access to everything. There aren't many app icons; some I recognize, some look foreign, but it's mainly just the in-house apps, no additions, no Candy Crush. I tap on Mail. An inbox bounces up. All the emails are in Russian. Shit. I thought something like this might happen. Okay, well, I guess they were Russian. Anyway, it's an alphabet I can't read. Okay. The easiest way to do this is to copy and paste into Google Translate, hardly elegant but, again, let me stress: I am not a spy.

I can't copy and paste the emails from this phone directly into

Translate because I can't let it go online, and I definitely can't forward them to my email account and do it from there.

I turn to the hotel computer and load Google Russia and type in the email provider that the emails have been sent to. It's the Russian email provider Yandex. The landing page means nothing to me; the writing is a mess of angular nonsense I don't understand, but in the top right-hand corner is a familiar box, containing space for a username and password. I type the email address on the phone into the first box and click the illegible squiggles below the password. Password reset. I fill it out and wait. I stare at the phone.

Oh bugger.

I'm not going to be able to get the reset email, obviously! What a fucking moron. I'm not online. The reset email won't get through. Why the fuck didn't I think of that? Idiot.

Okay.

Okay.

Hang on . . . I can turn Wi-Fi on while still in airplane mode. Of course! Mark showed me how to do that on the flight over so we could use the inflight Wi-Fi. Then I won't pick up any network signal. It won't be traceable. I can connect to the hotel Wi-Fi on the phone, collect the reset email, and then reset the password. Yes!

I run through it quickly, connect the phone to the hotel Wi-Fi network, and wait for the reset email to arrive. A batch of thirty-one messages download onto the handset, my password reset email being the last one to arrive. Nobody is missing these people yet. Nobody has accessed this account for days.

I reset through the email link and choose the password G650. It seems apt. Holding my breath, I wait for it to confirm. It works. Now only I can access their emails.

I scroll through the emails; the Google banner at the top of the page reads: *This page is in Russian. Would you like to translate it?* I click Translate.

I read.

Most of them appear to be statements or receipts of some sort. Some are meeting itineraries. Locations, times, and people. Some of the emails are spam. Funny that criminals get spam too. But none of the emails seems to be personal. No names in the emails. I see Aegys-Mutual Consultants referenced a couple of times. Another corporation, Carnwennan Holdings. Transactions between the two. Another called Themis Financial Management. I stop reading. I need something more, a person's name, something. I commit a few of the company names to memory; I'll look them up later.

I delete the emails created by my password reset and sign out of the email account; I clear the browser history on the hotel PC and sign out of the guest page.

Now text messages. I'm pretty sure I'll find something in the text messages. The green message icon shows there are forty-two new messages. I don't think I've ever had more than ten unread texts in my life, but then I suppose these guys aren't alive, are they? That can cause an unnaturally high buildup, I'd imagine.

I tap on messages. The phone has no saved numbers, so the messages all appear under phone numbers. I Google them. The +1 codes—America; +44 codes—UK; +7 codes—Russia; +352 codes—Luxemburg; and a +507 code—Panama. The Luxemburg number's text chain seems to be mainly written in French and German. The Panama text chain is in Spanish with the occasional English word cropping up. The American and Russian numbers seem to be purely English. Whoever this phone belonged to spoke a lot of languages and had a lot of balls in the air. So to speak. I tap on the first message, the most recent one, the American number. I read the chain:

THEY HAVE AGREED. THEY WILL EXPEDITE THE TRANSACTION. SAFE FLIGHT

INFORMATION NOT RECEIVED AS ADVISED

IS THERE A PROBLEM? WHERE ARE YOU?

CONTACT ME

THIS COULD TURN UGLY, ADVISE

I go back to the message menu. Choose the next message chain down. The Russian number:

MEETING LOCATION SET FOR TODAY

PICK-UP SET FOR 22:30 AT HELIPORT.

FLIGHT REDIRECTED? WHAT IS YOUR CURRENT LOCATION? IS THERE A PROBLEM?
CAN WE ASSIST?

THEY DID NOT RECEIVE. WHERE ARE YOU?

WHERE ARE YOU?

WE NEED TO TALK, RESPOND AS SOON AS YOU RECEIVE THIS.

RESPOND

Suddenly a dotted typing icon appears underneath. Oh my fucking God! Shit.

I forgot about the Wi-Fi connection. The three gray dots blink up at me. *Someone is there.* And then I remember, remember that iPhones send read receipts to the sender unless you specifically change the settings. And these messages have been marked read.

I scramble to turn it off. What if they've traced everything I've done? What if they find out who I am?

But they can't. There's no camera in here. I've used a public computer to read the emails. Anyone in the resort could have done it. There's no way they—whoever they are—could know it's me. But what if they're coming? What if they come here and review the

CCTV footage and see me coming in from the lobby at this time? I know there are security cameras in the lobby, in the hallway. Shit.

Okay, but realistically, Erin, *realistically*. Even if they know where the email account was accessed from, it takes at least a day to fly to Bora Bora from almost anywhere. A full day. And then they'd have to break into the hotel's security system and view the footage and then they'd have to figure out it was me from that footage. Would they do that? They don't even know I've seen the emails, do they? All they know is that their text messages have been read.

I need to read what they've written. I need to check.

I inhale deeply and push the power button again.

White screen, Apple icon, home screen, one unread message.

I tap it.

WHERE HAVE YOU BEEN?

They don't know I'm not whoever it is. Should I type something? Should I? Maybe I should tell them we found the bag?

No, I don't think that'd be a good idea. No.

Maybe I should pretend to be them? Should I? It would stop them looking for me, right? Send them off on a different track. Oh God. I wish I'd thought this through before. I can't think straight now. *Okay, think. Think.*

The three gray dots appear again. Shit! I have to say something. I tap on my text box. My text cursor pulsing.

Three gray dots will be appearing on his screen now. He'll know there's definitely someone there. Someone on the other end. I type.

REDIRECTED FLIGHT. UNAVAILABLE FOR TRANSACTION.

That seems okay, right? Fairly opaque. It should buy us enough time to get out of here before someone comes to find us. I press send. Gone. Off into the ether.

That seemed okay. Yeah. They might think the plane people are lying low or something, right?

And then reality hits me.

Lying low? What the actual fuck, Erin? What the actual, stupid, fuck are you doing? Lying low is not a thing. This is not *The Third Man*. You have absolutely no idea what you are doing right now. You are a film school graduate on your honeymoon. They will find you and they will kill you. You are going to die, Erin.

And then something very, very bad happens.

WHO IS THIS?

The gray dots pulse.

Pulse. Pulse. Pulse.

Oh no.

I stab the power button on the phone.

Oh God.

On the way back to the room I try to think of a good spin on what I've done. Some way to put it to Mark that doesn't make me sound like a liar and an idiot; but to be honest, at this stage it's fair to say that I am both those things. I just want his help. I'm scared. I need him to help me fix this.

18

Aftermath

"You did what?"

I stare at him. What can I say?

"Are you completely insane? Why on earth would you do that? Why did you lie? I don't . . . These are *real* people, Erin. Real dead people and real living people. We have no idea who they are or what kind of resources they have. I cannot believe you could be so stupid! Why? Why did you do it?"

I say nothing. I just stand there. I know! I'm an idiot, he's perfectly right, but we do need to fix this now. That's all I care about. I just want to fix it. I don't want to die.

He slumps down on the sofa. We're in the lounge. I called him over as soon as I opened the door and I told him everything. The companies, the emails, the texts—everything. He sits there thinking, frowning, his mind racing.

"All right," he finally says. "Okay. Erin, what does he know?"

I shrug, shake my head. I don't know. There's no way of being sure.

"No. Think about it, sweetheart. Stop, and think about it. What does he know?" He says it slowly, deliberately.

I swallow. Take a breath.

"He knows someone other than the plane people have the phone." That much I'm sure of.

"Great, and what will he infer from that?" he asks.

"That we stole the phone, I suppose. That we either killed them or we robbed them. They seem like the two most probable explanations." I look up at him.

He nods. "So he's going to want to find us, isn't he?" he says, thinking it through. "How can he find us?"

"Through the phone signal. Or through where we accessed the email account. They're the only links," I say.

"Okay. So, the hotel computer. The hotel computer room. And how will he know it was you on the computer? Rather than anyone else in the hotel?"

I see where Mark's going with this.

"The CCTV footage in the lobby and hallway. The time codes, me walking toward the room, away from the room. Before and after the access time." Shudder. Shit. Even though there weren't cameras in the business center itself, I'm still on film going in there for anyone to see. We need to get rid of the footage.

I notice my sudden jump in logic. From making a mistake to actively committing a crime. Just like that. I wonder if that's how it starts for a lot of criminals; I wonder if that's how it started with Eddie. A mistake, a cover-up, and then a slow inevitable chain of events. Nothing like this has ever crossed my mind before, the impulse to get rid of the evidence. I have no idea how one would even go about getting rid of footage. It's never occurred to me, of course, because I'm just an ordinary woman on her honeymoon, and aside from going over eighty on the motorway sometimes, I don't even consider breaking the rules. Maybe in my mind sometimes, but never in reality.

"So that's the only link to you personally, is it? That CCTV footage? Aside from that footage it could have been anyone in that room on the phone, on the computer?" Mark gives me an encouraging smile, not too much but enough.

"Yes, that's the only link," I assure him.

We go for a walk. We have no idea where they might keep the CCTV monitors and recording equipment, but we head for reception. It's a pretty logical assumption that it'll be in the room behind the reception counter. If not, we'll have to keep an eye out for a security guard and follow him back to wherever he goes.

The plan is simple. Of course it's simple, we're not actually criminal masterminds. If there's no one on the desk, then I'll slip into the back room, find the video system, and delete as far back as I can. It can't be that hard, right? If I can delete a whole month, so much the better. Cover our tracks completely, why not? If there's someone in the back room, we'll go with plan B.

There are two receptionists at the desk when we reach the main hotel. Mark takes my hand in his as we approach the lobby. He holds me firmly and leads me on, toward the library room. Plan B it is then.

Plan B is I have food poisoning and Mark wants to make a complaint. Hopefully, we'll be ushered into the back room so we can check if the system is in there. If it is, we'll need to get rid of the receptionist for a minute and deal with the footage. It's not foolproof for sure but I'm a film grad and Mark's an unemployed banker, so cut us some slack.

"Look sick," he whispers. I tilt my head back and inhale noisily through my nose. I put my hand to my head and exhale slowly through my mouth. Like someone desperately trying to hold it to-gether. I look around for a seat. Mark plays the concerned husband. Where do I want to go? What do I need? I am silent, I am pale. It must be bad, my illness. I sit gingerly down on a chair outside the hotel library. One of the receptionists glances up at us. Reads the situation. She throws a look to her colleague, who is slightly older, maybe her senior. The older woman nods, *You can deal with it,* then dips back into her paperwork. The younger receptionist makes her way over.

Here we go. My part here is easy, I just need to look distant and breathe deeply. Mark has the hard work.

He starts before she makes it to us.

"Excuse me. A little help here would be great if you're not too busy?" His tone is curt, tight. He's going to be difficult. A difficult customer.

The receptionist breaks into a dainty trot in order to get to us faster. Behind her the other woman, who can clearly see a shitstorm brewing, gathers up her papers and quietly heads off down the op-posite corridor. I bet they get a lot of arseholes here.

"Sorry, sir, is everything all right here?" Her tone is warm, an American accent.

Mark looks annoyed. "No actually, no, everything is not all right, to be honest with you . . ." He squints at her name badge. "Leila."

I see her sigh inwardly and steel herself. Credit to her, she keeps smiling.

"My wife and I are meant to be on a five-star honeymoon but we've been shut up in our room now for two days due to the food poisoning you've decided to give us. I don't know what kind of out-fit you think you're running here but we've had just about enough of it." This Mark is a genuine arsehole.

"I'm so sorry, sir! I wasn't aware of the situation. The issue hadn't been brought to my attention but I can guarantee you now that I will sort this all out for you and we'll make sure that whatever needs to happen happens."

"I appreciate that, Leila, and I know it's not your fault as such, but you should have been informed, really, shouldn't you? I raised this issue yesterday and no one has got back to us. Nothing has happened. This is supposed to be a luxury five-star resort but I honestly don't know how you managed to get those stars if you (a) don't communicate with each other and (b) ignore customers' complaints when they don't suit you. It's disgusting! Look at my wife, Leila. Look at her." His voice is raised now; it's very loud. I think we can officially call this a *scene* at this stage. Leila looks down at me. Somehow I've started to sweat; it's probably the stress of our plan but I'm guessing it looks pretty damn convincing. I stare up at her, dazed. She makes a decision.

"Sir, if you'll just come with me, we'll go somewhere a little quieter and perhaps I can fetch a glass of water for Mrs. . . . ?" Leila's doing really well. Extremely professional. God, this is a good hotel.

"Seriously? For Christ's sake, Leila. Roberts. It's Roberts. Mr. and Mrs. Roberts. Bungalow six. Jesus fucking Christ." Mark exhales loudly through his nose. A man contending with himself, staying just the right side of exasperated. Mark's good. If the banking doesn't work out, he could always be an actor.

"Mr. Roberts, of course! Well, if you would just come with me now, I'll make sure we get this all handled for you. Let's get you something to drink, Mrs. Roberts." Leila beckons us to follow her. Mark hoists me tenderly from the chair, supporting my weight, his hand bracing me under my armpit. We follow.

The back room is bigger than I'd imagined. Open plan. There's a door just off it that Leila leads us through. Into a plush, well-appointed meeting room. A special complaints room? More likely the VIP check-in room. For high-profile guests, the people that other people might want to stare at. I'm getting used to this world now, how it operates.

We sit. Leila turns the blinds on the windows that look back into the back room, slowly. As they close I catch sight of a black-and-white CCTV monitor and then it's gone.

She sits down in front of us.

"Okay, first things first, Mrs. Roberts, can I get you anything? An iced water? Something sugary? Anything at all?"

I try to speak but nothing comes out. I clear my throat; it's been a while since I've said anything. Big buildup. I nod.

"Thank you, Leila. I really appreciate it," I rasp. A good cop to Mark's bad. Poor Mrs. Roberts.

"Could I get a hot tea please, Leila? With sugar and lots of milk. If it's not too much trouble. Is that all right?" I peer up at her, apologetic. Sorry to be causing a problem.

Leila looks relieved. A friend, an ally. This might all have a positive resolution after all. She might get some great feedback later. A thank-you letter. Employee of the month. She smiles.

"No problem at all, Mrs. Roberts. I'm going to go and fetch it myself. Please just make yourselves comfortable and I'll be back shortly." She checks for Mark's approval before swishing out the door of the VIP check-in room, through the back room, and out into the lobby. The door shuts behind her. I jump to my feet and run out of the VIP room and into the back room. Mark stands in the meeting room doorway watching me. I get to the CCTV monitors in time to see, on the screen, Leila round the end of the lobby corridor off on her way to the bar. On the computer screen I minimize the windows and find the archived days. Sixty days' kept footage. Should I clear all? No. Just our stay? No. A month is fine. I highlight mid-August to mid-September and click delete. Am I sure I want to erase these files? the program asks. Yes. Yes, I am. I click. I then go into options, erase trash. Done. How are we doing? I click on the minimized screens. No sign of Leila yet. My heart is thundering. I go back into the program. Scroll through the options. There it is. Settings. Keep files for sixty days. I change the settings to six days. That should muddy the waters. By the time someone checks the archived data, they'll think it's a settings error. No one watches back hours of CCTV footage unless they're looking for something. I check the screens. There're no cameras in this room. We're fine. I return the screen to its original setup. Still no sign of Leila. I want to do one more thing. I scan the room.

"Have you done it?" Mark whispers, urgent. "Erin?"

"Yes, but one more thing. One more . . ." Then I see it. A filing cabinet across the room. I check the screen. Leila is leaving the restaurant bar, cup and saucer in hand. I've got less than a minute. I sprint across the room, dodging chairs. I yank open the *R* drawer and flick through the files. Roberts. There it is. I reach in and grab our passport photocopies. Our address forms. I hear heels tapping loudly across the marble lobby. Shit. I slam the cabinet shut and sprint back to the VIP room and dive into a chair. I shove the papers down the front of my shorts and Mark sits beside me as Leila opens the door. She enters with a warm smile.

"Here we go. Nice hot tea." She peers at me, concerned.

I'm breathing pretty erratically now due to the running and the adrenaline. I look terrified and sweaty. In a way I look perfect.

I wobble to my feet.

"I'm so sorry, Leila, but I really need to use the restroom again. Which is the nearest?" I implore breathily.

She puts the peace-offering tea down and instantly gives me an understanding smile. I suppose we've all been there.

"Just next to the library, on the right. We'll be in here when you're done, if you're up to it, Mrs. Roberts," she adds.

What a nice lady. I will leave feedback.

As I stagger out, hand lightly placed on the front of my shorts, I hear them start to duke it out over our imaginary grievances. *Well done, Mark. Keep it up.*

I waste a good ten minutes in the bathroom soaking the papers, then balling them into mush. I deposit them into separate sanitary disposal bins before heading back to our room.

19

Links

Eventually Mark bowls back into our suite, full of energy.

"Done."

He plops down on the sofa next to me. I let my head fall onto his shoulder, exhausted from the waiting, from the tension. I think we're friends again. Fight-or-flight stress endorphins have healed the rift I made by using the iPhone earlier. We're a team again. The Robertses versus the world.

"Great work," I breathe into his shoulder. I kiss it softly through his T-shirt.

"How did you leave it?" I ask. It doesn't really matter, I just want to hear the sound of his voice, the vibration from his chest. I already know he will have played it flawlessly.

"Very well, thanks. Leila and I are best friends. She's given us a letter for two free nights in any Four Seasons we choose. And I told her she was a credit to the hotel and we'd be passing that on to the manager. She seemed pretty pleased in the end." He kisses my temple.

"You did great, Erin," he says, tilting my head back to look up at him. "Seeing you like that . . . with the CCTV. I've never seen you like that. I can't believe we managed it. You got our ID's too, didn't you? I didn't even think of that. You did great. So great." He bends to kiss me.

Those were the only links to us being here. If they come. If they even come for us. The important thing is the hotel no longer has copies of our passports or London address on file. If anyone comes looking, then they won't be able to find any ID for us. Plus, the footage of who used the computer this morning no longer exists. A ghost took the phone and there will be no way to find the guests who stayed in our room except . . . it suddenly occurs to me. A terrifying flash out of nowhere.

My eyes flick up to Mark. "I forgot about the computers! Their computer system. We forgot! They've almost definitely put our check-in info on their system already, Mark. It doesn't matter that we took the file; they still have all our info."

He breaks my gaze, leans away from me. We have to go back. Shit! He knows it. He stands and starts pacing. We have to go back and somehow erase those files. *Shit shit shit.* And I thought we'd both done so well. I thought I'd been so clever. But in fact all we've been doing is making it more obvious. Highlighting who we are, who did it. If someone comes looking. And someone will come looking. They won't see our missing files, but they will find our details on the hotel database and they will know we tried to cover our tracks. We have flagged ourselves, nothing more. Unless. Unless we go back to that office right now and delete our names from the system completely. Unless one of us does that.

Mark looks down at me again. A thought is solidifying in his mind. He has to go; he has to be the one this time. I can't go back to reception. I'm supposed to be on my sickbed; that's the story we've sold. I've made my sickbed and now I have to lie in it.

Mark slowly paces, thinking. After a few minutes he heads into the bedroom and comes out holding an earring. One of my emerald earrings, a birthday present from the year before. He holds it up.

"You lost an earring. That's what's happened. I'll go and find it, shall I?" He nods. There's a finality to it. "Yeah, I'll go."

Forty-three minutes later he's back in the room.

"It's done. I changed our names, numbers, emails, and address. All of it. Done." He looks exhausted but relieved.

God knows how he did it but I knew he would. *Thank God.* I smile.

"We need to talk about the guy-on-the-phone problem, Mark." Time to stop congratulating ourselves and get back to the situation at hand. Since he's been gone I've been running it through in my mind.

He nods and sits down next to me on the sofa. He moistens his lips.

"Okay. What do we know? Let's start there. What do we know about him? Or her?" he asks. We're going to work it through.

"His phone number is registered in Russia, but his text messages are written in English. All the plane people's emails were Russian. They must have been Russian. But they wrote to the man in the text messages in English and he replied in English. So I'd hazard a guess he at least is either American or English. We don't know if he's the same person as on the American number too. He might just be the same guy with two phones. We don't know. It sounded like he was arranging the exchange for the plane people with the American number. He wanted the deal to go through. He knows we're not the plane people, and he knows we *pretended* to be. . . ." Mark's eyebrow is raised. I stutter to a stop.

"Huh, okay. He knows *I* pretended to be—" I correct myself. Mark nods.

I continue, "—the plane people. He will assume we've looked through the phone. He'll assume we've either killed them for whatever reason and kept the bag, or we've found it and seen things that we shouldn't have seen. Either way, we are a threat to him. Or them. And he'll try to find us."

Mark leans forward, elbows on knees, frowning. "Can they trace the phone signal? Well, not signal—you weren't using a signal, were you? Wi-Fi? Can they trace that somehow?" He's thinking out loud but I answer.

"No. No, they can't! There's no iCloud connection on the iPhone. You can only locate via Wi-Fi with a special app or through iCloud. I mean, he can trace the last place the signal was received but that was maybe before the plane people even got on the plane. Sometime before the crash, at any rate. The phone was packed away and turned off when the plane went down. So he may know it's somewhere near the Pacific but no more than that." I'm pretty sure that sounds right. Mark nods; he agrees.

"So the only link to here, to this hotel, is the accessing of the email account from the business center?" He's forming a plan, I can tell.

"Yeah, the IP address will be logged somewhere. It'll show where the account was accessed. I'm guessing these people probably have a way to find that out. At any rate they can certainly afford to get someone who can," I say.

They will come. It's just a matter of time really. They might have the IP address already. They might be on their way this very minute.

"So they're coming?" he says; he can read it off my face.

"Yes," I reply.

He nods thoughtfully. "In which case, we are going." He rises and heads for the laptop.

"Mark—?"

"It's fine," he tells me. "We've got the perfect excuse now. You got sick, food poisoning, so we cut the vacation short to get you home to the doctor."

I smile. It does solve a lot of problems.

"I'm going to change the flights. I booked flexible tickets, so it should be fine. I'll try and get seats for tomorrow. Sound okay?" he asks.

"Sounds ideal." I get up and head to the bedroom. Time to start packing, I guess. It's sad to be leaving, but if and when these people do arrive at the hotel, I'd rather be anywhere else on earth, but preferably in my own home.

I pull out our cases and empty out the contents of the wardrobes onto the bed.

I look up to the top shelf.

"Mark?" I wander back into the lounge.

"Yeah?" He looks up from the screen.

"Are we keeping it?" It's just a question. I don't know anymore. I don't know what we're doing. I don't know if we're running away from these people or if we're robbing them.

"Well, we can't just leave it in the room, can we?" he asks. "Unless we want to get arrested on the flight home. If we leave it, we'll need to hide it . . . I suppose? Under the bungalow, maybe? Or we could take it, keep it? Erin, once we're gone, there's no way to trace us." He studies my face. The question unanswered.

Two million pounds.

I don't want much in life. Just my house, my husband, the occasional vacation—economy flights are fine. Just a quiet life. Our life.

Two million is our whole house paid off. A startup fund for Mark if he wants to set up a business, or a cushion until he finds a new job. It could be a university fund for the child that might already be growing inside me.

I remember the vomit on the floor yesterday morning. Maybe? I've been off the pill for eight weeks now. No, no, it'd be too soon for symptoms. I'm fairly confident that yesterday's vomit will have been down to piña coladas and fear. I suppose time will tell.

And once we're gone, there's no way to trace us.

"Are you sure, Mark? Could they find us from the flights maybe?" Perhaps even though we've cleared our records here they could somehow check flight manifests for the whole island? Check all the incoming flights for names and find which two names don't appear in any hotel guest registers?

Mark looks out the French doors into the fading light across the lagoon. The sound of the waves lapping under the bungalow muffled and steady.

He answers slowly. "There are around thirty-six hotels on this island; it's coming up to peak season, so let's say they're running at half capacity. This hotel has one hundred suites, that's two hundred people—half capacity, one hundred people. One hundred times thirty-six hotels: give or take thirty-six hundred people. Five flights in and five flights out daily back to Tahiti. That's a lot of different people. A lot of names to check. Three thousand six hundred constantly changing names. They'll need more to go on than that. Trust me." He's right, there are too many variables.

We could take it and no one will ever find out.

"Yes. We'll keep it. I'll pack." I say it clearly, so that if at any time in the future the question rises as to whose idea this was, we'll remember it was mine. I'll take the weight for both of us.

Mark nods; he smiles softly.

We are keeping it.

20

Thursday, September 15

Customs

Our flights are booked, first-class back to Heathrow. Our last burst of luxury. The last of the honeymoon.

I packed our bags last night. Broke open the seal on the vacuum-packed cash and cut open the lining of my suitcase carefully along the seam with my nail scissors. We fill my lining and Mark's lining with half each and slot the iPhone and USB in mine too. I fold a towel over and under the layer of money so it feels like lining padding; I pack it in tight so it won't budge no matter how much the handlers throw the cases around. Then I sew the lining back up using the hotel mini sewing kit. We have to call for another one for Mark's case.

I pack the diamonds into five separate little baggies, the ones the shower caps come in. Then I slice open five sanitary towels, remove the filler and place the baggies, one each, into the absorbent lining, slip them back into their purple wrappers and back into their cardboard sanitary-pad box. The customs guys will have to be damn thorough to find this stuff, especially considering customs doesn't tend to open up first-class suitcases anyway. Sad but true—they just don't.

But even if they do, I think we'll be okay.

The main problem is the gun. Although part of me wishes we could keep it just in case this all goes wrong, there's no way we'd get it through customs, and we definitely don't want to draw any attention to ourselves, given what else we're carrying. So last night we bundled the gun up in a pillowcase with rocks from the beach and dropped it into the choppy water on the ocean side of the resort. Into the murky darkness.

Leila comes to collect our bags in the morning and see us off to the jetty. She's all smiles and get-well-soons. Mark hands her two hotel stationery envelopes. One has her name on it; it contains five hundred U.S. dollars. Not an unusually high tip for a resort of this sort; I'm sure they've had better. But it's big enough that she'll be pleased yet small enough to ensure we're not particularly memorable.

And we're off. Off to Tahiti, then LAX, then London. Then in a car to our house. I miss our home.

There's a moment when we're checking in our bags in Tahiti that I feel the check-in clerk's eyes catch mine. Just a fraction of a second, but I think *she sees*. She sees the way I'm looking at the bag, at her, and I know she knows. But then she shakes it off. A brief toss of the head. She probably thinks she's imagining things. Or maybe I imagined it? After all, what on earth could a honeymooner be smuggling back from Bora Bora? Hotel towels? I readjust my face to the way it's supposed to look and she hands our passports back over the counter with a smile.

At Heathrow we collect our bags again. Another lovely flight. And we're almost free. Almost home now. Just customs to walk through. I nip to the toilet before we go through. I check the lining inside my case; it's all still neatly stitched up. Safe. I zip it back up and head back to meet Mark by the luggage carousels. Then I feel my phone vibrate against my leg. I stop halfway out of the ladies' toilet. Something has happened. I freeze, then try to subtly make my way back into the washroom. I lock the cubicle and grab my phone.

But it's not Mark calling to tell me to flush the diamonds or run. It's just life flooding back in. Real life. Our real life. Emails from friends about the wedding, work, two missed calls from Phil. No emergency, just life-as-usual.

Mark senses my mood when I find him. He keeps me chatting. I know what he's doing and it works. And, thankfully, by the time I look up, we're through the "Nothing to Declare" aisle and out into the terminal concourse.

We did it, and it really wasn't that hard.

I look around at the brightly dressed, tanned people returning to the gray. Out through the giant glass panels of Terminal 5, damp England lies in wait for them. For us. God, I'm glad to be back. Outside, the scent of rain hangs in the air.

21

Home

We're back. The house is pristine, just the way we left it. Ready for our new married life. Lovely Nancy popped by and filled the fridge with a few essentials before we got home. She left our spare keys and a little note welcoming us. That was nice. I have to remember to call and thank her. I'll need to write it down or I know I'll forget, and it's important I don't. It's important I get back into my real life and I don't act differently. We all need structure.

I slept like a log last night; I wouldn't have predicted that at all. It's funny how the body seems to work completely of its own volition at certain times in our lives, isn't it? By rights I should have tossed and turned all night waiting for everything to come crashing down around us. But I didn't. I slipped back between our fresh sheets and sank into our mattress and slept the sleep of the righteous. Mark did too. I think he barely moved all night.

He's made us breakfast. Eggs and tomatoes on toast with warm butter and a tall steaming pot of coffee. The coffee we like. Everything the way we like it, so reassuring, so wonderfully familiar. The sun is shining through the windows onto him as he potters back and forth with tasty things. He looks calm, contented, shuffling about in his boxers and dressing gown. He sits down opposite me finally and we eat in silence as we sate ourselves with our less exotic but equally satisfying British food.

He reaches for my hand across the table as we eat, an unconscious gesture. We loosely clasp each other, our bodies seeking something to hold on to in this strange yet familiar new world.

After we finish I look out of the window at the trees outside, where the branches meet the clear blue sky. A clear crisp day. Mark squeezes my hand. He smiles across at me.

"I suppose we should get started then, shouldn't we?" he says.

I smile. We both don't want to. Get started, I mean. We don't want reality just yet. We'd rather sit here together and hold hands. But we'll do it together. We'll make it fun. Mark and I.

"Let's do it," I declare, and rise from the table. "Let's do it."

The first job is to unpack the bags, and by that I don't mean the clean and dirty clothes. We take scissors to the suitcase linings and remove the bundles of notes. Mark fetches an old weekend bag from his wardrobe and I begin to pack the bundles away into it. Of course, the original bag is gone now. Probably in a wheelie bin in the basement of the Four Seasons back in Bora Bora, torn and empty, its contents safely removed.

Next I remove the diamonds from their sanitary towel packaging. We empty them all into a thick plastic freezer baggie. Somehow they still manage to sparkle through the thick clouded plastic. Mark drops the phone and the USB into another freezer bag and then I place both of the plastic bags in the attic. I hide them under some loose insulation in the far corner of the eaves. They should be safe there. I remember when we first bought the house, all the forgotten things we found in the attic. Things can go unnoticed in lofts for decades, and no one really puts anything they actually care about in the attic, do they? They'll be safe there. As I climb down the ladder a wave a nausea rolls over me. I don't know why, maybe it's been bubbling away at the back of my mind, but I have a feeling I know what it is, instinctively.

I head to the bathroom and find what I'm looking for at the back of the cupboard. A pregnancy test. I keep a standby pack in the cupboard, just in case. I've always hated the idea of having to trudge to a shop and furtively buy one in an actual emergency situation. I like to be prepared, which I'm sure you've gathered by now. There are three sticks. I unwrap one and pee on it. I place it on the edge of the bathtub and wait. Sixty seconds. I think about our plan. About what comes next.

The hardest part will be the diamonds. Selling the diamonds. Converting the diamonds from beautiful sparkling possibilities into cold hard cash. That's going to take time and a certain amount of finesse. And of course a whole lot of Internet searches.

I have no idea how to sell diamonds or who to sell them to but we'll get to that. First we'll tackle the money. We'll get that dealt with and then we'll go from there. But even dealing with the money isn't a simple task.

You can't just wander up to a bank and hand the cashier one million U.S. dollars in cash unfortunately. It tends to raise concerns. Where you got it tends to be an issue. Tax is an issue. Hell, even currency conversion rate is an issue.

Luckily for us, Mark knows banks.

Sixty seconds up. I peer at the stick. The cross is blue.

Huh.

I try another one. Place it on the edge of the bathtub and wait.

It's probably faulty. Could be faulty. Best not to get too involved in that result just yet. Think about the plan. Yes. The plan.

According to Mark, here's what we need to do: we need to open a bank account where people won't ask questions, where that's the whole selling point of the bank. Not asking questions. Banks like that exist and Mark is going to find us one.

I'll give you one guess as to the type of person you don't ask questions to. Correct. Rich people. Very rich people. You're probably noticing a theme here. I'm beginning to realize that being rich doesn't really mean having money to buy nice things; it means having money to avoid the rules. The rules are there for the other people, the people without the money, the ones who drive you about in your cars, fly your planes, cook your food. Rules can be bypassed with money or even just the mystique surrounding money. Flights can vanish, people can find people, people can live or die without the hassle of police or doctors or paperwork.

If, and only if, you have the money to make things run smoothly for yourself. And with our bag we can make things run smoothly.

Sixty seconds done. I check the stick. That cross is definitely blue. Shit. How can that be, though? Isn't it supposed to take ages to get pregnant? I suppose it has been two whole months of trying. No, can't be. Must have done it wrong. I check the pack. No, I haven't got it wrong; a cross means pregnant. Blank is not pregnant. Huh.

One test left. Not much pee left.

Sixty seconds pass.

Blue cross.

Shit. I'm having a child.

When I finally get out of the bathroom Mark is in the study booking us two flights to Switzerland. I stand over his shoulder for a few minutes until he turns.

"You okay?" He smirks. I'm standing there in silence. I guess he thinks I'm shirking my duties while he's a hive of industry.

I try to speak but I can't say it. I can't tell him. It'll mess up the plan. I'll mess up all the plans.

"Yeah, I'm fine, sorry," I say. "Completely zoned out."

He chuckles as I head back out into the hallway to unpack the rest of our things.

22

Pretty Woman

It's 8 A.M. in Terminal 5 of Heathrow Airport. We're here early; our flight to Switzerland isn't due to depart for another two hours.

Mark is on the phone to a man called Tanguy. Richard, Mark's old Swiss banking colleague, put them in contact. You remember Richard. He was the one with Mark the first night we met, with the hooker? Well, it turns out all those hours of Mark babysitting Richard's dates with escorts finally paid off. This time Richard's hooking Mark up.

Tanguy works at UCB Banque Privée Suisse. Today I'll be setting up a business account. Our very own shell account. It'll be just a numbered account, no name, no questions. Innocuous. This way I can pay myself, or us, straight into my British business account through the shell account. Monthly. I can pay self-employment tax on those earnings. I can legitimatize the money. Once it hits my account it will just be plain old taxable income. There'll be a solid paper trail, all perfectly legal, if not entirely ethical. We can pay off the house, invest, plan for the future, for the little life growing slowly inside me. Half Mark, half me. With the money in the bank the pressure will be off Mark to get a new job straightaway, any job going. He can take his time, find the right fit. We can go back to the way we used to be. We'll have money for our new life together. Which I see is more important now than ever.

But first I need to get something appropriate to wear for our appointment. I have got to look like the kind of person who would be opening this sort of account, the kind of person who would have one million dollars in cash. We need to go shopping. I need a costume and Mark assured me we'd find something suitable here, in the designer stores of Terminal 5, hence our early arrival.

I look around the store options as Mark finishes up his call. The clean, fresh, gleaming glass fronts of Chanel, Hermès, Prada, Dior, Gucci, Burberry, Louis Vuitton, Bottega Veneta, as they bend all around the huge concourse. Their windows filled with beautiful, expensive things. Candy stores of shoes, jackets, dresses, and bags. Consumer heaven. Mark hangs up and turns to me, an eyebrow raised.

"Done. Right. Let's go shopping." He grins and takes my arm in his. "Where to first, Mrs. Roberts?"

I sweep the concourse with my eyes once more. Suddenly slightly nervous. We'll be using our own money to shop today, but ultimately we're spending the money we found. I think of the plane deep underwater, its passengers, and remember Mark's words: they were bad people. And we aren't bad people, are we? No. No, we are not. I shake the thoughts away.

"Chanel?" I offer. It looks like the biggest of the stores and easily the most impressive.

"Chanel it is." He notices my reticence and gives me an encouraging look. "Remember, you don't have to be nervous. Not about price tags. This is an investment; you need to look right or this isn't going to work. We can spend a lot here. Okay?" He pulls his American Express platinum card out of his leather wallet. "Let's go crazy."

I can't help but smile. Somewhere deep inside me a teenage girl is screaming.

Now, I'm sure you've seen the film; you know how this goes. My husband Richard Gere's me through the gauntlet of Heathrow Terminal 5's designer boutiques toward the glittering lights of Chanel. I like to flatter myself that I've always looked fairly stylish in my mid-price-range clothing. I'm usually happy to pay up to five hundred pounds for a special occasion. An event dress, a leather jacket, Jimmy Choos, but I would balk at paying, say, two thousand pounds for an embellished bustier. I know I spend more than I probably should, but even I don't tend to shop in stores that bring champagne on a tray into your carpeted dressing room. But today I will. And that's okay.

When we enter the shop it's empty save for the two shop assistants, one polishing the glass of the jewelry counter, the other dusting the handbags on the higher display shelves. Both look up as we enter. And both run their eyes up and down Mark and me, quickly assessing, calculating. I thought I'd left the house looking pretty good this morning, but as we walk toward them I suddenly feel distinctly pedestrian. I feel my usual confidence ebb away. The shop assistants' eyes slide off of me and onto Mark. All attention and focus is directed toward Mark: gorgeous Mark in his tasteful cashmere sweater, jeans, and jacket. His Rolex twinkling in the shop lights. We have been weighed and it has been astutely judged that my gentleman friend is the alpha here; my gentleman friend is the one with the money.

Mark bends and whispers in my ear.

"Go have a wander. I'll deal with this." He kisses my cheek and continues on to the now smiling assistants.

I drift over toward the racks and inspect a pink silk blouse, its tag clearly visible at £2,470. Mark's platinum card is going to get a hammering today.

On the opposite wall, I catch sight of a huge plasma screen playing Chanel's fall/winter catwalk show. Battalions of reedy girls clad in tweed, leather, and lace, a marching army of impeccable taste. I glance over at Mark; he's leaning over the counter now, talking to the assistants, who blush and giggle. Oh, Mark. They all look over at me, and beam. He's told them we're newlyweds, I can tell from their expressions. I beam back and give a little wave and the impeccably dressed delegation surges to meet me.

The blond assistant, the higher ranking of the two, speaks first. "Good morning, madam. Congratulations, by the way!" She looks back to Mark, smiling.

The redheaded assistant takes the cue and bobs her head in agreement as the blonde continues.

"So, we've spoken to your husband and we understand you are looking for *three* separate daywear options today. Is that right?" She sounds thrilled.

My eyes flick to Mark in surprise. *Three outfits.* He grins and shrugs. Okay, I see what we're doing; we're having fun. That's what we're doing. There's no messing around here; we really are going for this. I take a breath.

"*Yes.* Yes, three daywear options would be fantastic," I reply as if it's the sort of thing I usually say.

"Lovely, well, let me get the fall/winter collection book and you can take a look. We got the new collection in over the weekend, so we should have pretty much everything. Oh, what size do you take? We can measure you but just as a guide?"

"French 34," I say. Because I may not own any Chanel but I damn well know my French sizing.

The catalog is found and pored over. Sparkling water is supplied.

I need something appropriate to wear, something someone with a million dollars in cash, in a bag, might wear. I need to look polished, put together. Like someone you wouldn't question, someone you wouldn't mess with.

We start the fitting with a signature bouclé wool pencil skirt and the pink silk blouse. But Mark and I quickly come to the conclusion that it might be a tad too formal for our requirements. After all, I don't want to look like I *work* at the bank.

Next, we try a silk sundress in caramel from the spring/summer collection. It'll still be just about warm enough for it in Geneva, and paired with a jacket, it would work perfectly. It hangs from me in a way no item of clothing ever has, loosely draping from gossamer-thin spaghetti straps, showing just the right amount of South Pacific tan across my décolletage, and then plunging airily down between my breasts. The assistant pairs it with thick golden hoop earrings and cream espadrilles. When I look in the mirror I'm transformed, into someone else, another version of myself. A Greek heiress with a sugar daddy, Santorini-ready.

One outfit down. Two to go. The redhead arrives with champagne in tall crisp flutes. I think of my test yesterday and sip lightly.

The second outfit we decide on is a pairing of skintight black leather trousers and a thin black cashmere roll-neck, with a string of Chanel jewelry draped over me and finished with black ankle boots and a black cape coat. Minimal, sexy.

The final outfit we all decide on is a 1960-inspired bouclé top with a "space-suit neckline" in black and gray wool with hidden sparkles in the Chanel fabric. Underneath, tailored black culottes, ankle boots, and over it all a classic Chanel winter coat in the same fabric as the top. One hundred percent Emirates princess. Polished to perfection.

I finish off my sparkling water while Mark pays—I can't even imagine what the damage is—and we say our goodbyes, leaving two extremely happy sales assistants in our wake.

We head to Bottega Veneta next. We need a new bag for the money; I can't just take Mark's old weekend bag into the bank with me. I need something less conspicuous, more appropriate, something I might carry. We find the perfect size and shape, a Bottega Veneta oyster gray, woven-leather duffel bag. We can load it up with money, and I can change, once we're safely in our hotel room in Geneva. And with that we're done, just as our boarding call comes through.

● ● ●

23

The Money

I'm now sitting on the edge of a bed in the Four Seasons Hotel des Bergues in Geneva. The voucher Leila issued in Bora Bora came in handy really quickly. My heart is hammering.

Mark is on the phone to Tanguy from UCB Banque Privée Suisse again.

I'm dressed for the appointment now. There's a chill in the air here, so I decided on the second option, skintight leather trousers and soft cashmere. Smart, sophisticated, sexy, a woman who knows her own mind. I do look like the kind of person who would be opening this sort of account; beside me sits the Bottega Veneta duffel bag, a bag befitting the fortune inside it. I look across at myself in the floor-length mirror as Mark's voice drifts in from the suite's sitting room. The woman in the mirror is wealthy, she's confident. I certainly look the part even if I don't feel it.

Mark finishes the call and comes in to join me.

I'll be the one doing the heavy lifting today. I'm the one who has to walk into the bank alone and hand over one million dollars in a Bottega Veneta duffel bag. I feel my heart palpitate, deep inside my chest, at the very idea of it.

"Don't think of it like that," Mark tells me. "Don't think of it as you handing over a hugely suspicious bag in the middle of a bank. Because they won't see it that way. Seriously, Erin. If you'd seen half the stuff I'd seen in banking . . . Listen, I went out with some oil guys in Mayfair once and they carried a hundred thousand pounds in cash around in a gym bag. One hundred thousand pounds, for a night out. I know it seems unreal to us, and money in a duffel bag feels very illegal, but there's no law against carrying money around in bags. Is there? And you can't carry that much in a handbag, so of course it's a duffel bag. Right?"

I just stare at him. I might need to vomit again. I did earlier.

It's just nerves. The vomiting. Delicate flower that I am. It's only the deep shifting tidal cramps in my womb that are the first actual signs of the pregnancy. Yawning aches in the core of me. I Googled them this morning. Hormones. I worked out that from the first day of my last period I'm six weeks pregnant. Apparently the cramps are perfectly normal at this stage. I suppose my body is preparing to make a whole human being. I'm trying not to think about it too much. Mark doesn't know yet. And it hardly seems the time, does it?

The nausea washes over me. Waves of sickness followed by blissful calm.

"What if they ask me where I got it?" I ask.

"They won't, Erin. They just won't. If it's illegal, they definitely won't want to know, will they? Think about it. The law is: if you're aware the money is not legal, then you have to alert the authorities. If they asked every suspicious person who opened a Swiss bank account where they got their money from, Switzerland's economy would be fucked. Nobody opens a Swiss bank account with their birthday money, Erin, come on!" He's right, of course.

"I suppose they might just assume I'm an escort or something. Hence the cash . . ." I say.

"More likely they'll think you're siphoning off your husband's money before a divorce. I'm sure they get that a lot. At least that's what I'd think if I saw you." He smiles. Wow. It's at moments like that you wonder, Who did I marry? Judging by his face, I think he thinks he's just complimented me.

Another ripple of nausea. I am silent until it passes.

"And he's definitely expecting me?" I rise slowly from the bed, careful not to make any sudden movements.

"Yeah, he doesn't know we're married; I told him you're a new client. He knows it's a large cash deposit. That it's delicate, all that." He grabs an apple from the complimentary fruit basket and takes a bite.

I know Mark can't go himself, as he has a direct connection to the bank, but I can't help noticing that he really isn't leaving any trails back to himself. It's my face the bank will see, the memory of me that will be recalled. But then, the beauty of a Swiss account is that once the account is opened, that information will be protected. And my passport name is still Locke. I haven't changed it to Roberts yet. As far as Mark's old work links are concerned, the client he mentioned has no personal connection to him. Erin Locke will open an account today but my name will not be attached to the account at all. The account will bear only a number. Untraceable back to me. Untraceable back to either of us.

I stand and study myself one last time in the mirror. I've done a good job with the hair and makeup. I look right. Now that I think of it, I look like the type of person I had expected to see in the first-class lounge that morning two weeks ago. The kind of person that should have been in that lounge. If the world was a different place. If things always looked the way you imagined. But I guess, like in film-making, some things look more real when they're not.

For a second I see my mother in my reflection, my beautiful young mother, but it's only a flash, a ripple on the water, and she's gone, stowed safely away again.

The nausea's dissipating now. I'll be just fine.

"Off I go then," I say.

He nods, his energy high, and he hands me the bag.

"The car should be downstairs," he says as I take it from him.

And with that I'm on my own.

In the lift I stand alone, reflected ad infinitum in the mirrored box, dampened silence around me. The doors slide shut soundlessly and the hallway recedes.

What if I never see its lurid red swirling pattern again? What if I'm arrested at the bank as soon as I click across the marble lobby? What would happen to the little blue cross inside me?

Or worse, what if the person who sent that text is there, waiting for me? I remember the three pulsing gray dots.

What if somehow he knows what we're doing?

It is a "he" in my head. Of course, it could be a "she" or a "they." *They* could already know our movements, our plans. Why not? It's possible I've overlooked something. Or rather, *we've* overlooked something. That we've already made a mistake that means we've lost. After all, Mark and I are just two ordinary people from North London, normal, easy to find.

I do have a clearer idea of how their world works now, though, of how much more there is to everything than I could see before. My tiny life has been thrown into sharp relief. Who I was before, in the grand scheme of everything, versus who I am now.

We human beings are amazing in our capacity for adaptation, aren't we? Like plants, we grow to fit our pots. But more than that, sometimes, we can choose our own pots; some of us get that opportunity. I guess it really depends on how far you're willing to go, doesn't it? I've never properly understood that before. I think of

Alexa, her mother, their decision, their goodbye. Sometimes there's a stark beauty to the choices we make.

For our situation now, I have adapted. I've become a far different person. I see her all around me reflected in the glass. Solid. Implacable.

Or at least she is visibly. Inside is different. Inside there is only breath and silence. Because I'm scared. Plain and simple, sharks-in-the-water scared. But I will breathe through it, and I will not panic, and I will not think about what I can't control. It's not safe to think too much. I don't trust my mind right now, not until I get back in this elevator in a few hours' time. Then I can think.

But one thought does break through.

It has the echo of something familiar.

The thought is: I don't need to come back to this elevator at all, do I? I don't *need* to ever come back to this hotel. I could just leave. I could set up this bank account and leave. Leave my life. What if I just disappeared? Just left Mark in a hotel room in Geneva. I could slip off now, bag in hand, and melt away. Never even go to the bank. No one would miss me, really, would they? Would they? Life goes on. Life always just goes on. I'm sure I'd make a good life for myself, somewhere. They'd never find me—Mark, our friends, the plane people, the police. They'd never find me or the money, or our unborn child.

And there's the rub. Mark. And our life. That one cord. The way my whole body loosens when I think of him, like stepping into a patch of sun. Mark. The only thread connecting me to that old life, to my life. A life that I've just realized I could slough off like an old husk.

Mark and our life. And our baby. Our unborn baby. We can change together, right? We'll move forward together.

Mothers don't run. Wives don't run. Unless they're running away from something.

And Mark is all I have. Why would I run from him? If we run we'll run together. All three of us. I let my free hand rest on my lower abdomen, my womb. In there, safe, is everything worth fighting for. I squeeze my eyes shut tight; this is for our future, for us, for our family, for this family I am creating out of blood and bone inside me. I will tell Mark soon. I will. But for now I like this little connection. Just the two of us, me and my passenger, for just a little while longer. When all of this is done, then we'll share our secret. When it's safe. I tighten my grip around the duffel bag's handles, my knuckles blotching white and pink as the door pings open and I stride across the vast lobby and out into the chilly September air.

It's so much simpler than I'd ever have imagined!

Tanguy greets me on the steps of the bank. I'm introduced to Matilda, a petite and impeccably chignoned brunette who'll be handling my account today. She's polite and efficient as she explains the account setup procedures.

I feel a light tug of shame as I hand the duffel of cash over to her, even though we're already tucked away in the privacy of a client room and no one but she can see. Matilda takes it, unmoved; I needn't have bothered with the shame. I may as well have handed her my dry cleaning, for all the impact it has on her.

Her right shoulder slumps slightly with the weight of the bag. Business as usual, I suppose.

"I'll just be a moment." She nods curtly and clips out of the room.

She's taken it to be counted. Isn't it funny how in a world of electronic banking and constantly evolving technology, paper money still needs to be physically counted? Well, electronically counted, obviously, but you get my point.

They'll feed the crisp note-wedges into a machine, bundle by bundle, until they get the final figure of a million dollars. Perhaps there's a money handler back there whose only job is to run paper money through those little machines.

I sit alone. I wait. My mind wanders.

The vague thought that the notes might be marked, that they might be traceable back to whatever illegal practice they came from, flickers across my mind. Police, government agencies—anyone, really—can mark bills, either by physically marking them with a highlighter or a stamp, or by recording the serial number sequences. I've Googled it all, of course. I've checked the notes for sequences.

But more than that, I just *know* these bills are unmarked. There's no way the plane people would have had government-marked money, police-marked money. They obviously knew what they were doing. Granted, not in an aviationary sense, but they were doing well businesswise, all things considered.

Of course, they could have marked their own money, couldn't they? If they wanted to trace it for themselves. Why would they, though? They didn't know we'd find it. They didn't know we'd take it.

Sometimes I have to stop and remind myself that the plane people weren't omniscient. They didn't see any of this coming. What happened to them, and subsequently to us, was a random event. They couldn't have known they'd crash, that we'd find the bag. It was all unforeseen, unknowable. The money definitely isn't marked. No one is coming for it. No one is coming for Mark and me.

Matilda returns with the empty duffel bag neatly folded and places it next to a still-hot printout. It is the deposit amount receipt. She offers me a pen. The figure I'm looking for is in the far left column: *$1,000,000 USD—Cash Deposit.*

I sign.

We set up a monthly standing order into my own business account back in the UK. The Swiss account will pay me a nominal monthly retainer; the payment reference will be the name of a shell company. I'll explain the payment for tax purposes as freelance film consultancy. Then when we require larger amounts for the house or whatever, we'll transfer chunks out and call those project commissions. We'll bang out some company invoices for a shell company— something Arabic. It's got to look like someone who'd believably give a British documentarian large chunks of money through a Swiss account for short private filming projects. Don't worry, I'll pay tax on it all. I'll keep records. I'll be very, very careful, honest. All correspondence will be forwarded to a private mailbox on-site here at the bank. Matilda supplies me with two small keys for my mailbox.

After rather less paperwork than one would imagine, given the sheer quantity of cash I've just handed over, she twists the Montblanc ballpoint back into its housing and smiles. All finished.

We shake, businesslike, a deal done.

I am a millionaire. That money is safe; that money is, as they say, "in the bank."

I make my way out to the waiting car, gliding on success, unencumbered now by the physical weight of the bag. The numbered account information, SWIFT code, IBAN number, password, and keys all tucked safely in my purse.

As I clear the bank entrance and walk down the stone steps toward the Mercedes, that thought surfaces again, like a butterfly flitting in and out of sight: *Don't go back.* Don't get in the car. Don't go back to the hotel. *Ever.*

I don't know where these thoughts are coming from. Somewhere deep inside. My lizard brain. The limbic system, the part of the brain that wants things, the selfish part that doesn't want to share. Our instincts, our gut reactions, all those subconscious involuntary processes, offering up their wisdom. Primal wisdom. Lizards aren't pack animals, though. Humans are by nature pack animals. Yet I still feel the powerful tug to cut and run. To take what's not mine.

I imagine Mark waiting in our suite, pacing back and forth, checking his watch, moving to the window, peering down onto the streets of Geneva, the sunlight slowly fading into night, streetlights buzzing on, and no sign of me. What if I don't return?

I could go anywhere with this money; I could do anything now. I pause on the steps outside the bank. Out in the fresh air. I could be anyone. I have the means. I'm already this far in, why stop now? A thousand possible futures flood my brain. Beautiful lives, elsewhere.

Novelty. Adventure. A yawning chasm of potential. Terrifying freedom. The car sits there, waiting across the street.

I am my choices. Do I want this family? Do I? Or do I want something else?

I keep walking toward the car, I pull the door handle, and I slide into the leather seat and slam the door. Twenty minutes later I'm back in the suite, Mark's arms around me.

24

Sunday, September 18

Are We Dead Yet?

We've been back home for two days now. I won't lie; it feels odd. The weather. The light. Being back. Back where we started. The plan is to carry on as normal. Fulfill our obligations, see friends, talk about the wedding, and, of course, get back to work. Well, work for *me* anyway. We're filming with Holli tomorrow morning, in her home—technically, her mother's home—and I've got a lot to get through tonight. I need to get my head back in the game. It's important that nothing appears different.

Mark is beginning the process of setting up his own financial consultancy company. It's a great idea; he's got the skills, and he's certainly got the professional experience, to run a company focused on helping those who already have lots of money make even more through targeted investment. The idea's been brewing since Rafie's text. If Mark can't get a job, he's going to make one! And we've got the startup funds now. He's not going to take unemployment lying down; he's going to get out there and make stuff happen. His plan is to eventually partner with Hector, who's been working for a hedge fund since he was let go, once Mark has got the new company fully up and running. They met over the weekend to discuss potential client lists. For the sake of ease we're saying this "startup money" is the money Mark got as a redundancy payoff. Nobody knows Mark got nothing after being let go, except Caro. And fuck it, why not? The world's moved on from Mark; why shouldn't he try to catch up?

I need to read through my notes before going with Phil to interview Holli tomorrow. It's strange to think that while we bumped across the blue-green waves in the sunshine, Holli was stepping out into the chilly gray of North London for the first time in five years. Duncan, my sound guy, can't join us tomorrow, so Phil will be covering sound too. He's a trooper.

There's lots of work to be done before the morning. But it's hard to focus. My mind keeps juddering between two worlds. My old life and my new.

I glance at Mark, who's trawling through piles of old business cards. Hundreds, thousands of them, twelve years' worth of meetings, dinners, functions, networking drinks—each card a person. A person who could potentially be of help to us now. Mark's kept every business card he's ever received. I remember the first time I looked in the drawer he keeps them in, the horror. He studies them now, each one connecting with a time and place in his mind, a handshake, a conversation, a smile.

Mark's met a lot of people over the years, and we may be able to use some of his old work contacts to find a buyer for the stones. He's been looking into the legality of diamond sales; it's amazing how much you can learn from the Internet. I don't know how people managed without it. I honestly wouldn't be able to do my job without it. And we certainly wouldn't be able to do what we're doing now.

I Googled Hatton Garden, London's diamond district, in the airport lounge on our way back from Geneva. Absentmindedly, just looking at places to sell gemstones. It seemed like a fairly safe Google question. Not too suspicious. I could always argue that after the wedding Mark and I had agreed to sell my engagement ring to pay off some of the mortgage. It's an option, selling the diamonds ourselves, but it could raise suspicion; it would be better if we could sell the stones through a private dealer, a middleman.

Mark is trying to cover all our bases—well, as far as it's possible to do so. Apparently, it might be complicated but it's not illegal to sell diamonds. Just *very* delicate. He's been making tentative inquiries. After all this is done we're seriously going to have to consider wiping our hard drives.

I think of the computer back in the business center of our hotel in Bora Bora. I wonder if they found out where their emails where accessed from. If they figured out where we were. If they're even looking. Or have we just evaporated? I ran an Internet search on the company names I could remember from the translated emails, but I couldn't find out anything. These people are shadows. Ghosts.

It's getting late when the house phone rings. It's about six and the London light has already faded around us, leaving us in darkness lit only by the blue glow of our laptop screens. I leap up, the sound jolting me back to reality, but Mark beats me to it. He's been expecting a call back from someone about the diamonds.

His demeanor changes instantly at the sound of the voice on the other end of the line. He relaxes.

"Oh, hello, you." It's his mum. Susan. I can tell by the way he says "you," drawn out and playful. They're sweet together.

I try to dig back into my research while he tells Susan all about the honeymoon. She knows we came back a bit early because of my "food poisoning," but this is the first real chat they've had about our trip. I catch snippets. Sharks, massive rays, empty beaches, the helicopter trip, tans and relaxation. I don't know how long the conversation goes on for, but I snap back to attention at a sudden change in Mark's tone.

"They what?" He stands tense, transfixed in silence, his face tight, as her muffled voice repeats. He lifts his eyes to me. Something is up. Something is wrong.

He waves me over and I join him by the phone.

"Mum, here's Erin. I'm going to put her on; tell her what you just told me? No, just tell her what you just said. Please, Mum, just—" He hands me the phone. I take it, confused, and raise it to my ear.

"Susan?"

"Oh, hello, love." Her voice is mild and slightly confused by the situation. "I don't know what Mark's annoyed about. I was just saying about your honeymoon . . ."

"Oh?" I look back to Mark, leaning against the sofa now, as he nods me on.

"Yes, I was saying it's lucky you got ill, really, because of the news yesterday—" She breaks off like I might know what on earth she is talking about.

"What news, Susan?"

"In the paper. What happened." She pokes me toward understanding but I have no idea what she's—

Shit. What *news*? I look at Mark. Is it the plane crash? Have they found the plane? Is it in the paper?

"Sorry, Susan. What's in the paper?" I try to keep my voice steady.

"The accident. That poor young couple. I was saying it's lucky you weren't still out there, because I know you had an accident diving yourself a while ago and it's such a dangerous sport. It's lucky you weren't out there too."

Oh God. A couple. Are they okay?

"What exactly happened, Susan?" I signal to Mark to Google it.

"Er, let me think. Well, it was on Saturday the accident. I think

I read it in *The Mail on Sunday* this morning. I've got it somewhere around here. I didn't know you'd both be so interested. I mean, it's terribly sad, of course. It is. Here, let me find it." I hear her rustle around her paper-laden kitchen table as I look to Mark, his eyes now glued to the laptop screen.

He looks up at me—he's got it, he's found the story. He gestures to wrap it up with Susan. I hear her rustling and tutting at herself on the other end of the line. A muffled call of, "Graham, have you seen the *Mail* anywhere?"

I can't wait for this. "Susan, Susan? It's okay, don't worry about it. I can look it up later."

"Oh. Oh, okay, love. Sorry about that. It's awful, isn't it? I forget you might have met them. I can't recall the names but a young couple. Very sweet looking. There was a picture. Sad for the family. Yes, I was saying to Mark it's so lucky you weren't out there then. Very sad. But I don't want to spoil your nice memories, it sounds like you both had such a lovely time. Bring up the photos at Christmas, will you? I'd love to see them all."

"Yes, definitely. Will do." There's a natural pause and I grab it. "Look, Susan, I should go. Sorry, it's just I've left some pasta on and Mark's left the kitchen. Can Mark call you tomorrow?"

Mark raises an eyebrow regarding the pasta. I shrug, *What else can I say?*

"Of course, love, don't let me keep you. Yes, tell him I'm around in the evening tomorrow. I've got bridge in the morning, so late afternoon. Lovely. Bye then, love."

"Bye." I hang up and explode. *"Fuck!"*

"Come and take a look."

I plop down next to him on the sofa and we scan the articles in horror.

BRITISH COUPLE KILLED IN SCUBA-DIVING INCIDENT IN BORA BORA, *The Guardian*. DEATH IN PARADISE, *The Mail on Sunday*. BRITS' SCUBA DEATH TRAGEDY, the *Sun*.

It's not front-page stuff but most of the papers have covered it.

BRITS' SCUBA DEATH TRAGEDY

A British couple drowns while scuba diving together in Bora Bora after panicking underwater and removing their breathing gear

A BRITISH couple has died in a tragic scuba-diving accident while on holiday in the French Polynesian island of Bora Bora this week.

Daniel, 35, & Sally Sharpe, 32, died after the accident off the luxury resort island of Bora Bora. The couple were diving together along with their hotel resort dive instructor in a world-renowned scuba spot in the South Pacific when the incident occurred.

According to eyewitnesses the couple panicked, removing their breathing gear while eighteen meters underwater at the Four Seasons dive site.

A police spokesperson for the island said the couple had swallowed mouthfuls of seawater, while an autopsy later showed their lungs were also filled with water.

There were no signs of foul play, a local news website reported.

The Medical Examiner's Office examined the equipment worn by the couple and experts concluded there were no problems with any of the dive equipment but that both of the Brits' primary air tanks were empty.

While their secondary tanks did have air, the Sharpes were unable to access them in their panicked state, authorities explained.

The incident unfolded on the afternoon of Saturday, September 17, nine days into the tragic young couple's planned two-week trip.

Problems began ten minutes into the half-hour dive, when Investex UK fund manager, Sally, noticed her oxygen gauge had swung into the red zone and signaled to the dive leader that she was out of air. It was at this stage, Conrado Tenaglia, 31, the resort's dive instructor, tried to intervene. But it soon became apparent that Sally's husband, Daniel Sharpe, was also experiencing trouble. The instructor was unable to assist both divers simultaneously, and panic quickly took hold as the couple, realizing the desperate situation unfolding, fumbled with their own equipment. Eyewitness accounts from other dive group members state that "things escalated fast." According to fellow diver Kazia Vesely, 29, at some point the masks of both divers came completely off because "they were struggling," which may have caused both to panic further. The instructor tried to rectify the situation but it quickly spiraled out of control.

"We all started to panic too, the other divers, because we didn't know what we were supposed to do either. We didn't know what was happening. We thought there might be something wrong with all our tanks, so we broke off and ascended to call for help from the boat. The instructor signaled us to ascend slowly because we were all panicky. It was really scary," Kazia told local news agencies.

First responders at the scene where unable to revive the two tourists. Both were declared dead on arrival at Vaitape Medical Center.

The British embassy in the French Polynesian capital of Papeete said it was providing consular support to the family.

Bora Bora is a major international tourist destination, famous for its aqua-centric luxury resorts.

The location is a favorite amongst honeymooners and the jet set alike, with celebrity couples such as Jennifer Aniston and Justin Theroux, Benedict Cumberbatch and Sophie Hunter, Nicole Kidman and Keith Urban, and the Kardashian clan all flocking to its luxury hotels.

The resort also attracts divers from all around the world eager to see the island's tropical wildlife.

The dive site where the couple met their tragic end is an area described as suitable for divers of all experience levels, according to the International Dive Directory.

The directory says the site in question has "hardly any current" and a maximum depth of 18 meters—the deepest you can go without a PADI Advanced Open Water or equivalent diving license.

Mark and I sit in silence, stunned.

I | I

Oh my fucking God. The couple from the hike. The nice young couple from our hike are dead. And the way they died. Utterly horrific. I catch an echo of the panic they must have felt. Fuck. I push it down. Away.

The question hangs in the air. Two questions actually. We're both thinking it. Were they murdered? Did someone tamper with their diving gear?

"What do you think?" I finally break the thick atmosphere. We're sitting in the darkness, the half-light of the screen illuminating our pale faces.

"Could be an accident," he says. I'm not sure whether it's a question or a statement.

A couple in their thirties are dead in our resort three days after I accessed the plane people's email account. Two days after we left the island.

"Is it, Mark? I want it to be an accident. Tell me it's an accident, please."

He looks at me. There's doubt in his eyes, but he's thinking it through.

"Look, diving accidents aren't unusual. Sure, it's a huge coincidence, the timing and place, but that doesn't mean they were definitely murdered. The police are saying no foul play, right?"

"Their whole island economy is based on tourism, Mark! They're not going to tell the press that tourists get *murdered* out there."

"No, fair enough—but, come on, it's not the easiest way to kill someone, is it? By empty oxygen tank? I mean, anyone on the dive could have ended up with those tanks. They could have just not panicked and used their secondary tanks and just dealt with it, couldn't they? What if they'd just done that? They wouldn't be dead, would they? It doesn't really strike me as a targeted attack, does it?" He's starting to believe himself now. He's getting into it.

And he does have a point. It is a fairly blunt murder weapon, an empty oxygen tank.

"But they, the plane people, if *they* were there, they probably watched them, Mark. They probably knew the Sharpes couldn't dive, they might have watched them do their pool training? We don't know, they must have done this before. Made things look like accidents." It feels weird saying the Sharpes' surname out loud. I wish I hadn't. It hangs in the air of our home, strange and cumbersome. We didn't really know them, who they were. The idea of them feels odd and unwieldy, these two dead people we shared memories with. Strangers but like us, young, British, on honeymoon. Surrogate us's. Like us but dead.

I remember them from the resort. We were only on nodding terms. Small talk. Then again they'd only been there three days and we'd already found the bag. We weren't really paying attention.

Mark breaks the silence.

"I just don't think someone did this, Erin. I don't. It's beyond odd that this has happened, I won't argue with that, but why didn't they just kill them? If someone had wanted to kill them? I mean, come on, it's a bit convoluted, isn't it, honey? Why not do it in their sleep or poison or—I don't know! If these people are as rich and as powerful as we think they are, why do it like that? And why the Sharpes? Christ, they don't even look like us!" He's completely convinced now.

But one little thing keeps niggling at me.

"Mark. How would they know it was a *couple* that found the bag?" And then another thought strikes me.

"How would they know to look for a *British* couple, Mark?!" The fear rises in me. Because, how would they know? Unless we left a trail? Did I miss something? Did I leave some crucial piece of evidence behind?

Mark slowly closes his eyes. He knows why. Oh God. There's something he hasn't told me.

"What is it, Mark? Tell me!" I'm not messing around now; I'm up on my feet. I bang on the light switch, flooding the room with light.

He squints up at me, momentarily blinded.

"Sit down, Erin. It's . . . it's fine. Please, honey." He pats the seat cushion next to him wearily. This is a conversation he never wanted to have. I give him a hard look before sitting down next to him. This had better be good.

He rubs his face and leans back with a deep sigh. "Oh fuck. Okay, here it is. Um, when I went back, at the hotel, in Bora Bora, when I went back to erase the check-in info from their system—slash–look for your earring, er . . ." He blows out hard through his mouth. "Shit. I ran into the watersports guy." He looks at me.

"Paco?" I say.

He nods. "Yeah. He asked if we'd got our bag back."

Shit.

"He said one of the porters had mentioned we'd left our bag by the boat. Paco wondered if we got it back in the end. I guess the porter we left it with must have totally misunderstood."

"What did you do, Mark?" I demand. But I don't really want to hear the answer. Because if I hear it, it'll make it real.

"I had to say something. So, I don't know, I was thinking on my feet. I didn't, you know, think through the implications or whatever, I just . . . It just came out."

I say nothing. I wait.

"I asked Paco what he was talking about and acted confused and then suddenly remembered that the other British couple, the Sharpes I think they were called, had mentioned something about a bag on our hike. Something about finding a bag, or something. The porter must have mixed us up, I told him. I said it was funny that he'd confused us because we'd had a similar problem before, it must be our accents, I said. And he laughed. And we left it at that."

When he stops speaking, the silence floods the room again. We're submerged in it.

"And now they're dead," I say.

"And now they are dead," Mark echoes.

We let that and all its implications sink in.

Either the Sharpes had a diving accident or they were killed because someone thought they were us. We might have killed two people.

"Why did you say it?" I ask it with half-hearted intensity, because

I know he couldn't possibly have known this would happen, could he? I would have done the same thing, put on the spot like that, wouldn't I?

He shakes his head. "I don't know . . . I just did." He rubs his face again and groans.

"Do you think it was *them*? Do you think they killed them?"

He drops his hand and stares at me now. Sober, focused.

"Honestly? Honestly, Erin, there's no way of knowing. But it's a pretty elaborate way to kill someone. It could definitely have just been an accident. But—and I know this is awful—but if they were murdered, as terrible as that is, nobody will be looking for us now. As awful as that may sound . . . If it was deliberate—if they did come looking for and then killed 'the couple that found the bag'—then it's finished. Isn't it? The couple is dead. They couldn't find the missing bag. It's finished. We're safe. I made a mistake, definitely, but I'm glad with all my heart it wasn't us, Erin. I'm glad no one is coming for us." There's finality to what he says. He takes my hand in his and I look down at our tightly gripped fists. He's right. I'm glad it wasn't us too.

We're dead. They think we're dead. And—bizarrely, for just a second—it does make me feel safer.

I'm almost certain we left no trace, but that's the thing about slipups, isn't it, you don't know you've made one? I hear what Mark's saying but in my heart I know, I just know, that they are still looking for us. Maybe we should call the police?

But I don't say it out loud. Mark has made up his mind: no one is coming for us. He can tell me in a million different ways that it's over now, but I won't really hear them. I'll know they're coming for a long time yet.

So I don't pursue it. I let it go. I'll have to come to his conclusion on my own or not at all.

I nod.

"You're right," I say.

He wraps his solid arms around me and pulls me close in the silence of our home.

25

Holli's Follow-up

I press the entry buzzer.

Phil and I are standing outside the entrance of Holli Byford's council block. Or rather, Holli's mother's council block. It's raining a thin persistent mist that coats our clothes and hair. Not heavy enough for an umbrella but continuous enough to chill me to the bone. I'm still in that delicate post-vacation period right now where I know I'm going to come down with something; it's just a matter of time. Standing here in the rain might just do it.

I'm following our plan. The plan to carry on like normal. So here I am. Being normal.

I look out across the grassy wasteland surrounding the council-estate. What I hazard a guess may be called the "communal gardens."

I woke up this morning thinking about the Sharpes. I've been trying not to, but they're lurking in my mind, just out of sight. Flashes of the panic, bubbles in the water. And then two pale waterlogged corpses on stainless steel slabs. Our fault.

I feel as if I'm being watched. I have since we left the island. But more so since yesterday's news. I scan the bleak buildings and grounds for a source but we appear to be of little interest to the locals. No one is watching. If whoever killed the Sharpes has tracked us down somehow, if they're following us, they're not letting on yet. Of course, this feeling of being observed could be something else entirely. I think of the chilled champagne we drank in Bora Bora—was it only a week ago? Champagne sent from the other side of the world. Eddie is interested in me too, isn't he? Might he have someone following me now that I'm back? Checking up on me? Watching? I let my eyes wander across the complex. There's a young white guy pacing near the car park, a phone pressed to his ear. A black guy sitting in his work van about to leave. An old lady entering the building opposite, wheelie shopping bag in tow. No one suspicious. No one who looks like a killer. Nobody has found me; I am just a damp woman waiting for someone to answer a buzzer. I look up at the hundreds of windows reflecting gray sky back down onto us. So many windows. So far from the plane at the bottom of the South Pacific Ocean.

I push the buzzer again. A long slow push.

Phil sighs. The camera is fucking heavy. I don't blame him.

It's 9 A.M. They should definitely be up by now. I've been up since dawn and I can safely say this is not my idea of easing gently back into work. Today is going to be a slog. From the little I've seen of Holli I already know this will be exhausting. But in the words of Murakami, the master of the hard slog: "Pain is inevitable. Suffering is optional."

I press the buzzer again.

"WHAT!? What the fuck do you want? What?" The voice crackles through the metal grate of the entry system, abrupt and aggressive. It's female, older than Holli, gruffer, huskier. I'd venture a guess we've woken up Mrs. Byford.

I hold down the buzzer and speak.

"Hi there, is that Michelle Byford? This is Erin. Erin Roberts. I'm here to see Holli. We're supposed to be meeting her here at nine? To film?" I hear myself and I flinch inside. I know what people hear when they hear my voice. They hear privilege and condescension and bleeding-heart liberalism.

God, I'm in a funk today. Daniel and Sally Sharpe creep around my head. *Get it together, Erin.*

Silence. Phil sighs again.

"Oh, right." The tone has changed, resigned now. "Guess you'd better come up then," she mutters, annoyed. The door buzzes, clunks, and we push in.

I've told Phil what to expect here, but there's only so much you can relay; it's more of a general feeling you get from Holli than anything else, her stare, her smile. He's watched the first interview, so I'm sure he's picked up on it too. Anyway, he's been warned: don't get dragged into anything.

The Byford flat is on the sixth floor and predictably the lift is out of order. I'd be surprised if Phil has the energy to be dragged into anything after lugging the camera up six flights of stairs.

Michelle's standing out in the communal hallway in furry slippers, powder-blue robe, and a "But first give me coffee" pajamas set, scowling at us. She's clearly just got out of bed. No sign of Holli. Perhaps she's still asleep?

Michelle looks exhausted. My notes say that she works full time in a department store. Fifteen years, ever since Holli's dad left. Not to be rude but shouldn't she be at work by now?

"Hi, Michelle. Lovely to meet you. Sorry for the early start," I say, and to my surprise she takes my hand and shakes it.

A distracted smile. She seems worried about something. "I suppose you'd better go ahead and turn that on first." She gestures to Phil's camera.

Phil and I share a look and the camera is up on his shoulder. Red light on.

"I just don't want to say it all twice." Michelle looks at me and frowns to herself. "You'd better come in. I'll stick the kettle on." She shuffles in her pink booties into the linoleum-tiled flat. We follow. I'm starting to get the feeling that Holli isn't in there.

Michelle busies herself about the narrow kitchen space.

"I've got to call the police if anyone comes asking questions, that's the thing. Do you mind if I quickly call them up now?" She seems embarrassed, a woman forced into following rules she hasn't signed up for.

I shake my head, I don't mind. But the word *police* screams through my head. *Police* is not a word I wanted or expected to hear today.

"I'm sorry, Michelle, I really have no idea what's going on here. Has something happened?" I look back at Phil, in case he's figured it out. Have I missed something?

For a fraction of a second I think she might actually be calling the police because of me. Because of the plane. Because of the Sharpes. But that's absurd, of course. Michelle doesn't know. She doesn't know me from Adam. And any brief impulse I felt yesterday to call the police after finding out about the Sharpes has long since evaporated. Involving the police at this stage would definitely not be a good idea. Michelle holds up her finger, phone to her ear. *Wait.*

"Hi there, it's Michelle Byford. Can I speak to Andy, please?" There's another pause as we all wait, suspended, like the stale cigarette smoke in the kitchen air. "Thanks. Hello. Hi, Andy, yes, good, thanks. No, no, I haven't, no, nothing like that, but I've got some people here in the flat now asking about Holli. No, no, nothing like that. Yes, yes, I know." She laughs nervously. "No, they're from the prison charity. They interviewed Holli in prison for a film. Yes. Erin, yes . . ."

My eyes shoot to Phil at the mention of my name. This police officer she's talking to knows me. He knows *of* me. What the fuck is going on? Michelle holds up a finger, *wait.*

"Yes, and a man . . ." She doesn't know Phil's name. We skipped that formality.

"Phil," Phil supplies. "The cameraman." Pithy as ever.

"Phil, the cameraman. Yes, yes, I'll tell them, one second, right . . . here in ten, fifteen, okay, one second." She holds the phone away from her face and addresses us. "Andy says would you mind waiting ten, fifteen minutes and he'll swing by? He wants to ask you a couple of questions if he can?"

I look back at Phil; he shrugs.

"Sure," I answer.

What else can I do? Say no? *No, I'm afraid I can't actually stay to talk to the police, Michelle, because I've just stolen two million dollars and maybe caused the deaths of two innocent people.* I think my only move here is to just stay. Stay and try to act normal. "Sure" just about covers it.

First day back at work and I'm already being questioned by the police. My stomach rolls.

Michelle puts the phone back up to her ear and addresses Andy. It's becoming clear to me what's going on here; I credit myself that much. I'm guessing Holli's skipped parole. That's what it will be, something like that, but for some reason my palms are sweating.

Michelle continues into the phone. "Andy, yes, yes, that's all fine. They'll be here. No, no, I don't think they do. Of course. Of course I will. Yes. Okay then. See you soon. Okay then. Bye." She hangs up and smiles down at the inanimate phone. At Andy, I'd imagine, in an office somewhere.

Phil and I wait. Finally she looks up.

"Sorry. Sorry about that. Coffee?" She flicks on the kettle and it roars to life, recently boiled. "Okay, right, sorry. I suppose you've guessed that Holli's not here?" Michelle looks between us, business-like. We have.

She nods. "Yeah. She left yesterday. Just disappeared. I took her some toast in bed in the morning but she wasn't there. We've been looking since; we don't know where she is at the moment. Police are working on it. Andy's heading up the search right now. It's—" She breaks off and stares out the grimy double-glazed window above her sink. The kettle clicks off and bubbles to silence next to her. She snaps back into the room and smiles.

"Let's have a sit-down, shall we?"

She places the coffee mugs down with ceremony onto the pine fold-leaf table and we sit.

Phil continues to film her as she sips her steaming mug. According to the mug's inscription, "Coffee makes my day more beautiful." I do hope so; it doesn't seem to be going well so far, for any of us.

I peer down at the gray-brown stew before me, pellets of undissolved coffee still clinging for dear life to the white ceramic of my mug.

Shit. This is not a good situation. I could really do with not being here right now. I think of the bag hidden in our attic. And guilt, like the first domino, starts to topple one mistake into another. I need to center myself. I need to lock this feeling down before Andy, the policeman, gets here.

And where the hell is Holli?

Michelle sets her mug down carefully with two hands and explains.

"Okay. Here's what we know." She looks up with the certainty of someone toeing the official line. She's been over this a dozen times already, up all night. I can tell. She has that look. I've interviewed a lot of people so far in my career and she's been over these coals a few times. And now she's doing it again, for us.

"So, I met Holli, collected her, you know, out the back of the prison around 8 A.M. on the twelfth of September. That was seven days ago. She spent the week in the flat mainly. Watching TV, napping. I don't think she got much sleep in prison. She was exhausted. Then, day before yesterday, Saturday, we'd arranged to nip around to Sinéad's flat—she's a friend from work, used to be a hairdresser—so she could sort out Holli's hair. She'd, Holli had, been worried about her highlights in jail and Sinéad said she'd do them for free. So we went there. I'd brought her some other clothes—Adidas stuff, they all love that now." She smiles, a mother in the know. "And she changed into them. And then after that we went to Nando's for chicken. She'd been desperate for a Nando's. On about it forever. Really excited about the bleeding Nando's. I don't think the food was up to much in prison, you know. She was stick thin when she got home. Well, you saw her, you know yourself. Anyway, she loved it, had a half chicken and one each of all the sides. She was happy as a clam. Then we came home and she said she wanted to make a couple of calls on her laptop, so she went to her room and did that for a while and then we watched some old episodes of the Kardashians on catch-up. She was pretty tired and went to bed around nine. Nothing out of the ordinary. She seemed happy. Like her old self again. When I went into her room yesterday morning she was gone. She only took a couple of things. No note. Nothing. But I told Andy, she did take one thing: photo of us, me and her. The one she had in prison. She always kept it by her bed. She liked that photo. Said it made her happy whenever she missed me. She didn't say stuff like that very often, so I remember it." Michelle looks at us. That's all she's got. That's her side of it.

"Do you know where she might have gone?" I ask.

She looks down at her mug and tuts.

"No, not for certain. There's a theory. The police are looking into it and to be honest I'm not sure how much they're telling me about it all. Andy's part of SO15, so it's a bit tricky finding out anything from them really. I don't know if you both know about all that sort of thing? Counterterrorism stuff."

It comes so out of the blue that I almost laugh. Almost. Phil looks over. SO15. Fucking hell. I check Michelle's face but it's blank—drawn and tired. She's not joking. I shake my head. No. I know nothing about counterterrorism, obviously.

"I just . . . I find it very hard to believe my Holli'd be involved in any of this. She's never been involved in anything like that, never ever mentioned God or any sort of religion. Andy's lovely but he's wrong about this. I do trust him but—I don't know, he'll get her back and that's the most important thing. That's all that matters."

Michelle grabs a crumpled cigarette packet from her robe pocket and fumbles one out. I think fleetingly of the pregnancy test, the blue cross, as her lighter flashes and a fresh wave of smoke fills the tiny room. Michelle looks across the table at us both now, leans forward on her elbows. "Holli's not the brightest, you know. She's all mouth for sure but she's very easily led. Always has been. It's competitive, you know. Just a competitive streak. 'I'm tougher than you. I can do it better than you.' You know? But the 'it' could be anything. It could be dares or setting that bus on fire or whatever. She likes the drama of it. Just showing off. That's all it is. She's always been that way. It's just more extreme these days. The older she gets, the further she goes. I know, it's probably my fault. Her dad wasn't a great example and then she fell in with Ash—sorry, Ashar—and that lot. It's strange; Ash was such a good boy at school. Nice Turkish family. I met his mum once. I just don't understand it. Maybe I should have been around more. But someone had to work; her dad certainly wasn't going to." She stops herself. She's gone down the wrong track. She's gotten lost in her own tunnels and dragged us with her. She needs to head back to daylight.

"Did Holli go alone?" I ask. "Or with someone?" It's the next logical question. But I think I already know the answer.

"With Ash—Ashar," she corrects herself.

I nod. It's coming together now. Ash was Holli's friend from the bus video. It's not guilt in Michelle's tone but self-absolution. None of this is her fault. What could she have done to stop them? It's Holli and Ash. In her mind, the blame is halved. It's just the kids messing around. The threat's not real, in her eyes. Just two kids who may have gone a little bit too far this time.

Of course, it's impossible not to infer what's happened here. The pieces fall into place like the first level of Tetris. I'm sure SO15 Andy will enlighten us further once he arrives. But beyond a doubt he will not allow us to film him. We need to get as much footage as I can before he arrives, that's clear. Before we're asked to stop.

I stand up and take charge, changing the energy in the cramped flat. "Michelle. We need to take a look at her room now. Film in there." It's not a question. I am not asking her. My directing brain has kicked in and we need more for the film, as much as I can smash and grab. Look, I don't want to take advantage of her, but it's clear Michelle trusts and responds well to authority. If she feels it's for the best, then we'll get what we need. I want that footage of the room for the film and we're getting it. I hold her gaze slightly too long, deliberately. She looks away.

And it works. She rises, cowed.

"Yes, yes, of course. The police searched it already and took all their own pictures, so I'm sure it's fine to do what you need to do in there." She stares back up at me, searching for approval, reassurance. She wants us to know she's helping. That she's not going to be a problem like Holli.

She leads us out of the kitchen and down the hall. Phil throws me what I assume is meant to be an accusing glance. He didn't like that. What I just did. It wasn't like me. It was cruel.

Fuck it. I'm not sure I care today. I'm not feeling myself. Whatever that means. I'm not even sure who I am anymore. Maybe I died in the South Pacific with Sally Sharpe.

Holli's room is small. Teenaged. Basic. Phil scans it slowly with the camera. Magazine pictures Blu-Tacked to the walls. Hard-eyed fashion models clutching perfume bottles. Sexuality. Money. Glitter stickers. Dead flies on the windowsill. A doe-eyed Harry Styles foldout. Kanye posters. Wu-Tang Clan posters. Grandiose. Dangerous. A far cry from overcast Croydon: all pre-prison interior design, the faces on the posters sun-bleached after almost five years of staring back into an empty room.

But I'm looking for other things. I sense Phil is too. Even if he disapproves of my methods, I know he's thinking what I'm thinking: Is there anything religious in this room? Anything at all? I look but I don't see it. A stack of books by the bed. A Victoria Beckham fashion book, a dog-eared Garfield book, *The Power of Now*, *The Little Book of Calm*. The last thing I'd expect Holli to read. But then maybe not. A stab at self-knowledge? Or a gift from a well-meaning mum? Either way, neither of the self-help books looks read. But then, who am I to judge? I haven't read them either. And anyway, they definitely aren't the cause of what's happening now. They are not exactly terrorist textbooks.

Then it hits me. We won't find anything here. Holli was only eighteen when she lived in this room. These are the relics of who she was. She's twenty-three now. Growing up changes you. Five years in prison changes you. Who knows what happened to her in that time?

I mean, look at me, my whole life has changed in nine days. I've become a liar and a thief. God knows where or who I'll be in five years. Hopefully not in prison.

The doorbell chimes and our eyes flick to Michelle. She nods and trots off to let Andy in.

Phil lowers the camera.

"Do you see anything?" he whispers. There's a new urgency in his eyes now too. To him this documentary just became very interesting. He can already sniff awards in the future.

"No. I don't think there's anything here, Phil. She'd only been back a week before she left. We need to look elsewhere: Facebook, Twitter, all that. But Holli's not an idiot—not anymore anyway. If there is something here, it won't be easy to find." I scan the room again but I know I'm right on this one; there are no clues here.

As we enter the hallway a stocky man and Michelle are talking quietly by the front door. Andy. He's shorter than I'd imagined, but attractive. There's an easy charm about him as he turns to greet us, the flash of a winning smile; perhaps that's why he got the job. A people person. Michelle's right, he does inspire trust. I'd say he's early fifties. Good head of hair. An almost illusory whiff of expensive soap. I'm going to have to be extremely careful now. He's clearly very good at what he does; he's playing Michelle like an old pro. I'd hazard a guess that Andy is one of life's winners. I think perhaps everything comes up roses for Andy. Well, let's go, Andy. Let's do this, because I am not going to prison. I will not lose this fight. I run my hand subtly inside my coat and push gently against my belly. *It's okay in there. Mummy's got you.*

I fix my game face as he steps toward us, smiling.

"Erin, Phil, I'm Detective Chief Inspector Foster. Call me Andy. Nice to meet you both; thanks for sticking around." He shakes our hands firmly. We make our way into Michelle's living room, leaving the camera in the hall. Phil's not filming anymore.

Phil, Michelle, and I take the sofa while DCI Andy perches facing us on a low leather pouf on the other side of the cluttered coffee table.

"So, I'm not sure how much Michelle has told you, but Holli was on probation after her release. She's violated that by leaving the house. And she most certainly violated it now by leaving the country." He says it lightly.

Fuck. This is a little more serious than I had hoped. I didn't think it'd get that far. Holli's fled the country?

He continues: "That's one thing. The probation violation is a separate issue, though. The main issue we're facing right now is that we're extremely concerned Holli may be trying to make her way into Syria with Ashar Farooq. That appears to be her plan. Both her and Ash's plan. We know she boarded a flight at Stansted Airport fourteen hours ago to Istanbul. We've got CCTV footage of them leaving the airport in Istanbul and boarding a bus. It's safe to say we're concerned. So that's where we are." His tone is serious now, businesslike.

Syria. This is huge. And the awful truth is: this is a documentarian's wet dream. Events superseding planned narrative structure. Filmmaking heaven.

But I definitely don't feel that as I sit here. I see what a great story this could be. I see it, but all I feel now is dread. A barreling wall of horror speeding toward me. This is real. Holli has done something really bad. There will be a full investigation. I am involved. We are all involved. And there is a large bag of loose diamonds under my loft insulation. Which will look fairly incriminating if the police decide to search our house. Very incriminating.

With every bone in my body I wish that Holli would just breeze back in through the door, right this moment, sullen and vicious, and just be a bit rude to us all.

"Our job is simple," DCI Foster continues.

"First, we need to find out where Holli is, make sure she's safe, if possible bring her home. Second, we need to find out who she's been associating with, at what stage she became radicalized in prison, and how she managed to leave the UK. That's the information I'm currently interested in."

How does he think we can help with that?

"Now, I want to be clear: in terms of Holli herself, as of now she hasn't done anything wrong. The probation violation is very small fry compared to the other things at play here; we're not interested in punishing Holli for running away. It's more important to get her home and talking to us about what's gone on. How she managed to obtain her documents, her contacts. We're looking to help her, and any other girls like her in this situation. You'll have to trust me when I say this: it's not the place they think it is out there. They tend to target younger girls, problem girls, promise great things, and by the time the girls get out there it's too late to change their minds and they're trapped. Holli's going to find that all out pretty soon, if she hasn't already. They don't care about these girls; they're trophies. They are expendable." Andy looks to Michelle, holds her gaze. "Which is why we need to get her home as soon as we can."

Michelle has gone quite pale. Her hand fumbles a journey down to her cigarette pocket; she's forgotten that she left them on the kitchen table, and for some reason, this thought makes me incredibly sad.

"Now, Erin—" The DCI turns his high beams on me. "We weren't aware you were filming this morning. I guess Holli didn't pass that information on to her mother. We've been talking to the guys down at Holloway Prison about your interview footage of Holli. Obviously, no one's seen it yet, but we'd be extremely interested to take a look at it. I think what you have there might be the only up-to-date footage we have of Holli. Aside from CCTV footage, which isn't any real help to us, if I'm honest. I've got a lot of departments that are fairly eager to see what you've got. Do you still have the footage?"

I nod. "It's not edited. It's just raw footage at the moment. I haven't gone through it myself yet, so I can't say if there's anything that stood out in terms of—"

"That's not a problem," he interrupts. He hands me a card. Detective Chief Inspector Andrew Foster. His number and email. "Transfer whatever you've got as soon as you can."

"No problem." I take the card and make a show of pocketing it safely. Policemen make me nervous. They always have. I feel him searching my face, scanning me for something, anything, a peg to hang guilt on. I struggle to keep my face open, blank.

Andy turns to Phil. "You weren't present at the interview in Holloway, were you? You never met Holli yourself?"

"No, never met Holli. I'm meeting Alexa tomorrow," he answers, unfazed. But then, he's not connected to a plane crash, two murders, theft, fraud, and smuggling. I think the worst Phil's ever done is smoke the occasional joint. And maybe an illegal download or two.

The DCI's gaze shifts back to me. "Ah, yes, your documentary." He smiles. I can't quite tell the smile's meaning. "Who else's in it again?"

He knows. He's almost certainly checked. I hold his gaze.

"Eddie Bishop at Pentonville, Alexa Fuller at Holloway, and Holli," I reel off. Everything is on record; I've got a paper trail to prove it.

Andy gives a little nod. It's a good group. I know it's a good group. He turns back to Phil.

"Anyway, Phil, you're actually okay to knock off early if you want. It's just Erin I need. I don't want to keep you any longer than I have to. So feel free to scarper." A flash of that smile again.

Phil eyes me. I nod. *I'll be fine.* As he leaves he glances back, eyebrows raised. It's been a weird morning.

This documentary could be bigger than either of us imagined. I know it. Phil knows it too. He'll be on his MacBook trawling Holli's social media platforms as soon as he can find a café with Wi-Fi.

Michelle is sent off by Andy, ostensibly to make more bad coffee. Once she's gone he leans in toward me, elbows on knees, serious.

"So, Erin, your time with Holli, did you notice anything? Anything at all that might have seemed unusual? That might have struck you as odd? Did she mention anything at all?" He looks older when he's not smiling. Slacker, beaten down, more like I'd expect a detective to look.

I think back to the interview. Two months ago now. It may as well be a year ago for all that's happened since. Did I notice anything that might suggest her traveling to the Middle East? Did I?

Amal's image flashes into my mind. The prison guard that day. Middle Eastern Amal. Amal, meaning "hope" in Arabic. Amal, with the kind eyes.

I instantly feel shame.

I push the thought away. I'm not that sort of person. I refuse to be that sort of person. Amal is just an average Londoner trying to do his job; he just happens to have an Arabic name. *Stop it, Erin.*

Andy sits waiting for an answer.

"I wouldn't say anything specific, no. Holli was . . . she was, you know, slightly unnerving, I'll admit that. I can't say there was anything definitive but I did get a general feeling from her." I stop talking. Shit. I replay my words in my head. I probably should have just said "No, nothing" and left it at that. Idiot. I really don't need the scrutiny of being part of a police investigation right now. Mark and I can only stand up to so much background-delving before the shit hits the fan. My first retainer payment from my Saudi Arabian shell company will be transferring into my bank account in eight days. Money from the Middle East after a girl goes missing won't look good to a man like DCI Andy Foster.

"Unnerving? In what way?" He looks worried now. I've made him concerned. Yes, I seem to have snagged an invisible trip wire. Damn.

"Just her attitude, you know, in light of her previous crime. The video of her watching things burn. Her attitude the day of the interview. She's . . ." Again words fail me. What is she?

"Sorry, Andy. There's no other way to say it. She's a very creepy girl. Sorry, but there it is." In for a penny, in for a pound. And you know what? If I'm a prejudiced witness, then at least I'll never make it to court.

He chuckles.

Thank God.

His face is light again. I'm just a girl making a documentary.

"Yeah. I've seen the bus stuff." He nods and we're on the same page again. "*Creepy*'s the word all right, Erin. Creepy, but not bad, I don't think, just easily led. I hope she has a change of heart before she crosses that border, because once you cross those sorts of lines there's no way back. We won't be able to help her after that. We won't be looking to bring her back, if you know what I mean." He keeps his voice low. I can hear Michelle puttering about alone in her kitchen, cigarette smoke trailing through to us. He sighs.

We share a look.

"We do what we can, Erin. But some people won't help themselves."

I think we're bonding. I think we're getting along.

"To be fair to Michelle, she has no idea who her daughter is anymore. She couldn't have seen this coming. A prison visit once a week for five years does not an attentive mother make." He glances off toward the kitchen. I take the opportunity to swallow. My desire to look like a normal person, while under scrutiny, has rendered everyday bodily functions tricky. He continues.

"Holli changed about five months before release. We have statements from prison guards and counselors. Two things happened around that time. She signed up for the prison charity scheme and she agreed to take part in your documentary. I can fairly confidently say that you're not heading up a London cell of Al Qaeda, Erin, but I'd lose my job if I didn't follow up a bit." Silence. He's watching me. The hint of a smile plays at the corners of his mouth.

So they have been looking into me already, shit. How much?

"Am I a suspect?" I know you're not supposed to ask, but am I?

I feel my cheeks reddening, my neck grow hot. My body now officially out of my control.

He chuckles, satisfied.

"No. No, Erin, you're definitely not a suspect. You've never even met Ashar Farooq, your only meeting with Holli is on film, and all your phone calls to the prison were recorded and monitored at the time. I've listened to them all."

Shit.

"You've done nothing. But you do need to let me have a copy of that footage as soon as possible today—and then we'll be out of your hair. We're not interested in you, as such. At this stage." Another shadow of a smile. With that he stands and brushes down his trousers. Then he looks up.

"Oh, and it goes without saying, but don't share that footage with anyone else. No news agencies, no press, obviously. And you won't be able to use the footage for your documentary until our investigation is concluded. And you know what, even then, do me a favor and call me beforehand, okay? Check in. Don't be a stranger." He smiles. It really is a winning smile. He's not bad looking by any stretch of the imagination.

Then, I don't know why I say what I say next, but I do.

"Andy. When it's done I want to get an exclusive on this, okay? Before anyone else. An interview would be fantastic." There it is. I've nailed my colors to the post.

His smile broadens. Surprised. Amused.

"Don't see why not. Once it's all public record. Couldn't hurt. It sounds like a nice little film you're making, Erin. Interesting. Call me." And with that he's gone.

When I get home the first thing I do is race up to the attic. Thankfully, Mark isn't home yet. He's meeting old colleagues today, testing the waters for contacts to sell the diamonds to. But in the meantime the diamonds are still in our attic and I'm worried about them. Our stash. If they decide to search the house they will find them. I move an old sewing machine on top of the loose insulation. I sit cross-legged on the splintered floor agonizing about whether putting the sewing machine over it makes it more noticeable or less. If SO15 searches our house, will the sewing machine draw the eye or hide the loose section of insulation? I Googled SO15 on my way home: they're a Specialist Operations branch of the Met, Counter Terror-ism Command, a department created from the merger of the Special Branch and the old Anti-Terrorist Branch. They're *serious* police.

I move the sewing machine off again.

There is definitely nowhere in this house the police won't look if they decide I'm of interest. I can't bury the diamonds in the garden now either. The soil will be disturbed and police love to dig up a patio, don't they? I've seen enough crime dramas to know that. And now there's no chance I can fly to Switzerland and store them in a safety deposit box, not now that I'm a part of Andy's investigation. That would raise more flags than anything else. We just need to get this stuff out of our home as soon as we can. That's the only answer. We need to get rid of the diamonds.

I think of the plane. The people still down there, strapped in tight, safe in their seats. In the dark nighttime water. I can't help wondering about them. Who were they? Were they bad, like Mark said? Did they *look* like terrible people? I'm glad I didn't see them; I don't think I would ever forget something like that. It's hard keeping my thoughts at bay as it is. I see faces of my own imagining, gray and waterlogged.

I wish there was some way to find out who they were. We tried everything we could think of, we trawled those Interpol and missing-person websites out in Bora Bora. Mark is the only one who would be able to pick them out of a lineup. And he's looked. Maybe I should ask him to look again? Maybe *I* should search Russian news sites for missing people?

26

The Stones

Mark has a contact for the stones. One of the old work colleagues he met with yesterday, while I was filming at Holli's, has suggested a possible solution. Just in time. Once the diamonds are sold we can get the money wired straight to Switzerland and we'll be all done. Our nest egg secured. I haven't told Mark about Holli or DCI Foster. I want to get today out of the way first; I don't want him worrying about the police until this deal is done. I'm certain they're not looking into me yet, and if we get the diamonds sorted today, it's over. I still haven't told Mark about the baby either. I'm not deliberately keeping secrets; I just want to wait until the time is right. It's such big news, I don't want it tarnished by worry. I want it to be special. Pure.

I'll tell him once this is done. When we sell the diamonds today, all traces of the bag will be gone, all traces of the plane gone. The diamonds are the last loose end.

Mark's contact has come through a girl called Victoria—she was in the same training program as Mark at J.P. Morgan. She dropped out pretty early, specialized, and now she's a quant trader in the Equity Algorithmic Trading team at HSBC. She's Persian and has a half brother who advises and trades in tangible assets: that's art and luxury goods, jewelry, Ming vases, Napoleon's hat, that kind of stuff. Only joking, not Napoleon's hat. Well, actually, yeah, maybe Napoleon's hat, who knows? The liquid assets of the super-rich, whatever form they may take.

Victoria's half brother has a website.

Naiman Sardy Art & Asset Advisors. My favorite page on the website is titled "Art as Collateral." I wonder what Monet, de Kooning, Pollock, Bacon, and Cézanne, being the most liquid of all the assets, would have thought about being collateral.

According to the website:

In the wake of the international financial crisis, investors have begun to see the benefits of allowing nonmonetary assets such as art, yachts, jewelry, and other collectibles into their overall investment portfolios. These tangible assets, however, need expert care and delicate management, not just in the areas of storage, display, preservation, and insurance, but primarily as tradable assets of substantial value. They require the same level of oversight needed by solely financial investment portfolios. Here at Naiman Sardy we will ensure you achieve and maintain a balanced portfolio, by advising and making you, the investor, aware of current market values and advising on when to buy, to sell, or to hold while assisting at every stage with procurements and sales.

Well, there you go. A protective shell of art. Art being used like cigarettes in prison.

I suddenly realize the double meaning of "oversight." *"They require the same level of oversight needed by solely financial investment portfolios."* One of life's ironies, I suppose.

I fear the clients of Naiman Sardy Art & Asset Advisors will be first against the wall when the revolution comes, collateral or no.

Anyway, Mark has asked Victoria to contact her brother Charles for "a client" of his. They're LinkedIn friends, Mark and Victoria, and after a brief catch-up over coffee Mark brought it up. Would her brother be interested in meeting a potential new client who is looking to dissolve some assets over the next few months? The idea seemed to go down well. Mark said she sat up a little taller in the café and very much enjoyed playing the role of middleman. Her brother's business had been hit quite hard by the current climate, apparently, and Charles could really use the commission right now. Victoria handed over one of Charles's business cards and told Mark to pass it on to his "client." She even thanked Mark for thinking of Charles for it.

Mark made the call, set up the meeting. I was to go, not as the client but as the client's PA, Sara. So far so standard; I knew from Caro's stories that most of her gallery sales came over the phone or through personal assistants buying at openings. Why go to buy your own collateral if you can send someone else?

I'm meeting Charles this morning. I leave Mark in the Patisserie Valerie at Green Park and make my way, alone, down onto Pall Mall.

The showroom in Pall Mall is discreet. As you enter, it looks more like a high-end private auction house than anything else. Self-contained display plinths pepper the room, housing treasures that I'm guessing probably aren't for sale. Just totems placed to reassure clients that this is the right place for them, class-related dog whistles, trophies, emblems. But, to be fair, I'd imagine everything in there can be bought for the right price.

In one case, an Incan death mask glimmers warm in the glow of spotlights behind a good inch of thick glass.

In another case a Japanese suit of armor.

In another a necklace with one glistening briolette diamond hanging as thick and as fat as a sherbet lemon from a string of lesser diamonds twinkling in the showroom lights.

Charles greets me. He's a healthy, ruddy, well-haired red-trouser-wearer, with the hint of a South of France tan.

He appears to be the only one around. Perhaps they only open the shop for meetings. I can't believe there's much foot traffic, even in Pall Mall.

We sit nestled at the back of the room at an oversized mahogany partners desk. If it's not a Chippendale, it's definitely in the manner of Thomas Chippendale. I guess you're meant to notice these things. I guess that's the point of them; that's probably why they're chosen.

We sit and make light small talk deep inside the thickly carpeted showroom, Charles makes me a pod coffee, and I figure the business conversation ball is in my court. I'm sure Charles could keep the small talk going and divert me all day if I don't cut to the chase. He's definitely not the sort to bring up business first—it wouldn't be the done thing in his trade, I'd imagine, cutting to the chase.

Even East End market-stall traders love the patter, don't they? Of course, Charles is no market-stall trader, let's be clear. He's Oxbridge through and through: precise, sharp, but riddled with the self-imposed shame of underperforming his own potential. It seems that the one drawback of having every opportunity in life is that you can never fulfill that level of expectation. You'll always fall short of your own potential. Any achievement will be the minimum expected of you, considering the circumstances, and any failure will be purely due to character weakness.

To be clear, I personally think Charles is doing really well. He's got a lovely place here. It seems like a lovely job. I'd be a proud mother. That's another thing about private school boys. They tug at the heartstrings, don't they? They bypass the sexual and hotline the maternal. They never grow up.

I pop the diamond pouch out of my coat pocket and onto the desktop. The stones are now safely stored away in the soft cream leather wallet that Mark and I purchased for the purpose. The plastic baggie was not appropriate, and although the pouch set us back £150 it gives a wholly different tone to the current endeavor.

Charles clicks to attention. It's the reason he's here, after all, and it has been a bad year.

I explain that the family I work for is looking to liquidate some assets over the next months. The stones will be an initial sale to test the waters, to see how receptive the market is at the moment.

Of course, in reality there are no other assets. I wish there were. I wish we'd found more bags. But I figure the prospect of more sales to come for Charles will (a) get us the best price for the stones today and (b) lessen the suspicious nature of a one-off sale.

Charles's interest is piqued. I knew the leather pouch was worth it.

He fetches a jewelry tray. I pass him the pouch. I want him to pour it out himself. To have the feeling I had the first time I saw hundreds of diamond pills pour out into the refracting light.

He shakes the pouch gently and they tumble out onto the green felt tray.

He feels it.

The hairs on the back of my arms rise. I feel it.

Opportunity. Possibility. He moistens his lips before he looks up.

"Very nice, lovely." A hint of joy bubbles just under the surface of his deadpan expression. He's no poker player, that's for sure.

A rate of ten percent commission is agreed upon. He'll get started as soon as I leave and should have some offers by the afternoon. Things move very fast in the diamond market. He can have a sale arranged by the end of the day if that's something the family I work for would be interested in.

I leave with a handwritten receipt in lieu of the stones and head back to the café to meet Mark. And then I feel it: eyes on my back. I stop on the corner of Pall Mall and St. James's Street, and with nerves fizzing pretend to look for my phone in my bag. The two men behind me pass by. They're not police, and they aren't following me, they're just two well-dressed men on their way to a long lunch.

I check over my shoulder, back all the way down the Mall to Trafalgar Square, my eyes searching for DCI Foster's stocky frame among
the few pedestrians. Of the twenty or so passersby, no one fits the
bill. DCI Foster's not here. He's not watching me.

Stop it, Erin. Don't be paranoid.

My heart flutters in my chest. A ghost instinct, nothing more. I
head off up St. James's to meet Mark.

He lights up when he sees me enter. He wants to know how it
went with Charles.

"Very, very good," I assure him. "He's looking for buyers as we
speak. He was really excited. He was trying to hide it but I could tell.
This might be done in a couple of hours! He's going to call me this
afternoon with some offers." My hands are shaking ever so slightly.
Mark slides his hand over the café table and rests his palm over mine.

"You're doing really well, honey. I'm impressed." He undercuts it
with a grin. I can't help breaking into one too. What are we doing?
It's scary but it's also completely thrilling. I can't speak for Mark,
obviously, but I've only ever gotten the occasional parking fine before now. I'm not a criminal. But it's amazing how smoothly we're
taking to all this. I console myself that it's okay to be paranoid every
now and then, it'd be crazy if I weren't, considering what we're
doing. We've brought all of this danger home with us, to England.

"Listen, Erin, honey, why don't we just stay in town and wait for
Charles's call together? And if an offer comes through, we'll just take
it, okay? And you can pop back down there and do the deal and we
could be completely done by this evening. Diamonds out of the
house, done. We can go back to our normal lives. Well, normal-ish."
That smile again.

My mobile rings at around one-thirty. It's Charles, calling back already. I recognize the final three digits from Mark's call this morning.
Mark gives me the nod and I answer after four rings. We don't want
to sound too desperate.

"Hello?" I answer, brusquely. Sara, my imaginary PA character, has much more important things to be getting on with than waiting for Charles's call.

"Hello there, Sara, it's Charles from Naiman Sardy?" He's tentative.

"Oh, fantastic. Hello, Charles, what can I do for you?" I sound breezy, aloof, and professional. Mark catches my eye and smiles. He likes this character. Very sexy.

Charles hesitates again ever so slightly, but I catch it. An infinitesimal pause down the line before he plunges in. "Sara, I'm ever so sorry. But unfortunately I'm not going to be able to help with this. As much as I'd love to, I'll have to sit this one out, I'm afraid."

My stomach flips and my eyes dart to Mark. He's already caught the change in energy from me and he quietly scans the faces in the café. Are we busted? Is it finished?

I've been silent a beat too long on the phone. I focus and continue calmly. "Is there some sort of problem, Charles?" I manage to sound slightly passive-aggressive. Sara isn't sure why Charles has been wasting her goddamn time if he isn't capable of selling diamonds.

Mark's eyes are on me again.

"I'm terribly sorry, Sara. It's just a small issue of provenance, that's all. I'm sure you can understand. I'm embarrassed to mention it really. I'm certain your clients are unaware that they are in possession of . . . well, needless to say there have been quite a few red flags regarding the provenance of the stones, which may cause potential problems further down the line. So I'm going to have to bow out at this stage. I'm sure you understand?" Charles leaves a silence for me to fill.

I shake my head at Mark. No sale. *Provenance.* I frown. And then I get it. Charles is letting me know that he thinks we're dealing with blood diamonds. That our stones come from some ethical void or another in Africa. Of course, with no papers, no trail, that's what they must look like. And I'd rather Charles thinks they're blood diamonds than that their lack of provenance is due to the fact that we simply stole them. Of course he must have suspected something was off when I handed them over. But I'd wager his concerns are more to do with potential heat than ethics. If he'd been able to offload the stones to literally anyone over the past few hours, I'm guessing he'd have done it. I don't blame him at all for balking. If I were Charles I'd run a mile, especially if he's having a bad year. People like Charles don't last long in prison.

"I see. Well, thank you, Charles, that's all extremely helpful. I'm sure my clients will be very interested to hear that. You're correct in assuming they would be completely unaware of any complications of that nature. So, thank you for your discretion." I oil him. I know he's not going to tell anyone, but he's worth greasing if it makes life easier.

"Not a problem at all, Sara." I hear a relieved smile in his voice. "Could I ask, though, that you inform your clients that I'm very happy to look into any other assets they'd be interested in liquidating? I'm happy to be of use if they need me for anything else. You do have my details, don't you?" He wants the spoils but he doesn't want to get his hands dirty. Join the queue, Charles, join the queue.

"Yes, of course, and I know they'll appreciate your discretion in this matter," I say.

Mark shakes his head. I'm smoothing the ego of a man who just told us we're criminals, and it's working. People are strange, aren't they?

"Wonderful, many thanks. Oh, Sara—would you mind awfully collecting them from my office now? I'll have them bagged and ready. It's probably best."

I hang up and slump onto the café table. God, being a criminal is exhausting. Mark ruffles my hair and I raise my eyes slowly to him.

"No sale." I keep my tone hushed. "He thinks they're blood diamonds. He's fine, though. No intention of telling. I've got to go get them back now."

"Dammit!" It's not what Mark wanted to hear. He put a lot of work into smoothing that transaction. "This part was supposed to be the easy part. He doesn't know it's us selling, does he?"

"No," I reply quickly. "There's no way he could know. And if he does, he's definitely not the kind to ever mention it. I'm sure people bring him all sorts. Blood diamonds are probably the least of his worries. If he's too scared to try and sell the diamonds for us, then he'll definitely be too scared to shoot his mouth off about them. Who knows who my clients could be? Who knows what they might be capable of?" I'm not concerned in the least about Charles ratting on us.

Mark's frown fades and he flashes me a little smile. "So, what the hell are we going to do now?" He says it lightly, the absurdity of our situation evident in his tone. Because what are we going to do now? We don't know anyone else. We don't know how to sell diamonds.

I let out a giggle. He grins back, eyes crinkling around the edges. God, he's gorgeous.

"I really thought that Charles was it; I half expected him to make an offer on the spot," I say. "God, why can't it just be that easy?"

"I kind of thought it would be too. Switzerland spoiled us, I think; that went almost too smooth. We're going to have to look down other avenues for these, though. We're not done yet. I'll get on it now. You go get the stones back." He nods toward the door.

I leave Mark brainstorming while I head back to Charles's office to pick up our diamonds. And suddenly this feels fun again. I could do this forever with Mark, a Daisy to his Gatsby.

When I get back to the gallery, Charles isn't there. A security guard answers the bell and hands me the offending pouch in exchange for Charles's receipt. It seems Charles wants to cover his bases, distance himself. Mark will have to feign ignorance of the whole thing if he ever meets Victoria again. Act shocked and dismayed that his contact was trying to offload blood diamonds. Who knew! It's perfectly plausible. Mark's been far enough away from the action to plead ignorance, and there are a lot of bad rich people out there. Aside from being my husband, Mark has no tangible connection to anything that just happened. But then, I wasn't here either. Sara was here.

A flicker of a voice in my head reminds me that I consistently am the one closest to all this, in terms of traceability, if it all goes sour. I am the one on CCTV in Switzerland, I am the one on CCTV in Pall Mall. Not my name, but my face. As I walk back with the stones to meet Mark, I wonder: Was this my idea, to get so close? Or did I just fall into my role? Am I braver, am I more adept than Mark? Or am I stupider? Why is it always me?

But then, Mark's the one with the contacts, so he can't do the transactions, can he? It does make sense. And to be honest, I don't like taking the back seat on things. We're actually a perfect team.

Mark's fresh out of diamond ideas when I get back, so we decide to call it a day. His brain seems to have shifted back to business concerns now. He has to meet another old work friend this afternoon about financial regulation in private consultancy; setting up the new business is going to mean jumping through a lot of hoops. I tell him to go. We really need more time to think about our next move with the diamonds anyway. I kiss him goodbye and head back home, the diamonds cocooned inside their buttery leather and my cold, pocketed hand.

It's while I'm walking back to the tube that the idea comes to me.

So, if slow-moving Charles can sell diamonds, why can't we do it ourselves? Charles is a middleman, someone who takes the things very rich people don't want anymore and finds other people to buy those things. He trades with other people's money. If Charles can pick up the basics of trading assets alongside his BA in Fine Art, I'm pretty sure it's not rocket science. Like Mark used to do in the City, but Charles does it on a much smaller scale. And we've certainly bought diamonds before; we know our four C's from all the extensive diamond searching we did together after our engagement. We know approximately how much these stones are worth, so we just need to find someone willing to buy them. And fancy that, there's a whole street in London entirely devoted to buying and selling dia-

monds. We just need someone who isn't too concerned about provenance to show an interest. Someone a little more, shall we say,
proactive than Charles. We can at least test the waters.

I dip into an alleyway off Piccadilly, shake one fat diamond out
into my palm and pocket the rest.

At Farringdon Station I walk up through a warren of side streets
into busy Hatton Garden. It's cold today, with a fierce sharp wind.
The road is bustling with Hasidic Jews, hands holding down their
wide-brimmed hats against the wind, and moneyed cockney traders
muffled to the chin in cashmere coats, all in a hurry to get somewhere.

It's probably a stupid idea, coming here, but again I don't exactly
look like a jewel thief, do I? Why would a well-dressed woman in
her early thirties draw attention by having a diamond valued in Hatton Garden? People do it every day.

I look down at my engagement ring; it's beautiful. Mark did
spend too much on it really. It's easy to see that now. But at the time,
I remember thinking how much he loved me. How much he'd sac-
rificed to buy it. The hours he'd worked for it. How beautiful it is.
How sparkly.

Now I see a trophy. A game head. Mark's hard work mounted on
my finger. If we'd needed the money, I would have sold it in a heartbeat for us. For our house. For our baby. The thin gold band beneath
it means more than the sparkle above. But after the bag I won't ever
need to do that. And I suppose if I manage to sell the stones there'll
never be any need for me to sell anything again.

I try the open-fronted diamond exchange market first. It's a cavernous space filled with many different store counters, different traders specializing in different gems and metals. Orthodox Jews sit
leaning over counters next to sharp-suited cockney traders, a smor-
gasbord of family businesses cheek to cheek.

I don't get far before a trader motions me over. Although no one
appears to be looking at me, I know I'm a fox that's just wandered
into a hunt.

"What you after, darling?" He's bald, cockney, shirt, tie, fleece. Practical: a man who dresses for the weather. He's got a friendly enough smile. He'll do.

"I'm looking to sell, actually. I've got a two-carat stone. Used to be in an engagement ring." I figure that's a fairly foolproof story. No one's going to ask whose engagement ring, are they? I mean, logically, whoever once owned it is either dead or not married anymore. Not the kind of sales patter anyone wants. Not that useful in oiling the cogs of commerce. And the fact that the stone is not in a ring anymore is fairly ominous too, ominous enough that it would be inappropriate to ask. Well, here's hoping. I came up with my story on the tube. I think it's pretty good.

"Two carat? Lovely. Let's have a look then." He's genuinely excited. I guess it's the kind of job where you never know from day to day what might turn up. Something about his expression as I fish out the single stone from my pocket reminds me of that famous episode of *Only Fools and Horses*. You know, the one where Del and Rodney find the watch and they finally become millionaires? He's bought my story.

I place it on the felt tray on his counter. It barely hits the felt before he snaps it up. Lens out, studying it. His eyes flick up to me again, assessing. I'm just a woman, middle class, well dressed, late twenties/early thirties. Whatever was worrying him is allayed by my appearance; he squints back at the stone.

He calls a colleague over. Martin. Martin gestures a friendly hello. He's younger than the guy in the fleece, who now passes him the stone. His son, perhaps? A nephew? Martin pulls out his own lens and inspects the diamond from all angles. He throws a look to me too. Sizes me up.

"How much are you after?" Martin's chillier now than his initial hello, businesslike. I suppose that means it's something they want. Game faces are set.

"I'm not too sure, to be honest. I know it's two carat. The cut and color are pretty flawless. I'm guessing around . . . five grand?" I aim low, low, low. I'm testing the water. I'm pretending I don't know what I've got. I know what I've got. Charles confirmed what we've got before he bowed out. This diamond, like all the others in the pouch, is color D (colorless), clarity IF (internally flawless) or VVS1 (very, very slightly included). Charles wrote the specs very precisely on the receipt he gave me. A basic round stone with those specs would reach eight grand per stone wholesale, nine and a half grand with tax. But the stone they hold in their hands now is a radiant-cut diamond, rectangular and cut to enhance brilliance and sparkle. These stones are rarer, they're brighter. They come in, wholesale, at about eighteen to twenty grand before tax.

These guys can't believe their luck.

The guy with the fleece juts out his lower lip as if to say five grand seems reasonable. He glances at Martin.

"What do you think, Martin? Can we stretch? It's a nice stone." He's playing it well—if I didn't know any better I'd think they were doing me a favor.

Martin eyes the stone again before exhaling loudly. He looks at me, his mouth pursed, weighing up the decision.

"Yeah, we can do that. Why not? Sure, let's do it. I'll get it written up." He nods at the fleecy man.

Fleecy Man smiles over at me, brisk. "You happy with that, love?" he asks.

I'm happy in that I've achieved here what I wanted to achieve. These stones can be sold. There are people who will overlook where they might come from, if there's a bargain to be made. Even if we let them all go for five thousand each, that'll still give us a cool million. We could get more than that, I know we could, but a million is fine. Let's not be too greedy.

I nod my head sagely, having a think, and I let them stew a moment.

"That sounds great, guys. Fantastic. I'll have a chat with my husband about it tonight and see what he says and maybe pop back in tomorrow?" I give them a chummy smile—we're all friends here—and pocket my stone.

Of course, I have no intention of coming back. I have no intention of selling two hundred diamonds one by one at various diamond markets. And as we've learned, the high-end traders won't touch them with a barge pole. So, what we need is to find someone who will look the other way for the right percentage. I think of all the stories Mark's told me over the years about the people he's worked with, the people he's worked for. The things they do, the things they've done. I'm certain we can find somebody.

Mark's in the living room when I get home, full of renewed vigor. His business meeting went really well, apparently: thankfully, most of the industry regulations encourage and support new business; people are setting up their own firms more than ever before, and there's plenty of demand for them in the current climate. He's been working on his potential client list too. It's looking very healthy, he says with a smile. His luck finally seems to have turned. A rich fug of coffee hangs in the air. He hands me a cup too, a welcome-home gift.

"Any luck with anything?" he asks. He leans against the side of the sofa, his arms folded across his chest with the low light from the setting sun illuminating him. We'll have to turn the lamps on in a minute.

It's funny how much we're both enjoying this. It's become a game; sometimes a game of skill, sometimes a game of chance. Maybe we like it so much because we're winning it right now.

"I had an idea after I left you," I say tentatively. "Bear with me. I went to Hatton Garden. Don't worry—I didn't do anything crazy. I just wanted to test the waters. I wanted to see if there were people who might be willing to look the other way on provenance. And, Mark, there are! There definitely are." I smile at him, feeling my face flush. He doesn't smile back.

I persist. "What we need is someone just the wrong side of legal to buy them off of us. Someone who wants the money and isn't too worried about where they came from." I try another tentative smile but he looks back at me blankly. Why isn't he going with me on this?

He rises and starts to pace the room, lost in thought. Something's not quite right. I bite my bottom lip and wait.

After a moment he turns and looks at me, his face unreadable.

"What is it, Mark? What's bothering you?" It comes out slightly sharper than I'd expected. He looks away. I guess I can only hold so much in before it starts to seep out. I'm keeping too many secrets right now, the pressure too heavy in my head. We need to sell these diamonds as soon as we can so we can go back to our real lives. I don't understand why he doesn't see that. We were having so much fun together earlier. I don't understand the sudden withdrawal.

He turns back to me. "I just can't believe how incredibly stu— Nothing. It's fine. No. You just carry on, Erin." He stops and goes to his desk; he busies himself with work papers.

"How stupid what, Mark? What? Sorry if I'm not getting this but . . . Just say what you want to say to me, please. Today has been tough and I think I've played it pretty well, so if you have a problem with what I'm doing, then could you please tell me? Or better yet, why don't you tell me *your* ideas, Mark?" I demand.

He stops what he's doing and looks up at me.

"Erin, I found DCI Foster's card in the pocket of your other coat." He says this softly; he's not angry, he's disappointed, which is worse. He didn't think we did things like this, kept things from each other. "I needed change, before you ask. When were you going to tell me about him, Erin? You scared the shit out of me! When did you stop telling me things?" Mark looks at me, hurt in his eyes. "First of all, I thought you'd been to talk to the police about the bag. I thought you'd told them everything. I had to Google the guy. Then I saw it was counterterrorism and I didn't know what the hell was going on. And then I started thinking, is she having an affair with this guy or something? Why does she have his card? And then, like a pathetic moron, I look through your emails—and thank God! Thank

God I saw your email to Phil about yesterday. About Holli. So, at least now, I know it's just work you're keeping from me. Which is fine, Erin, but don't freeze me out, okay? I have a right to know what's going on. Keeping secrets, especially about the police at a time like this, that . . . that is how things start to go wrong." He frowns at me accusingly. "I wasn't going to mention it, I was going to let you get around to telling me in your own time, but I guess we'll just have to talk about it now. So, I'm sorry if I'm not completely ecstatic about what you've been up to all day, but I think you can see where I'm coming from, right? You'll be all over CCTV in Hatton Garden, you know that, right?" He says this calmly, but his words pound in my head. "It's not going to look good if they start looking into you. And it will definitely not look good if DCI Foster finds footage of you."

He's right, of course. I am acting like an idiot. I am so incredibly screwed if everything goes wrong.

"Just tell me we're in this together, Erin. You're not keeping anything else from me, are you? It's just you and me, right?" It's a serious question that requires a serious answer. I feel the importance of this moment. He's putting himself on the line; I must take him or I leave him, he's not offering half measures.

I still haven't told him about the pregnancy, about Eddie knowing where we live, knowing everything about us, but I can't tell him now, can I? I'm already on shaky ground. I'm the irresponsible one; I'm the one running around town risking everything, lying. Imagine if he knew I was doing it while I carry our unborn child. If I tell him now, I might break this fragile thing we have that we've spent so long creating.

He's waiting for my answer. He's genuinely concerned. I feel bad. So bad.

"I'm sorry, Mark. I'm so sorry. I was going to tell you after we'd sold the diamonds. I just didn't want you to worry. And if I genuinely thought Andy—sorry, DCI Foster—was having me followed, I wouldn't have gone to Hatton Garden, I promise. We really need to get the diamonds out of the house, though, you see that, right? Especially now."

He's hurt. I see that, even though he doesn't want me to see that. But after a moment, he nods. He knows we need them gone.

I nod back in reply. "So we agree. We need to sell the stones as soon as we can. We need them gone, out of this house, and we need the money in the bank ASAP?" It's a question. If he wants me to end all this now, I will end it. I love him too much to push it.

He pauses, briefly, and then nods again. "Agreed."

"I should have told you about DCI Foster. I'm so sorry, Mark." I angle for a half smile and he doesn't let me down. God, I love him.

I cross the room to him and put my arms around him.

"Just don't make a habit of it, Mrs. Roberts." He pulls me close. "Let's sell some sodding diamonds then."

I press against him, relieved. "Do you know anyone who could help us do that?" I ask.

He looks down at me. "Do you?"

27

Wednesday, September 21

Alexa's Follow-up

They lay her things out on the counter. Souvenirs of a life. We stand back and let her look through it all. She signs it out.

We pull camera focus to the counter. A Nokia 6100, one of the first mobile phones to have Internet connectivity. It was 2002's most desired phone; Alexa was an early adopter. But there's no charger. God knows how she'll ever find one for it now.

A Mulberry brown leather purse. She opens it. Obsolete Amex cards, notes, coins. I wonder if any of the notes are obsolete now too. The five-pound notes changed again last September; they're always changing. I think of all those wallets back there, in the prison store-room, with five-pound notes that are now, or soon will be, utterly worthless.

A black collapsible umbrella. Half a pack of Wrigley's Extra chewing gum. A faded zone 1–2 travel card. And that is it. Alexa's life.

"Thank you very much." Alexa gives the Trinidadian warden a warm smile. They seem to be getting on well.

"My pleasure, darling. Now, you have a lovely day. And I hope I never have to see you again, if you know what I mean." He gives a throaty laugh and grins back at the beautiful woman before him.

Alexa gathers up her belongings into a small cream canvas bag and makes her way toward the exit.

She pauses by the door while the final officer signs her out. Phil, Duncan, and I stand in a cluster behind her. This is the only actual release we've been given the go-ahead to film. Alexa is the only prisoner who has allowed us this much access. We all feel the intimacy of the gesture. We slip out past her, out into the rain, the camera trained back toward her on the doorway as she steps out into the damp autumn air and the door shuts behind her.

She's outside.

She looks up, the rain misting her face, the breeze ruffling her hair. She breathes, her chest rising and falling gently. The muffled sound of traffic rumbling past down Camden Road. Wind in the trees.

When she finally looks down again, her eyes are wet with tears. She doesn't speak. We all remain silent as we walk backward in convoy toward the road, filming her.

And as we reach the road a smile bursts bright across her face and the tears start to roll freely down her cheeks. She lifts her head and laughs.

It's contagious. We're all smiling now.

In the great gaping chasm of Alexa's new freedom, our plan must come as a welcome guide rail. We're off to Waterloo East Station, where Alexa will be getting the train down to Folkestone in Kent. Her new home. Her family home. We're traveling down there together and we'll be filming her on and off for the next two days. It's a relief to be getting away from London for a night. I keep expecting Andy to burst through the door at any moment. It's unbelievably exhausting, the diamonds burning a hole through our attic floor like Poe's telltale heart. This trip will take my mind off that. It will focus me.

I've booked a car to take us to the station, but first Alexa wants to walk for a bit. So we walk in the light rain.

She stops at a café to buy a freshly squeezed orange juice. We all stand watching the bright orange crescents turn through the juicing machine and press into liquid. She sips it through a straw. She nods.

"It's good." She smiles.

She buys three more, one for each of us, using some of her fourteen-year-old legal tender, and we walk on.

We stop at Caledonian Park, where she finds a wet bench to sit on and we pull back, out of her sightline as she looks at the trees, the skyline, dog walkers, joggers. She takes it all in.

Finally she breaks the silence. She turns back toward us.

"Can we stop for a minute, guys? Come sit with me." She pats the rain-darkened bench.

We're an odd sight, the four of us, all side by side on the park bench: slender Alexa, stocky Glaswegian Duncan on sound, Steadicam operator Phil, and me. We all look out ahead across the drizzly park, Phil still filming our view, the camera resting on his lap.

"Thank you for being here," Alexa says as we stare out at a gray London. "This is the best day of my life."

And, yes, we capture the audio.

Thankfully, our train's not too busy. We catch moments where we can along the journey: Alexa's first newspaper, Alexa's first G&T, Alexa's first bar of chocolate.

Then on to the quiet village of Hawkinge, where Alexa's father, David, stands waiting in his driveway. She fumbles at the door handle of the taxi, finds it, and springs out into the Kent countryside. Father and daughter run to each other. The ruddy-faced seventy-year-old enveloping his daughter in a bear hug. They cling together.

"Home now," he says, like a promise. "Home safe." He squeezes her hard.

Finally David turns back toward us, Alexa's head fitting perfectly in the crook of his arm. Both beaming.

"Come on then, you lot. Let's get some hot tea in you." He motions to the house and shepherds us inside, Phil, still filming, bringing up the rear.

We leave them to it as the light starts to fade, and make our way to the glamorous lights of Folkestone and the Premier Inn, where we'll be sleeping tonight.

Nothing's Premier here except the prices. The soap is antibacterial foam that comes out of a wall dispenser. I call Mark, almost reluctantly. I feel so awful about hurting him yesterday, but he'll be worried, so I force myself to call. Mark tells me he's had some terrific news about the business. A potential client got in touch today; he'd heard about Mark's new firm through a colleague and he said he'd be looking to move over to Mark once he's up and running. Plus, Hector has confirmed he's definitely going to move companies; he's delighted to be joining Mark. It's going to be a new start for both of them. I'm so glad he's decided to take matters into his own hands. He's had no new ideas about the diamonds; he's been too busy. I tell him we'll work something out, we always do. We just need to hold tight. I just need to finish here with Alexa and get through Eddie's filming on Saturday. Then I'll have time to work something out.

This new company is a real lifeline for Mark. The job market is dead right now, and I really don't know what he would have done without this. I kiss him goodnight down the phone and go to sleep on my rock-hard bed, smiling like an idiot.

Alexa's fertility clinic appointment is at 10:35 the next morning back in London. It seems funny that since we last spoke about getting pregnant, I am pregnant. My secret passenger will be joining us on our visit.

Alexa is quiet this morning, nervous, her hands tightly clasped as we sit in the Lister Hospital's waiting room. We have permission to film today's doctor's appointment. I've done some reading around fertility, but I have no idea what to expect really.

After a certain amount of reshuffling we all manage to squeeze ourselves and the filming equipment into the small consultancy room.

Dr. Prahani, a well-groomed doctor in her forties with a reassuringly serious smile, offers Alexa a seat.

She folds her manicured hands and rests them lightly over Alexa's paperwork, which covers her desk.

"Now, the main aim of our consultation today is to ascertain whether you actually need IVF treatment or if we can proceed with the less invasive method of insemination, IUI for short. IUI is much simpler than IVF; it's the process of selecting the best sperm from your selected donor sample in the lab and then introducing that sample directly into your uterus via a catheter. It would be a very minimal, noninvasive process, which we could do for you in about five minutes. Obviously that would be our preferred method!"

Alexa raises her eyebrows hopefully and nods in hypothetical agreement.

The tests are easy and surprisingly quick. A vial of blood is taken. Then the curtain around the bed is drawn and Phil, Duncan and I watch the extra monitor as it shows grainy black-and-white footage of Alexa's uterus.

It's funny how little we all know about fertility, pregnancy. It's the single most important subject for the whole of humanity and yet I feel like I'm trying to read Urdu.

Her egg count is good. Alexa's body softens in relief. They'll need to get her AMH levels back from the blood work tomorrow to be sure, but it looks very promising so far.

We hug outside the clinic. I've somehow slipped from professional to personal with her. It's been an emotional two days. Alexa jokes that she'd like to keep Duncan as her emotional support animal. I laugh. She's funny. And Duncan does have a pretty outdoorsy beard these days. I arrange to Skype her, off the record, tomorrow night once she's back in Kent. See how she's doing.

It's strange; I feel like I know her. Really know her. And I feel like she might know me. She falls somewhere between my old life and this new one I'm creating. Alexa seems more alive than anyone I've ever met. And suddenly I realize I care very much what happens to her next.

28

Strange Things

When I got home yesterday, Mark was working in his study. He stopped when I came in and we went and sat in the kitchen together. We'd been given tea bags and biscuits from Fortnum & Mason as a wedding gift, so I made us a pot. He only managed a few sips and a bite of orange rind biscuit. I don't know why, but being away from him, even for a night, made me desperate for him. I led him upstairs and we made love as the daylight faded. Perhaps it's all these new hormones; that, and the fact that we hadn't slept together since Geneva five days previous. As I've said before, disgusting as it may seem, that's a long time for us. I needed it. I hadn't known I needed it but I did. After, as we lay tangled together on the sheets, I thought about telling him. About our baby. But I couldn't seem to form the words.

I didn't want to spoil the moment. I didn't want him to stop me trying to do what I need to do. And it's still early days. The pregnancy
may come to nothing. Anyway, I've made a promise to myself: I will
go to the doctor and I will tell Mark everything, as soon as the diamonds are out of our house and we're safe.

In preparation for Eddie's interview tomorrow, I was called to Pentonville Prison at seven forty-five this morning. It's been a week of
early starts.

As Pentonville is a male facility, I've been told there are a few
slightly different angles I need to be aware of, as I can now imagine.
For example, I've been told to wear trousers tomorrow, that sort of
thing. Best not to analyze it.

After a lot of listening, nodding, and paper signing, I make it out
of the final security door and back into the icy wind on Roman
Road. I wrap myself up in my coat, winding my scarf tight, trying to
remember where I need to be next, when a voice behind me calls
out.

"Excuse me? Hello?"

I pivot back toward the gates to see a friendly looking man in a
suit jogging toward me.

"Sorry, one second—sorry to slow you down there," he huffs,
ruddy-cheeked in the cold, his hand extended. "Patrick."

I take his hand in mine. I don't think we've met before. "Erin
Roberts," I say.

Patrick beams back at me, a firm grip, my warm hand in his cold
one. "Yes, yes. Miss Roberts. Of course," he says, catching his breath.
He gestures back to the prison building.

"Did I forget something?" I prompt.

"Sorry—yes. I'm just wondering what exactly you're doing here
today, Miss Roberts. I saw your name in the register but I think
there's been some confusion in administration and for some reason I
think I've been cut out of the loop." He looks embarrassed.

"Oh God, sorry. Yes, I was visiting the warden, Alison Butler, about the Eddie Bishop interview tomorrow."

His eyes flare with understanding. "Right, yes, of course! The interview. And you're a reporter, aren't you?" He looks at me suspiciously.

Oh great. The last thing I need right now is for them to revoke the filming permission. People warned me Pentonville would be a pain in the arse. And it has been plain sailing up until now.

"No, no. It's for the documentary. The prisoner documentary. We got the permissions late last year? Should I maybe email the info to you, Patrick? Alison has it all already. I'm pretty sure." I can hear a hint of disbelief at the situation in my own voice. I mean, I don't want to piss him off, but they should be on top of this. I mean, it's a prison, for God's sake, they should bloody well know who's coming and going. Seriously. I think of Holli and suddenly her breaking parole doesn't seem quite so implausible.

He catches my tone but doesn't seem offended. If anything, he's apologetic. "Ah, I see. Right, that'll be it. My office has been having some issues with visitor log-ins, but that's by the by. I'm so sorry, Miss Roberts. I'll make sure we're all on the same page for next week. What day did you say it was?" He squints at me in the cold September light.

"It's tomorrow. Not next week. Saturday, the twenty-fourth. Eddie Bishop." I say it slowly and clearly.

Patrick smiles and nods. "Perfect. I guess we'll see you then. Sorry about the confusion, Erin." He shakes my hand again and heads back toward the prison.

I turn and start to walk away. Should I send a confirmation email to him once I get home? Just in case. That way I'm definitely covered, right? There'll be a paper trail. And then I realize I don't know his surname. I turn to catch him but he's no longer there, disappeared back into the bowels of Pentonville. Damn.

Patrick what? I run the conversation through in my mind. He didn't mention his surname, did he?

And then a doubt suddenly flickers across my mind. I remember how cold his hand was in mine. His cold hand in my hot one. He didn't come out of the prison, did he? If he had, then his hands would have been warm like mine.

But why would he pretend to be coming out of the prison? And then it hits me. He knows my name and what I do and where I'll be tomorrow. Who the hell was he?

I head back to the prison gates and buzz in. A voice comes loud over the intercom.

"Hello."

"Hi there. Did Patrick just come back in?"

"Who?"

"Patrick?"

"Patrick who?"

"Er, I don't know, Patrick . . . er . . . I don't know his last name," I stammer. Better to be honest.

"Um, right. Sorry, who is this?"

"It's Erin Roberts. I was just here?" I try not to sound too desperate but I'm keenly aware I sound fully deranged about now.

"Oh yeah, you just signed out. Sorry. What's the problem?" The guard sounds cheerier now. He remembers me and I didn't look crazy a minute ago.

"Um, no, no, there's no problem. It's just . . . Has anyone come through since I left?"

There's a second's silence. I suppose he's weighing up whether I am crazy after all. Either that or he's thinking about lying? "No, ma'am, just you. Should I get someone to come out to help you?" he asks tentatively. He's popped out a "ma'am" now, shit. I'm being handled. I need to go before this escalates.

"No, no, I'm fine. Thank you." I leave it at that.

Patrick doesn't work for the prison. And if Patrick doesn't work for the prison, who the hell does Patrick work for? He wanted my name and he wanted to find out why I was here. A cold nasty thought forms in my head: does Patrick want his bag back?

| | |

When I get home something is not quite right. The house is empty and when I walk into the kitchen an icy breeze is blowing in through the slightly ajar back door. It's open. Mark would never leave the back door open. Someone else has left the back door open. Someone else has been in here. And might still be in here.

I stand there for a second frozen in disbelief, unwilling to accept the implications of what this means. I sense something shifting in the corner of the room behind me. I spin around but, of course, there is no one there, just the fridge clicking on in my silent empty house.

Room by room I check. I nudge open doors, bursting in, Mark's cricket bat in hand, for all the good a cricket bat will do me. My adrenaline is off the charts as it pounds through my system. Room by room I search for someone, or something, evidence that someone was here. I scan for anything missing, anything disturbed, but nothing obvious stands out.

Finally, once I've checked the whole house is empty, I make my way to the landing and pull down the attic ladder. I need to check under the insulation. As I ascend, a simple sentence repeats over and over in my head. *Please don't be gone. Please don't be gone.* But as I approach the loose section where the diamonds are hidden, the mantra shifts, without a second thought, to: *Please be gone. Please be gone.* Because if the diamonds are gone, then whoever came in through our back door has no reason to come back again. Unless, that is, they want their money back too.

Under the dry insulation everything remains as it was. The diamonds sit sparkling in their warm pouch, the phone and the USB still safely tucked in its casing. We weren't robbed. Whoever broke in was checking up on us, not stealing.

But the seed of doubt is now firmly planted in my mind. Perhaps I'm missing something. I search the whole house again, every room. I look harder this time, searching for any signs of interference, any possible clue as to who has been here. And then I see it.

In our bedroom, on the mantelpiece of our Georgian fireplace, next to our concert tickets and our antique clock, there is an empty space. An empty rectangular shape left in the mantel dust. Our photo. Gone. A photo taken the day of our engagement, us smiling into the camera, Mark and me. Someone has stolen a photo of Mark and me. And that is all they took.

Down in the living room the answerphone's red message light is flashing. Five messages. I sit in silence and listen.

The most recent is from Alexa. She's been given the go-ahead for IUI. It's good news. Her appointment is next week.

The answering machine segues into the next message. At first I think it must be a pocket dial. I hear the sounds of some unknown location. Muffled background noises, the occasional snippet of barely audible conversation. The low hum of a large busy place. A station perhaps? An airport. The phone is on the move. I wonder if maybe I pocket-dialed myself at Waterloo East. The call came on Wednesday when we were on our way to Folkestone. I listen harder for our voices. Ghosts from the past. But I can't hear us. I listen to the whole message. Two and a half minutes of muffled life, somewhere. Until the line finally clicks out. I stare at the answering machine. There's nothing that strange about a pocket dial really, is there? I mean, they happen all the time. Don't they? But they do feel eerie, even at the best of times, like gateways back through life. Or maybe not, maybe I'm just creeping myself out.

The next message starts and things get really weird.

It's the same. Well, almost.

I know what you're thinking, that's perfectly normal. Whoever pocket-dialed the first time must have just kept leaning on the same button. But the second message is from the next day. At the same time, exactly—11:03.

I was in the clinic then with Alexa and the crew. My phone was off. So it definitely can't have been me pocket-dialing myself. This call is different; it's outdoors. A park maybe. The gentle whistle of breeze over the receiver. The occasional shriek of kids in a playground. The caller is walking. At a minute in, I hear the rattle of an overground train. Or it could be just a train; nothing tells me this call was made from London but my own mind. The walker reaches a road. The sound of cars passing. And then the line clicks out again. Why would someone call two days in a row at exactly 11:03 and not speak? Why indeed. They could still be pocket dials, of course, but they're not, are they? Somebody is checking to see if we're in.

The next message begins. Left at 8:42 this morning while I was in my meeting with Alison Butler, the warden at Pentonville. This one is quieter. Indoors. A café perhaps. I think I can just about make out the clink of cutlery on plates, and the mumble of conversation in the background. Breakfast for someone. I strain to hear more, a snatch of context, and then it comes. A voice, not the caller but someone speaking to the caller. It's so soft I might have missed it if I weren't listening so hard.

"Are you still waiting? Shall I come back in a moment?"

The caller gives a low mumble of ascent and the rest is just background noise. So I know that this morning whoever called me was waiting for someone to meet them. At around 8:45, in a restaurant. A restaurant somewhere in London, judging by the waiter's accent.

But it's the final message at 9:45 today that scares me the most.

It's inside again. The low hum of something electrical. An industrial freezer, cold storage, something like that. Muffled conversation in the background again. An irregular electrical beeping. People shuffling about. And then, suddenly, a noise that I recognize. A noise that I know very, very well. It cuts through all of the other background sounds: the automatic two-tone *beep-bleep* of our newsagent's door when it opens. This call was made from inside our newsagent's. It's just around the corner from our house. A tingle runs straight down my spine and I have to sit down hard on the study chair.

I got home about fifteen minutes after that message was made. Whoever left that message was *here*. I think about calling Mark. Calling the police, maybe? But what on earth would I tell them? Everything? I'd have to. No, I can't do that.

I guarantee Mark hasn't got any idea that these messages exist; he never checks the house phone, he never even gives anyone this number. This is essentially my work number.

I think of Patrick's cold hand in mine. Number unknown. Could Patrick have come here after leaving me? Or did he come here before going to Pentonville? Is that how he knew what I looked like? But why would he come back here after meeting me? Or maybe Patrick was only supposed to hold me up while whoever was in the house could do what they needed to do. I sit in the fading afternoon light and listen to the messages again. Straining to catch a hint of anything I may have missed.

I try to remember Patrick's face. His hair, his clothes. Oh God. It's funny how little we pick up, isn't it? There's nothing I can cling on to. Middle-aged, a suit, a firm handshake. His voice British, with a hint of something else. French? European of some sort? I want to cry. I'm such an idiot. Why didn't I pay more attention? I guess the situation was distracting; I wanted to smooth the transaction so I didn't really look.

What did he want? To show himself? To scare me? Or maybe to find out my connection to the prison? If I was visiting anyone else inside? Could this be about Eddie? Maybe that's it. Maybe it's nothing to do with the bag at all. Maybe this is something to do with Holli—Holli and SO15?

When Mark gets home I know I have to tell him everything.

29

Strange People

I tell Mark *almost* everything. He takes it all in, calmly, nodding me on. I tell him about Patrick, about the calls. He checks his own phone, to check it wasn't him pocket-dialing. I tell him about the open door, about the missing photo. I hold back on my suspicions about Eddie—I know he'll stop me going to the interview tomorrow if I tell him about how Eddie knew where we were from the other side of the world. How he may be monitoring my every move. I don't want Mark to stop that interview.

I don't tell him about the pregnancy either. Once I tell him that news, I'll have to stop it all—the documentary, the diamonds, everything. He'll want me to stop it all.

When I finish talking he leans back against the sofa, arms folded across his chest. He takes a long beat before speaking.

"All right, here's how I see it. First of all, that photo is in the study. I scanned it the other day for Mum. So that explains that."

"Oh my God, Mark! No one took the photo?!"

He gives me an amused grin and I feel my cheeks flush with color. Oh God, how embarrassing. I slump my head down into my hands. What a paranoid idiot. And suddenly I'm not sure how much of this situation is real at all, and how much is just adrenaline-based fabrication.

Mark snorts a chuckle before continuing, "Yeah, the picture is safe! Second, I'm not sure we should read too much into forgetting to lock the back door. You know, the mind does funny stuff when we're stressed out. *But,* having said that, I think the guy you met today does sound like he could be a serious issue. I think you're right to be concerned about that. I mean, my initial thought, obviously, is that Patrick's connected with DCI Foster and the SO15 investigation into Holli. Don't you think? I mean, that's the only logical explanation really. He's been following you and he's seen you at Pentonville Prison a day before you should be there for your big interview, so he decides to intervene and ask you some questions. That makes sense. He wouldn't know Pentonville called you in a day early for that meeting; you only found out last night. I'd say that's it."

It makes sense, what he's saying. But I can't quite shake the feeling that this is something else entirely.

"But why wouldn't he introduce himself as police, Mark? And what about the answerphone messages? Do the police leave weird answerphone messages?"

"Listen, I know you think it's the plane people, but think about it logically, Erin: If it was the plane people, if they knew where you were, do you think we'd still be here? Do you think the stuff in the attic would still be here?" He lets the questions hang in the still air.

I shake my head. "No, I don't think we would be." I answer slowly, realizing the truth of it as I say it out loud.

He continues briskly. "I don't know why he didn't say. I guess he hoped you'd believe he worked for the prison, like he said, I mean he was undercover, right? And the messages: they could just be a prank. I don't know, pocket dials. And, I mean, come on, you know that's not really our newsagent, right? Most of the corner shops in London have that noise. I really don't think someone is threatening us via door noise. Maybe it's something to do with one of your interviewees? I mean, that's definitely a possibility, right?"

I think of Eddie again and the champagne. Yes, it's definitely a possibility. Maybe Eddie needs to speak to me? But how could he be calling from an unknown number from prison? They wouldn't agree to let him have his own phone in prison. And then it hits me. Eddie is a criminal. Of course he has a way to call me. I remember reading about the methods gang members use to get burner phones smuggled into prison. It's certainly not a comfortable process for the smuggler, but they are handsomely rewarded for their troubles, or at the very least not murdered in their beds. It could definitely be Eddie leaving me those messages.

"Erin, you need to focus on the real situation here. The man you spoke to today, Patrick. Let's say SO15 is doing some checking up on you. Forget the missing photo and our back door. The photo's fine and as far as the door goes, well, sometimes we just forget to lock things—"

"Mark, I don't. I don't forget to lock things," I interrupt, but I can feel my conviction flagging.

"Er, yeah, you do, Erin." He studies me for a second, frowning, surprised. "Sorry, honey, but you have definitely done that before. You know that door blows open if it's not locked properly. Trust me—you've forgotten to lock it before."

Have I? That door does blow open if it's not locked, he's right. How would I know that unless I'd seen it do that? I guess I must have left it unlocked at some point. Then I think of our photo. It probably hasn't been in our room for days; I didn't notice that it was missing at all, not until now. I hadn't even checked the answerphone until today. Shit. I am probably not half as observant as I think I am and I have been pretty preoccupied lately. Oh my God, I hope I haven't been wandering around London making too many mistakes.

"Don't worry about it, Erin, it's fine. Just concentrate on the actual *person* you met today. The facts. This Patrick guy is probably SO15. I don't know, maybe they think there's a vague possibility that you're running information between prisons or something like that. I mean, your dad does live in Saudi, right?"

I give him a hard look. We don't talk about my family. It's weird that he's brought them up now.

"Erin, the police have to follow up on possibilities like that even if they don't suspect you. They have to at least check. It would be ludicrous for the police not to check up on you. So, in light of that, honey, I think you seriously need to drop the Holli storyline. Just drop it. There's too much attention on her right now. All it will take is the smallest amount of digging by DCI Foster to bring up some fairly awkward questions about us. To put it mildly." He holds my gaze expectantly, brows furrowed.

He's right, of course. They'll want to know why we traveled to Switzerland last week. And who is suddenly paying me a monthly retainer.

"Okay." I nod, reluctantly.

"Good. Drop the Holli storyline, drop it from the doc, stop the research entirely, distance yourself, distance us." There's finality to it. He's so clear about this being the solution. The last I'd heard was that Andy, and SO15, now had CCTV footage of Holli and Ash leaving the Istanbul airport and boarding a bus to Gaziantep, a small Turkish village near the Syrian border. It's all gotten very serious.

"Consider it dropped." I plop down on the sofa opposite him. My brain is whirring. I'll come back to Holli once our situation has settled down. But something doesn't quite fit in my mind. I don't agree about Patrick being linked to DCI Foster. I don't think the man I met today had anything to do with the police. I can't shake the feeling that what happened today is because of the bag. That some-one did come to our home. Even if they didn't take that picture, I think they were here. No matter what Mark says. Yeah, I'm aware of how paranoid that sounds. Maybe the plane people know we're not dead. And now maybe they know we still have the diamonds and the phone in our home. It's true that we're still alive, but maybe they're just taking their time. Working out the best way to do it. I think about the Sharpes; they took their time with the Sharpes. Worked out a safe way to get rid of them. Because they needed to make their deaths look like an accident. But then again, maybe what happened to the Sharpes was just an accident. Mark seems convinced it was.

Later that night, before bed, Mark sits on the edge of the bathtub watching me while I brush my teeth, a single sock in his hand. I can tell he wants to say something but he's having trouble putting it into words. He takes a breath.

"Honey, I'm worried now. And please don't take this the wrong way, you know how much I love you, but I think you might be getting a little bit overwhelmed by all of this. That photo business today and the answerphone. Erin, you know no one is coming for us, right, honey? No one is watching us except the police. And you are refusing to acknowledge how dangerous that is. This Patrick guy today. You need to stop doing things that might attract attention from now on, sweetheart. Will you promise me that, Erin? I need you to stop doing things that the police might notice. We're sailing close to the wind here already." He looks at me, softly. I feel foolish and so guilty about the things I haven't told him.

He's worried about me. He's worried about us. He continues, "You asked me before what I thought we should do about the diamonds, and I've been thinking about it a lot. You're not going to like it, I know, but I think we should dump them. Just get rid of them. This is getting crazy. We should cut our losses, stop trying to sell them, and just dump them somewhere. I don't think it's worth the risk we're running right now. We already have the other money, Erin. We're good. We have enough. We should stop."

Something bubbles up inside me when he says this. I don't know why, but I'm annoyed with him. It's the first time I've ever really been frustrated by something Mark has said or done. Dump the dia-monds? Why would we do that? We've come this far. What about his business, his plans, our plans? He was so concerned about our finances before, why isn't he anymore? What we've got in Switzerland won't last forever; we'll need the diamond money too, to get his company up and running and keep all of this going. We could just store the diamonds somewhere, couldn't we? Why would we dump them? But then, realis-tically, I know there'll never be a later date when we can magically find an easier way to sell them. And once we have a child we won't be able to take any risks at all. Either we try to sell them now or it'll be too late.

I look at him in his boxers, the sock still dangling from his hand. I love him so much. He is right, it is dangerous, but I don't want to just give up. Not after everything he's been through in the past couple of months. And what if, God forbid, his new business falls through like all those job offers that never seemed to materialize. No, we need to keep going. But . . . cautiously.

"All right, yes, I see your point of view, Mark. I do, but can we please try one last thing? I'll come up with something, okay? Some-thing safe. Just give me a few more days. I really think I can make something work. I do. Isn't that a better outcome overall, if we get the money from the stones too?" I try to say it gently, calmly, but I'm not calm. To give up now would make no sense at all.

He holds my gaze for a beat, then looks away. He's disappointed, again. He tries to hide it but I saw the flicker of it in his eyes. I've let him down, again.

"Fine," he concedes. "But that's it, all right? If this doesn't work, Erin, you'll stop? Please don't take it any further, honey. Don't keep *pushing*." He doesn't look at me then, he just stands and walks to the bathroom door. Distant. Alone. I feel like this is the closest we've got to an honest conversation for a while and it hasn't brought us any closer together. A rift has opened between us. The more I tell him, the wider it will get. He knows about Andy now, he knows about Holli, he knows about the man outside the prison, Patrick. I can't just let him walk away. I need to bring us back together; I need to share a bit more of myself.

"Mark. Do you really think they're not looking for us?" I blurt out. He turns back, surprised.

"Who, honey?" He looks confused.

I don't know why I choose the plane people of all things to get closer to him. But they're on my mind. "The plane people. Maybe you're right, maybe I'm crazy, but I feel like something is closing in on me, Mark, on us. Not just the police. Maybe it's something I haven't even thought of yet. I don't know. I know it sounds stupid and paranoid and I have no evidence to back this feeling up, but I can just sense it all around me. Like it's just waiting for something. I can't see it yet, but I can feel it coming. . . ."

I falter, seeing his concerned face. I must sound totally insane. And I know if I feel this way about things, then I should definitely stop all of this—the diamonds, the interviews, everything, like he says. But instead of stopping, I'm just diving deeper and deeper in.

Mark steps back into the bathroom and circles his arms around me; I let my head rest gently against his bare chest, listening to his heartbeat. He knows I need him.

"They're not coming for us, Erin. Whoever they are, they'd never be able to find us. And even if they could find us, they already think we're dead. Honey, they aren't the ones we should be worried about. We should be worried about the SO15 investigation. And this Patrick character is almost definitely part of DCI Foster's team. I mean, think about it. If Patrick were related in some way to the bag, then I'm pretty certain the police would have noticed him hanging around by now too, wouldn't they?"

I nod mutely against his shoulder. He's right; in a way, DCI Foster might be keeping us safe. Mark places a tender kiss on my forehead and leads me to bed. Magically we've come together again. I seem to have fixed the rift. For now.

But as I lie in bed beside him I wonder. Would the police notice someone following me? They didn't notice a vulnerable young woman being radicalized right under their noses. They haven't noticed Eddie looking into my life. They haven't noticed a lot.

30

Interview Three

My coffee steams in the sharp chill of the interview room. This September has been arctic. The guard in the room with me here in Pentonville looks like an extra from the TV series *T. J. Hooker*. His physique appears to be ten percent hat and ninety percent barrel chest. Maybe I'm being unfair? He's definitely more focused this morning than I am. I feel like I'm half asleep, stuck in an extended jet lag. I remember the sky back in Bora Bora, the heat on my limbs, the bright clear days.

I hope I wake up soon.

What if the rest of my life is just a waking dream, trapped here forever? I think of Mark, out there in the cold, somewhere on the bustling streets of London. He's looking into office spaces for the new firm this morning. It all seems to be becoming a reality now. He's meeting Hector at a notary later today to sign some paperwork. It's all getting very exciting.

My phone vibrates in my pocket. I decline the call. It's Phil again. He's furious we're dropping Holli from the doc; I emailed him first thing this morning and he's already called three times. He's not happy. There's a missed call from Fred too. He wants to see the footage I've got so far. He's interested. He'll want to dissect the wedding too, no doubt. It's pretty rare that a BAFTA-winning, Oscar-nominated director would ever have even a passing interest in a first-time film like mine, but that's nepotism for you. Or maybe it's not. I mean, we're not related; he just gave me my first job, somehow I managed not to fuck it up, and he's been watching over me ever since. Plus he gave me away. I'd love to give him some of the footage, but of course, SO15 has most of my footage. Explaining that to Fred will take more time than I have right now.

The cage buzzer in the hall rumbles. Unlike the room at Holloway, this one has no door, only an archway leading out into the corridor. I wince at the off-white prison walls and tell myself to perk up. Life could definitely be worse. It could always be worse.

The buzzer sounds again.

I look up and see Eddie Bishop, sixty-nine, handsome, through the archway as he heads down the squeaky linoleum corridor, led by another guard.

Although Eddie's wearing the same gray marl tracksuit that all the inmates wear, it doesn't quite hang the same on Eddie. He might as well be wearing one of the three-piece suits I've seen him wear in countless research photos. He's got gravitas. But perhaps I think that because I know his crimes, his history.

He looks like a cockney Cary Grant; God knows how he stays so tanned in prison.

He sees me, gives me a smile. Why are bad boys always so attractive?

I suppose, at the end of the day, if you're not good-looking you don't get away with being a bad boy. You just get called a thug.

244 | Catherine Steadman

He pulls out his chair and sits. Here we finally are. Me and Eddie Bishop.

There're smiles all around. Then T. J. Hooker pipes up.

"You all right, Eddie? Need anything? Water?" His tone is friendly, pally. We're all friends here.

Eddie turns back, slow, smooth.

"Nah, Jimmy. All good here. Thanks very much." His voice is cheery. Today's a good day.

"No problem. Just give us a shout if you need anything." Jimmy looks to the other guard now, the one who brought Eddie in, and gives him a nod. Both wander through the archway and out into the corridor. "We'll be down the hall in the break room." Jimmy's talking to Eddie, not me. And with that they both disappear from view, their shoes squeaking away, leaving me staring wide-eyed after them.

Why are they leaving? I haven't even turned on the camera yet! This is definitely not normal. No one mentioned this to me in the briefing yesterday. They've left me alone in a room with Eddie Bishop.

I wonder if I should be scared. I think of the answerphone messages. Eddie's killed a lot of people, or had a lot of people killed. There are stories—books full of stories—of torture, kidnap, assault, and everything else that happened in the Richardson Gang and Eddie's forty years at large. Urban myths. Nothing provable, of course, no solid evidence, no witnesses.

I suppose I should be scared but I'm not. And suddenly it dawns on me: I never could figure out why Eddie had agreed to do the documentary with me. He must have had a million offers to tell his story but he's never said yes. He has no need to, and no inclination, from what I can work out. But now, sitting across from him, unguarded, the camera beside me still not turned on, I realize I missed something important. There must be something in this meeting for him. Eddie needs something. And I suppose I need something too, don't I? My heart skips a beat. There it is. Fear.

I turn on the camera. He smiles.

"Lights, camera, action, aye?" He extends a hand across the table, slow. He's being careful not to spook me. He must know the effect he has on people. His singular brand of magic.

"Nice to finally meet you, Erin, sweetheart." *Sweetheart.* I'm a millennial woman, I've read my Adichie, my Greer, my Wollstone-craft, but him calling me "sweetheart" is, somehow, fine. It seems strangely innocent coming from him, of another time.

"Nice to finally meet you, Mr. Bishop," I answer. I take his hand across the Formica tabletop; he rotates my hand to the top, his thumb over the back of my hand—it's a squeeze, not a shake, a delicate squeeze. I'm a lady and he's a man and he's letting me know.

"Call me Eddie." The whole display is so old school it's laugh-able, but it works.

I smile in spite of myself. I blush.

"Nice to meet you, Eddie," I say, almost giggling. Excellent, I'm an idiot. I take back my hand.

Focus, Erin. Down to business now. I sort out my tone. Reset my professional face.

"I suppose we should get this out of the way first, shouldn't we? Thank you for the champagne. Much appreciated." I meet his gaze; I want him to know I'm not intimidated.

He gives me a sly smile. He nods. *You're welcome.* After a pause he replies, for the camera, "I'm afraid I don't know what you're talking about, sweetheart. If they don't sell it in the prison tuckshop, it ain't from me. It sounds like a nice little present, though. What's the oc-casion?" He raises his eyebrows innocently.

I understand. The camera is rolling, so we're playing it like this. We won't be mentioning the answerphone messages either then? Very good. I give him a nod. I understand.

I get back on script. "Is there anything you want to ask before we get going?" I'm eager to move on now; we don't have as much time as I'd like.

He straightens up in his seat, readies himself, rolls up his sleeves.

"No questions. Ready when you are, sweetheart."

"Okay, then. If you could give us your name, conviction, and sentence please, Eddie."

"Eddie Bishop. Convicted for money laundering. Seven years. Release is coming up before Christmas. Which'll be nice. My favorite time of year." And we're off. He looks relaxed, at ease.

He raises his brows, *What next?*

"What do you think about your trial, Eddie? The sentencing?" He's not going to incriminate himself on film, I know that, but he'll give as much as he can; he likes playing chicken with authority—I've read his court transcripts.

"What do I think of the sentence? Well, Erin, interesting that you should ask that." The smile is sardonic now. He's amused, playful. "I'll be honest with you: not much. Don't think much of the sentence. They'd been trying to get me on something for thirty years, tried all sorts and I've been acquitted of all sorts over the years, as I'm sure you know. It seems to me they've got a problem with a Lambeth lad making good, making an honest living. It's not supposed to go that way, is it? They couldn't make any of it stick till now; any other man might have got slightly offended, if you know what I mean. Only a matter of time before something stuck. If you want to find something enough, it always turns up in the end. One way or another, if you catch my meaning." He leaves that floating in the air. I think we all know enough about the sixties and seventies to guess that the police force might have been a little shadier then. He's suggesting they planted evidence to frame him. I don't disagree.

"But what can I say? My bookkeeping isn't what it should be, at the end of the day. Yeah, never was very good with numbers. Dyscalculic. Didn't pay much attention in school," he continues, tongue, quite obviously, in cheek.

"Course it wasn't diagnosed back then, was it? Dyscalculia? They just thought you were messing about, or retarded. And I was a quick kid, you know, in other ways, so they just thought I was pissing about. Winding 'em up. Different story in schools now, though, ain't it? Got two grandkids. I didn't stay in school too long, wasn't suited to it. So in a way I suppose it was only a matter of time before I slipped up on my sums, wasn't it?" He smiles warm and wide.

I'm pretty sure he's got an accountant. I'm pretty sure that accountant was at the trial.

It's astonishing that he can stick his finger right up in everyone's faces the way he has for the past few decades—bait the system and get away with it. But not only does he get away with it, I *want* him to get away with it. I'm rooting for him. Everyone is. For his brand of jaunty cockney psychopathy. It's *fun.* It doesn't seem like real modern, raw, bone-and-gristle crime; it seems like the Pearly Kings, and pie and mash, and *I'll-be-mother.* Good old-fashioned British crime. Homegrown, Brexit crime. Bob Hoskins, Danny Dyer, Barbara Windsor, *The Italian Job,* hatchet-in-the-trunk-of-the-car crime.

"Okay." I lean forward. I want him to know I'll play his game. "You're not going to tell me about the Richardsons or any of it, are you, Eddie?" I just need to know what game we're playing.

"Erin, sweetheart, I will tell you anything you ask, my darling. I'm an open book. I might not know the answers to some of your questions, but I'll certainly give it a go. So, how 'bout a smile?" He gives me a roguish tilt of the head.

I really can't help myself; it's ludicrous, but I'm enjoying this. I smile, with all my teeth.

"Thanks very much, Eddie. In that case, can you tell us about Charlie Richardson, head of the Richardson Gang, what was he like?" I think I understand the rules now. Ask around things, ask opinions, no facts.

"He was an awful fucking human being . . . but in the nicest possible way. Awful fucking human beings sometimes are." He sighs. "It's all been said about the Richardsons already. Everyone involved in all that old East End stuff is dead now anyway. You can't rat on the dead and I certainly wouldn't speak ill of the dead . . . but Charlie was a nasty fella. I never physically saw him do any torture. But he'd talk about it. He used the power generator from a dismantled WWII bomber to electrocute them. He'd torture 'em, slice 'em, scare 'em until they told him whatever he wanted. I asked him once, 'How do you know they're not lying to you if you torture 'em?' He said, 'They lie until they get to the point where they turn into little children and all they can do is tell the truth.' But you see, that's not what I was asking him. What I meant was: what if they'd told you the truth to begin with and you kept on torturing 'em until they made up some old shit? That never occurred to Charlie. I didn't ask again. Different generation, Charlie was. Thought he knew what was what. But torture's never worked. You've got to respect people, right, Erin? If you want respect, then you need to make sure you're respectful. Let people die with a little dignity. It's up to them if they lived with it. No one can say you did wrong in this life if you treated people with respect."

I'm not sure that's entirely true, but I push on.

"Did you treat people with respect, Eddie?" I ask. It seems important to ask.

He looks up at me, eyes hooded.

"Yeah. Always have, always will. But you don't sign up for certain things without knowing the rules, Erin. And if you've signed up for the game, then you can't complain when you lose. You got to lose with dignity is all; a good sportsman always lets people lose with dignity." He pauses, studies me.

He's weighing me up. He wants to say something. I give him a moment but he looks away, changes his mind.

There's silence. He seems distracted, his mind elsewhere. We're getting close to dangerous territory. I can feel it.

I change the subject to something lighter.

"What do you think you'll do first? When they let you out. Do you have anything in particular you'd like to do?" I plow on. I need to keep the energy up.

"Turn it off." He looks at me hard, unflinching. His charm has suddenly vanished. I instantly feel sweat prickling along the back of my neck.

The silence is thick between us. My heart is hammering. I can't interpret this situation anymore. There are no social cues to read; I have no frame of reference.

"Turn the camera off. Now." He is motionless. Solid, immovable. Dangerous.

I fumble to turn it off. I don't know why, but I do as I'm told. It's the worst possible idea in this situation but there is no other option. I could call out to the guards, but this isn't like that. It's not that sort of situation. Something else is going on here. I want to know what it is. I do what he says.

The red light fades out.

"Is everything all right, Eddie?" I don't know why I ask him this. He's clearly fine. I'm the one whose hands are shaking.

"You're all right, sweetheart. Calm down." His face has softened. His tone is gentle now. My shoulders slowly release. I hadn't realized that they were clenched.

"Sorry if I scared you, love. But here it is . . . I, um? Right, well . . ." He seems engaged in an internal battle.

And then it comes. "I want to ask you something. I wanted to ask you before, over the phone, but it wasn't possible to discuss at the time and I don't want it on camera. I'm going to ask you for a favor. If I'm totally honest, sweetheart, it's the only reason I'm doing this interview with you. You give me what I want, I'll give you what you want. So there we are. Now listen up; I'm not going to say it twice."

I can't believe this is happening. Although, to be honest, I haven't got a clue what is happening. I wonder if this is the reason he's been leaving me those messages. *If* he has been leaving me messages?

"I'm not used to asking favors, so bear with me." He clears his throat. "It's a personal matter. I find this sort of thing quite . . . stressful. And at my age I try and steer clear of stress, you know how it is. I need you to do something for me. Will you do something for me, sweetheart?"

He is watching me. I swallow. And then I remember that he probably wants an actual answer. My mind kicks up into another gear. What will I have to do? Oh God. Please do not be sexual.

Shut up, Erin. Of course it's not going to be sexual.

"Um, I'm . . . What kind of thing?" I keep my tone as steady as I can manage.

"I made some mistakes, in my life, you know. With my family. Maybe. My wife, definitely, but I know that's all done, that's over. Fine. I'm okay with that." He brushes it aside. "But I've got a daughter. My Charlotte. Lottie. She's . . . she's twenty-eight. Looks a bit like you. Dark hair, pretty, world at her feet. Beautiful girl. We're not talking right now, Lottie and I. She doesn't want me in her life, around her family. I'm sure you understand. And I don't blame her; she's a smart girl. We raised her smart. She's got a lovely fella now; he's good to her and she's got two girls of her own now too. Look—I wasn't the best dad, obviously. I'm sure you've probably picked up on that. Anyway, long story short, I want you to talk to her." He gives himself a little nod. He got there in the end.

He wants me to talk to his estranged daughter. Excellent. More family drama. Not what I need right now. I've got enough at home.

But this is definitely not as bad as it could have been. I can talk to his daughter. I was actually planning on interviewing her anyway. Unless what he's really asking is some kind of a euphemism? Is it a euphemism? Do I have to kill? Does he want me to kill her? God. I'm hoping not! He would have been more explicit about that, right? *Right?* This is weird.

"Eddie, you're going to have to be slightly more specific here. What do you want me to *talk* to Charlotte about? Talk to her for the documentary? Or about something else?" I choose my words carefully.

He's obviously finding this conversation hard, having to ask politely for something of a personal nature. I can't imagine he's had much need to do it before. I really don't want to piss him off.

"No, not about the documentary. Sorry, sweetheart, I couldn't give a sweet F.A. about the documentary. I looked you up after they first mentioned the whole thing, had you looked into a bit; you seem like a nice enough girl, kind of girl my daughter might be friends with. She'll trust you, maybe. This isn't my fucking forte; I just want her to see I'm trying here. Let her know I'm together, I'm a good guy, I've got it all under control. Erin, you'll make an old man very happy if you do this for me. There isn't anyone else to ask, do you understand? It's not as if I've got women friends knocking about, and even if I did Lottie'd run a bloody mile from them lot. She needs to know that I'll be better in the future, once I'm out. That I'll be there for her. That I want to be part of her life again. Help her with stuff. See the kids. My grandkids. All that. I just need you to talk some sense into her. Get her to give me another chance. She'll listen to you. I know her. Tell her I'm different, tell her I've changed." He stops talking. The room falls silent.

Why on earth would his daughter listen to me? Why would he think that? Maybe he's not as together as I thought? And then I catch sight of my reflection in the Perspex glass of a poster screwed into the prison wall. Suit, blouse, heels, glossy hair, sunlight bouncing off my new wedding band. I see what he sees. I look together. A young woman in control of her life, on the cusp of something. Professional but still open, hard but still soft, in that magical period after youth and before age. He might be right. His daughter might listen to me.

I can't hear the guards at all. I wonder where they are. Do they care what's happening in here? Did Eddie arrange for them not to be here, ask them not to interrupt? He still has power outside prison, doesn't he? I look at him. Of course he does. They probably have to be careful around him; he'll be free again in two and a half months. Untouchable. And he's just asked me for a favor.

"I'll do it." Screw it, fortune favors the brave.

"That's a girl." He smiles.

My stomach flips as I realize there's a chance here for Mark and me. I could ask a favor in return. But should I? Is that a good idea?

"Eddie?" I lower my voice, lean in. Just in case someone's listening, just in case. "If I help you, will you help me? I don't know anybody else who can help me with this." My voice sounds different, to my ears, more serious but thinner than usual. Needy.

His eyes narrow. He studies me. I'm a pretty readable mark. What possible threat could I ever be? He sees that, then shows that glint of a smile.

"What is it?"

"Well, okay, long story short . . . I have some gemstones that I . . . found. Okay, that sounds . . . I can't sell them. They're illegal. So there it is. And I need to sell them . . . off the record. Do you know someone, maybe who could . . ." My whisper trails off. Turns out it's not just former gang leaders who find favors hard to ask for.

He's grinning at me now.

"You naughty girl. It's always the quiet ones, ain't it! I tell you what, it's fucking hard to surprise me, love, but I didn't see that one coming. Sounds like a quality problem you've got there, Erin, sweetheart. How many stones we talking and what kind?" Eddie's enjoying himself. He's back in the game.

"Around two hundred, diamonds, all cut, all flawless, all two carat." I keep my voice low but I know from his demeanor that there's no one listening.

"Fucking hell! Where the fuck did you get those?" His voice echoes out of the archway and down the corridor. I really hope no one's there or I'm so fucked.

He's looking at me differently now. He's impressed. A million is a million. But then again a million's not what it used to be.

"Ha!" He laughs. "I'm not usually wrong about people. But every day's a school day, aye? Very nice. Yes, Erin, sweetheart, I can help you out with your little problem. Got a numbered account?"

I nod.

He laughs again, delighted.

"Of course you fucking 'ave. Brilliant. You're a find, Erin, sweetheart, you're a bloody find. Right, you'll get a call next week. Do what he tells you. He'll sort you out; I'll have a word. All right?" He's beaming at me. I'm glad it's gone this way, but it is all slightly disconcerting. And all so easy. I'm not really sure how it happened.

And now there's my end of the deal to keep.

"I can pop around to visit your daughter next week. I'll call Charlotte this afternoon, arrange a meeting." I know she'll accept. I haven't told Eddie but we've already spoken briefly. She seems nice.

"You got her number? Address?" His bravado is gone. He sounds like an old man again, scared and hopeful.

"Yes, I got it from your info. I'll have a proper chat with her."

Suddenly another thought occurs. It's so simple but I think it'll do the job nicely.

"Eddie, here's a thought. Why don't I turn the camera back on and you can record a message for Lottie? I'll edit it off the rest of the interview and she can watch it when I meet with her. I think that would make a big difference. Hearing it directly from you. I know it would to me. If it was my father, you know?" It's worth a shot. He'll say it better than I would, that's for sure.

He thinks, drumming his fingers lightly on the table. Then he nods.

"Yeah, you're right, let's do that." He's nervous. Bless him, he's actually nervous.

"Okay. I'm going to turn the camera back on now, Eddie. Is that all right?"

He nods, sorts his sweatshirt out, sits up, leans in.

I stop, my finger poised over the record button. "Eddie, can I just check one last thing? You haven't been leaving messages on my home phone, have you?"

"No, love. Not me."

Well, that solves that.

"Oh, okay. Never mind. Right, ready when you are, Eddie."

I turn the camera on.

When I get home I tell Mark what I've done. The deal I've made for us. I know what should be coming; I brace myself for it. I know what I've done is insane, I know it's dangerous, but I trust Eddie, I just do. And now that I know he's not the one calling us and leaving messages, he doesn't seem half so threatening.

But it doesn't come. Mark doesn't shout even though I can see he wants to. He stays calm. He lays it out.

"I know you were just thinking on the spot, and you took your chance while you could, but that's when people make mistakes, Erin. If anyone sees this transaction happening . . . If this Holli thing comes to anything, aren't the intelligence services going to try to find as much CCTV of you as they can? We just need to be more careful. Sure, if this contact Eddie gives us works out, it's fantastic. But if not, there's no recourse if they rob us. There's no getting out of it if DCI Foster is watching and sees any of this."

He's not saying anything I haven't already thought through myself. "But, if Eddie's contact robs us, then we're no worse off, are we? If you want us to get rid of the diamonds, to just throw them out, then at least this way we stand a chance of making something from them? Right?"

He's silent. When he speaks again, his tone is grim. "Erin, Eddie's contact could kill you."

"I know that, Mark, but do you really think that I would have made this deal with someone I genuinely believed would kill me? Give me some credit, please!"

He sighs. "You're not necessarily the best judge of character, honey. You do tend to see the best in people, which isn't always a good thing. I'm just saying we need to be far more careful than you are being. If the police managed to find footage of Holli in some tiny village in Turkey, then they can definitely manage zone one of London. You need to be more careful, honey. They'll see the bank payments into your account from the Swiss account after Holli's missing, they'll see you in Hatton Garden trying to sell diamonds. And then the next week you're back talking to more criminals? For all they know, meeting contacts, paying people off to recruit, maybe, who knows? It won't look great."

He's talking like I've already been caught and sentenced some-how. Like I'm beyond help. He doesn't seem to care about the money at all anymore. I need to explain it to him; he's just not understand-ing.

"I know, Mark. I know all those things. And trust me, I am being as careful as it is possible to be. I know it's terribly risky. I know it's a gamble, but I am doing it for us. For both of us. And, I'm doing it for . . ." I almost say "our baby," almost. But I stop myself. I can't tell him about the baby now, can I? He already thinks I'm reckless. I can't tell him I'm putting his unborn child at risk too.

Am I putting his child at risk? It's the first time I've really thought about it that way. Fuck, maybe I am. I was sure I was doing this for all of us, but now I wonder. Maybe it is all just for me? That thought sucks the air straight out of me. I stand and stare at him. Empty. I feel my eyes fill. His face softens.

What he sees are tears of repentance, tears of remorse. But that's not what these are. These are tears of confusion. My hot tears of confusion because I can't tell anymore why I'm doing any of this.

31

Lottie

I suppose I'm on the wrong side of the table this time.

Sitting across from Charlotte McInroy, in her lovely family kitchen, I wonder what I am now. Less than a month ago I was just an average person, a civilian, someone with no angle. I belonged on the good side of the table, and on the other side were the bad people. Whether they were innately bad or just bad because of the choices they made was a subject of theoretical debate. But either way, they were different from me, different to the core. I was a normal person. Now it's Lottie on the good side of the table.

But was I ever a normal person? Because I really haven't changed that much inside, have I? I think the same way. I act the same way. I want what I want. I have only acted in line with the way I have always lived my life. Was that all wrong? Am I all wrong? I have broken a lot of laws, not serious ones, I hope, but ones that mean I should definitely be in prison. Eddie got seven years just for money laundering; the thought makes me shudder.

Lottie is soft and bright and as smart as you'd expect Eddie Bishop's daughter to be.

We do look similar.

She is the associate specialist emergency medicine doctor at Lewisham's ER. She works long days but she's happy to fit me in. I'm not sure I'd be quite so magnanimous in her place, but she wants to help. She's a good person. She wants to do things the right way. Not like her dad.

I wonder suddenly in what inventive ways Mark and I will mess up our kids. If Mark will even want kids with me when I finally tell him. My hand falls down over my stomach and I leave it there, an extra barrier of skin, flesh, and bone to protect my unborn child from the outside world.

I spoke to Alexa yesterday evening after her IUI appointment. She may well be pregnant by now. She'll have a test in two weeks' time and we should find out. I know I shouldn't have, but I told her about my baby. I somehow got caught up in her excitement and that's when I told her my secret. I had to share it with someone. I'm eight weeks pregnant now. She told me I have to go and see a doctor, take folic acid, not eat soft cheese.

I have been taking folic acid since we got back from Geneva. It's hidden at the back of the bathroom cupboard. But she's right, I should go to the doctor. It's important, Alexa insists. I tell her I'm too busy right now. Stuff has come up. I want to tell her what has come up too, but of course, I don't. I can't.

The rift between Mark and me is growing. I've been pushing him. I don't want the diamonds to break our marriage.

"Are we a team?" he'd whispered to me in bed last night.

And I'd nodded, of course, but he shook his head. "Then I say we dump the diamonds." His voice was tight. "We still have time to back out of this deal. The police might already be watching us, Erin. Who knows, you might be right, the plane people might already be watching us too. And now you want an East End crime syndicate to get involved with us as well. You're being willfully stupid, Erin. You're putting us both in danger. Keep your side of the deal with Eddie, sure, do his favor, but tell him you don't need his help with the diamonds anymore."

He's right about one thing. Someone's definitely watching us, I'm certain of it now. There have been two more silent phone messages this week already, and it's not Eddie. Whether it's something to do with the plane people or SO15, I don't know. But someone is watching. Someone is sending a message.

It's too late to back out of my deal with Eddie now, you can't pull out of these kind of contracts, it doesn't work that way, and Mark will thank me later, I know he will. So here I am. Fulfilling my end of the bargain. And this *will* work.

Eddie's daughter sips her tea thoughtfully as I set up the tripod and camera.

In the shot Lottie is side-lit by the French windows that lead into her wet, autumnal garden. A clean diffused light. Stark, but delicate as filigree.

Through the viewfinder lens, she looks relaxed. At home. A contrast to the tense energy of my prison interviews.

I turn the camera on.

"Lottie, I visited your father last week in Pentonville. He spoke about you very fondly. Were you close, when you were growing up?" I'm going to take it slow. Ease her in. After all, I really have no idea how she feels about him.

She takes a soft breath.

She knew there would be questions, but now that they're here the reality of this interview is finally dawning on her. Big questions require big answers. A steep trudge uphill into the past.

"We were close, Erin. It's hard to say if we were closer than other families. I don't have much to compare it to. People sort of kept away from me at school. I get it now. I've got kids myself and there's no way I'd let them be around people like my dad. But at the time, I thought it was me, that I wasn't quite right. That none of us were, my whole family not quite right. And it definitely made us closer, Dad and I. I was closer to my dad than my mum. Mum was . . . difficult. Always was. I think that's why Dad loved her, though. He liked the challenge. Liked the payoff. He used to say high maintenance means high performance. You know, like a car. Anyway, Mum was tricky. Especially with me. But I was Dad's little angel. He was a good dad. He was. Told me stories. Put me to bed. He was very good to me. So, yes, we were close."

She watches me expectantly, waiting for the next question.

"Did you know much about his work? His life outside of his time with you?"

Interviewees usually need a while to gather their thoughts, to consider what they want to say. But Lottie knows what she wants to say; she's just waiting for the chance to say it.

She looks out at the garden for a microsecond, then back to me.

"Nothing, until I was maybe thirteen. I changed schools. They sent me to private school. Dad was doing well. I guess, before, I thought he was a businessman. Everyone looked up to him, everyone trusted his opinion. He seemed to be everyone's boss. There were always people around the house. Smartly dressed. They had meetings in Dad's living room. Mum and Dad had separate living rooms. That's what it was like, you know?" She looks at me, eyebrows raised.

I nod. I get it. It was a rocky marriage.

Her mother remarried while Eddie was in prison. The family split after the trial, each going their separate ways.

"Yeah, so did I know about Dad?" She refocuses. "I remember the night I finally figured it out. As I said, I was about thirteen; I'd just started at the new school. It was the weekend; there were people around, the usual lot and someone new. They'd gone into Dad's living room together and I'd been in Mum's watching a film. I came out to get more popcorn from the kitchen. It was a big house, you know. I heard a weird noise like crying, but creepy crying, coming from the hall. I assumed the visitors had all gone already and Dad was watching *Saving Private Ryan* or something like that on loud, I don't know. He watched it a lot. He loves Tom Hanks. So I grabbed my popcorn and went into his living room. Dad was there leaning against his desk. Three of his work colleagues were there too. The TV wasn't on. There was another man on the floor in front of him. The man was on his knees. He was kneeling on this plastic sheeting and there was blood pouring from his mouth. He was sobbing. Everyone else in the room was staring at me, standing there frozen in the doorway, but this guy just kept crying like he couldn't stop. Dad didn't look surprised to see me. Just blank. And he still had his overcoat on. That's always stuck with me. He'd kept it on, like he might leave at any moment. Like he wasn't staying. At that point Mum happened to come around the corner, she saw that I'd wandered in on something and grabbed me. Took me upstairs. She was gentle about the whole thing—well, for her. Told me the man I'd seen was a bad man, that Daddy was handling everything. Dad came upstairs about ten minutes later. He asked if I was okay. I hugged him so hard. For ages. Like I was trying to somehow squeeze something back into him. Or out of him. But that's when I knew. That *he* was the bad man. That good people just don't do things like that. Even if someone else is bad. They just don't. After that, I was different with him. Wary, I suppose. I'd like to credit my younger self that he never even noticed the difference in me. I didn't want him to. You know? I still loved him. I wouldn't ever want to hurt him." She stops, her focus snapping back from the past to me.

"Wait—I'm not sure you can use that stuff. I don't want to have to go to court or anything, you know. I don't really know what I saw. It was just . . . enough for me to know." She gives me a tremulous smile.

"It's okay. I need to run a lot of stuff by the lawyers before we release the documentary anyway. I'll flag this for them. If it can't be used for legal reasons, we can easily scrap it. Are you worried about upsetting Eddie?" I prompt.

She lets out a little laugh of surprise. "No, I'm definitely not worried about upsetting Dad. These things happened; if he doesn't like them, that's his problem. I just won't give evidence against him. There's a line. And I won't cross it." She says it calmly. I realize not much in life upsets Lottie. The apple doesn't fall far from the tree. Maybe they have more in common, she and Eddie, than she'd like to believe.

I think now is the time.

"Lottie. What I want to do now, if it's okay with you, is show you a video. It's a message your father made for you during our interview on Saturday. I know it was your choice not to see him over the past seven years, and if you're not comfortable doing this, that's fine. We just won't."

I take it easy. I do want Eddie's help, but I'm not going to be a complete arsehole to get it. If she doesn't want to see him again, that's his problem, not mine.

She nods, slow at first but then faster. She wants it. She wants to see it.

"Okay, if you're sure." I whip out my laptop and slide it onto the table. "I'll load it up for you and we'll just leave the camera rolling if that's okay?" I want the footage of her watching Eddie. I want the reaction. I want people to see it.

I want his favor and I want the footage.

I slide it around to her and she hits play. Her hands fly up to her mouth.

Maybe he looks older? Maybe he looks sadder? Maybe it's the tracksuit or the empty off-white room. Maybe he's thinner, weaker than she remembers. I don't know. But seven years is a long time. I track into her eyes. Transfixed. I hear his words from last week.

He's seen photos of Ben, their wedding.

Her eyes crease. A smile behind her hands.

Ben's a good man, she did well.

He's proud of her job.

262 | Catherine Steadman

She frowns.

He's proud of her choices.

She drops her hands, lets them lie lifeless on the table before her. Rapt.

Then the meat of his message.

He did things he regrets. He will change.

Her eyes fill with tears. She is frozen now. Mesmerized. The tears drip from lash to table.

I'm no longer here in the room for her. Nobody exists but them, father and daughter.

He won't bring that world to her. She'll be safe. Separate.

She wipes her tears away. Sits up. Solemn. Inhales.

He'll be a great granddad.

Nothing.

Sweets all round.

A burst of laughter, gone as quick as a burnt magnesium strip.

He loves her.

Silence. Nothing.

She pushes down the laptop screen until it clicks.

She gives me a tight smile.

"I'll just get some tissues. One second." She exits frame.

Her eyes are still red when she returns, but she's back to her usual self. A bit embarrassed by her display of emotion. I turn the camera back on.

"So how does that make you feel, Lottie? Do you think you could give your father another chance? Let him back into your life once he's out?" Now, I want to know for myself as much as for Eddie.

I don't know what I'd do if I were her. I could speculate, but reality never matches speculation, does it? At least not in the big things.

She smiles. Gives a self-deprecating chuckle.

"Sorry—it's a lot to process. God, I thought I was over all this! I really did. Um, what was the question? Will I let him back in my life? Huh, no. No, I really don't think that's a great idea. I'm sure people will watch this and root for my dad. Root for the underdog. He's a charmer, I should know. But no, no, I won't. And I'll tell you why. Because he's actually killed people, real people. Sorry, alleged, alleged! Don't use that, please. Fuck. Look, he's a convicted criminal. He is unreliable, he is manipulative, he is dangerous, and I have children. Two little children, and a husband I love. And my husband has family, who don't want to meet him either. I love my life. I like it just the way it is. I made it for myself, from scratch. So, don't get me wrong, Erin, I am thankful for my education, the opportunities afforded to me, but I put in the work. I turned up every day, in spite of my family, not because of them."

She looks directly into the lens.

"Dad, I know you'll watch this. So here it is. I love you. I love you so much, but I can't be responsible for you. You made your choices. I'm glad you're proud of me. I'm going to keep making you proud, but I don't want you in my life. Know that and respect that decision." She's finished. She nods at me; that's all she's got. I turn off the camera.

"I know you're thinking that he's a good guy, but you don't really know him, Erin. Trust me. I think it's lovely that you want a happy ending for us all, but things don't work like that. *He* isn't like that. He's careless. He's careless with people. People drop off the radar and to him, that's fine. Well, I don't think that's fine. So I'd rather not. I appreciate the effort, though. I really do. When you see him again, tell him he looks well. He'll like that."

We make more small talk as I gather my bags. I pack away my footage, like gold dust.

I did all I could do. She's not an idiot, and if I'd championed him any more, she'd have realized something was up. I gave her the information, passed along his request, and let her choose. That's all I could do. I just hope that's enough for Eddie.

32

A Man at the Door

The house phone starts ringing the moment I unlock the front door. Mark is out looking at more office rental spaces this afternoon. He should be home in an hour or so; I asked him to come back around three just in case it all went wrong with Lottie.

The phone rings twice before I can reach it, racing across the front room. It could be the silent caller again. It could be Patrick. I might catch him this time.

"Hello, is this Erin?" It's a gruff voice, forties, cockney. It's something to do with Eddie, I know it instantly.

"Uh, yes, yes, speaking." I try to sound professional, as if this might still be a legitimate work call. I really hope Andy Foster isn't monitoring my calls, because if he is, this one could very quickly become incriminating.

"Hello, Erin. My name's Simon. I'm meant to be picking up a package from you, I think?" A second's silence on the line. "Now, I know you're busy but I'm in the area at the moment; would now be a convenient time for you?" He must suspect a phone tap too because he's working around it; he just sounds like a courier. Or at least that's what we can argue in court, if we have to.

"Yes, that would be—now would be fantastic. Five, ten minutes?" I try to mask my relief, my excitement at the prospect of finally being free of the diamonds.

They will be out of our home in less than an hour. It will be finished. The bag, the plane. Only the USB and the phone nestling under the attic insulation left as evidence.

I cradle the phone against my shoulder and hastily jot down the Swiss bank account number on a slip of paper. I've learned it by heart now. There is no paper trace of the number. I burned all the paperwork over a week ago, in the garden in our fire pit. All the relevant information is memorized. The number and the password. On his end, I hear a car engine come to life.

"Right then. Ten minutes it is. See you then." The line goes dead.

He seemed friendly enough, sounded pretty easygoing. I suppose he must know the situation. My favor. Eddie's favor. Our mutual favors.

Hell, who am I kidding; Simon's probably been following me all day, hasn't he? From here to Lottie's and back again. I wonder who else has been following me as I go about my day. SO15, Patrick, and now Simon. They can't all be following me. If one of them found out about the others, the whole house of cards would come tumbling down around me. But Simon must have been tailing me today; how else would he know I just got home? That's why he's *in the area*.

I grimace. I might actually be the world's most naïve criminal. Completely oblivious. I'm lucky I'm not dead yet.

I have less than ten minutes to prepare before he arrives. I stuff the slip of paper with the account number into my trouser pocket.

The stones are up in the attic where I left them after I got them back from Charles. I take the stairs up, two at a time. I need to be ready before Simon gets here. I don't want to have to leave him unattended in the house while I go up to the attic alone. I don't want him wandering around. I can't trust him.

Suddenly a thought occurs. What if this guy isn't connected with Eddie at all?

Or what if he is connected but somehow I've misread Eddie's personality entirely and this situation isn't going to end well for me? Maybe this isn't safe.

I imagine Mark coming home to find my dead body crumpled, like a fleshy rag doll, in the hallway, a single shot to the head, execution-style. Job done.

But that won't happen. My instincts tell me. And if I can't trust my instincts, what can I trust? I'm sure it's fine. I'm sure. I'm sure I'm sure.

Even so, I dash back downstairs and grab my phone. I dial Mark's number.

Three rings in he picks up. He sounds distant, distracted, the background noise muffled.

"Mark?"

"Yeah, what's happening? You okay? How did it go?" He means with Charlotte.

"Um, yeah, really good. Listen, quickly, someone called. Someone called about—" Shit. I suddenly realize I can't say this over the phone, can I? I can't mention the diamonds or Eddie. If Andy's tapped my mobile, then we'll be screwed. *Okay, think. Think fast. Talk around it.*

"Someone, um, wants to collect the honeymoon souvenirs." Is it okay to say that? Sure, it's fine—we bought souvenirs for Mark's folks; if I get them FedExed this afternoon to East Riding, this call is perfectly explainable. God! This is complicated. Being a criminal is mentally exhausting.

On the other end of the line Mark is silent. I imagine he's trying to work out what he can and can't say over the phone too. I'm glad I married someone shrewd.

"Okay, that's great. Can you manage by yourself, honey, or should I come back to help?" He keeps his tone even but I can tell he's worried. He made his feelings about Eddie clear. He doesn't trust Eddie at all.

"No, I'm fine. Everything's great, Mark. I just wanted you to know that was happening now. It's all fine, I can manage. I have to dash now, though, he'll be around here in a minute. Okay?" I want to give Mark a chance to stop me if I'm being stupid. Am I being stupid? Giving a man I don't know a million pounds' worth of diamonds? In my own home, our home?

"Great. Sure, okay. It sounds like you've got it covered, honey. I'll see you a bit later then, all right? I love you?" It's a question. Sometimes it is a question, isn't it? In the question there's a lot of stuff.

"I love you too," I answer. In the answer there's a lot of stuff. And then he's gone.

Shit, I didn't ask how he was. I didn't even ask where he was. It sounded outdoorsy, busy, crowded, maybe a station but—

I really don't have time for this. I race up to the top landing, fumble the loft ladder stick into its hook in the ceiling, and pull.

I find them up in the loft, exactly where I left them, tucked under a loose layer of pastel yellow insulation, in their pouch. Glittering in the cream leather, gently warmed by the heating pipes. I seize them and push the insulation back into place.

As I'm making my way down the ladder, the doorbell rings. I freeze, mid–ladder rung.

A flash of terror, like a shot through my system.

I suddenly wish we still had that gun—the one we dumped in the sea in Bora Bora. Were we stupid not to keep it? Do I need it?

But then, what the hell would I do with a gun? I don't know how to use one. I wouldn't even know if it was loaded or how to do the safety catch or anything.

No, I don't need a gun. This will be fine. I'm being paranoid. It's broad daylight. I continue down the ladder from the loft, jumping the last three rungs and sprinting back down to the hall.

Hot-cheeked, I pull open the front door, grateful for the blast of September wind it lets in. And there stands Simon.

Simon looks harmless. Suit, tie, smile. Not the smile of a predator, just the smile of an iffy friend of your dad's, maybe. A little bit too knowing a smile, but ultimately harmless.

I don't need a gun, of that I'm suddenly sure.

His manner suggests we're both in this together; I'm part of the gang now.

"Simon?" I have to say something; we've been standing in silence for slightly too long now.

"Guilty as charged." He grins. I'm pretty sure he's used that one before. But the inoffensive humor settles me.

"Great." I nod. I really don't know what we do next. "Do you want to come in?" I hazard. From my tone I think it's fairly clear to Simon I have no idea how this situation is usually supposed to go. I'm hoping he'll take the lead quite soon.

"Nah, gotta dash. Thanks though, love. I'll just grab the stuff and get out of your hair, if that's all right?" He's dealing with me beautifully. I appreciate this delicate handling of my obvious ineptitude; in an odd way, it's very reassuring. I hand him the pouch. I'm relieved to be unburdened. That's half the battle. He takes it.

But what about the money? Should I say something? Is that rude? But he beats me to it.

"You got a number for me?" He's one step ahead. He's obviously done this before.

"Yes, yes, here we go." I fish the paper slip out of my pocket and smooth it out on my upper thigh. "Sorry, it's creased. You can still see the numbers, though, can't you?" I pass it to him.

We both stare down at the slip of paper in his hand, very clearly legible through the slight folds. I'm an absolute moron.

"Hmm, yep, yep, that should be fine," he mumbles, over-feigning interest in the rumpled slip. "Right, I should be off then." He weights both hands: a note in one, a million-pound pouch in the other. He grins and turns to leave, then stops.

"One quick question, love. How did it go today? Eddie wants to know."

"Um, I don't think it's going to work out." I say it gently, as if I'm personally heartbroken about the cruel twist of fate. Eddie the re-formed hero denied a second chance with his daughter.

Simon seems confused by my answer.

"Why, what did she do?" He looks at me quizzically.

"Well, she watched it. The video. She cried. She was extremely upset but she was concerned about her children and—"

"Oh, the kids," he interrupts. "Oh well, fair enough." He seems satisfied. I wonder if this was an official inquiry about Lottie or if I've spoken out of turn.

"Don't worry about the kids." Simon's smiling again. Order re-stored. "He can get round all that. Good work, though, sweetheart. She cried, aye? Nice. Very good sign. Eddie's gonna bloody love that. That'll cheer him right up. If she's crying, we're halfway there." He beams at me. Today's going well for him.

"Right, darling, I'm off then. Take care." And with a cheery hand raise, he's away.

"Um, thank you, Simon!" I call after him. I don't know why. I have to say something, don't I? I can't just stand in silence as he strides back toward his black Mercedes with my diamonds in the palm of his hand.

33

Loose Ends

An extremely large bunch of flowers arrives in the morning.

Thanks for your help. Shan't forget it. E. He's got style, I'll give him that. But Mark is less sure.

"It's not exactly covert, is it?" he asks over breakfast. He's worried about police surveillance.

"They're only flowers, Mark. They could be for doing the interview, for all anyone knows. Through a lawyer or something? I'm pretty sure Eddie knows how to cover his tracks at this point in his career. Well, except for the bookkeeping, obviously." I smile. We've done it, after all. Haven't we? The full payment for the diamonds hit the numbered account at midnight last night. Much more than we expected. Certainly a lot more than I thought we'd ever be able to get by ourselves. Two million. Two. Sterling. I literally cannot keep the smile off my face. Ten grand a pop per stone. Eddie barely took a cut. The payment came from another numbered account. Wherever Eddie's money is squirreled away, I guess. Great minds think alike.

Mark's worried.

"I'm sure the gift trail will be well covered from his end, Erin. It's our end I'm worried about. If SO15 is watching you, they'll wonder . . ." He gestures to the massive bouquet. "It's not exactly low-key, is it?" He has a point, I suppose. The flowers look ridiculously ostentatious.

"But can the police really be monitoring me twenty-four hours a day, Mark? Seriously? Why would they? And how would Eddie not know that?"

"Yes. Potentially yes, they could be, Erin, if they think Holli might contact you. If they notice anything strange. They might be watching you in case she tries to call you, or God forbid shows up on our doorstep."

"But, why on earth would she do that, Mark? We weren't exactly close, were we? We met once. I interviewed her for thirty minutes, *once*. I don't think the police think that will happen and I don't think we're being watched by them. At least not to the extent you think. Maybe they're monitoring our home phone, but I really feel like that's something Eddie might have looked into before helping us, something he might have mentioned. He's not an idiot. If SO15 is watching us, I think we'd be aware of it by now. If anything, I feel like Eddie's presence is protecting us from a lot of things right now."

Mark looks distractedly out the window, watching the rain, his thoughts whirring away, silently.

Why isn't Mark happy?

I tentatively touch his arm across the table. "It's done. We have all the bag money. It's safe. With the paper money and the diamonds combined, we have just under three million pounds. Untraceable. Completely secure. We did it, Mark. We actually did it!" I look at him, expectant.

A smile breaks across his face. A small one.

I squeeze his arm.

His smile widens to a grin.

He nods, reaching for his mug of tea. "I'm pleased it worked out, I am. Obviously! But, Erin, you can't do any more stuff like this. You just can't. It's worked out this time, but no more, right? No more risks. We're done now?" He is happy, of course, but I worry him and I can't blame him for not trusting me, really. I have been keeping secrets. And there were definitely a couple of moments there when I thought he might be right, that I might have gone too far. But now the money's in the bank.

"Yes. Yes, I'm done now. I promise. There's nothing more to take risks for." I lean across the table and plant a kiss on his warm lips. I can tell he's not entirely convinced, but he smiles and kisses me back. He wants things the way they were. Hopefully, we can go back to that now. Finally.

But no sooner does that thought settle in than I remember. Those loose ends, up in the attic. A trail of evidence leading all the way back to the bottom of the South Pacific.

It isn't quite over yet.

"But—what should we do with the phone, Mark? The USB? Should we dump them? They're the only link back to us. We need to finish things properly, don't we? We don't want loose ends."

He squeezes his eyes shut as the realization sinks in; we're not quite finished. He'd forgotten them. "Damn. Okay, let's think."

He takes a moment, gazes through the rain-speckled window out into the wet garden. "Maybe we should keep the phone. Just in case. There's no harm in keeping it. And if anything ever happens, we'll have it as evidence of who these people are. Or leverage against them. Not that I'm saying we'll need it but, maybe, just for insurance." He pauses, then shakes his head. "You know what? No. We'll dump it too. Dump it all: the USB and the phone; we need them out of the house. In case, for any reason, the police want to search the house. We need it all out of our lives." His tone is firm. There will be no further discussion of this. And that's okay with me. I'm done now. All done. Three million done.

"Perhaps we can drive up to Norfolk together, right now, stay the night, take out a boat in the morning, and drop them into the sea. Make a day of it, the last loose ends?" I suggest.

His expression doesn't change. I feel a tug of fear.

I continue. "We need to dump them somewhere, right? We could stay up there a few days. It would be nice to get away. To just be together for a while. We need it. I miss you. I miss us."

He gets up and walks around the table and cups my face in his hands. He kisses me on the lips, ever so gently.

"I love that idea. It feels like a long time ago, just you and me, the honeymoon."

I know what he means. Our real honeymoon, before the bag came along, before it turned into something else. All I want right now is just to be near him. I miss my skin on his skin. I miss the closeness.

"If we go up to Norfolk today, then that's it. The phone and the flash drive are the last things, and it's done after we've got rid of them. Finished," I promise. "We can go back to the way we were. But better, because this time we'll never have to worry about money again."

Mark will never have to worry about losing everything ever again. He'll never have to worry about having to work in a bar or stack shelves ever again. Up in Norfolk, I can finally tell him about our baby.

He looks down at me, studying my face; there's a ghost of sadness in his eyes. I suppose he's not convinced I've truly decided to stop being so reckless. Perhaps we can't get back to where we were? I need to prove to him that I am focused on us now, so I press him: "We need the time together, Mark. Please?"

His eyes fill almost imperceptibly and suddenly I realize how much I've pushed him away over the past few weeks. I have very nearly broken this thing we have. This bond needs to be handled with care, nursed back to health. He stoops down again and kisses my forehead. "I know. And as much as I love the idea, honey, I can't go away today. You know that. Remember?"

Oh God, I totally forgot. He told me this last week. He mentioned it. I feel awful. As if I didn't feel awful enough already. He's flying to New York this afternoon, an overnight stay. I wasn't listening properly when he said it, obviously. I wonder what else I've totally missed. I am the worst wife. He's meeting new clients in New York City all day tomorrow and then traveling straight back that evening on the overnight flight. A literal flying visit.

I'll be here alone. I can't help, all of a sudden, feeling frightened that Mark's moving forward with his life without me. It's my fault, of course. I should have shown more interest in his new business instead of spending all my time thinking about the documentary, the money, the diamonds. I should have been present more; I should have been with him. Self-recrimination washes over me. I will have to do better. I will have to be better. It'll all be fine. We can go away the following weekend together. It's not a big deal; it just feels like one now.

I lie on the bed while he packs, watching. He tells me all about the new office spaces he's considering. His big plans.

"Will you come and see them with me next week?" he asks. He's so excited.

"Of course! I can't wait," I assure him. I'm glad he's letting me back in. I'm glad he's this happy again. Maybe the rift is finally starting to close up. "I'm sorry, Mark, if I've been absent. If I haven't been here for you . . . I'm so sorry." I look up at him.

"It's all okay, Erin." His face is alive with the future and everything that's laid out ahead. "You've had a lot on your plate. It's fine. I love you." He holds my gaze and I feel forgiven. I'm a very lucky person. I think again about telling him everything. About the pregnancy. But I don't want to tip the balance. I'll tell him once he's back. When we're alone together next weekend.

"I love you, Mark," I tell him instead, scrambling off the bed and wrapping myself around him. And I mean it with all that I am. My hormones must be doing something crazy inside me right now, because it physically hurts later as his airport taxi pulls away from the curb outside our house. My whole body keens for him. The ghost of his arms around me, the scent of his cologne still clinging to my skin.

After he's gone I make my way up to the loft. To inspect the last remaining evidence.

It's hot in the attic. Under the insulation the phone is toasty warm. The separate envelope containing the USB drive lies next to it. Is the heat of the loft bad for the memory of the phone or drive? I finger the USB through the plastic of the envelope.

It's warm to the touch.

I stare at the phone's inert screen, and remember the text message from two weeks ago. The way it made me feel in my stomach. Those three gray dots, pulsing.

WHO IS THIS?

Again, I wonder who *they* are. The dead people on the plane, the person on the other end of the phone, the plane people. I've tried to ignore this question, to listen to Mark's advice, but here on my own, in the hot, dusty loft, the thought grows stronger. Who are they? I've searched Russian websites, news sites—nothing. Is Patrick one of them? Or is Mark right? Could he be an undercover SO15 officer? Is it him who is calling me and leaving silent messages? The sickening thought flashed through my mind the other day that the calls might be from Holli. Silent, desperate phone messages, from somewhere out there; maybe she's back in England. But then I remember the low mumbled reply to the waiter in the message. And besides, Holli's never even had my phone number, so it can't be her.

My mind gravitates back to the plane people. Could it be them? Mark was certain it wasn't. But maybe they found the hotel's IP address? Maybe they went there? Maybe they killed the Sharpes—but would they have stopped looking after that?

For how long would they have kept looking? What were the bag and its contents worth to them? And then it hits me with stunning clarity. They're *still* looking. And I'm alone now. I think of Mark's face as he drove away in the taxi. They might still be out there, searching for us. Maybe they realized they killed the wrong couple. And now here I am, alone in the house. I've been so concerned with keeping ahead of the police, of converting what we found into real money, that I've completely forgotten about the reality of being found by the people we stole from. The reality of a knock at the door, a shot to the head.

I think of the open back door, six days ago. It's just me here now, alone. And I don't want to die. I need to find out what I'm dealing with. I need to find out who might be coming for me. And with that I take their phone downstairs, slip on my coat, and leave the house.

It's time to turn it on again. Somewhere safe. Somewhere busy.

When I get to Leicester Square I weave through and around the crowds and head for the garden at its center. I find a group of foreign exchange students talking on and playing with their phones while they eat their lunches on the grass. I stand as close as acceptable and only then do I turn the phone on. It struggles back to life, slowly. The screen flashes white. The Apple symbol. Then the home screen. I don't even attempt to put it on airplane mode. I let it find signal. And it does. The signal bars fill to five.

You see, my thinking is this: Leicester Square is the busiest pedestrianized thoroughfare in Europe. I Googled it on my own phone, before I turned it off, outside our underground station. More people move through Leicester Square in a day than anywhere else in Europe. On average 250,000 a day. As I enter the garden area it's full of people on their phones, weaving past one another deep in conversation or heads down, tapping away and surfing. There are 109 CCTV cameras in Leicester Square, but I challenge anyone to guess which person is on which phone. There are fuckloads of us. I'm hiding in plain sight. Let them find the signal; it won't help them.

The screen flares to life. Text messages ping up on the phone. Two messages.

THE OFFER STILL STANDS

CONTACT ME

From the same number as before. The number that knows someone has the bag.

But I don't understand what the message means. What offer? I scroll up for more but I see only the old messages I read in Bora Bora. Then I notice a small red circle over the call icon. I check the missed call log. There have been two missed calls from the same number since we have been in possession of the bag, since I sent that ridiculous text message in Bora Bora. Two missed calls . . . and one voicemail.

I sit down on a bench, hit the voicemail icon, and lift the phone to my ear.

The first voice I hear is the voice of the network carrier's automated system. It's female, but in a language I don't understand. Eastern European? Russian. Then silence, followed by a long beep.

It connects. I hear the closed-in silence of a room, someone waiting close to the receiver to speak.

Then the voice comes thick and calm. It's male. The language is English but with an accent that's hard to distinguish.

"You received the previous message. The offer stands. Contact us."

The message ends. I have no idea what it's referring to. What previous message? What offer? The system voice prattles on in Russian. And then the man's voice returns. A saved message. The previous message.

"You have something that belongs to us. We would like it returned."

I feel my breath catch in my throat.

"I'm not sure how you came into contact with it. It's not important at this stage but it will be in your interests to return it to us," he says.

It suddenly occurs to me that someone has already listened to this voicemail; that's why it didn't show up as new. Someone has heard it. I think of our back door standing ajar, I think of Patrick's cold hand in my warm one, I think of SO15, I think of Simon and Eddie. Has someone been in our attic? Who? But then I realize there's only really one other person who could have listened to this. Because why would the man on the phone right now, if he really was searching for us, break into our house and listen to his own message? And if it was DCI Foster and SO15, why would they not have immediately seized everything they found as evidence? And if it had been someone to do with Eddie who heard this, then why would Eddie still have paid us two million pounds if he could have just taken everything? The truth—the truth is that no one else has been in our attic. Which must mean that I'm not the only one who's been keeping secrets. Mark has already listened to this voicemail.

"We will reimburse you. A finder's fee for your troubles."

I glance around the square, heart pounding through my chest. It's crazy, I know, but all at once I'm certain that someone is watching me again. I scan the faces in the crowd, but no one seems interested in me, no one is looking. I suddenly feel utterly alone, alone in a sea of strangers. I snap back to the voice.

"If you have the flash drive, contact me. On this number. The offer is two million euros."

Euros. That means he's in Europe, right? Or he knows we are. Does he know we're in the UK? He'll have traced this phone's signal whenever Mark last accessed it. He'll know we're in London by now.

"The amount is nonnegotiable. If you can supply this, we will make the exchange. We are not interested in pursuing you; we require only the USB. Whether you choose to assist us in retrieving it or not, however, is up to you. Contact me."

The message ends.

The flash drive? I had completely forgotten about the USB. No mention of the bag money? No mention of the diamonds. They just want the USB? More than the diamonds, more than the money. What the fuck is on the USB? I can't catch my breath. Do I even want to know? Holy shit.

I turn off the phone. Just in case. You never know.

Why didn't Mark tell me about this? Why did he turn the phone on in the first place? And where did he turn it on? Of course, he's far more cautious than I am. He'd have gone to a crowded area too. He's a clever guy. But why? Why look? And then I realize. He too was worried about them coming for us. Of course he was worried. After the Sharpes' accident, he felt responsible, in a way, for what happened to them. He knew that it was deliberate and it scared him. So he pretended, for me. Mark's very convincing when he wants to be. So he checked the phone. He checked to see if they were still looking for us. And they were and he kept it to himself. To protect me. To keep me from being terrified. The guilt makes my chest ache. I can't believe Mark's been going through all of this alone. And with me running around so recklessly.

But then I realize that's probably why he didn't tell me, isn't it? He wanted to stop me finding out about this offer. He knew I'd want to do it, to make the exchange, and now that I think about it, yes, yes, I do want to do it. Because if we can play it right, if we can just play this last situation right, we'll win it all. We can't stop now anyway; it's not safe to stop. If we don't give them back what they want, they'll never stop looking for us.

And I know Mark didn't tell me about the voicemail because it's clearly a stupid idea. And I know it's stupid because they don't really know where we are or they'd have just taken the USB already. And it's stupid because we don't need any more money. And I'm stupid because I have been driving this whole thing from the very beginning, and now that I've heard this voice message all I want in the whole world is to make that deal. They might not know where we are now, but they will keep looking and I want them to stop. And I want that extra two million euros.

Mark knows me so well, better than I know myself, and that is why he didn't tell me. Because he knows I will definitely do something reckless.

What did they say in the message? *"We are not interested in pursuing you; we require only the USB. Whether you choose to assist us in retrieving it or not, however, is up to you."* Is that a threat? Not exactly. A warning: they don't want *us;* they just want their memory stick. But if we make that hard for them, then maybe it becomes a threat.

Wait, wait, wait. Two million euros? What the actual fuck is on that USB? And that is the question that propels me as I sprint out of Leicester Square and toward our attic back in North London.

34

A Damsel in Distress

I lift the insulation, pull out the warm envelope, and open it.

There is no USB. It's not there. The stubby object I felt through the plastic earlier is just the long-empty casing. The USB itself is gone from inside it. Gone.

I stare, bewildered. What does it mean? I stand in the attic, winded by the run from the tube station, sweat rolling down my skin, gasping for breath. Where has it gone? Have they already come for it? No, they can't have. They'd have taken the phone too. They'd have done something to us. I remind myself that no one else has been in the house but Mark and me. It must be Mark. What has he done? Has he thrown it out? Has he hidden it elsewhere? In case I listened to the message and tried to find it? What has he done with it? I turn on my own phone and check the time. He'll be on his flight now. I can't reach him. I feel another wave of nausea and slump down on one of the attic beams. I should take it easy. Less running.

I look down at the screen of my phone again. I'll text him.

> I heard the voicemails!
> Why didn't you tell me?
> Where is it?

I stare down at the message, thumb posed over send. No—this isn't right. Too furious. Too panicked. He must have a pretty serious reason why he hasn't told me—and I haven't told him a lot of things too. I delete the message. And type instead . . .

> Mark call me when you land.
> I love you xxx

I press send. That's better. He can explain later. He'll have hidden the USB in case I try to do something stupid. I think about where it could be. I wonder if he knows what's on it. I want to know what's on it. It'll be in the house somewhere. It has to be.

I start in the bedroom. I try all his usual hiding places. We've lived together for four years now and I'm pretty sure I know them all. I check his bedside drawer, the small combination box inside it. The code is his birthday, but there's nothing inside apart from some foreign currency. I peer under his side of the mattress—he once hid some Patti Smith concert tickets there for my birthday—nothing. I fish through the pockets of his grandfather's overcoat in the wardrobe, old shoeboxes in the top cupboard.

Then I move to the bathroom, an aftershave box at the back of the bathroom cabinet, his desk, his old briefcase—nothing, nothing, nothing. He's hidden it well. Or maybe he's taken it with him. Maybe he doesn't trust me at all. But I know he wouldn't have taken the

USB with him; if there's a chance he might lose it, he wouldn't take it. If he's hidden it from me, it'll be here—somewhere in this house.

And that's when I get angry. I turn the house upside down. I search every inch. I pull out everything. I empty full bags of rice, I strip beds, I check the linings of curtains and bags.

Nothing.

I stand sweating and disheveled in a house torn apart. I'm dizzy and nauseous. This is not me taking it easy. I need to raise my blood sugar, right now, if not for me then for what's trying to grow inside me. I plonk down where I am in the middle of the living room and drag a Liberty of London bag full of wedding gifts toward me. I fish down to the bottom and grab a tin of truffles. Rose champagne truffles. They'll do. I prize off the lid and dig in. And then I find it. Just like that. Nestled on the bottom deck of the truffle box. *Fuck, Mark. What are you playing at?*

Exhausted, I eat my truffles in triumphant silence. The USB as company. The daylight fading around me.

At some point in the darkness my phone starts to bleat. I fumble it out from under the detritus of my search. It's Mark. He must have landed.

"Hello?"

"Hi, honey? Is everything okay?" He sounds worried. Could he know I found it?

"Mark. Why did you hide it?" There's no point beating around the bush. I'm drained. I'm hurt.

"Hide what? What are you talking about?" He sounds amused. I can hear bustle in the background behind him. He's on the other side of the world.

"Mark, I found the USB. Why did you lie? Why did you hide it? Why didn't you tell me about the messages?" I can feel my eyes welling. But I will not cry.

"Ah, right . . . I was wondering when this might come up. You found it? Have you looked at what's on it?"

"Yes. No. I only just found it." I stare at it in the half-light, sitting innocently in the palm of my hand: a mystery.

"I'm sorry, Erin, honey, but I know you too well. I listened to the message. I had to after what happened to the Sharpes. In the voicemail he said he wanted just the flash drive, nothing else. I needed to see what was on it, why it meant so much to him. So I looked and, Erin, what I saw really worried me. All of it scared me. I just wanted to protect you. But I knew that sooner or later you'd look too, and if you heard that voicemail you wouldn't be able to not look at the USB. So I hid it." He gives me a second to process what he's said. "But obviously not well enough," he jokes, and laughs. He's struggling to lighten the mood.

"Erin. I'm sorry, but will you promise me you won't look on it, honey? Please. Just leave it alone until I get back. Can you promise me that?" I've never heard his voice sound so serious, so worried. "Promise me. Just put it back where you found it, honey. And once I'm back we'll burn it together. Don't do anything. We'll put the phone and the USB in the fire pit and together we'll watch them burn. Okay?" he says soothingly.

God, he really does know me so well.

"All right," I whisper. I feel sad and I'm not sure why. Maybe because I can't be trusted. "I love you, Mark."

"Great. Listen, Erin—I'm sorry. I didn't know what else to do. Maybe I should have told you?"

No, he was right. I would have done all those things.

"No, you did the right thing and I love you," I say again.

"I love you too, honey. Call me if you need anything."

"Love you." And then he's gone.

I'm broken, confused, and incredibly thirsty. I pour myself a tall glass of ice water from the fridge door. I stare at our beautiful kitchen. The handmade work surfaces, the integrated wine refrigerator, the slate tile floor, radiating underfloor heating up through my socks. I look at our kitchen decimated by my crazed search, pots and pans, packets of food, and cleaning products scattered everywhere. And there among it all is my laptop. I don't stop to think; I stumble across to it and I flip the lid on the computer, pull the USB out of its wrapping and slide it into the port.

A new device icon flashes up on my desktop. I double-click. A window opens. Files. I click on the first. It opens. Text.

Encrypted. Pages and pages of encrypted text. Files on files of encrypted text. Nonsense stares back at me. I don't know what it says. I don't even know what it *is*.

I don't understand it, I can't make it work, and it terrifies me. Perhaps Mark knows what it means? Perhaps it's a banking thing? A numbers thing? But why then warn me away? I don't know what I'm looking at. But my breath is shallow now because even I can tell that this is important. Even I can see that. We shouldn't have this USB. It's not for people like us. And I can't tell Mark I looked. Now I know with crystal clarity that I am completely out of my depth.

Who are they? And what is this? Is this what they killed the Sharpes for? Why is it so important to them? Why aren't they concerned about the money or the diamonds? Why is this worth two million euros?

Are we going to die for this?

I need to think. I eject the drive and place it carefully back into its plastic. *Breathe, Erin. Think.*

Okay. What should I do?

First of all, I really need to know what is on this USB. If I can find out, I'll know the kind of people I'm dealing with. I remember the emails I saw in Bora Bora. The shell companies. The papers floating in the water. Who are these people? What are they capable of? How much danger are we in? If somehow I can get these files unencrypted, I'll know. If it's something awful, maybe I should go to the police? Maybe I should go now? But I want to know. I need to know what this is.

I haven't the faintest idea how to decrypt files. But I think I might know someone who does. I stuff the USB into my pocket, grab my coat. Eddie's mobile number is scrawled on the back of the card that came with his bouquet this morning. I, Erin Roberts, have direct access to Eddie Bishop's illegal prison burner phone. And what's the point of having contacts if you're not going to use them? I pluck the card from the flowers as I pass them in the hall and dash out of the house.

There's a smashed-up phone box on Lordship Road. I've driven by it enough times to wonder (a) why no one ever sweeps up or repairs the broken glass and (b) who on earth uses the terrifying-looking thing. Well, I realize as I stride purposely down the long stretch of suburban road toward it, today that lucky someone is me.

I honestly can't remember the last time I used a pay phone. Maybe school? Calling home with my ten-pence pieces lined up along the shelf in the booth.

When I reach the phone box, it's worse than I remembered. The booth is a hollow plastic cage carpeted with milky shards of glass, and clumps of weeds have burst through the cracked tarmac. There are spiders suspended from the empty windowpanes, slow and befuddled in the wet air. At least the open air diffuses the stale stench of piss.

I rattle my coat for change. A fat two-pound coin hits my palm. Perfect. I dial Eddie's number.

When he answers he's chewing something. I look at my watch: 1:18, lunchtime. Oops.

"Hi, Eddie, sorry to bother you. It's Erin. I got this number from the flowers; I'm on a pay phone, so . . ." I think that means we can talk safely but what do I know; he'll be the judge of that.

"Oh, right. Hello, darling. You all right, sweetheart? Problems?" He's stopped chewing. Somewhere in Pentonville I hear Eddie wipe his mouth with a paper napkin. Do the guards know about Eddie's burner phone? I wouldn't be surprised if they did and they just looked the other way.

"Um, no, no problems really. But I've got a question. I don't know if you'd know—or if you know someone else who might know—but . . ." I stop. "Can I talk on this?" I don't want to incriminate myself. I don't want to make things worse.

"Uh, yeah, should be fine, sweetheart. Anyone near you? Watching you? Street cameras?"

I scan the tops of lampposts along the residential street, my breath catching in my throat. I chose this road because it's the emptiest road near us, hardly any passersby, but now I start to wonder: do all London streets have CCTV in some form? But the angled cameras or small circular pods I'm searching for are nowhere to be seen here.

I think we're safe. "No people, no cameras," I say into the receiver.

"Then it's fine." I hear a smile in his voice. I've caught his interest.

"I'm sorry to bother you again, it's just I've got a slight, well—a situation. Um, do you know anything about file encryption, Eddie? Do you know anyone I could talk to about it? It's important." I need to mask the urgency in my voice. I don't want to scare him off. I don't want to seem overly familiar either. At the end of the day, I'm asking for another favor and this time I really have nothing to give in exchange for it.

"Computer stuff, right? Yeah, we've got a guy. Here, look, tell me the gist and I'll give my guy a ring and we'll go from there. You like those flowers, by the way, sweetheart? I asked 'em for something nice and tasteful but you never know with those places, do you?" Eddie's a very sweet man. I think of my monstrous bouquet back in the hall. Under different circumstances I think Eddie and I would have really gotten along.

"Sorry, Eddie. Yes, yes, I did. They were gorgeous, very tasteful, thank you so much. I'm just glad I could help out."

"You did, sweetheart, you did. My daughter means the world to me. Now, what's the problem then?"

"Okay, so, I've got an encrypted USB. In a nutshell, I'm not really sure what I'm dealing with here. I need to know what's on that stick." I lay it out for him. A problem shared . . .

Eddie clears his throat.

"Where did you get it?" His tone has turned serious.

"I can't say. I'm not sure who exactly I'm dealing with. I need to know what's on the USB in order to know what I need to do now."

"Listen, Erin, I'm going to stop you there, sweetheart. You *don't* need to know anything. So, do everyone a favor and drop that idea. If that thing belongs to someone else and they've gone to all the trouble of encrypting it, you don't need to know what's on it. Because it's bad, it's bad stuff they don't want people reading." Did Mark read it? I wonder. I think of the pages and pages of scrambled text. Could Mark have figured out what they meant? Does he already know too much?

Eddie continues: "My gut says you copy what you've got. I'm guessing you'll be handing the original on? Exchanging?"

"Umm . . . yes. Yes, I will." I hadn't thought that far ahead. For a second, I feel so much relief I'm dizzy. Calling Eddie was the right thing to do. He knows how to deal with these kind of people.

"Right, well . . . You exchange one-on-one. You take backup in case they don't want to play nice. You do *exactly* what they say. And don't hand anything over until you've got the money. You made that mistake the other day with Simon; I heard all about it. It's very endearing, sweetheart, but it's not the way things get done. You exchange *after* the money's gone into your account, not before. You understand?" The question hangs on the line between us.

"Yes, yes. Thank you, Eddie," I say. It feels weird being this honest with a criminal. I can tell him more than I'd ever tell Mark. I know he's right. I should just take the offer. Make sure I cover all my bases and go for it. It's what Eddie would do.

"Do you need anyone to help you with the handover? I could get Simon round to help out?" he asks, his voice soft now. I feel like this is personal. Eddie's worried about me.

"Um, I think I've got it covered, Eddie. But can I let you know?" I'm aware I sound fragile. A damsel in distress. I'd like to say it's a deliberate manipulative move to garner assistance, but it's not. As I've said, I'm just way out of my depth. But I can't let Simon and Eddie help me. I can't take on more than one front at a time. I don't know if I can trust Eddie and his gang with this. He's a criminal, at the end of the day. I understand the irony of that statement, but you know what I mean. I need to figure this out myself first, alone.

"Okay, sweetheart. Well, you know where I am if you need me."

"Oh, Eddie, do you know where I could get, um, you know, er, protection?" That's probably the least persuasive request for a firearm ever uttered, but I think I might definitely need it now.

He's silent for a second.

"You know how to use one?" he asks, businesslike.

"Yes," I lie. "Yes, I do."

"Well, well, I said you were full of surprises. Not a problem, sweetheart. Simon will drop what you need round tonight. Look after yourself, sweetheart. Stay safe. You need to talk again, next time you call use a different box, different area. No more Lordship Road. Mix it up."

How does he know where I'm calling from? For an instant, I feel sick. "I will. Thanks, Eddie. Really appreciate it."

"All right, love. Ta-ta." The line goes dead.

I'm going to end this situation. I'm going to end it for both of us, Mark and me. We can't hide from what's coming. Mark doesn't know what he's doing. We can't just squirrel the USB away in chocolate boxes and hope for the best. We need to finish what we have started and properly, because now I'm absolutely certain that they won't stop until they have the USB. We've turned the phone on two times now; they must know we're in London. Now it's just a question of when and where we meet. And on whose terms.

I think of the Sharpes: of their fate. Those last desperate gasping breaths of seawater, and then—nothing. But the difference between the Sharpes and me is that the Sharpes weren't expecting what happened to them, they weren't prepared, they panicked. They didn't stand a chance. But I do.

I head to St. Pancras Station and in the crowd below the giant clock I turn on the phone. Passengers spill from the Eurostar through the glass in front of me. I tap on messages, tap on the text box of the most recent message, and write:

I HAVE FLASH DRIVE.

HAPPY TO EXCHANGE.

MEETING INSTRUCTIONS TO FOLLOW.

I tap send, turn off the phone, and slip it into my coat pocket. Now I just need somewhere to meet.

At home I spend the night trawling YouTube videos to prepare. If there's one thing I'm good at, it's doing my research, and it never ceases to amaze me what you can learn off the Internet. I watch videos on handgun assembly, specifically Glock 22 assembly and disassembly.

Simon dropped off a Glock 22 with two boxes of bullets two hours ago; I made him a cup of tea, and he left with the cup.

I've been watching the videos ever since: Glock cleaning, how to handle a handgun, Glock safety features, how to shoot a handgun, how to make your handgun safe pre- and post-usage. And two hours in, I'm happy to say that it is about as hard to take apart a handgun and reassemble it as it is to change a Brita water filter. If you're interested.

Apparently WD-40 is an acceptable substitute for gun oil as long as you intend to re-lube and clean after a three- to four-day period. My gun only needs to work for one day and I'm hoping that it doesn't actually need to work at all. I can't risk going into a Holland & Holland in Piccadilly tomorrow morning and buying gun oil. Just in case. Just in case SO15 is watching. Or Patrick. Or someone else entirely.

I miss another call from Phil. He's already rung twice today to argue with me about why I'm dropping the Holli stuff. He's been fuming since I told him and I've got the voicemails to prove it. I still haven't called him back. He can wait. Everyone can wait.

Glock 22s are absurdly easy to use. Not many buttons. Not much you can fuck up. The thing about a Glock is it doesn't have a safety catch. You know that bit in films when the heroine finally needs to use her gun and she raises it to the looming bad guy, squeezes the trigger, and *click* . . . nothing? The safety's on. Well, that won't happen with a Glock. With a Glock, his head explodes. If the magazine is in and it's cocked, that's it. Point and shoot. And it'll only fire if a finger pulls the trigger. You can drop it, or snag the trigger, or shove it in your waistband, whatever, it won't go off. The double-trigger system means your finger has to go into the trigger bed and pull all the way back. That's the only way a Glock fires. But if you grab the gun out of that waistband and accidentally touch that trigger bed on the way, you'll almost certainly never have kids. No safety means no safety.

My mobile bursts to life again. This time it's Nancy, Fred's wife. Goddamn it. I forgot to thank her for watching the house for us while we were on honeymoon, and for the food she left us. I haven't got back to Fred either about the footage. They're probably worried. Mark is right: I am forgetful. I let it go to voicemail.

If you ever find a Glock, you'll know it's a Glock because of the logo on the bottom right of the handgrip. A big "G," little "lock" written inside it. If you find one, then here's what you do: First, keeping your hand away from the trigger, pick up the gun. There should be a small button right by your thumb on the grip. That's the magazine release. Place your other hand under the butt and push the thumb button. The magazine will pop out of the butt and into your hand. If the magazine is full, you'll see a bullet at the top of the magazine. Now pop that magazine down somewhere safe. Next you need to check/empty the chamber. In other words, see if there's a bullet in there and if there is, eject it. You do this by pulling the top section of the barrel backward away from the tip of the gun. The little window should open up on the top of the gun as you cock back. If there's a bullet, it should pop safely up and out of the top as you cock. Cock back again to double-check the chamber is clear. Now your gun is safe. Then, to load it, pop that bullet into the top of the magazine you set aside. Slide the whole magazine back into the butt of the gun until it clicks, cock it again, point, and shoot. Practice that routine about twenty times and you'll be as convincing as any actor in *Full Metal Jacket*. Besides, it keeps your thoughts from buzzing around the reasons you may need the gun in the first place.

Mark calls before bed to check on me. It's the one call I do take.

"Yeah, I'm fine. Just watching stuff on the computer." Technically true.

"How are you feeling?" he probes. He doesn't want to push it but he's still uneasy, I can tell.

"I'm fine, honey, seriously. Don't worry about me. I'm absolutely fine."

I tell him I love him and he tells me he loves me too.

When I feel confident enough with the gun, I clean it thoroughly again and apply silver duct tape from Mark's toolbox to the gun handle. The checked grip sections on gun butts can't retain prints but the smooth areas at the front and back can. The Internet tells me that it will be easier to pull duct tape off after firing than it would be to wipe the gun down after an altercation. I know myself well enough to know I won't be thinking straight after that happens. If that happens. The tape will help.

I leave Mark a note on the stairs in the hallway. He'll get back from New York tomorrow night and I won't be here. The note says I love him with all my heart, I'm sorry about the mess, I didn't want to stay in the house alone, and I'll be sleeping over at Caro's that night. Not to worry. I'll see him soon.

I start to gather what I'll need from the shambles that is our home. I download a GPS coordinate location app onto my phone; I'll need it to find the coordinates of the meeting location. I fill a rucksack with the gun, bullets, phone, and USB. I pack a change of clothes. Toiletries. An old yellow travel alarm clock I've had since I was a kid, my hiking clothes and boots, and a flashlight. As I wander the house gathering these items, I wonder at what stage all of this started. If I could wind it back, how far back would I have to wind? To before I turned on the phone? To before we opened the bag? To the circle of floating papers? To the wedding? To the day Mark called me from the men's loo? Would that be far enough?

35

Point and Squeeze

At 7 A.M. I pack the car and go. The road to Norfolk is nearly empty, the soft mumble of Radio 4 filling the car as I work things through in my head. Norfolk, I figure, is my safest bet. It's isolated. There's no real police presence. I know my way through those woods. And there's no CCTV. No one will be watching me. If someone follows me, I'm sure I'll know it. I pull over on the hard shoulder of the motorway and text the number again from the phone. I specify only a time for tomorrow and general location. I will send more detailed GPS coordinates on the morning of the meeting.

| | |

Mark's not leaving from New York until this evening and he won't get back to our house until after midnight tonight. I try not to picture his face, his eyes when he sees me tomorrow morning, when I finally get home, after this is over. He'll know I've been lying to him. He'll know I wasn't at Caro's; he's not an idiot. And I'll have to tell him everything. I promise myself that once this is all over I'll be honest; I'll never lie again. I'll be the best wife in the world. I promise.

I've booked a hotel room. It's not the same hotel we stayed in before; it's one I've never been to. I plan to stay just one night. I've set the meeting time for six tomorrow morning and they've confirmed. I also received a new voicemail. The same male voice as before. He wants me to hand over the coordinates for the downed plane tomorrow too. That's part of the deal now. Luckily, I have that information.

They'll be able to get here by the meeting time tomorrow, wherever they are. A private jet flight from most places in the world would only take a few hours, not days. Russia is a four-hour flight. They have more than enough time to get here, wherever they're coming from.

I've chosen an isolated area to meet, in the woods, and I've chosen 6 A.M. because the earlier the better. I don't want any interruptions; I'll have enough to worry about as it is. My backpack lies across the back seat of the car, my thick coat draped protectively over it. Inside, a small bag of emergency food and a bottle of water. It's cold out and there's a lot to be done today. The memory stick is nestled in the rucksack's front zip pocket, safe, easy to access. In the internal computer compartment of the rucksack, the gun waits in its case, next to the bullets and the phone. Everything I need for tomorrow.

I get to the hotel at 10 A.M. I have no more voicemails. Check-in runs smoothly. The receptionist is sweet but this is obviously a gap-year job. She's totally uninterested, which works out perfectly for me with the hours I'll be keeping.

My room is small and cozy. The bed is a thick, deep nest of crisp cotton sheets and down feathers. There's a gleaming copper tub in the bathroom. Very nice. Perfect.

I double-check I have the flash drive and gun, slip on my thick outdoor coat, pull on my backpack, and head out. I'm going to walk the route for tomorrow's meeting.

According to my own phone's GPS, I can get the whole way to the woods without using any roads. That's the safest option, if I stick to the fields and woods.

It takes me an hour at a brisk walking pace to reach the woodland area I'm after. I'll need to make a note of two sets of GPS coordinates on my phone for the exchange. I'll send the first one, the meeting point, once I've set off tomorrow. It would be silly to give them extra time to look around before we meet in the morning. The second set of coordinates is for the exact location of the USB. I'm going to bury the USB today near the meeting point. Once they give me the money, once it hits our Swiss account, I'll text them the second set of coordinates, just like Eddie said. This way I'll avoid a direct face-to-face confrontation. After that I will finally text them the plane coordinates, and then we're done.

I chose this area because I know it's isolated. Mark and I have hiked through these woods enough times. You can walk half the day without ever coming across another person. The only noises this far from the village are the sounds of things scuttling in the undergrowth and the distant crack of rifle shots carried on the wind. No one thinks twice about gunshots out here. It's part of everyday life. Another reason I chose this spot.

I'm deep in the woods, about twenty minutes' walk to the nearest B road. I shrug off the backpack and carefully remove the gun box. I take an A4 sheet of paper out of the back section of the bag—the hotel welcome letter—and a thumbtack that I pocketed from the tourist information board in the hotel lobby. I pin the sheet of paper to the widest tree in the clearing.

I need to practice. I need to at least fire the bloody thing before I point it at a person.

Eddie mentioned backup. *Don't do it without backup.* Well, this is my backup.

I have one magazine preloaded with fifteen bullets, plus another fresh pack in a little cardboard box. That makes twenty-seven bullets. Simon didn't scrimp on bullets, thank God. Perhaps he guessed I'd need the practice.

I'll need a full mag for the meeting. In case I do actually need to use the gun.

So here's a math problem for you: if Erin wants to keep a mags' worth of ammo, for tomorrow, how much ammo can Erin use today?

Erin can use twelve bullets today. Twelve practice shots to work with. I carefully remove three bullets from my full mag and place them safely with the fresh twelve-pack in the pocket of my rucksack.

Hopefully, I won't need to put this practice session in use at all tomorrow, but I'd rather be over-prepared than under.

I slide the mag back in, hold the gun out in front of me, arms extended, the gun leveled in front of my dominant eye. I line up the white dot and the box that make up the Glock's sights with the paper target on the tree ahead.

I've been warned in the videos about the kickback on Glocks, but the stance you're supposed to adopt to counteract it isn't what you'd expect. Not like you've seen on TV. Not like you've seen in films. You stand straight on, not to the side, not like a sidestepping, flashlight-carrying FBI cadet. Your feet need to be hip-width apart, knees soft. My right hand on the grip, my trigger finger along the barrel, safely away from the trigger, my left hand held high, bracing the right on the grip, shoulders forward, elbows locked. You might not look cool but you will hit what you're aiming for. At least that's the idea. . . .

298 I Catherine Steadman

I breathe. Slow in. Slow out. It will be loud. So much louder than you'd expect. It will kick, buck back against you like a punch. But you need to stay solid, give slightly but hold your ground.

I inhale deeply. Slide my finger into the trigger well. Exhale and pull.

The crack rips through the woods around me. The gun kicks back like a grown man slamming into me. My heart explodes with adrenaline, my eyes are dazzled. Astonishingly, I hold my position. I am fine. Ahead of me I see the very edge of the paper shredded, a large clump of bark splintered upward at a crazy angle. I got it. If that were a man, I'd have got him. An odd flush of joy. I shake it off and focus. I realign.

And then I pull the trigger eleven more times.

By the end of the afternoon there is no paper left and the tree is a mess. I decide perhaps I'll walk a little farther before I note down a GPS location. I definitely don't want them to see this tree. I find a good spot another five minutes in, a small muddy clearing. I jot down the GPS coordinates from the app into my iPhone notes. Then I try to find another location where I'll actually bury the USB in a plastic bag. I choose a distinctive oak tree, away from the clearing, near a ditch. I should be safe to hide there unseen tomorrow. I squat down by the oak and dig a small hole in the topsoil with my bare hands; I place the USB in its little plastic bag in the ground and cover it over with soil and leaves, blending it back into the forest floor. I note the coordinates of where it's buried on my iPhone. And then I head back to the hotel.

In my hotel room I lay everything out for tomorrow. I test my travel alarm clock a couple of times, and miraculously, it still works. I set it for 4:30 A.M. and place it on the nightstand next to the hotel's ornate bedside lamp. I place the gun and remaining ammo in the safe.

After ordering room service, I ring Mark's mobile but it runs straight to voicemail.

"Hi, Mark, it's me. I guess you've already taken off but I just wanted you to know everything is fine. I'm fine. I miss you. I love you. Um, listen, the house is an absolute tip, by the way. Just to warn you. I'll tidy it tomorrow. Safe flight. Love you. See you soon. Can't wait." I hang up. When he gets home he'll get my note on the stairs saying I'm staying over at Caro's tonight. I hope this all works. I really do.

My food comes and I eat in silence. No TV or music for company. I think of Eddie and Lottie, of Holli and her friend Ash out there somewhere, who knows where. I think of Mark in his plane high over the Atlantic, of the people in their plane deep under the South Pacific. I think of Alexa and her potential pregnancy. How happy she must be. I think of what I am carrying inside myself. I'm in a kind of daze but I force myself to eat, for what's growing there. I need to look after us both better. With that in mind, after dinner I run a hot bubble bath in the roll-top tub and lower myself slowly into its soft warmth. I let the heat soak in and I let my mind wander as I stare absentmindedly at the etched frosted-glass section of the bathroom door: entwined climbing flowers and engraved wild birds, a forest scene. It's pretty. This is a lovely hotel. Mark would like it here. Or maybe he wouldn't. After all, right now I'm doing the exact thing I absolutely promised him I would not do. And with that thought I rise red-skinned from the water, towel myself off, and prepare to get an early night.

36

Something in the Dark

My eyes shoot open in the darkness. I can't see anything in the thick black except the dull glow of the alarm clock's luminous hands. I don't know what's woken me but it was sudden. Now, I am wide-awake. Something is not right in the darkness. There's some-one in the room with me, I can feel it. I'm not sure how long I've been asleep, but light is no longer spilling from the edges of the curtains. The gun is where I left it, tucked away in the safe, in the wardrobe. I would never get to it in time. I should have kept it out. Should have, would have, could have. I can't hear anything. No movement. No sound but the muffled *tuck tuck* of the plastic clock. Then a rustle, a brush of fabric, in the right-hand corner.

Oh shit, shit, shit. There *is* someone here. There's someone in my room.

Adrenaline instantly fizzes through my system, through the other tiny heart inside me. Absolute fear. It takes every fiber of my being to stop myself from leaping up. I freeze. I realize that, whoever they are, they believe I'm asleep. That gives me time to think. To plan. Maybe if I don't move they'll leave. They'll just take what they want and go. Except I'm not sleeping. It seems impossible they'd not sense the change in the air now, suddenly thick with terror. The soft rustling sound comes again.

What are they doing?

What should *I* do? Am I going to die, here, in a weekend-getaway hotel, alone? *Is that the way you want to go, Erin?*

Think.

I keep my breathing low, deep, as if I'm still asleep.

It's him, it's the man on the other end of the phone, it must be. They've found me.

Was it the last text I sent? The one with tomorrow's meeting location? I think desperately about how that could have happened, but I don't know how, my mind won't focus. And does it matter? He's tracked me down somehow. Oh God. I'm such an idiot.

There's no way he will just take what he wants and leave me sleeping. I know this. I know this because what he wants isn't here. It's buried in the woods. He won't just leave me. He'll have to wake me up eventually. He'll make me tell him where it is.

I'm going to die.

He'll do it quietly, perhaps he'll smother me with a pillow or hold me down in the bath. Something that looks accidental. Something that'll raise no suspicions. As if he were never here.

My chest screams under the tension of controlling and slowing my breath. My fingers are itching to crawl through the dark to my phone charging on the bedside table. Sweat soaks my T-shirt under the heavy duck-down duvet. I need to think.

I don't want to die.

The sound of a zip. I can't ignore it. I can't ignore this sound—it's too loud. I let out a heavy sigh and turn in the bed. Disturbed but not awake. He pauses.

What the fuck is he unzipping? *Think, think, think. Think!*

I need to use the element of surprise; it's all I've got. If I can surprise him. Hit him with something, something hard, just once, then I'll have the upper hand. One good swing.

But what? A fucking pillow?

There's a glass of water by the lamp. I could throw that?

And what, Erin? Get him a bit wet?

Okay, maybe not. The lamp?

I remember it's a big baroque thing, metal with a marble base. Yes! If I grab and yank hard enough, the plug might pull out as I swing.

The noises are coming from over by the bathroom door now. Near my backpack. Suddenly my phone, sitting innocently on the bedside table, lights up in the darkness of the room. The rustling stops and both of us turn our eyes to the light. I catch a glimpse of the text in that split second. It's Mark.

I know where you are. I'll be—

But I don't have time to read the rest. The man in my room knows I'm awake. It's now or never. I squeeze my eyes shut, tense my palms against the mattress, and push myself up and over to the side table.

A sudden burst of movement races toward me. He's running at me. I scrabble for the lamp and swing blindly toward the intruder with all my might, my full weight behind it.

I feel the tension and the pull of the plug coming away from the socket, followed by the dull thump of the marble base grazing flesh.

A guttural shout. He stumbles back, away from me. A curse.

"You fucking bitch." The voice is low, filled with hate. But there's something familiar about it. He comes at me again. In the darkness I can't tell how close he is, or if he has a weapon. All I can do is swing again. Swing with all my strength. It connects. Marble on bone, a wet smacking sound.

He stumbles. I hear his labored breathing, low to the floor now; he's on his knees.

I need light. I need to see what's going on, to see him, to find out if he has a weapon. I sprint toward the bathroom door and fumble inside for the switch.

The cool bathroom light floods the room.

There he is. Crouched at the end of the bed, hand to head. Dark hair, black coat. He's white, large, strong. I can't see his face. Is there stubble? A beard?

The lamp still hangs in my hand, ready. A glimmering smear of blood across its base. He's coming around now. He raises his face slowly to the light. I falter. It's Patrick. The man from outside the prison. I wasn't paranoid. He has been following me. And now I know, he's definitely not SO15. He's definitely not police. Blood runs from the fresh wound above his eye, streaming down his face, smeared in his hair; he swipes it away from his eyes, then looks up at me, blank, cold. There's only one way this is going to end.

I can't believe how stupid I've been. I think of all the mistakes I've made. I should have seen this coming. A huge wave of nausea breaks over me. I'm going to die. My heart thunders in my ears, my knees buckle.

And as I'm falling, he lurches toward me.

I lose consciousness.

37

Saturday, October 1

Mark Is Coming

When I open my eyes, all I see is white. I'm sprawled on the bathroom floor, the bright ceiling lights glaring, my cheek pressed to cold white tile. I bolt upright but I'm alone. The bathroom door is shut; there is only darkness visible through the ornate glass that makes up its top half. My head spins from the sudden movement. On the side of the basin next to me: blood, a long ugly smear, a half handprint. There's pain coming from the side of my head, and when I touch my forehead my hand comes back dark red and gummy. He must have smashed my head into the porcelain washbasin. A blow to the head. Head wounds bleed a lot, I've heard, or perhaps I saw it in a film. I can't remember. But it means they're often not as serious as they look, right? Then again I could have a concussion. I try to estimate the damage, the pain. It feels like I'm drunk and hungover all at the same time. I think of the baby and put my hand to my stomach. And then quickly down between my legs. My fingers come away without blood this time. No blood, no miscarriage. Thank God. *Be safe in there, little one. Please be okay.*

I pull myself over to the door, head throbbing, waves of nausea. I can't hear anything coming from the next room. I gingerly wipe the sting of sweat and blood away from my eyes with my T-shirt, then I press my ear to the door, and I wait. Nothing. I think he's gone. I pray he's gone. I don't know how long I've been unconscious but it must have been a while. The blood on the white tiles has crusted and dried. I rise up slightly to kneel and peer into the dark glass of the door. There is no movement in the next room.

I try the door handle but I know it's locked even before I pull back. The small metal key that's usually on the inside of the bathroom door isn't there anymore. He's locked me in.

I try the handle again. Solid. I'm trapped. He wants to keep me here. He's gone but he wants me to stay. In case they can't find the USB. That's the only reason I'm still alive. He'll be back, after he's got what he needs.

Who is Patrick? Is he the man on the other end of the phone? Whoever he is, I know now that he's working for whoever owned that bag. I've lost. They have everything. My phone with the location coordinates was by the bed. They'll know to look for something as obvious as my phone. With enough time they'll find the GPS coordinates for the USB on it, and they'll check both areas in that clearing until they find it. I've led them straight there.

I need to get out of here before they come back. I need to walk away from this. Leave all of it, go home. Run. Then Mark and I can call the police. We'll explain everything. At this stage I don't care what the consequences of that may be. We can work that out later; maybe we can bargain with the information we have. Either way, we need police protection now. I don't want to end up like the Sharpes.

But then I remember Mark's text. He is on his way. Where?

Here? But how can he know where I am? How can he know I'm here, in Norfolk? I thought he might work out what I was up to once he got home, but how can he know it's happening *here*? I rack my brain and then I remember. It's so simple. About three years ago I lost my mobile phone after a night out, and when I got a new phone Mark installed a phone finder app for me so we could track the new one if I ever lost it. All he needed to do was open up my laptop at home and click on the app. And *bing,* there I am.

And he's on his way here to meet me right now. Thank God.

We'll ring the police as soon as he gets here, and he should be here soon, very soon. And then it hits me. He won't be coming here. He'll be going to wherever my phone is. Oh my God. He'll be going straight to them.

I have to stop him. I have to get to where they are before he does. I have to warn him or he'll walk right into it. I need to save him. This is all my fault.

I shake the bathroom door, hard this time. I'm trapped and I hear myself let out a muted whimper of frustration. I peer through the empty keyhole. The key's not on the outside either. No key to poke out of the lock onto the floor and pull under the door like they do in the movies. Patrick has tossed it or taken it. I look up at the window in the door. The intricately engraved birds of paradise frozen in song above me.

I rise clumsily to my feet as the bathroom spins sickeningly around me. I wait for the burst of dizziness to pass.

I grab a thick hotel towel off the rail and wrap it around the ceramic soap dish. Hopefully the noise won't wake anyone. I turn on the shower to muffle the sound, just in case.

A rain of glass smashes and patters across the bathroom tiles and the plush carpet of the bedroom. Shards pepper across my cheeks and my hair. I turn off the shower and hold my breath, listen. I hear nothing. No doors open along the corridor, no voices. I drag the bathroom garbage pail over to the door and step carefully onto it, laying another towel over the jagged window frame to protect myself from cuts. Then I clamber as quickly as I can through the shattered window, back into the main room. As expected, my mobile phone is gone. Ignoring the fresh cut I've opened on my arm, I run to the bedside phone to call Mark, to warn him. But then I stop. I can't call Mark. His number is in my iPhone. I don't know it by heart. Modern technology. I don't even know my husband's phone number. I wish more than anything I had memorized it. But I haven't. So, I can't call him. I can't warn him. The only way I can reach Mark now is to go to the buried USB coordinates myself. I need to go there, find Mark, and warn him before it's too late. I need to stop him from following my phone right into the middle of all this, right into danger.

I scan the room. My rucksack is gone. Dammit. But it's something else that makes me pause. The safe door is open and the safe empty. This throws me. That's where the Glock was. It's gone. How did Patrick know the code? But of course, I always use the same code. I use the code we have at home, one that is so easy to figure out it's laughable. Mark's birthday. Maybe Patrick did come to our house that day. Either way, somehow he knew Mark's date of birth; he must have gone through the obvious choices and then struck gold. And now I have no gun. I have no gun, no phone, no plan.

There's broken glass on the carpet. There's blood on the bedspread. We've made quite a mess in here; I'll have to clean it up at some point but right now I don't have time. The clock on the bedside cabinet reads 4:18. It will go off in twelve minutes. I slam the off button and toss it onto the bed. I'll need to take it with me; it's the only way I've got of telling the time now.

In the mirror, the top left corner of my forehead on the hairline is red, swollen, crusted with black. For a second, feeling overwhelmed, I think about calling the police. Sending them to the woods. But I need to get Mark away from there first. I don't want him caught in the chaos of police gunfire.

Instead I dress hastily, jam shoes on, then pull on the beanie hat that will cover the rest of the mess Patrick has made of my head.

Twelve minutes later I silently lift the latch on the front entrance of the hotel. The Do Not Disturb sign left hanging cn the door to my highly incriminating room is the only thing between me and police interference. It will take me an hour to get to that spot in the woods, and I have no phone to call Mark, or Eddie, or anyone else who might help, no GPS to guide me, and no plan of what I'll do when or if I get there. Just one simple thought: *Save Mark.*

It's still dark outside. My breath fogs in the air. Five A.M. is already the sort of hour that prompts you to question your life choices. This morning, that feeling is particularly apt. I really have made bad choices in my life, but at least now that I know that, I'm in a position to rectify them.

With no phone or watch, I have to rely on the little plastic alarm clock. If I run, it should halve my time. I run. I run for a long time.

At 5:43 I start to panic. I've made my way as far as the tiny layby on the B road. I must have passed the spot and missed it. I head back into the forest.

At 5:57 I hear voices. They're coming from the right, about a hundred yards away over a sloped area. I drop to my knees and crawl up the slope to the top of the incline and peek over. In the clearing, two figures stand talking. No conflict. No guns in sight.

I can't make out the figures in the predawn light but I listen. I inch closer, desperate to remain hidden even as the leaves and forest debris crunch beneath my weight. The voices are clearer now, but something stops me short.

That voice. I know it. I love it. It's Mark. Mark is here already. I want to leap up, charge into the clearing and into his arms. If he's in danger, we'll face it together.

But something stops me.

His tone.

His voice is cautious, businesslike. He's clearly doing what he's told. I'm too late. Shit. He must have run into them, trying to find me. They're making him help them find the USB. I slide farther along the ridge. In the thin light I see that Mark and another man are now down on their knees, scraping at the forest floor, leather gloves brushing through leaves, scrabbling soil. The second man has read the notes on my phone, he knows I buried the USB, and now he's making Mark help him look for it. He has both sets of coordinates; it's only a matter of minutes before they find it. Shit. I need to think of some way to get Mark out of this.

Then in the half-light I see the face of the man holding my phone. I bite back a gasp. This man isn't Patrick. This is not the man who attacked me in my hotel room. Panic jolts through me. There's more of them. Does Mark know? Where *is* Patrick? I chance a glance behind me but the wood is deathly silent. Has Patrick gone? Has he done his part and left, or is he out in the darkness somewhere, keeping watch? Mark and the man stand and wander over to another patch of the clearing. This new man is taller than Mark, his dark hair peppered with gray; beneath his overcoat I catch a glimpse of a suit and tie. Expensively dressed—even as he slowly kneels near Mark and continues to search in the dirt and leaves. He reminds me of Eddie, but with a continental slant. This must be the man who was on the other end of the phone, I'm sure of it. Patrick has delivered my phone to him and they've been looking for the USB ever since. My phone app must have led Mark straight to them and now he's been forced to take part in their search too.

Now I can see Mark's features, grim and determined, as he scratches around on the forest floor. Is he wondering where I am? Is he scared? He's hiding it well but I can still see the fear playing across his face. I know him so well: I know he's using all his will to hold it together. Maybe he has a plan. I remember the way he fooled the receptionist at the Four Seasons just a couple of weeks ago, how good he was at playing his character. He's smart; he'll have a plan. God, I hope he has a plan.

I scan the clearing, desperate to come up with my own plan, but what can I do? I have no gun. I can't just charge in. I'd end up getting us both killed. I need to think of something. I have to stop what's happening, before they find the USB and Mark becomes dispensable. Before Patrick comes back, if indeed he's out there. We can do this together, Mark and I, if I just think.

I decide to crawl nearer to the USB. I've been able to use the darkness as cover, but the light is relentlessly building and I'll be exposed soon. I wriggle awkwardly back down the slope and toward the second GPS spot, to the tree I'd picked yesterday as my landmark, where the USB is buried. Their voices fade away and I pray I'm right that the tall man won't do anything to Mark at least until they've found the USB. I find a spot out of sight, in the sunken hollow behind my tree. A perfect view of the GPS location.

There's movement now, snaps of twigs, footsteps coming closer. I press flat against the hard, cold ground; I can just see them over the crest of the ditch. They have given up in the first spot and are moving toward the second set of coordinates. They head right for me and sink to the ground to continue their search. They start digging in silence. Mark's so close to me now. I want to scream, "Run, Mark, please run!" but I know our lives depend on me not doing something stupid like that. What's his plan? I don't know what to do. This is all my fault. God, he must be so worried about me. Where does he think I am? Does he think they have me? That they've killed me? He's almost close enough to touch. I could just reach out, let him know that I'm here—

It's then that Mark finds the USB. I see it happen in slow motion.

He palms it and throws a glance over his shoulder to the tall man, who continues searching, still oblivious. *Good work, honey,* I think. *Come on, drop it in your pocket, buy us some time. Hit him when he's not looking.*

But he doesn't do that. Mark doesn't do that. Because what Mark does next astonishes me.

Instead of pocketing the USB, he laughs. He laughs and holds it up! A child with treasure. His smile broad and genuine. Delighted, he stands, brushing the leaves and muck off his knees. What is going on? The tall man nods. His face breaking into a tight smile, he tosses my iPhone down into the leaves near Mark's feet. He doesn't need it now; he's got what he wanted. Mark bends to pick it up.

The tall man reaches into his pocket and I strain to see what he's reaching for, praying not to see a familiar glint of gun metal. "No copies of the files?" he asks Mark.

I notice I'm trembling; the leaves around my arms rustle ever so slightly.

Mark shakes his head. "No copies," he says as he slips my phone safely into his pocket.

Is Mark acting? I don't get it. I don't understand what's going on.

The tall man nods, pleased.

Something about Mark's tone of voice. His posture. This is not right. He doesn't sound scared. He doesn't even sound worried. What is he doing? Doesn't he know they will kill him?

Oh my God. I think Mark's plan is to try to do the deal. How has he managed that? What happened before I got here; what have I missed? Why would they do the deal when they already hold all the cards?

The other man is on the phone now, talking in a language I don't understand, his tone curt. When he seems satisfied, he hangs up.

"Done. Check your account," he tells Mark.

Mark pulls out another phone now, slowly, demonstratively, showing that it's not a weapon. He looks calm, fully in control. Every inch the businessman. Not one part of him scared, or panicked. I have this disconcerting thought. The two men look the same, the tall man and Mark. The same breed.

The man looks off into the treeline. "Where is she? Your wife?" he asks conversationally.

I catch my breath. *Careful, Mark. Don't be fooled.* That man knows exactly where I am, where Patrick left me. Mark has no idea what they've done to me. No idea that Patrick attacked me and took everything. He knows they had my phone, though. He knows that's how he ended up here; he tracked it here. He'll know this is a trick question. *Don't let them trap you.*

Mark scrolls and taps on the phone. He looks up briefly. "She doesn't know anything. I've taken care of her. Trust me. She won't be a problem anymore." His voice is bored. His eyes flick lazily back down to the phone. *That's right, Mark. Well played.* God, he's good at this. I watch him as he scrolls away at his phone waiting for the payment to come through. So calm, so together.

But wait, hang on. Something's wrong here. Why are they paying him? Why would they attack me and steal the coordinates and then still pay us? They have everything they want. Why pay Mark? I mean, Mark's not pointing a gun at them or anything; why would they give him the money?

A depth charge of sadness surges through me, leaving in its wake an emptiness the likes of which I've never known. And all at once it all starts to make sense.

Mark didn't come here to save me. He came here to stop me from making the deal. To take over the deal. He doesn't care what they've done to me. He doesn't care that they've hurt me. He doesn't care about me at all. And now he's doing the deal with them behind my back. Oh God. Mark has made the trade for just himself.

I want to cry out, I want to scream; I slap my gloved hand over my mouth. Because this man, standing here in the woods, is Mark, but it's not my Mark. This man is a stranger.

My mind races over the facts. Who is this man I married? How long has he been lying to me? How did he do this? My mind retraces everything that's happened over the past month. When did this start? Mark was the only one who saw inside the plane. What did he see in the wreckage? It was Mark who left a trail that led to the Sharpes. He's the reason those people are dead. It was Mark who sent me to set up the bank account, sent me to meet with Charles. Mark insisted no one was looking for us or for the bag. He wanted to dump the diamonds. So he could sell them himself? He kept the voicemails about the USB a secret. He hid the USB from me. He wanted it for himself. He's been covering his own tracks since we left Bora Bora, setting everything up so I've been the front man all along, but he can still access all the money without me.

I'm numb with shock. I can't believe how stupid I've been. I never even noticed. I never noticed any of it. But I loved him, I trusted him, he's my husband, and we were supposed to be in this together. But then, I never really was very good at reading people, was I? And he always, *always,* was. Silly me. Silly Erin. I feel my heart thrashing in my throat as I realize. I don't know this man at all. The man I thought I knew, the man I fell in love with, the man I married: he never really existed.

"It's gone through," Mark says, nodding, and he pockets the phone. The money has hit our Swiss account.

"Flash drive," he says, holding it out at arm's length to the tall man.

"You don't mind if I check too?" the man asks, indicating the drive. He wants to make sure it works. He doesn't trust Mark. But then, why should he? I don't trust Mark now and I'm married to him.

The man walks away from Mark, careful not to turn his back on him. I see now he's heading toward a black canvas bag left at the clearing's edge. He bends. He pulls out a slim silver laptop.

With the laptop open in the crook of his arm, he inserts the flash drive. Both men stand silent in the woods as the sun rises and they wait for the USB to load.

The tall man finally looks up.

"You opened it, I see? But you didn't decrypt it. Very wise. That makes things easier, right?" He smiles at Mark, a smile devoid of humor.

Mark smirks. So he'd lied to me about that too. He didn't decrypt it either. He just guessed. He has no more idea than I do what is on the USB. He just knows it's worth two million euros.

"None of my business. I'd rather not know," Mark answers.

314 | Catherine Steadman

The other man seems momentarily distracted; he's focusing on his computer. I wonder what he sees flashing up on that screen. I wonder what secrets worth two million euros look like. I suppose I'll never know now.

"Happy?" Mark asks. The transaction feels like it's coming to a close.

"Yes, happy." The man places the laptop and USB safely back in his bag.

And it's at this point I realize I'm never going to see Mark again. I'll never get to touch him, kiss him; I'll never fall asleep beside him ever again. We'll never watch our children grow up; we'll never move to the countryside and get a big dog; we'll never see a film together or go for a drink. And we'll never grow old together. Every good thing I've ever felt was a lie. And now there is no recourse. He took all of our life together from me. And now he'll take the rest of it too. Not that it matters now really, but he has access to the Swiss account too. I haven't checked it for days. He could have syphoned off all the money already, sent it to another account somewhere. That might be where he's just had the two million euros sent.

And what was he doing in New York yesterday? He can't have been planning to make an exchange with the Russians, because he didn't take the USB with him. Maybe he was just trying to find somewhere to live? Maybe that's where his new life will be? I wonder what he's really been doing for the past three weeks.

Questions I can't answer. I should have paid more attention. I should have been less trusting. Too late now.

Mark will disappear and I'll be left alone, with nothing but an empty house I can't afford.

Or maybe he will come for me. Maybe he'll want to clear up the loose ends.

How long has he been planning this?

"I just need the other coordinates now."

An awkward silence.

A bird screeches in the distance.

"What coordinates?" Mark is frowning.

Ha. Mark has no idea what the guy is talking about. I want to laugh. Schadenfreude. He doesn't know the tall man needs the plane coordinates too. That last voicemail, the one I got yesterday morning—only I listened to it. Mark only knows about the USB exchange. He has no idea what coordinates the other man is talking about.

"The crash coordinates," the older man replies. He watches Mark expectantly.

Mark doesn't know the coordinates. He wrote them down originally, but I was the one who memorized them, in case we ever needed to go back. It had seemed important at the time, in case someone cared for those people. I burned that information the day I burned everything in connection with the Swiss account in our fire pit. I am the only person in the world who knows where that plane is, where those dead passengers lie.

Mark's made a mistake. He doesn't know what to say now, so he'll fake it, he'll bluff, I know it. I know him.

The silence lengthens. The tall man is beginning to realize something is not quite right. Mark has created a problem.

I hold my breath. Even now, after everything, my heart wants me to shout out and help, but my head screams, *Shut the fuck up.*

"The plane coordinates. I asked you for the coordinates of the plane. Where did you find this drive? Where is the plane fuselage? We want the location, you understand?"

The situation has shifted up a gear. There's a sense in the air that things are about to go bad. Very bad.

Mark has no other hand to play. He doesn't know where the plane is. He must bluff or fold.

He tries doing both.

"I don't have the coordinates. I don't have them anymore. But I can give you a rough idea of the—"

"Stop," the man barks. "Stop talking."

Mark obeys.

"In your message you said you had the coordinates, and now you don't. Please explain to me why? Unless you plan to sell the coordinates elsewhere? I hope you understand that this money is for the flash drive *and* the plane location. You don't get to pick and choose, I'm afraid. You give me the location or we are going to have a very serious problem." He holds Mark's gaze. He's called his bluff.

They stand in silence, the tension building toward something inevitable.

In the blink of an eye the older man's hand dips into his pocket and pulls out a gun. That's not a surprise; I think we all knew it was there. The surprise is how swiftly things have escalated. He levels it squarely at Mark. Mark stands frozen, bewildered by this ugly turn of events.

With all my heart, I wish for my gun. But I have no gun. Patrick has it. Wherever Patrick is.

Instinctively I glance behind me but there's no one there. When I look back at the scene, Mark has moved. His body has turned sideways, and in his hand now is a gun. My gun. I see the silver duct tape. Somehow, he's got my Glock from Patrick. Oh my God. *Mark sent Patrick.* That's how Mark *took care of me.* That's why I *wouldn't be a problem:* he sent Patrick to take care of me. A small wood pigeon suddenly bursts up into the air behind them. And then a lot of things happen all at once.

Mark jolts at the unexpected movement. He must have slid his finger into the trigger bed of the gun, because as he jerks in surprise it discharges, sending a thunderous crack of recoil echoing through the woods. I told you: Glocks don't have safeties.

The tall man fires almost instantaneously. What he will no doubt later regard as self-defense. As far as he is concerned, Mark's bullet barely missed him and he fired to protect himself.

A red bloom opens in Mark's chest. It happens so fast and I try to tell myself I didn't see it. Mark stumbles, one arm flailing out, grasping at a tree. He leans his whole weight into it but his knees buckle.

In a heartbeat Mark is on the ground. The two gunshots still echoing in my ears.

The tall man scans the trees around the clearing before approaching Mark's hand, which now lies outstretched on the mud of the clearing floor. The man bends. Mark is groaning, his breath rasping in and out, frosting in the cold air.

The man pockets the Glock. My Glock. I have to clench every muscle in my body as hard as I can to stop myself from screaming.

He takes a moment to stare down at Mark. He fires one more time, down into Mark's body. It jerks awkwardly against the leaves.

I have stopped breathing. I can't remember when I stopped breathing. Next to me a dribble of fresh blood trails down my wrist from my balled-up fist. My nails have dug in so hard they've broken my skin. I stay as still as I can. I will not cry. I will not call out. I will not die for Mark.

He wouldn't have died for me.

I let myself sink down farther into the leaves, squeeze my eyes shut and pray for this to be over.

I hear rustling in the clearing as the man wanders about collecting his things. I press my cheek into the musky earth. And then I hear the slow recession of his footsteps, away through the woods, over dead leaves and broken twigs. And then silence.

I lie there unmoving for minutes that stretch like decades, but no one comes. After a time I raise myself slowly. There he lies, in the mud and crumpled leaves, in his best suit and coat. My Mark. Near his motionless body is my rucksack. The rucksack Patrick took. I hadn't noticed it till now. I guess Mark had it all along. I stumble toward him.

It's a strange feeling. I'm not sure I can describe it. The love I feel for him is still there. I would do anything to go back in time, but we can't. I approach warily, timidly. If he's still alive he may try to kill me. Finish what he started. But as I near him, he doesn't stir. And somehow that's worse.

I crouch beside him, and look at him. The same handsome face, the same hair, lips, eyes. The same warm skin.

I gently touch his arm. He doesn't respond. I become braver, lowering my head toward his. My cheek toward his mouth, the reversal of a gesture we've made a thousand times. But instead of being kissed by him now, I try to feel his warm breath on my cheek; I try to hear it. I bend my head to his chest, careful to avoid the hot pooling puddle of blood. I hear a gently muffled beat. He's still here. He's still alive.

I push his hair tenderly back, away from his forehead.

"Mark? Mark, can you hear me?" I whisper. Nothing.

I lean closer.

"Mark. Mark? It's Erin. Can you—" and then his eyes flutter open. He gazes up at me, slow and dazed. He coughs hard and winces deeply at the pain. He's going to die. We only have a moment.

His eyes meet mine and for an instant, like the flashing recognition of an Alzheimer's patient, there's my Mark. And then it fades. Another look passes like a cloud across his eyes. He looks at me in a way I'll never forget. I see it now. How he really feels about me. It's fleeting but irrefutable. And then he is gone.

A bird screeches deep in the forest and I flinch. I scan the trees again; there's no one there. I stumble to my feet and stand there. Lost, broken, unmoving.

And then I grab my rucksack and I run.

At first I don't know where I'm running to, but as I move, the plan forms. Self-preservation kicks in. I need to find a pay phone. A phone that can't be traced. Halfway back to the road, I nearly stumble over Patrick's body. He's crumpled to the ground, arms outflung. His throat cut. I run on.

Eventually I reach the road, exhausted, trembling. I tidy myself up. Pull my wool hat down low over my injured forehead. Wipe Mark's blood from my cheek and head toward the little village pay phone.

The time is 6:53. He picks up after eight rings.

"Eddie? It's Erin. I'm on a pay phone. Er, it went wrong. Um, the, um, it went wrong." The wobble in my voice makes my eyes fill with tears. I sound like someone on the news, like a refugee, like a bombing victim. I'm in shock, I guess. Shaky, reedy, breathless. Trying desperately to cling to some semblance of normality even after my entire life has been torn apart. I notice my hand vibrating, poised over the slot, clenching the next coin and Eddie's crumpled phone number between trembling fingers. What the fuck just happened?

"All right, love. Slow down. It's all right now, right? You all right? You safe?" He's with me. His tone concerned, supportive. *It's all going to be okay now. Eddie's here.*

"Er, yes. Yes, I'm fine. My head—but it's okay. I don't know what to do, Eddie. . . ." I'm finding it hard to know what to focus on. What's important. How much to say or not say.

"About what, love? About what? The money?" He's patient but I can tell I'm making no sense. He's not a mind reader.

"He's . . . he's, um, and someone else. I don't know what I'm supposed to do. I don't want to go to prison, Eddie." And there it is. The heart of it. The reason I called him and not the police.

"It's all right. No questions. Don't say anything else about it. First of all, Erin, I need you to calm down, all right? Can you do that for me, sweetheart?" I think I can hear him getting out of bed, the squeak of springs. Somewhere in Pentonville two bare feet hit the floor.

"Yes. Okay. I understand. Calm." I struggle to concentrate on my breathing, to slow it down. I start to notice the hedges along the road, the early morning hush. I hear the murmur of a yawn down the line and the clank of metal echo around his cell. I imagine Eddie sitting, hairy-chested, in the heart of Pentonville, on his smuggled-in burner phone.

"Good. Now where is he? Them? Where are you?" He's going to sort it out. I can feel it.

"Norfolk. The woods," I manage.

Silence. I guess that wasn't what he was expecting.

"Right. Fair enough. And it's just you?"

"Just me. And him. And there's another one." It's clear from my tone that I am now talking about *bodies*. Not people.

"Two. Gunshot?"

"Yes. No, one gunshot. And the other one is, er, knife. Knife wound." I'm aware that I'm not coming across well in this conversation. I breathe in again, exhale.

"Okay. You're alone?"

"Yes."

"Isolated there?"

"Very."

"Perfect. Now, Erin, here's what you need to do, sweetheart. You need to bury them. Do you understand? Go back and bury them. That's going to take a while, all right?"

I can't focus right now. I can't think. I'm just glad of any direction. I'll do whatever I need to do.

"Are you near any houses right now, love?"

I look around. Opposite the phone box is a church. Farther down the lane is one other building. A run-down cottage, shabby and overgrown.

"One house. Yes," I say.

"Okay. Nip around the back and see if there's a shovel or something. Take it with you. Now listen to me: be careful, sweetheart. You're going to have to bury them properly. It won't be easy but you'll do it. And call me back once you're done. Different phone box, remember. We'll sort this all out, don't you worry." He sounds confident. It's so unbelievably reassuring I want to cry. Right now I'd do anything for Eddie.

"Okay. Okay. I'll call you after. Bye." I hang up and head for the cottage garden.

And you know what happens next.

●●●

38

Saturday, October 1

Tidying Up

I'm ruddy-cheeked and covered in mud by the time I get back to the hotel, but my wound is safely hidden under my hat and my appearance is nothing that can't be explained by some pretty hard-core hiking. I've got the sweat to prove it.

In my rucksack are bleach and other cleaning products that I bought from a petrol station on the long walk back from the forest. If you ever need to buy anything suspicious, it helps to buy some Super Plus Tampax at the same time. Cashiers seem to get so flustered by them they rarely pay attention to the rest of your purchases. They'll want to get that box in a bag for you as fast as possible. Try it.

Thankfully, my room is as undisturbed as my door sign requested. It's a mess. Blood, glass, signs of a struggle. I find the bathroom key in the bin. Patrick must have dropped it in there on his way out last night. I looked through Patrick's burner phone before I dragged him into the grave with Mark. Patrick wasn't working for the plane people at all. Mark was the one paying him to follow me. Patrick attacked me last night on Mark's orders. Mark wanted me put out of action—not killed, to be fair, but hurt enough to stay away. Was he planning on killing me himself later? I push the question away for another time.

The texts between their burner phones stretched back as far as our second day back from honeymoon. But Mark's tone changes after I had the diamond valued in Hatton Garden and he found out about DCI Foster and the SO15 investigation into Holli. It gets darker then, angrier, as he tells Patrick what to do, to keep an eye on me, to frighten me. I remember Mark trying to make me believe I was in danger, trying to make me believe that Patrick was part of SO15's investigation into Holli. It was Patrick calling the house, leaving those answerphone messages. Mark was the person Patrick was waiting for in that restaurant in that message. Mark was trying to spook me, really scare me. He's the one who left the back door open. Who moved our photo. Who tried to convince me I was going crazy. He wanted me to back off the diamonds. He wanted us to dump them. So he could go back alone, retrieve them, and sell them himself, without raising my suspicions. He must have feared I'd ruin his plans if the investigation into Holli's disappearance got too close to me and thus to him. He created his own Swiss account; he must have done it while I was out of the hotel depositing the money and setting up our Swiss account. I'd find that out from Mark's burner phone. He planned to put the money from the diamonds in it, and then start syphoning the mutual Swiss account dry over the next few months, and, finally, he was planning on trading the USB himself. But, oblivious as I was, I kept finding new ways to keep us both in the game. I sold the diamonds through Eddie. And then I found the USB and planned to sell that too. It must have infuriated him. I interfered with his plans and he had to act.

Before I buried him I searched his pockets. Looking for a clue, I suppose, something, anything that might prove it was all a huge misunderstanding. That he loved me really. I hoped I'd find something that would, somehow, show that Mark had actually done it all for me, for us. Of course, I didn't find anything like that. But Mark had two phones on him. His iPhone and the new burner phone he'd been using to contact Patrick, the phone he'd checked our Swiss account with during the deal. He was clever. His own phone was on airplane mode; he must have done that after he texted me that night. Turned airplane mode on in London, no doubt, before he came for me, so that no signal towers would ever know where he was. The last text he sent me was cleverly vague as well, all circumstantial in a court of law. *I know where you are. I'll be back soon, honey xxx*. If I had happened to go missing for some reason on my trip to Norfolk, Mark could have pleaded ignorance. He'd covered his bases.

A brief scan of his emails, on the burner, revealed he'd been looking at apartments in Manhattan over the past two days. New houses. For his new life. Without me.

I wonder what I did. When exactly it was that I drove him away. I wonder how I could have been so wrong about us. About him. I truly believed he loved me. More than that, I saw it. I swear I saw it. I knew he loved me. Didn't I?

But now is not the time. I have to sort this out, because things can get much, much worse if I'm not fast and careful now. I have to tidy up. Mistakes come down to three things: (1) lack of time, (2) lack of initiative, (3) lack of care.

I strip the bed and soak out the bloodstained sheets in the sink. I let them dry on the heated rail and get started on bleaching the basin and tiles. I scrub the lamp base and replace it on the nightstand, its thick marble still intact after connecting with Patrick's skull. I clean everything, put it all in order, remake the bed, and then strip down for the shower.

I let the streaming water run over my forehead. The cut throbbing. All my muscles pound and sing under the hot shower, but I can't relax yet. In the mirror I pick open my scabbing forehead cut until a drop of blood beads out. I make sure there is water on the floor and then I smash the largest remaining shard of the bathroom door. A satisfying crack.

I phone down to reception. My voice is shaky. I need help.

The receptionist runs up to assist. It's a different girl from yesterday, older, more friendly. I stand trembling in my towel. I explain how I just got out of the shower and slipped on the wet floor into the glass of the door. My forehead dribbles red onto my cheek and into my hairline.

She's appalled on my behalf: "Floor tiles shouldn't be that slippery!" She can't apologize enough. Refunds are offered.

I say it's fine. I'm fine. Just shaken up.

She calls her manager, who offers me a free stay. I decline. They offer me a free dinner. Shivering in my towel, I accept. My blood sugar is low; I do need to eat. I already ate all the cookies in the minibar about an hour ago. I dress and go down to eat in the pub restaurant below.

The problem of the broken door is solved. The problem of food is solved. I am given a dressing for my wound. The receptionist insists on helping me apply it.

It's not until I am safely on the motorway home that I stop at a service station and call Eddie back from a pay phone.

"It's done. Thank you. Thank you for helping me. I really appreciate it." I feel very close to Eddie. We've been through something together.

"That's all right, sweetheart. Happy to help. Just, you know, don't make a habit of it." He snorts lightly into the receiver.

I smile silently. I definitely won't be making a habit of it. "I won't," I promise gently.

There's no way really to tell him how much he's helped me. How much I owe him. Yet he seems to glean it down the line.

"Listen, love, I didn't tell you anything you wouldn't have worked out for yourself. It's just shock. I remember the first time for me.

That feeling. Shock does some—yeah, it does some funny stuff to the brain. But you're all right now?" He's gruff again, back to reality. Enough of the mushy stuff.

"Yes, I'm better. I just need to ask you one last thing, Eddie. How long do you wait to report someone missing?"

Silence from the other end. I can almost hear him blink.

"You don't," he says simply.

"But what if you have to?" I insist.

There's a moment's silence on the line and then I hear him put two and two together. The penny drops. Someone I know isn't coming back.

"Right. I see. Right," he says, and starts to talk me through it.

As soon as I get back home I call Mark's iPhone. It goes straight to voicemail, of course. Buried three feet deep in the Norfolk woods. I clear my throat.

"Hi, honey, I just got home. Just wondering where you are. Hope New York was great. I just got back from Norfolk. Wondering where you are? Let me know if you want some dinner left out. See you soon. Love you." I make a kissing sound and hang up.

Phase one: done.

Phase two: get my house in order. I burn the note I left on the stairs in our fireplace. I was never at Caro's. I'll tell the police I was in Norfolk. A minibreak while Mark was traveling for work. I tidy our home. I undo all the mess I created searching for the USB before I left.

Finally, when it's all done, I slump down exhausted on the sofa in my empty house and stare at the walls—painted York Stone White, the color we chose together.

39

Missing Person

The next morning I wake early. I slept deeply and now every muscle in my body aches, torn and battered from hours of stress and exertion. I rise and make myself a hot chocolate. I need the sugar. I need the warmth.

At five past seven I call Mark's mobile again.

"Mark, it's Erin. I'm not sure what's up. I'm getting a bit worried now, so can you call me please?" I hang up.

I go to the living room and light the fire. I'm staying in today. All day.

I check the Swiss account. Two million euros went in yesterday morning. He must have planned to transfer it all over to his new account after the handover. But I do notice around £800,000 is missing from the account. I do not find it in Mark's savings account. I do not find it in his current account. It must already be nestling in his Swiss account, somewhere out there, God knows where. There's no way to find out now. But so much the better for my current purposes.

Now that I think about it, it all fits perfectly. The story of Mark will hang together nicely.

Mark has been asking around about a client wanting to shift diamonds, a client needing help with certain assets. It will look suspicious. It will. Which is ideal. My husband has stumbled into something he shouldn't have and run away. Or something worse has happened. Perhaps he got involved with the wrong people. We'll never know. They will look, the police, but they will never find anything.

There are three stages in documentary filmmaking, and they are: research and preparation, patience while the narrative unfolds, and, finally and arguably most important, editing your footage to create a lucid and compelling narrative. I know life isn't a documentary—but if the process works, then why not use it? And believe me, this story is not a story I ever wanted to tell, but here I am; this is what I have to work with and this is the narrative I have chosen. And it's a narrative I'm sure the police will buy into.

In his online bank account I see he took out three hundred pounds from the cash point near our house after he got back from New York. It's the largest cash withdrawal you can make. My guess is he hailed a cab to take him all the way up to Norfolk—he knew where I was because of my phone, or because of Patrick. Patrick was following me; he followed me up to Norfolk. He texted Mark to let him know but he must have been in the air by then. Mark would have known I was there even without turning on the find-my-phone app.

Patrick is the bit I can't understand. I'm not sure who killed Patrick and left him crumpled in the woods. Mark or the tall man? Perhaps Mark met up with Patrick after Patrick had attacked me at the hotel, maybe that's when Mark collected my rucksack, phone, and gun. Maybe that's when Mark slit his throat? I found the knife in some leaves near the body and buried it with them both. Perhaps Mark didn't want to risk having to share his earnings? Or perhaps the tall man killed Patrick? Maybe Patrick heard the gunshots, came to investigate, but ran into the man as he left. Too close to the road to fire his gun, perhaps the tall man cut Patrick's throat and let him bleed out onto the leaves.

Either way, Patrick is hard evidence of what kind of man I married. I can't quite believe Mark did what he did: having me followed, terrifying me, making me doubt myself. Hiring Patrick to attack and rob me. And now they're both dead.

I've been trying to pin down the exact moment it all changed between Mark and me. But maybe Mark never trusted me. It's funny: the more I question his reasons for betraying me, the clearer his story becomes. To the extent that it shocks me I didn't see this entire thing coming. How could I not have noticed? But I was so happy; I loved him so much.

As I tidied the house I kept replaying an argument we had two months ago, after our wedding menu tasting. The worst argument we ever had. I've tried to forget that argument, what he said that day. I nearly had. I chalked it up at the time to stress, to fear after he lost his job. But now I wonder if that is when all this really started.

I remember I didn't know what to do to absorb his fury at me. Everything was going wrong that day. And there was nothing I could do to fix it.

I remember him shouting at me—my heart skipping a beat in my chest. I remember thinking *Mark has gone,* just like that, and someone else is standing in my living room. My breathing was shallow and I remember such a strong feeling of being alone. Completely alone. I told myself not to cry, to be strong. That it wasn't his fault. That it was probably mine. But I remember feeling the sharp prickle of tears behind my eyes. He looked at me then, like a stranger, and turned away.

"I can't believe you just said that, Mark," I had said.

But now, of course, it makes perfect sense.

Nothing links Mark to Norfolk. Good luck to the police trying to track the cabbie down who drove Mark all the way to Norfolk, especially when they don't know he even took a cab anywhere. As far as they can ever find out, Mark got off his flight at Heathrow, cabbed home, and then took money from the cash machine and vanished. He never called me; he never saw me. His last text simply said he knew where I was and that he'd see me later and then he disappeared.

And while all this was happening I was in Norfolk. I have credit card receipts. Witnesses. The hotel receptionist can even vouch for my head wound, a slip in the bathroom. I am safe.

I back up all the files I want to keep from my laptop onto a hard drive. Eddie's sending someone to wipe my computers and reinstall after lunch.

I cancel the impending payment from the Swiss account into my account. I'll stay away from it until everything is done.

An hour and a half after the first call of the day, I call Mark again.

"Mark. Where are you? Call me, please. I've checked your flights and there weren't any delays. Did you miss your flight, honey? Getting really worried, can you call me? I'm going to call the airline and check now." I hang up. I call BA. They, of course, confirm he made the flight.

So where is Mark?

I call Mark's parents. I have to hang up the first time around, when his mum answers, and run to the toilet to vomit bile into the bowl. The second time around I manage to hold it together.

"Hi, Susan. Yes, yes, it is. Hi, hi. Um, strange question, Susan, but have you heard from Mark?"

I explain the New York business trip and how he was definitely on the flight home but that he hasn't turned up today. She sounds slightly concerned but assures me he'll turn up. He's probably lost his phone or he's got a work thing on. That gives me an idea.

I call Hector. He's been spending so much time with Mark that it seems appropriate to check in with him next.

Hector hasn't heard from him either.

"So the last time you saw him was the weekend?" I ask.

Silence from the other end. And then Hector says something I wasn't expecting at all.

"Erin, I haven't seen Mark since your wedding." He sounds bewildered. And for the first time since what happened in Norfolk, I feel genuinely surprised.

Where the fuck was Mark going all those days he said he was meeting Hector? Checking in with Patrick? Setting up his new life in New York?

"He hasn't called you about work?" I ask.

"Um, no, no. Has he found something new?" he asks, cheered by the apparent change of subject. Perhaps he suspects Mark has been cheating on me and using him as an excuse. Who knows? But it's clear Mark wasn't setting up a business with him. Good. I can use that. I move on.

One last call.

"Mark. I don't know if you're listening to these but no one knows where you are. I just spoke to Hector and he says he hasn't seen you since the wedding. He doesn't know anything about a new business. What the fuck is going on? I need you to call me, please. I am freaking out here. Call me." I hang up. The trail has been laid. My husband has run off.

Tomorrow morning I will call the police.

• • •

40

Empty

After the call I sit in silence, the empty house a shell around me. The police will be here in about an hour, they said. There is nothing for me to do but wait.

I miss him. It's funny how the brain works, isn't it? I miss him so much I ache.

It hurts and I don't really understand it. I don't understand what happened. I suppose you can never really know a person, can you?

When did it change? Did it change the day he lost his job? Or was it always like this?

It's impossible to know if we were a good thing that we broke somehow or a bad thing that eventually became exposed. But either way, if I could just go back now to the way we were, I would. I

332 | Catherine Steadman

would, without a moment's hesitation. If I could just lie in his arms one last time, I could live with an illusion the rest of my life. If I could, I would.

I don't know why I reach for the phone. It's not part of the plan. I just want to speak to him. One last time. And it can't possibly hurt. I dial Mark's mobile number and for an instant when it connects, my breath catches in my throat and I think he's answered, that he's alive after all, and everything that happened before was just some kind of trick. He'll explain everything and he'll be on his way home to me and I'll get to hold him in my arms again. But of course it's not him, he's not alive, it wasn't a trick, and he's not coming home to me—it's just his voicemail message. His deep assured voice, my favorite sound in all the world. And when the tone sounds at the end of it I can hardly speak.

"Mark?" My voice comes out cracked and thick. "I miss you *so* much. I wish you would just come home. Please come home, Mark. Please, please, please. I don't know why this happened, why you went away from me. But I'm sorry. I'm sorry if I wasn't good to you, if I didn't do the right things . . . say the right things. I'm sorry. But I love you more than you will ever, ever know. And I always will." I put down the phone and cry in my empty house.

I made a lot of bargains with a God I don't believe in last night in bed. I would give back all of the money for how it was before. Everything back the way it was.

Before the police arrive I pore through our photo albums. We put them together last Christmas after the engagement. For our future kids: Mum and Dad when they were young.

So many memories. His face in the firelight, blurred Christmas lights behind him. The smell of smoke. Mulled wine. Pine. My fingers running across his thick sweater. His hair on my cheek. The scent of him, close. His weight. His kisses. His love.

Wasn't it real? Any of it? It felt real. It felt so real.

They were the best days of my life. Each day with him.

In my heart I believe it was real. He was scared of failing. He was flawed. I know. I'm flawed too. I wish I could have saved him. I wish I could have saved us. He lost his job. That's all that happened, really. But I know what that means to some men. People died after the financial crash. Some jumped and some took pills or alcohol. Mark survived. He survived eight years longer than some of his friends.

He knew he couldn't go back to what he did before and he didn't want to start over. He didn't want to be less than he had been. He was terrified, I see that now, of going backward, going back home to East Riding, back to the bottom, back to where he started. And fear is corrosive.

I wish I had seen it. I wish I could have fixed it.

But it's done. He's gone. And I am alone. I don't think I'll try again. I don't think I could. I'll love Mark until my dying day. Whether we were real or not, I loved him.

Fuck, I miss him.

When the police arrive I'm a mess.

41

What Happened Next

I made that missing-person call over two months ago now. The missing-persons team wanted everything. His friends' phone numbers, addresses, family, work contacts. I gave them his computer, his bank information, told them all the places he frequented. I told them about the bank letting him go. The arguments we'd had about it and how I believed we'd come through it. I told them about his new business plans. I told them about Hector. What Hector said to me on the phone that day. I told them everything they wanted to know. They even took his old toothbrush, for DNA.

Three days after that, DCI Foster turned up on my doorstep too. My connection with another investigation had been flagged by his office. Mark's disappearance wasn't being investigated by SO15, of course, but it had piqued their interest. Andy wasn't there on official business, he told me, but he did have a few questions for me. I answered them, remembering the calls from him I hadn't returned, guilt flushing my cheeks. I suppose it is hard to believe that one person can be connected to two missing persons and not be involved in both disappearances. But then, if I've learned anything recently, it's that life sometimes is weirdly random.

Convincing Andy that there was nothing to see was difficult. But in the end, I'm a lot of things but I'm not part of a terrorist organization. I never had anything to do with Holli and her flight to Syria. And Mark was a lot of things too, but he certainly didn't flee to Syria like Holli. It took me a while to convince Andy of that fact, though, and if the police weren't bugging me before that day, they definitely started bugging me after.

I keep my eyes peeled in the news for anything about a missing plane but nothing has surfaced in the past two months. The plane people seem to have vanished without a trace. I often think about those people deep underwater; I wonder if they're still down there in the darkness, still safely strapped in their seats. I try not to, but I do.

I can't help but wonder what was on that USB, why it meant so much to the man in the woods and, I'm assuming, to whoever he worked for? I've thought about it a lot. Those endless files full of encrypted text: were they accounts, details of companies, individuals' names, addresses? I remember those emails I found in the Russian account back in Bora Bora. Shell companies. Arms. Hacked data. I don't know. Maybe. But I'm glad I didn't get a chance to decrypt it; I'm thankful for Eddie's advice—I'm pretty sure they would have come looking for me if we'd actually read or copied whatever was on that USB. And what would I have done with that information anyway?

I steered clear of calling Eddie after the police came. Luckily, my follow-up interview with him was booked for the beginning of this month. Phil and I went to his house. Eddie Bishop's actual house. Simon was there too. Lottie was there. I guess Eddie and his daugh-

ter made up, God knows how. Simon had been right—Lottie's crying must have been a good start. I suppose Eddie is a pretty persuasive
guy, and Lottie seemed happy enough.

After filming, Phil left us alone for a couple of minutes while he
nipped to the loo. Lottie was with her kids watching cartoons in the
TV room. Eddie thanked me again for the favor, for talking to his
daughter. He pulled me into a hug.

And as he pulled me close he whispered in my ear. "All sorted
now, sweetheart?"

"All sorted, Eddie, all sorted," I whispered back.

"Glad to hear it. Listen, I'm going to need you to do me another
favor, sweetheart. At some point. Nothing too big. Nothing you
can't handle," he said, and released me from the hug with a sly smile.

Simon grinned at us. "You better watch yourself, Erin. He's a
wrong'un, you know."

So am I, I thought. It was nice there. I felt welcome. I felt ac-
cepted. I suppose I'm part of the group now. Another favor. I should
have seen that one coming. He's got my back, though. I know that.
And I owe him, don't I?

I'm staying at Alexa's house at the moment. For this week anyway. A
fugitive from my own life, I suppose. I just don't want to be alone in
our house on Christmas morning. Not for all the money in the
world.

Alexa and her father invited me. I can hear them pottering around
in the kitchen downstairs. We're having ham tonight. Apparently it's
a Christmas Eve tradition. New traditions. New beginnings. They've
both been really supportive since it's all happened. Since Mark disappeared.

I know what you're thinking. I'm starting to believe my own lies.
And, yeah, you're right. But I'd rather believe my lies than the truth
in Mark's eyes in that clearing.

Sometimes I think I can hear him at night rustling around in the darkness of our bedroom. I sleep with the hall light on now. I keep something heavy by the bed.

I'm having Mark's child. Our child. I'm twenty-one weeks pregnant. Second trimester. I have a bump. According to my app, the baby is the size of a grapefruit now. Her little heart is fully formed and it's beating at three times the speed of mine. She's more alive right now than I'll ever be again. I don't know how, but I know she's a girl. I just know.

Alexa's IUI worked. Two weeks after the police came to my house, Phil, Duncan, and I crowded back into Dr. Prahani's consultancy room to film Alexa receiving the news. It was a good day. Her pregnancy is not too far behind mine. It's funny how things work out. It's going to be nice to have someone to go through it all with and I haven't heard from Caro once since everything happened. Well, a few phone calls, a coffee, but nothing really. Not that I mind—Caro reminds me of who I used to be, and I'm not sure I understand that person anymore.

I don't think I'll ever tell Alexa everything about what happened, even though she's become a good friend now. She told me not to let it all get to me; of course, she thinks Mark has just run off—my missing husband. But her advice still worked for me: she told me not to let it make me angry, not to let it break my heart, but to remember that we all lose the things we love the most and how we have to remember that we were lucky to have them at all in the first place. Sometimes you're the lamppost; sometimes you're the dog. I could definitely take a leaf out of Alexa's book. She makes me laugh, which is something I realize I haven't done for quite a while. Sometimes the right people come into your life at just the right time. But then I think of Mark, and, of course, the wrong people do too—don't they? Sometimes it's hard to tell them apart. Maybe I will share all of what happened with Alexa one day. We'll see. After all, she did tell me her story.

I'm going to leave the money alone until after the baby's born. I can handle the mortgage until then. I'll be able to sell the house as soon as I am granted guardianship over Mark's financial affairs in a couple of months. Although it will be a full seven years until they can officially declare him dead.

But I can wait that long. I'm patient. I'll keep working, keep filming. I'll do one more favor for Eddie. I'll use the Swiss money to help once she's born, and when my daughter is seven, and I'm legally free, maybe we'll leave this country. Maybe we'll take the money and disappear. I don't know yet. We'll see. But I'm excited for the future. Our future.

It's 7:39 that evening when Alexa calls out my name from the kitchen; I'm upstairs napping in the guest room, my room. She calls my name just once. Clearly. Loudly. And I get a feeling in my chest I haven't had for two months. Fear. Tight and sharp and sudden. I know from her tone. Something is happening. The sounds of Christmas Eve cooking have ceased now. The house is eerily still. I follow the sound of the television downstairs and into their cozy kitchen. The scent of our Christmas maple-roasted ham wafts from the closed Aga. Alexa and her father stand frozen, their backs to me, staring wordlessly at the wall-mounted television. They do not turn when I enter. I slow to a halt as I join them and the sense of what I'm seeing hits me. On screen, BBC News 24, a live feed to a shop-lined street—a deserted London street, maybe Oxford Street. But it's abandoned. So it can't be Oxford Street, can it? Oxford Street wouldn't be abandoned on Christmas Eve. Then I see the police cordon. Police tape across the entire road. An ongoing event. A breaking news event.

We watch in horror as a crouching figure makes a sudden break from the safety of a shopfront bright with Christmas lights. Stumbling blindly out from cover and into the wide empty expanse of the road. The shadow sprints low and fast, terrified, toward the cordon. Away from something we can't see, away from something terrible.

The crawl scrolls across the bottom of the screen. ONGOING INCIDENT . . . FATALITIES. TWO ATTACKERS. ARMED POLICE PRESENCE.

If there's a reporter speaking, I don't hear them. Everything around me muffles to silence as two photos flash up in the corner of the TV screen. The identities of the attackers. I recognize one of the faces instantly.

Alexa turns her head now to look back at me. To make sure I see what she sees. The photo is of Holli. My Holli. I look back at the screen. At Holli's pale young face. It's not a mugshot they've used for her picture; that's the first thing that occurs to me—I don't know why that's the first thing that occurs to me, but it is. The photo they've used is a holiday snap. From before prison. Before the burning bus. Before any of this. And then it hits me so hard my breath catches in my throat. Something awful has happened. She's done something terrible this time. Something truly, truly terrible.

Her words come back to me. That day in prison when I asked her what she planned to do next. "You'll have to wait and see, won't you? But expect . . . great things, Erin. Great things."

She told me. She told me she would do this, didn't she? I knew. In a way I always knew—not something like this, obviously—but I knew.

But what could I have done? What can you do? You can't save everyone. Sometimes you just have to save yourself.

Acknowledgments

To Ross, thank you for leading by example and inspiring me to start along this road. Thank you for your energy, your knowledge, and your advice.

To my mum, my first reader, thank you for checking it wasn't awful! Thank you for all your encouragement, for supporting my reading habit when I was younger, and for inspiring me to go for things.

Special thanks go to Camilla Wray, my wonderful agent. Thank you so much for replying to that first synopsis email I sent you, for reading the first three chapters, and then, the next day, the full manuscript. Thank you for all your brilliant thoughts, ideas, and guidance and being a strong cheerleader for Erin. I can't thank you enough for introducing me to a whole new, exciting world.

To the brilliant Kate Miciak, my editor at Ballantine, thank you for reading the manuscript so quickly, thank you for your belief and your enthusiasm from our very first phone conversation and through the whole process. Thank you for your editing genius, your eagle eye, and your love of a good story—it's an absolute pleasure working with you. Thank you for making this book its sparkling best.

To the excellent Anne Perry, my British editor, thank you for falling in love with this book and being such a complete joy to work with. I'm so happy SITW has such a fantastic UK home with Simon & Schuster.

Thank you to everyone who has helped to bring about the book you now hold in your hands! It has been a warm-sanded, sun-soaked dream working with you all.

About the Author

CATHERINE STEADMAN is an actress and writer based in the UK. She is best known for her role as Mabel Lane Fox in *Downton Abbey*. She grew up in the New Forest, UK, and now lives in North London with a small dog and an average-sized man. *Something in the Water* is her first novel.

Twitter: @CatSteadman